Dead Romantic

by

D1743700

Ruth Saberton

Copyright

Also by Ruth Saberton

Music Mad interview with Rafe and Alex Thorne, 23rd December 2009

Thorne take Christmas number one

Music Mad *feared that the days of unmanufactured music basking in the Christmas limelight were long gone. In these bleak times of mass-production stranglehold it seemed unlikely that a genuine band would ever take the Christmas number one again.* **Thorne**'s *festive hit,* **"One Christmas Kiss"**, *has taken the music world by very welcome storm. The haunting lyrics and soul-wrenching vocals have kicked saccharine pop right back to the eighties dustbin where it belongs. With Rafe Thorne widely regarded as one of the foremost songwriting talents on the British music scene, and with "One Christmas Kiss" playing at parties the length and breadth of the UK and being downloaded every nine seconds, what's the secret of his success?*

"Honesty," Rafe Thorne is quick to answer. "When you don't write from the soul your music doesn't ring true. Sure, there's a formula, but people aren't stupid. They soon figure out music by numbers."

With this Christmas number one Rafe has spilled not only his musical guts but his emotional ones too. His face clouds when pressed about the origins of the song. "Yes, it's written from the heart. It's very personal. What more can I say? The song is about something that really happened." He pauses. "It's about somebody I knew was really special."

So the Christmas kiss was real?

Rafe nods. "It was Christmas Eve and I was travelling home to London from a crappy gig – without Alex, for once. I think some girl had taken pity on him and he'd got lucky!"

At this point Alex Thorne stubs out his cigarette and punches his brother on the arm. "There had to be some perks to playing the outskirts of Watford for forty quid! And anyway, she liked you best. You're just too picky!"

The brothers banter. They finish one another's sentences and clearly know each other inside out. Noel and Liam they are not.

Back to the song?

Alex grins. "Yeah, don't stop now, bro. Tell them about how your eyes met across the snowy track and the angels sang. It's pure Mills and fuckin' Boon!"

Rafe laughs. "Mills and Boon just bought you an Aston! Anyhow, my train home was cancelled and I was stranded at this godforsaken branch-line station miles from anywhere, waiting ages for the next one. It had been snowing and there was nobody about for miles."

Just like in your song?

"Yeah, just like that. This girl was waiting for her lift, this goddamn amazing girl. She had the greenest eyes and sunset-red hair." He hesitates. Gone is the rasping anger of his hits "Dead Lines" or "Killed". "We sat on this bench and she was shaking with cold. Her mum was really poorly and she'd come home for Christmas to spend some time with her. She was so upset and I couldn't help it; I put my arms around her." He shrugs. "I expect you can guess the rest."

We don't need to guess; Thorne's lyrics speak for themselves.

Rafe sighs, clearly exasperated with himself. "One Christmas Eve kiss was all we had. Man, like an idiot I never even asked her name. Then her father arrived all distraught and my train pulled in. She'd scribbled her number down but it blew away in the snow. I haunted that station for months but I never saw her again. I knew, though. She was the one. The only one."

And that's Rafe Thorne's gift: he can wrap raw emotion up in notes and lyrics that echo through the heart and soul. The opening bars of "One Christmas Kiss" are filled with the bitter-sweetness of lost love, the magic of Christmas Eve and the pain of unfulfilled dreams. *Music Mad* predicts that for many Christmases to come this song will be right up there with Wham! and Slade.

With his brother lost in reminiscences it's up to Alex to lighten the mood. "Yeah, the song's about Rafe's famous 'one that got away'! Who knows, maybe she'll read this and recognise herself? Then she'll find him and they can live happily ever after!"

Rafe's girlfriend, *FHM* favourite Natasha Lacey, will no doubt have something to say about that. Still, with "One Christmas Kiss" outselling everything else in the charts and set to become a Christmas classic, Rafe Thorne seems very likely to live happily ever after, with or without his mystery girl.

"But if I could," Alex says quietly to his brother, "I'd move heaven and earth to find her for you."

Chapter 1

November

"Is that a normal latte, Madam, or one of our seasonal lattes?"

The teenager behind the counter pauses to allow me to make this challenging decision. He needn't have bothered. Seasonal latte in early November? What's that about? I've enough problems dealing with Christmas in December; foisting it on me now is nothing short of cruelty.

"It comes with a mince pie," the helpful teen adds, in case this is enough to tip the balance.

I nearly walk out. All I want is a quiet coffee while I wait for Susie to arrive. The last thing I need is a festive reminder that before long Dad will be on the phone wondering what I'm planning to do for the holiday, the silences between us filling with unspoken disappointments and memories. *Are you coming home, Cleo Rose?* he'll ask and, as usual, I'll pretend I have to work or am planning to go away. He'll know I'm just making excuses because I never go away, unless you count my annual Christmas guilt trip.

"Skinny latte," I say firmly. "And absolutely no mince pies."

I shuffle past the till and alongside the counter to collect my drink, trying to ignore the strains of "Last Christmas", and concentrating instead on the dismal day beyond the steamy window. The early afternoon sunshine has turned a sickly yellow and the sky is bruised with lemon-hued clouds. Pedestrians huddling under umbrellas scuttle past and cars swish through puddles, their sidelights scattering diamonds over the road. Across the street sodden tourists pour into the Henry Wellby Museum, my workplace, where they'll be dripping all over the tiled floor, as excited to be out of the rain as they are about seeing the exhibits. Then they'll be testing the security guards' patience by touching the statues with moist fingers and fogging up the display cases. The Ancient World Gallery will be even more crowded than usual, a press of faces peering through the glass at the mummies as the tide of visitors sweeps through the dimly lit space, starfish hands leaving sticky kisses behind.

Settling onto a sofa, I decide I'm glad to be away from the Wellby Museum for a while on this soggy Saturday. I'm even gladder Aamon's sarcophagus is currently hidden away from public view. There'll be plenty of time for the hordes to see the boy pharaoh once I've finished my research, but until then Aamon and his secrets are my personal challenges. I love trying to decipher the hieroglyphics and symbolism and untangling stories that for millennia have lain buried under the desert sands; it's the ultimate Sudoku.

Susie doesn't get this at all. She thinks I should be socialising rather than spending every spare minute at work or reading up on the latest academic papers. Mum always understood, though. From the moment she first showed me her collection of artefacts I was hooked. Being named Cleopatra probably helped me too, as did the family holidays to places near my mother's archaeological digs in Egypt and Sudan. Anyway, I pored over her books, was glued to the History Channel rather than CBBC and spent hours mummifying my unlucky Barbies. It was worth working my socks off and being the school boffin to see how proud Mum was of me.

I stir my drink violently, sloshing coffee onto the table. I'm not going to think about Mum right now. Not here in a café and in full view of everyone. And neither am I going to think about the empty space at the Christmas dinner table.

No. Way.

Where's Susie when I need her to take my mind off things? I fish my iPhone out of my satchel. I'm going to call her.

"I'm so sorry!" Susie says breathlessly when she finally answers. "I'm on my way! I'm just running a bit late."

"Where are you?"

"I'm in Neal Street. I've found the best shoe shop! They've got leopard-print thigh boots and everything!"

"Never mind the boots, Susie. How long until you get here?"

Susie pauses, torn between trying on the boots and meeting me sometime this week. "Err, maybe half an hour? Size four, please. Oh, yes, can I try the purple ones too?"

"Are you trying shoes on while I'm sitting here like a lemon, waiting for you?"

"I'm multitasking," Susie says quickly. "You should approve, Cleo. You were only telling me yesterday to be more organised."

"I meant you should keep your purse, Oyster Card and door keys in the same place, not buy multiple pairs of shoes! Susie Maxwell! What are you like?"

"A disaster," she says cheerfully. "I just can't be as anal as you, Cleo Rose Carpenter!"

"I'm not anal!" I protest.

"Babes, you write lists about what lists you need to write! I'd say that makes you pretty anal."

"Rubbish! I'd say that makes me *organised*. And at least being on time means *I'm* warm and dry in the coffee shop, whereas you're going to get soaked now traipsing around trying to get here."

"But will you have leopard-skin thigh boots?" she counters.

I start to laugh in spite of myself. "No, we can safely say I won't have a pair of those!"

When she rings off, promising faithfully to be with me in half an hour, I'm still smiling. Susie drives me nuts but I can never be cross with her for long, because she's like a small blonde sunbeam – or rather, a pink-haired one, now that she's discovered dye. We may be very different but there's nothing like being misfits in a posh girls' school to bond two opposites. We were the class weirdos: the skinny, speccy ginger girl and the short, plump blonde. It was bad enough being called Cleopatra without having a passion for all things ancient

Egypt, but luckily for me Susie always had a reply as sharp as a samurai sword for any bitchy comment slung at us. Before long, the other students learned to leave us alone rather than risk her scathing putdowns. I left the verbal battles to Susie and did her homework, which seemed to me more than a fair exchange for being left in peace. Nearly twenty years on we're still friends, and when I returned to England sharing a London flat seemed like a good idea.

At least, it did until I discovered just how messy she could be…

Deciding I may as well make good use of the time while I wait, I delve into my satchel, fish out a folder and settle down to read through the first few thousand words of my notes on Aamon. Or rather, I try to read but I'm being deafened by Christmas music.

> *When once I had an angel's kiss*
> *Never knew love could hurt like this*

How depressing are the lyrics of this Christmas song they're playing now? Add as many sleigh bells as you want; it's still utterly miserable. Come back George Michael and Andrew Ridgeley: all is forgiven. At least Pepsi and Shirley looked like they were having fun playing snowballs and wearing earmuffs.

> *On my own, out in the cold*
> *No one to love, no one to hold*

I put my hands over my ears. The words remind me of a chance meeting, one long-ago Christmas Eve that had been the worst of my life.

I close my eyes and let the memories wash over me. I'd taken a last-minute flight from Cairo and then journeyed to my home village in Buckinghamshire, in a desperate race against time to see Mum. It had been truly awful. The single carriage that posed for a train had deposited me on the platform with my luggage and then trundled away into the night, taking with it all light and life. For a moment I'd stood dazed, numb with grief and the cold alike, before managing to gather my wits about me sufficiently to drag my case towards a bench. There I'd shivered and wept while the snow whirled down and distant church bells pealed, summoning the faithful to worship.

"May I join you?" a voice had asked, out of the whiteness.

The flurry of needle-sharp wind and swirling snow had snatched my breath way. Or maybe what took my breath was the sight of him, silhouetted against the night sky; a tall figure with a guitar slung across his back and violet eyes set above sharp, jutting cheekbones. It was as though he'd walked straight off the cover of one of the trashy romances that Susie devoured. I'd looked away, firstly because I couldn't trust myself to meet those eyes and secondly because I never liked anyone to see me crying.

"Hey," he'd said, sitting down beside me and shaking the snowflakes from his dark curls, "you're sad. Nobody should be sad at Christmas."

I'd dabbed my eyes with the back of my gloved hand and tried to paste a smile onto my face, but I'd seen from the concern in his eyes that I was failing miserably. For a moment I'd teetered on the brink of pretending to be polite, being the usual Cleo Carpenter who just got on with everything and took all life's blows in her stride – but there was something about the tenderness in his face that had pulled me back. It was late and I was jetlagged, half frozen and worried sick. Uncharacteristically, I'd found myself pouring out my heart and telling him everything: how Dad's frantic phone call to Cairo, where I was doing my field studies, had sent me tearing across time zones in the desperate hope that I might make it back in time; how I knew in my heart that Mum wouldn't last through Christmas; how I should never have gone so far away; how I couldn't believe my father hadn't called me home earlier. Before I'd even known it, I'd been sobbing in earnest, with the arms of the compassionate traveller holding me close. It should have felt wrong – he'd been a total stranger, after all – but it hadn't felt that way at all.

And I'd never even asked his name…

"Sorry! Sorry! Sorry!" Susie charges though the coffee shop like a paratrooper with pink dreadlocks and hurls herself next to me on the sofa. My daydream evaporates abruptly and for a second I'm bewildered to be back in the coffee shop rather than at the cold railway station.

"Aren't these totally worth being late for?" Rummaging through her bags, Susie plucks out a pair of platforms that even the Spice Girls in their heyday would have baulked at.

"Let me go and buy us some lunch," I say hastily when Susie starts to show me her other purchases. I know from experience that she's about to unpack every single item. "Latte? Cheese and ham panini?

"Lovely, but a skinny latte, please! I'm on a diet."

I smile. Susie lost all the weight she carried at school a long time ago, but old habits die hard. I leave her gloating over her shopping, but when I return she's peering at my Kindle, her brow corrugated with concentration.

"Why can't you read *Heat* like everybody else? You're such a brainbox."

"Stop talking and eat your lunch," I order, plonking down the tray. "I've got to get back to work soon."

"Work? But it's Saturday! Your day off, remember? We're going to Oxford Street and then clubbing. You promised!"

"Suse, I can't afford a day off right now. There's an exhibition coming up and the post of Assistant Directorship of the Egyptology Department in the offing. I'm flat out."

"I don't know how you can bear working with those mummies," shudders Susie. "It'd creep me out, especially if I was on my own at night. I'd be pooing myself."

Late at night has to be my favourite time at the museum. No visitors and no noise. Just my laptop, my research and me. Perfect.

"What on earth would you be worried about?"

"Seeing a ghost, of course! The museum must be crawling with them."

Susie loves all things paranormal. Our flat's crammed with crystals and psychic magazines. Her idea of heaven is to curl up in front of the TV show *Totally Spooked* and watch celebrity medium Lilac Delaney trying to commune with the dead, although why any dead people would want to talk to a woman who wears more make-up than a drag queen and rolls her eyes like a dying horse is beyond me.

"Suse," I say patiently, "there's no such thing as ghosts. When you're dead you're dead."

"So *you* say, but nobody's actually scientifically proven that ghosts don't exist either."

"That's a fair point," I concede, "but since I spend most of my time in a museum that, according to you, is crawling with ghosts, surely I'd have seen something by now? Maybe a mummy stumbling down the corridor like something out of *Scooby-Doo*?"

"OK, that does sound daft." Looking abashed, Susie returns her attention to her lunch. "So, if you're not coming shopping I suppose you're going to blow me out tonight as well?"

"I'll be there," I promise, rashly. "It just might be a bit later, that's all. I promised Simon I'd go through some notes this evening."

Susie's eyebrows shoot into her fringe. "Sexy Dr Simon? Is there something I should know?"

"Simon's just a colleague." I say, as I do an impression of an Edam cheese. Drat. Why do redheads blush so easily? It's so unfair. As if corpse-white skin and freckles aren't enough to contend with.

Susie stretches out her hands and pretends to warm them on my scarlet face.

"Wow! Look at the colour of you! You really fancy him, don't you?"

"What are we? Fifteen?"

"Don't change the subject, Cleo Rose Carpenter. This is *me* you're talking to, remember? You looked just like that when you fancied Duncan from Blue!"

That's the problem with having a best friend who's known you since you were eleven – you can't get away with anything. I've spent years trying to live down my embarrassing teenage crushes and fashion errors, or at least live them down as much as I can when I have Susie on hand to remind me.

Thanks goodness I never told her about my Christmas stranger. She'd still be on about him now.

Unable to meet her gaze, I look down at the table, suddenly fascinated by the muffin crumbs scattered across the sticky surface. If Susie takes one look at me now she'll know the truth – the painful, awkward, unprofessional truth: I do indeed fancy my newest colleague. Since he arrived I've struggled to focus on anything else. This is most unlike me. Normally I'm entirely career focused and, give or take a few dates now and then, pretty happy with being single. Life might be a little lonely sometimes but at least it's under control. Usually my pulse never races, and I certainly don't find myself checking my hair and make-up in the display cases every five minutes just in case I bump into a particular person. Until now, I've never regarded my colleagues as anything other than respected academics, probably because they're only slightly younger than some of our exhibits – so to suddenly be working with an Egyptologist who's not only brainy but also sex on a stick has thrown me completely.

"You do fancy him!"

I sigh. Right. I admit defeat. Of course I fancy our new Egyptologist – not that there's much mileage in it, given that every female with a pulse in the Henry Wellby Museum fancies Simon Welsh.

"Come on, babes, ask him out!" Susie urges. "He sounds perfect. After all, what are the chances of you ever meeting a fit guy who's as obsessed with dead Egyptians as you are?"

She has a point. The odds of my winning the EuroMillions are probably higher – and I don't even buy tickets. But ask Simon out? No way! Never! Imagine if he said no? Just thinking about how humiliating this would be makes my skin prickle with horror.

"I don't think so," I say.

"Chicken," says Susie.

She's right. I'm such a chicken it's a miracle Colonel Sanders hasn't coated me in eleven secret herbs and spices and served me up in a KFC Bargain

Bucket. When it comes to guys I'm useless. Unlike Susie, who can flirt for England, I just get quieter and quieter. Men probably think I'm aloof, when the truth is I'm just shy.

Dr Simon Welsh is the newest addition to our department. I don't think anyone's arrival has ever caused such a stir at the Wellby. Not only does he have very recent field experience and an impressive list of published papers behind him, but he's also exceptionally good-looking, in a dishevelled, stubbly sort of way. When Simon was introduced at his first department meeting, our Departmental Assistant, Dawn, was practically drooling all over the minutes and her eyelids were batting so much she looked deranged. Even our secretary looked flustered and gave him all the custard creams. I'd kept my face impassive and listened intently to Dr Welsh's presentation – but I hadn't heard a word because I'd been far too busy sneaking glimpses at those sleepy denim-blue eyes and that slow, sexy smile. When a lock of corn-coloured hair flopped across his face I'd had to practically sit on my hands to stop myself leaping forward to brush it away.

So for the past few weeks I've been a nervous wreck. I've done my best to avoid Simon, but on the few occasions we have met, my tongue's turned itself into a pretzel and I've hardly been able to say a word. Which is ridiculous. I'm twenty-nine! Surely I'll be back to normal soon?

"Anyway, never mind Simon," continues Susie, who knows me well enough not to push the issue. "I'm your oldest friend and deserve some quality time. You even blew me out on my birthday last week, so you have some serious grovelling to do."

"I was working!"

"That's a crap excuse, but because I love you I'm going to let you off. On one condition."

Susie's conditions are not for the faint-hearted. The last one involved me tackling a pile of ironing so high that NASA could have used it for the Mars mission.

"Which is?"

My best friend reaches into her bag and pulls out two tickets. Passing one to me, she says quickly, "Annie from work got them for my birthday but she's going away and I really don't want to go on my own. Please come with me, Cleo! Please!"

"Lilac Delaney: An evening of clairvoyance and mediumship," I read. "You have got to be joking."

"Come on, Cleo, please! You're always letting me down."

"Just because I don't always want to join in your social whirl doesn't mean I'm letting you down. I pay all my bills and the rent on time, don't I? And who bailed you out last month when you'd forgotten to pay the council tax and spent the money on some ridiculous new bag?"

"It was really funky," mutters Susie sulkily.

"So *you* get a brand new bag and *I* get to pay the council tax? I think that makes me the world's best flatmate."

"You'd be an even better one if you came to see Lilac Delaney with me. What have you got to lose? It's not as though you actually believe in any of it." Susie narrows her blue eyes thoughtfully. "Unless you're scared that something'll happen and you'll be proved wrong, Mrs I'm-Such-a-Sceptic."

"Hardly," I snort. "I just don't want to see you get ripped off, that's all. And before you say it, I know you believe this woman's genuine, you poor deluded girl."

"So prove me wrong? If we go and it's total bollocks I promise I'll agree with you, forever. I'll never ever mention paranormal stuff again!"

Because this sounds too good to resist, I find myself agreeing to accompany her to see the famous psychic. All in the name of research, obviously. I have absolutely no doubt in my mind whatsoever that I'll be proven right.

In twenty-nine years, the only thing that hasn't let me down is my research.

Chapter 2

"Are you still here?" the security guard scolds. "It's gone half eight. Haven't you got a home to go to, Dr Carpenter?"

Ripping my attention away from my computer I'm amazed to discover the hours since three o'clock have melted away. The day has bled from the sky and now buttery lamplight spills from the Anglepoise, pooling across my notes and casting long shadows against the walls. The voices and footfalls of visitors faded away hours ago and quietness seeped into their absence, but absorbed in my work I hadn't noticed.

"I'm so sorry, Tom. I didn't realise it was so late." I pull off my reading glasses and grind my knuckles into my eyes. "Give me five minutes and I'll be out of here."

"I don't know why you don't just move in," the guard grumbles as he shuffles back into the corridor.

"It's official. I have no life," I say to a photograph of Aamon's sarcophagus. "Maybe Susie has a point? I should get out more."

Aamon doesn't reply, of course, but the cheeky sloe-black painted eyes in the photo seem to follow me as I scoot around my office putting my books away and powering down my laptop.

"And what about this?" I wonder aloud, looking at the unfilled application for the Assistant Director's job. "Shall I apply?"

The silence is heavy around me. Somewhere in the depths of the museum a door bangs and a draught sighs through the empty spaces; it breathes its way towards me, lifting the application forms from the desk and scattering them at my feet.

"If I was Susie I'd take that as a yes," I laugh. Susie loves to imagine signs and spiritual interventions at every turn. Nothing so mundane as a draught driven by a slamming door for her: it would have been the spirit of a long-dead Egyptian telling me I should apply for the post.

How ridiculous!

I pick up the application forms and place them back on the desk. I'm ready for this promotion. I know I am. My research into Aamon is ground-breaking, and out of everyone in the department I'm by far the most qualified for the role. Or at least I was until Simon arrived. He's the only member of the team who's my equal, and even then I know my paper on Aamon, the Boy Pharaoh, gives me the edge. I wonder if Simon will apply too? And if he does, how will he feel about having some competition? We've hardly spoken – mostly because my vocal cords tend to do macramé whenever he's about – but he strikes me as being ambitious and fiercely intelligent.

As well as drop-dead gorgeous, of course…

I need to get over this. And soon. Time to leave the building and have a few drinks with my best friend. Swinging my bag onto my shoulder, I cast a quick glance around the room and check everything's in order. The mummified cat and Aamon are side by side on the examination bench. My microscope and reference books are returned neatly to the shelf and my collection of papyri is locked inside a special case. I find this little routine very satisfying because I do like to keep everything neat and in order. That's not being anal, it's being organised.

That's odd. How come my wheelie chair is on the far side of the room rather than tucked neatly under my desk? I must have been scooting about on it at some stage and forgotten. It sounds crazy but I seem to do that a lot, move things around to bizarre locations without being conscious of it. That's what happens when I get immersed in my research. Only yesterday I came to work and found all my pens stuck into a lump of Blu Tack like a hedgehog. And the day before that, my ball of elastic bands was on top of the cupboard. I must have bounced it up there and forgotten.

Oh dear. Maybe Susie's right and I am working too hard. Just as well I'm off clubbing to relieve the old intellectual stresses, then.

Shaking my head, I click off the lamp; inky fingers of darkness wrap themselves around the office. I lock the door, check it twice before pocketing the key, then slip into the Ancient World Gallery to make a handy shortcut to the stairs. The mummies slumber behind the polished glass and as I pass by I mentally tick each one off until I'm happy that they're all present and correct in their carefully controlled environment. The stillness in the vaulted rooms and the dust falling silently through the air always soothes me after a busy day: the ancient peace is like a balm to my busy scuttling mind.

Creepy and crawling with ghosts? Hardly.

It's my favourite place in the world.

Calling goodnight to the security guard, who secures the heavy door behind me, I step into the drizzly darkness and switch on my mobile. Seconds later text alerts are buzzing like wasps and I scroll through everything, unsurprised to see three texts from Susie and several answerphone messages. Crossing the road, my head bowed against the rain and with my hood pulled up, I listen to the messages and my heart plops into my loafers when Susie's cheerful voice is followed by my dad's quieter tones.

"Hello, darling, just wondering if you wanted to pop over for Sunday lunch? I thought I'd do a chicken and all the trimmings. I expect you're very busy but I'd love to see you." This is followed by a long pause and I imagine my father tugging his beard as he wonders what to say next. Then there's a sigh before he continues, "I know this time of year is hard but, well… I just thought it might be nice. Take care, Cleo Rose."

Oh Lord. How bad do I feel now? It's not as though I'm avoiding him; I've just got so much on at the moment. There's the job application to think about and an exhibition to start arranging, not to mention all the research on Aamon, which is starting to fall behind schedule. I really don't have time to trek all the way to Buckinghamshire just for a roast chicken.

Battling guilt, and losing as usual, I arrive at Museum underground station and make my way down to the Piccadilly Line. It's eerily quiet on the platform today. It's that odd time of the evening when everyone's either at home or busy out and about. They're certainly not down here on the westbound platform, anyway. There's a rumble of a distant Tube train, but apart from that it's silent and the blind eye of the tunnel gapes into nothingness. I peer up at the neon announcements board and then return to my reading – but my mind keeps slipping away from the words. I know it's silly but I feel on edge being alone down here now, rather than it being me and hundreds of other people. If I were Susie I'd think it was a spooky place, which of course would be absurd. It's only a Tube station, even if it is all deserted and echoey.

Fascinating as my reading is, I can't help glancing up when I hear footsteps approaching. There's a second passenger now: a man in a black coat who's walking towards me from the far end of the platform, his scuffed Doc Martens boots crunching through the litter as he mutters to himself. A weirdo. Just my luck. Surely he isn't going to sit on my bench when there are three others to choose from?

I'm not going to make eye contact (I'm a Londoner using the Underground system and we don't communicate with one another here), but I can't help noticing a livid scar on his left cheek. He's younger than I first thought too, and even though he's balding his hands are matted with black hair. Hairy hands. Eugh.

I look away hastily and bury my nose back in my book, but it's too late. He's caught me staring.

"Are you looking at me?" he demands. His voice is harsh and as cracked as ancient papyri.

I swallow nervously and pretend not to hear.

"I said *are you looking at me?*" Heavy footfalls move nearer. Unease crawls over my skin.

Come on train. Hurry up. I don't want to be left here with a weirdo. You hear all sorts of stories about flashers and stuff on the Tube.

The man draws alongside my bench and pauses. A tangy, citrusy scent fills the air, which surprises me. He looks grubby and unkempt, not the type to wallow in aftershave – especially not a sexy sharp fragrance like this.

I'm stereotyping, aren't I? All those equality lectures I've attended seem to have gone right over my head. He looks like a weirdo and every nerve I possess is telling me to run, because something about him feels very wrong. There's no logic to this whatsoever, but I just know he's dangerous. Is he going to mug me for the eight quid in my purse and my museum pass? Or something worse?

Come on train! I thought Boris had improved the service?

For a terrifying moment it looks as though the man's going to seat himself next to me. He even stops and looks down at the bench. My heart's beating so loudly it seems to echo in the emptiness and I'm paralysed with fear, no more able to move than the bolted-down bench.

"Oh! Sorry!" A surprised expression crosses the man's face and he raises his eyebrows. For a second confusion pleats his brow, then as abruptly as he arrived, he passes by, picking up speed as though keen to leave me behind. He can't go away quickly enough for me. I know it sounds crazy, but if I had to describe him the word that springs to mind is *evil*.

But I'm getting carried away. I've watched too many episodes of *CSI* while up late working, that's all. I'm being ridiculous. Still, ridiculous or not, I stare after him as he continues along the platform and I will him to keep going. He pauses momentarily, glancing over his shoulder at me and staring hard before turning sharp left and vanishing into the exit.

Thank God he's gone. And brrr! I must have been worried because I feel chilled to the bone. Actually it's really cold down here, so cold I can see my breath making puffy clouds, which is odd; it's normally warmer down in the Underground than it is on the surface. Even more peculiar, my left shoulder feels especially icy. Maybe I have a cramp from being hunched up, or perhaps it's a result of feeling so on edge.

Breathe, Cleo, breathe. It's OK now. He's gone and the platform is starting to fill with other passengers. What a silly overreaction. First of all Christmas rage in a coffee shop, and now this. Maybe I do need a holiday; I must be way more stressed than I'd realised. For a moment there I'd really thought…

Actually, I don't know what I'd thought. It was more a feeling of creeping unease. Just a daft illogical feeling. Susie would call it a sixth sense, whereas I would say I read too many newspapers and have seen too many episodes of *Crimewatch*. There's always a logical explanation if you look for it.

A rush of stale air announces the imminent arrival of my train and, sure enough, moments later it rumbles out of the tunnel, all yellow lights and crowds of commuters. The doors hiss open and I'm relieved to abandon my lonely bench for the fug of the carriage. Finding a seat and settling into it, I shake my head at my unusual reaction. So a man walked past and looked at me. Big deal.

I return to my reading. I may as well use the journey to get some more work done. With any luck, concentrating on ancient history will make me feel much more like my usual self.

My plan works. By the time my train arrives at Ealing Common the stranger on the platform couldn't be further from my mind; the only evidence I ever saw him are the eight red crescent moons my nails scored into my palms.

Chapter 3

It's a Monday afternoon and I'm sitting at my desk studying a CT scan of Aamon. Lunchtime's been and gone but the cheese roll I picked up from the café remains uneaten in its wrapper. The greasy stain on the brown paper puts me off and, anyway, I'm way too busy to eat. I can't remember ever feeling so absorbed by a subject. Aamon's mummified body has never been removed from the cartonnage and it's awesome to be one of the first people to see what's within, after thousands of years. So far the scan's revealed the presence of amulets and artificial eyes within the wrappings, and has enabled me to estimate Aamon's age at between eight and thirteen. But there's so much more to discover and I can't think about stopping yet. My grandmother led the team that discovered the tomb; it's always been my dream to finish her work, and my mother's research on this too.

I'm just returning my attention to the scan when a sheaf of papers drifts off my desk and onto the floor. That draught is so annoying. I must get something done about it before my notes get well and truly muddled. It keeps catching the chair and making it spin too, which is very distracting. Making a mental note to speak to maintenance, I get back to work, alternately jotting notes onto my pad and chewing thoughtfully on the end of my pencil. Every now and then the chair squeaks or a biro rolls onto the floor, making me jump. It would be worth getting the promotion just to secure a draught-free office.

A loud knock on my door makes me start. All the creaks and noises here are putting me off my work.

"Come in," I say. I hope it isn't Simon coming to have a chat. He tried to do this earlier and I had to make a swift excuse about being needed in the Ancient World Gallery. I dread making a fool of myself in front of him;

Simon looks at me with such intensity that when he's near the articulate Dr Cleo vanishes and I'm right back to my gawky teenage alter ego. Until I figure out a way of banishing her, my only tactic is to avoid him. Unfortunately this is proving to be pretty tricky because he's constantly seeking me out on the strangest pretexts. It's a nightmare.

Luckily the head peeking round the door isn't Simon's golden one but belongs to Dawn, the department's assistant and all-round dogsbody, who has the unenviable task of conducting school tours around the department dressed as an Egyptian. Today she's in full Cleopatra mode, complete with a jet-black wig and white robes that almost conceal the billowing body underneath.

"Sorry to interrupt, Cleo. I did try calling but your phone isn't working again."

I glance across the office to the black Bakelite phone which, according to rumour, once belonged to our museum's founder himself, Henry Wellby the renowned Egyptologist. The phone is certainly old, like most of the furniture and fittings in the Wellby, but I don't believe this story for a second. Henry Wellby, famous for his archaeological work in the 1920s when he discovered the famous lost city of Nephet, surveys us all from the portrait hanging in the museum's entrance concourse. A portly gentleman with a bushy ginger moustache and shrewd blue eyes, he looks to me like the type who'd have the good sense to bin a phone with a receiver that continually falls off the hook.

"The phone must be on the blink again." Leaving my desk I replace the receiver in the cradle. "I don't know why it always does that."

Dawn's eyes flicker nervously. "It's the cursed phone, isn't it? The one Mr Wellby used? Is it true it's cursed because of Tutankhamun?"

Oh Lord. Here we go again. What I should mention about Dawn is that she's utterly credulous, falling hook, line and sinker for all the museum myths about moving exhibits and pharaohs' curses, which I once overheard her repeating to a group of open-mouthed visitors. I had to have a sharp word with her about that. The Wellby might be smaller than the British Museum or the Ashmolean, but it is a highly respected place of learning and discovery, not the latest setting of *Totally Spooked*.

"Dawn," I say patiently. "Henry Wellby was nothing to do with Tutankhamun. He found a lost city, not a lost tomb."

"I knew he'd found something lost," says Dawn as though two of the greatest archaeological discoveries of the last century are interchangeable. Above the rumbling traffic outside I swear I can hear Henry Wellby spinning in his grave. Then she frowns. "But you must admit it's a bit weird that the phone is always off the hook."

God give me strength. "I've knocked it off the hook, that's all. It's nothing sinister."

She doesn't look convinced. "It's really cold in here though, isn't it?"

Is it cold? I suppose so, but it is November after all and – unlike Dawn, who usually sports short-sleeved crop tops from beneath which her pallid midriff ripples like Viennetta – I'm wearing a polo neck.

"We're in a building that's over two hundred years old," I point out. "When Henry Wellby's family purchased it to house his private collection they weren't really thinking about whether or not it was centrally heated."

Dawn rubs her arms. "But your office is way colder than all the others." She huffs a great lungful of air at me. "I can see my breath!"

"Dawn, was there a reason you're here? Or do you just want to chat about the lack of central heating?"

"I do witter on, don't I?" Dawn giggles. "Natter, natter, natter! That's me!"

I fix her with my sternest stare, the one that usually makes Susie confess to eating my chocolate/using up the milk/borrowing my perfume. It's never failed yet and Dawn instantly pulls herself together.

"Anyway... Look, I'm really sorry, Cleo, but I've just had a call from my Gary. He's caught in a big traffic jam on the Westway and there's no way he'll be on time to pick our Ellie up from school. I'll have to leave now or I'll never make it."

I glance at the clock. It's one fifty. "But aren't you supposed to be doing a school tour at two?"

She nods. "There's thirty Year Eights downstairs and they're really excited."

"You'll just have to let them down gently," I tell her.

Dawn looks shocked. "We can't do that; they'll be gutted! And anyway we've got that reporter joining us, remember? He's waiting too."

I do remember because I was the genius who organised this. It seemed like a good idea at the time, in the abstract way that these things always do. It would raise our profile, tick all the right boxes for funding initiatives and hopefully generate lots more educational visits. There's no way we can put today's tour off. I need to find another sucker, I mean volunteer, to dress up as an Egyptian and do battle with stroppy teenagers.

"We'll have to find somebody else then," I say. "But who?"

Dawn starts to unwind her costume. "You'll have to do it."

"Me?"

I'm an academic. There's no way I'm dressing up and parading around the museum. No way at all. Nobody will ever take me seriously again. But by the time I open my mouth to protest Dawn is down to her knickers, tugging off her wig and pulling on her leggings.

"You'll be brilliant, Cleo!" she insists, two-thirds dressed now and on her way to the door while I stare at her, appalled. "Nobody knows more about ancient Egypt than you do. You've even got the right name!"

The robes are shoved into my arms, followed by the wig and a bag of grotty make-up. I'm beyond horrified.

"Dawn, I can't!"

"Of course you can," says Dawn cheerfully. Of course she's looking cheerful; she's halfway out of the door isn't she? "Just remember to stay in role and have fun! Bye!"

Stay in role and have fun? I stare after her, lost for words. Fun? I hated drama at school and, as I recall, I didn't much like the other kids either. I can't imagine anything has changed significantly since then. There's nothing else for it: I'll have to cancel the journalist and the tour.

I pick up the phone, which is somehow off the hook yet again, and dial down to reception.

"Dr Carpenter! Thank goodness!" The receptionist sounds stressed. "We've been trying to ring up for ages! There's a journalist here who says he's supposed to be having a tour of the department." She lowers her voice. "He's really irate."

Great. This is all I need. There's nothing else for it. I'm going to have to do this tour myself and pray nobody I know ever finds out.

Dawn's right, my office is Baltic – so I don't waste any time getting changed. In seconds my polo neck and black trousers are folded up on the chair and I'm wearing nothing but my underwear. What a day to have chosen to wear my big red and white polka-dot pants! That's what happens when you share a flat with a girl who constantly breaks the washing machine – and until we get it fixed I'm down to the last few random odds and ends of underwear that I'd never normally dream of wearing. Today's beauties were bought by a well-meaning ex who never did grasp the fact that I prefer white undies. Or quiet nights in to being deafened in crowded pubs. Or Radio Four over Radio One. Coloured pants aside, it's easy to see why we didn't go the distance.

Anyway, I really hope the pants don't show through the robes. Luckily Dawn's quite a bit bigger than me, so the costume wraps around several times and covers everything. I can't find the brooch she uses to fasten it and I haven't got time to search either, so I improvise with some unravelled paperclips and tuck the surplus fabric under my bra strap. It's not a great look but it's just going to have to do.

Right: make-up time. I don't tend to wear a lot of make-up, so my attempt at Cleopatra eyes is more Alice Cooper than Elizabeth Taylor. Still, too late to worry now. I've just about got enough time to shove on my black wig and grab the golden staff before dashing downstairs. I glance in the mirror and a drag queen peers back. Not a good look. My only consolation is that nobody will recognise me like this.

There's no mistaking which group is waiting for me downstairs. Kids in school uniform are running around, scattering through the crowd like mercury beads. Others are sprawled on the floor, a few are having a scrap on the staircase, Jane from the Wellby Museum shop is evicting a couple more and the rest are waiting in a huddle, snapping gum and texting while their teachers look increasingly nervous. That sour-looking guy, scribbling notes and glowering, must be the journalist. He looks about as cheesed off as I feel, which is saying something.

I'll just think of the children and remember that nobody knows it's me underneath the wig.

"Hello, everyone!" I say brightly, "Welcome to the Wellby Museum. I hope you're all ready to come back thousands of years in time with me?"

"Is that why you took so long to get here?" asks the journalist. All the kids snigger and I feel myself turn red. Not a great start.

I'll stick to the script. Things can't go too wrong if I do that.

"My name's Cleopatra," I begin, "I'm the last of the pharaohs."

"And I'm Prince William," sneers the journalist. "Call that a costume?"

Sod this. I'm standing in the lobby of one of the nation's most established museums wearing what is in essence a bed sheet, plus a comedy wig. My reputation as a serious academic is hanging in the balance and I'm freezing cold. I'm not in the mood for this smart Alec, even if I do want him to give us a fantastic write-up. Time to get into role...

"Listen, peasant," I hiss, pretending to prod him in the chest with my staff, "I'm Cleopatra the seventh, Thea Philopator and incarnation of Isis, and if I say my name is Cleopatra then you don't argue with me. Any more disrespect and I'll have you mummified alive! Or boiled in oil and fed to locusts! Maybe I'll even bury you in the sand?"

"Cool!" says one of the kids.

"It's like *Horrible Histories*!" gasps another.

"Perhaps your eyeballs can be plucked out and fed to scarabs," I improvise. "Or your brains hooked out through your nostrils. If, indeed, you have a brain?"

The journalist steps backwards hastily. "Sounds painful! Sorry, Your Highness!"

"You will be," I threaten. "I have a thousand agonising ways to kill you, worm!"

Well, this does it: the kids are riveted by the gory details of Egyptian torture and want to know about all of them. As I shepherd them around the museum I tell them as many gross-out facts as possible. By the time we exit the Ancient World Gallery they all look a little green and I don't think it's down to the lighting, either. They ask questions, take pictures and seem utterly fascinated. I'm actually quite enjoying myself. Even the grumpy journalist has cracked a smile and told me how much he likes the tour. I'm just leading them all back down the stairs before finishing, and congratulating myself on surviving, when somebody calls my name.

"Cleo? Dr Carpenter? Is that you?"

Please, no, anything but this…

I turn around slowly. Simon Welsh is standing at the top of the staircase and looking down at me in absolute amazement. Of all the people to spot me it has to be him, doesn't it?

"Dr Carpenter?" Simon is descending the stairs now, his blue eyes crinkling with mirth. "Is that really you underneath that cunning disguise?"

They say that life is comprised of choices and I have one now: to stay and brazen it out or to do a runner. Actually, that's not a choice at all. I haven't even been able to face Simon when I've been at my professional best. I double my speed on the stairs, figuring that once I'm in the concourse I can dive into the crowd and lose him. I'll just deny everything when I see him next – if I don't die of embarrassment first, that is.

Unfortunately, in my haste to escape I catch my heel in the robes. There's a sharp jolt as I stagger forward. For a hideous moment I teeter on the step before somehow recovering my balance and continuing my descent with my head held high, even though the bloody kids are shrieking with mirth. How on earth do teachers cope with this on a daily basis?

It's strange, though; either I'm super paranoid or something very strange is happening. The concourse is the beating heart of the museum – a busy, noisy hub of excited visitors and enthusiastic staff – and my ears normally ring for ages if I spend too much time here. Yet today the place is unusually quiet, and the further I get down the stairs the more a hush descends. Everyone seems to be looking at me.

Is my costume really that interesting?

I glance down just to check it and this is when my day lurches from bad to horrendous.

I don't seem to be wearing my costume.

It's like one of those awful nightmares when you suddenly find yourself naked in a shopping centre, only worse because I'm not dreaming. No, I'm wide awake and I really am standing on the staircase wearing nothing except my big polka-dot pants and bra! Turning slowly I see my robe abandoned halfway up the stairs.

The school kids are practically wetting themselves while below me people are staring and pointing. Laughter spreads through the place like ripples on a pond.

With a wail of horror I sprint for the robe, but Simon is quicker. He leaps down the stairs three at a time, snatches up the fabric and seconds later is draping it around my shoulders. An hour earlier the idea of Simon touching me would have been enough to make me feel giddy but now I'm just mortified. The guy has seen me in my *pants*. My big spotty pants! And when did I last shave my legs? Far too long ago for me to remember, that's for sure.

What must he be thinking?

Clutching the robe around me I tear up the steps towards the safety of my office. En route I spot school kids snapping away on their mobile phones and the journalist grinning from ear to ear as he jots down what's probably going to be a highly amusing story. I'll be a hashtag on Twitter by the time I reach my office door. My professional reputation is ruined.

And, almost worse, how can I ever face Simon Welsh again?

Chapter 4

Once in the safety of my office I slam the door shut and lean my back against it. I don't think I'll ever leave again, at least not in daylight.

My skin is crawling with mortification. I can't believe what just happened. As soon as my computer boots up I'm off to surf Cairo Uni's website to look for vacancies. It's just a shame the ancient Egyptians never lived on the moon, although the way I feel right now even that wouldn't be far enough…

I'm pulling on my clothes when there's a knock on the door.

"I'm busy," I call. For the next millennia or two. "Come back later."

"Cleo? It's me, Simon. Can I come in?"

Simon? What on earth does he want?

"Please go away," I say.

"Not until I know you're OK."

"I'm fine," I reply. I'm trying to scrub off the eyeliner, which is easier said than done. What on earth is it made of? Indelible ink?

"I know you're embarrassed, but it really isn't as bad as you think," Simon says kindly.

Embarrassed doesn't even come close. I could be in therapy for a year and still have issues after today. And as for *not as bad as I think?* I just paraded through the Wellby Museum in my smalls! It doesn't get any worse than this.

"You'll look back on this and laugh," he adds.

Yeah, right. That's about as likely as Susie becoming a neat freak.

"I'm absolutely OK," I fib. "Honestly. I'm just getting changed."

"Well, if you're really sure, I'll leave you in peace," Simon says doubtfully. "But just for the record, I thought you looked amazing. Easily the best exhibit in the entire place."

His footsteps retreat down the corridor leaving me stunned. Did Simon Welsh just tell me that I looked amazing in my underwear? Seriously? Did he just flirt with me?

I'm trying to get my head around this when the phone shrills. Oh great. It's probably the Museum Director wanting an explanation. With a heavy heart I lift the receiver.

"Dr Carpenter? It's reception. There's a call for you. It's the police."

The police? I feel the colour drain from my face. My robe fell off. It was an accident. Surely the police don't need to be involved? Or has something awful happened to Dad or Tolly?

"Hello? Cleo?" The disembodied voice of the receptionist crackles through the receiver. "There's a WPC Moore on the line for you. Shall I put her through?"

"Please," I say. I take a deep breath and wind a coil of my hair around my finger.

"Dr Cleopatra Rose Carpenter?" The voice on the end of the line doesn't sound as though it's about to impart bad news, but you can never be too sure.

"Speaking."

"Hello, Dr Carpenter, thanks for taking the time to speak to me. I'm WPC Moore. I'm hoping you may be able to help us with an investigation."

I'm taken aback. "Me? How can I help?"

I hear papers rustle. "I believe you were at Museum Tube station at approximately 9.20pm last Saturday? You caught a westbound train?"

"I don't know whether to be impressed or scared," I say. "How on earth do you know that?"

"A mixture of CCTV and good detective work, Dr Carpenter. Sometimes the Big Brother culture does come in handy. We've been able to trace most people who passed through the station that evening."

"In that case I'm impressed! But what's all this got to do with me?"

There's a soft intake of breath at the other end of the line. "Dr Carpenter, this may come as something of a shock but there was a violent attack that night, not far from the station. A brutal assault on a young girl. She was left for dead."

"That's awful." I twirl another spiral of hair around my forefinger. Would you believe it, another sheaf of papers has slipped to the floor. What is it with this draught? "I'm afraid I didn't see anything. The CCTV must show that."

"What it shows, Dr Carpenter, is that you were on the platform with the alleged attacker only ten minutes before the assault took place, which makes you the one person who may be able to confirm the identity of the suspect."

I sink onto the tatty office sofa. Stuffing oozes onto the carpet and a spring pokes me in the kidneys but I hardly notice. Instead I see in my mind's eye the deserted platform, the skittering litter and the odd man with the scar who paused by the bench.

"I know this must be difficult," continues the WPC, "but we really need you to come to the station and have a look at an ID parade. You're the only person who can confirm the victim's positive identification of the suspect."

Cold sweat trickles between my shoulder blades. The air of menace that had radiated from the stranger had made me feel very uneasy. Why did he pass me by? The platform was empty, so what stopped him? Why did I escape?

"Dr Carpenter?"

"Sorry. I'm a bit taken aback. Of course I'll come over."

The WPC gives me some directions, which I scribble onto my pad, but my hands are shaking so much that the writing looks like a drunken spider has staggered across the page. Once we've confirmed the destination and the time I need to arrive, I put the telephone down abruptly and start to chew the skin round my thumbnail. I've no doubt at all that last Saturday night I had a very lucky escape indeed. The question, though, is why?

Suddenly my embarrassing afternoon seems like a very small issue indeed.

* * *

"Do you want a coffee, Dr Carpenter? You look very pale."

WPC Moore's eyes are wide with concern. Placing her hand on my elbow, she gently guides me to a seat before fetching a pallid cup of coffee from a machine. I wrap my shaking hands round the cup and draw some comfort from the warmth.

"You did a good job in there," she adds.

I take a sip of the tasteless liquid. "I'd have known him anywhere."

It hadn't been difficult to pick the man I'd seen from the line-up of eight similar-looking men. They may all have had the same hair colour, height and build, but as I'd looked through the one-way glass I'd recognised him instantly. The scar, the set of his lips, the hairy hands; I have a good eye for detail and I could have picked that man out of a hundred others.

"Why didn't he choose me?" I wonder aloud. I've only been told a few details about the attack but it's enough to turn my stomach. The poor girl who was assaulted will be in hospital for weeks and in therapy for a lot longer. All of a sudden my spotty pants trauma doesn't seem quite so important after all.

WPC Moore shrugs. "We've asked him that already. He told us you weren't alone and that's why he left you."

"But that's nonsense! Of course I was alone!"

She nods. "I know you were. We've got the footage to prove it too, as if there was ever any doubt."

A headache starts to beat above my right eye.

"So who did he think I was with?"

"He said you were with a young man in a leather jacket, with dark hair and green eyes. He was adamant about the eye colour." She gives me a reassuring smile. "But please don't worry too much about it. He's obviously not well."

My head's spinning. It's still spinning twenty minutes later when I step out of the police station and into the evening gloom and drizzle.

This has to be one of the weirdest days of my life.

I shrug my bag onto my shoulder. The headache's spread from my right eye across the whole of my forehead, where it thumps and thuds like something Susie would dance to. The scene from the Tube station keeps spooling past my vision and I watch over and over again the man's slow passage along the platform, and see him pause alongside me before he continues his journey. I'm so very thankful he imagined I wasn't alone. The thought of what could have happened makes me feel sick and shaky.

I'll never be able to work feeling like this. I'll head home, take a couple of Nurofen and go to bed. With any luck Susie's on a night shift and I'll be able to have a hot bath in peace, and a good night's sleep.

Spotting a chemist just across the road I decide I'll cross over, pop in to buy some Nurofen and then I'll...

There's a scream of brakes as headlights blaze across the wet road. Hands bite into my shoulders, pulling me sideways, and wheels swish by so close to my face that I can smell the rubber against the tarmac.

My head slams onto the road, fireworks shoot across my vision and I hear a high, unearthly screaming. I think it's me.

Big green eyes are staring down at me. A wide generous mouth makes an o of surprise.

"You can see me!" I hear a voice gasp. "My God, you can really see me!"

And then there's nothing.

Chapter 5

Where am I? Did I fall asleep at work again? I really must stop doing that.

I feel awful. What on earth was I doing last night to have a headache like this? It feels like Black Sabbath is playing a set inside my skull. Was I out drinking with Susie again? If I was, it must have been some night. My head hurts like hell and my brain seems to be swivelling; it's making me nauseous.

That's it. I'm giving up alcohol. Forever. And ever. And ever…

Or maybe I've got the flu? My mouth's dry and my limbs have all the strength of overcooked pasta. My throat's a bit sore too, come to think of it, and my neck feels unusually stiff.

I don't think I can face opening my eyes…

Have I dropped off again? What time is it? For a second I just lie still while Ozzy Osbourne continues to play inside my cranium. I can't ever remember having such an evil headache. It's like someone's trying to split my brain open with a chisel. I need to get out of bed and find some Nurofen.

Wait a minute; that thought feels familiar. Wasn't I looking for Nurofen when… when…

No. It's gone. Thought I was onto something there.

My head hurts. Maybe just a bit more sleep?

Ouch! Ouch! Who's shining a light into my eyes? Even peeling open one eyelid just a fraction hurts so much that I screw my eyes shut again.

"Cleo?" says a voice. "Hey, Dad! I think she blinked!"

OK. So now I know I'm ill. I'm so delirious I'm hallucinating; that voice sounds just like my brother, Ptolemy. There's no way Tolly would come all the way from Canary Wharf just because I've got flu. Not when there are stocks and shares and gilts to buy, anyway.

Buying things. Wait! I try to force my mind to hang onto that thought. I was buying something. The memory surfaces for a moment then flickers like a silvery fish, diving back into the depths of my splitting headache.

"It's just an automatic response; you heard what the doctors said. Come on, son, have a break. Let's get a coffee."

This dream is just getting weirder by the minute. The second speaker sounds exactly like my dad, except that Dad and Tolly haven't been this chatty since Mum died…

But I'm not going to think about *that*. If I can't remember what it was I was doing moments ago then there's no bloody way I'm going to think about stuff that happened when I was nineteen. I was going to buy something. I walked down some steps and then–

Damn. All I can see now are pictures from ten years ago, so vivid they may as well be tattooed on my retinas.

A plain wooden coffin covered in red roses, tears running down Dad's cheeks, curling ham sandwiches and tepid tea, people mouthing platitudes…

Mum's empty study, dust falling through the air onto the precious books that she rarely used but so needed; Dad with his head on her desk sobbing. Relatives looking at me with awkward sympathy, patting me on the shoulder and saying "It'll help to talk about it, Cleo."

That's where they'd been wrong. In my experience, talking only makes things worse. Much better to bury it deep inside and think instead about degrees, masters and PhDs – and if that makes me a cold unfeeling bitch, as Tolly once put it, then I guess that's what I am. But at least I'm holding it together without the need for booze or the buzz of gambling on the money markets and buying fast cars.

Fast cars. Wait!

There's a memory, more slippery than an eel coated in butter, but I grasp for it anyway. Yes! That's it! There was a car, wheels passing by my face, strong hands on my shoulders pulling me out of harm's way and shocked sea-green eyes holding mine.

I was nearly killed and some passerby saved my life. I must have slammed down on the road like a tonne of bricks. No wonder I'm in pain. From what I remember I'm pretty lucky *to* be in pain. But where am I?

Prising open eyes that feel as though they've been Pritt Sticked, I discover I'm in a darkened room and lying in a metal-framed bed. Stiff white sheets are pulled up to my chest, the starched cotton only slightly paler than my hands, and with a shudder I see that the back of my left hand is black with bruises fanning out from a cannula, and a drip is hooked up to my right arm. A machine bleeps rhythmically from a control panel somewhere above my head and the smell of antiseptic hangs heavy in the air. Closer inspection reveals that I'm wearing a plain blue robe and no underpants.

Where have my knickers gone? Actually, never mind my knickers; where's my laptop? I've got months' and months' worth of notes on that; I can't have lost them all! They're irreplaceable! Maybe my clothes and the rest of my stuff are in the locker over by the door? If I can manage to swing my legs out of bed, fight this riptide of pain and maybe drag my drip with me, then perhaps I can check it out?

OK, Cleo. On the count of three, then: one, two–

"Hey!" A cool hand lands on my shoulder, gently pushing me back onto the scratchy pillow. "Take it easy! You've had a really nasty accident. There's no way you're up to moving about yet."

A young man is staring down at me. He's ridiculously good-looking, with sharp cheekbones, floppy dark hair and sparkling jade eyes in a crinkly face that must smile a lot. Stubble sprinkles his strong jaw and he smells of a delicious citrusy scent.

"Where am I?" I ask. Gorgeous-man heaven? Susie will be so jealous.

"You're in hospital. You had a nasty bump on the head," the mystery guy explains. I guess he's some kind of doctor. "You've been unconscious too, so try to keep calm."

I'm in hospital? Wow. That must have been some bump to the head. There would have been an ambulance and everything. Tentatively I raise my fingers to my temple and feel something prickly.

"Stitches," explains the man when my hand recoils. "They had to take you into theatre. Brace yourself: you've had surgery."

"No way!"

He nods then sits next to me on the bed. The cloying antiseptic smell is replaced by that lovely tangy aftershave. His hand brushes my cheek; it feels blissfully cool in contrast to the tropical hospital atmosphere. "Do you remember anything that happened?"

I close my eyes and see again the busy rush-hour traffic. I'm running down the steps towards the chemist across the road; there's a hideous screech of brakes, hands on my shoulders and a flash of jade green as my head slams onto the tarmac.

My eyes fly open.

"You saved my life!"

He looks exceedingly pleased. "You did see me. I knew it!"

"It's the last thing I remember before I woke up here," I say. "You shoved me out of the way of that car, goodness knows how. You must be my guardian angel."

"Um, err, yeah." He blushes and runs a hand through his hair, leaving a few clumps standing to attention. "I guess you could put it that way."

I struggle to sit up. What do I look like? Is my hair a mess? Make-up all over my face? I wouldn't normally care but this is the man who saved my life and I think the least I can do is make an effort to look human. God, I hope my hospital gown isn't gaping.

"I'm Cleo Carpenter," I hold out my hand but this yanks at the drip. Annoyed, I give it a sharp tug and instantly an alarm starts to wail. Oops, I don't think I should have done that.

"Look, Cleo," he says, "I should really tell you something–"

"Too right you should! You saved my life and I don't even know your name!"

"I'm Alex. Alex Thorne. You don't recognise me?"

Just as I'm about to ask Alex why I should recognise him, the door swings open and in comes my father, spilling coffee all over the floor and with his bearded chin practically splashing into the cup when he sees me sitting up.

"Cleo! You're awake! Look, Tolly! She's come round."

Am I still unconscious? I guess I must be because here's my workaholic brother hard on Dad's heels, his bespoke shoes and Turnbull & Asser shirts totally incongruous with the NHS starkness. The sunshine peeking through the blinds suggests it's the middle of the day too – and we all know Tolly doesn't leave his merchant bank until the pubs are kicking out.

I'm dreaming, then. My handsome rescuer and concerned family are nothing but a fantasy. But ouch! The jabbing needle in my right arm doesn't feel much like a dream. The blood welling up into the tube around it looks pretty real too, as does the nurse who's shining a light into my eyes. Any minute now she'll say they have ways of making me talk…

"Just sit still," she says, putting down the torch and fiddling with the drip. "There'll be a sharp scratch–"

"Ouch!"

"All done." The nurse flicks a switch on the control panel and the wailing alarm is silenced. "How do you feel?"

"OK," I say. Actually, I'm not sure to be honest. I feel weird, not quite like myself.

The nurse is unconvinced. "We'll send the doctor to have a look at you. In the meantime, can I get you anything?"

I consider asking for my knickers but this is a bit too embarrassing in front of the green-eyed stranger, never mind my dad.

"My laptop?" I say eventually.

"Cleo! Absolutely not!" Dad marches to my bedside. "You've been unconscious for forty-eight hours! The last thing you need to do is worry about work."

I'm horrified. If I've been unconscious for forty-eight hours I must be really behind.

"He's right," agrees my rescuer. "There's more to life than work."

I can't think what, but my head's starting to pound again and it seems easier just to ask for a glass of water and gulp down a couple of mouthfuls.

"How are you feeling, darling?" Dad asks. "You gave us such a scare."

"My head aches, but I think I'll live."

"You might not if you catch a superbug. How clean is it in here?" Tolly's peering distastefully at the room through his designer glasses, as though he can see MRSA tap-dancing towards my sick bed. "Maybe we should move her to the Nuffield, Dad?"

"I don't believe in private healthcare," snaps my father.

"It exists, believe me," Tolly says through clenched teeth. "And you can have Sky there."

"It's fine, Tolly; I can live without Sky," I say hastily. The last thing I need is my dad and my brother having a full-scale row about socialist principles. For a pacifist, Dad can get pretty violent when challenged.

Tolly looks doubtful. He's probably having withdrawal symptoms from Bloomberg as we speak.

To distract them before things get ugly I say, "Dad, Tolly, I want you to meet Alex. He saved me from getting run over."

Alex is looking awkward. "Really, there's no need."

"There's every need! If it weren't for you I'd have died. You're a hero, Alex."

I reach out to touch his arm but somehow my fingers seem to slither right through his sleeve. That's weird. My vision must be funny from the bang on my head. "Seriously, Alex, we really can't thank you enough. Can we Dad?"

But Dad and Tolly aren't looking at Alex. They're staring at each other, Dad mouthing "concussion" and shaking his head in a very rude manner.

Charming.

"Hello?" I say, impatiently. "Alex saved my life! At least thank him."

"We can't, Cleo," Tolly says slowly. "There's no one here."

"Don't be ridiculous! He's right here sitting next to me!" Honestly, a girl gets knocked out for forty-eight hours and her entire family flips. Embarrassed, I turn to Alex to apologise.

But Alex isn't there.

"Where's he gone?" I look around wildly. The window's shut and there's no way he could have pushed past Tolly and Dad without being noticed. Where's he hiding? Under the bed?

"Christ, don't fall out!" Tolly shoots forward and grabs me. For a second the room dips and rolls sickeningly. "Your brain's come loose, sis. There's nobody here."

"But there was!" I shake my head and my brain really does swivel in my skull. Where's Alex gone? I can still see him vividly: his laughing green eyes and smiling mouth hover in front of me like something from *Alice in Wonderland*. He can't just disappear. "He was here! He saved me from falling under a car. I remember that bit really clearly."

Dad and Tolly exchange a look.

"What?"

Dad sits at my bedside and takes my hand in his. "Sweetheart, no one saved you from that car. You tripped on the kerb and fell sideways."

"I fell sideways because Alex pulled me out the way!"

"Cleo, that really wasn't how it happened! There were witnesses who made statements; even the driver said you were alone when you fell over. There wasn't anyone else involved."

I clutch the bed covers. My knuckles glow through the skin, even whiter than the sheets.

"But he was here! I saw him."

Dad shakes his head. "Sweetheart, you've had a really nasty crack on the skull. The doctors said you were extremely lucky not to have done more damage. You're bound to be a bit muddled for a while."

I stare at my father. I don't feel muddled. Alex *was* here. I know he was. I could see him.

"Hallucinations are quite usual after a head injury," Tolly states without looking up from his BlackBerry. "You just need some rest."

I think I need more than rest if I'm having long conversations with imaginary men.

"The false memories are a symptom of the concussion," my brother continues smugly. "The doctors have told us all about it. Confusion is to be expected, they said."

Tolly's lucky I'm bedbound, otherwise I'd probably bop him on the nose. Then he could see for himself just how confusing a head injury is.

I close my eyes wearily. I know what I saw. Only minutes ago Alex Thorne was sitting on my bed and chatting to me, every bit as real as my family or the busy nurses.

"He was here," I insist. "I really did see him."

Dad drops a kiss onto my forehead.

"Try to get some sleep, Cleo," he says softly. "Things are bound to be a bit confused. You just need to rest."

I'm too weary to keep arguing but I know I'm not confused. Alex Thorne was here sitting on my bed and he was with me when I had my accident. It's not my memory that's the issue here – it's everybody else's! I know what I saw.

What on earth is going on?

Chapter 6

I've had it with hospitals. I want my life back. I'm through with people clucking round me, shining lights in my eyes and telling me I need to rest a bit more. How can I possibly rest when I'm so behind with my work? I've spent the last few days begging Dad to bring in my laptop but I may as well be talking to the wall.

I *need* my work. Don't they get it? I'm going mad in here with nothing to do except watch endless property shows and flipping Christmas adverts on daytime TV. If I don't escape soon I'll be forced to take knitting lessons from the old lady in the bed next to me. Seriously, does she ever give up? All day and half the night she's been at it, clicking away with those infuriating needles until the tapping seems to be right inside my skull. I keep asking the nurses if they can get her to stop but they don't seem worried, preferring to take my pulse or tend to the rest of the patients. They've completely ignored her, poor old soul. It's just as well I'm here to chat to her. I guess Susie was right when she once told me that there's no time to care in the caring profession.

Where is Susie, anyway? She's supposed to be coming over, hopefully to take me home if I can find someone to discharge me.

"Are you all right, pet?" asks Knitting Lady, peering at me over a tangle of cat-sick-yellow wool. "You look at bit peaky."

"I'm fine, just a bit tired."

I can't really tell her I'm exhausted from listening to her clicking needles all night and I certainly can't mention how I keep seeing things out of the corner of my eyes. If the doctors get so much of a whiff that I'm having visions they'll never let me out, and so far I've done a sterling job of pretending I feel fine. I've even laughed off thinking I saw a man at the foot of my bed when I woke up. "Ha! Ha! As if!", "In my dreams!", "I should be so lucky!" etc., etc., which I think has just about convinced them.

But Alex was so real, just as real as Knitting Lady smiling at me over her needles or as the elderly doctor who walks up and down the ward all day and night, only pausing to pore over the charts that hang on the foot of each bed.

"Excuse me!" I call. "Can you discharge me?"

But the doctor ignores me, as he has done for every lap of the ward. Charming.

"Don't mind him, dear," Knitting Lady sighs. "He doesn't mean to be rude. He's obsessed with making sure he doesn't miss anything important. It worries him that he could make another mistake."

"It worries me I might be stuck here forever," I mutter.

"There are worse places," she smiles.

I'm sure she's right but I've got so much work to do. I managed to get Susie to liberate my laptop, so that's something. Simon's phoned twice and updated me on the preparations for the exhibition and offered to come and visit too. I haven't taken him up on this; I may have had a wallop on the head but the memory of him seeing me in my red and white spotty pants is mortifyingly fresh. Where's a nice spot of amnesia when a girl needs it?

"Cleo, babes! How are you feeling?"

It's Susie, stomping across the ward in platform boots.

"I feel much better," I tell her. "I'm hoping to go home today."

Susie's brow crinkles. "Is that a good idea? You've had–"

"I know, I know; a really nasty bump on the head. But I'm going crazy in here, Suse! I need to get home. There's only so much daytime telly a girl can watch."

"There is?" Susie looks amazed, but then she would. Phil, Holly and Jeremy Kyle are practically her best friends.

"Suse, do me a favour?" I say, leaning across to my bedside cupboard and delving for my clothes. "While I get dressed would you be an angel and grab that old doctor for me? I've been calling him for ages but he keeps ignoring me. I think he's a bit deaf actually."

"What doctor?" Susie screws up her eyes and scans the room. I wish she'd stop being so vain and admit she needs glasses. Not only is her short-sightedness bloody annoying but it also makes driving with her a hair-raising experience on a par with anything offered at Alton Towers.

"He's over there at the end of the ward, by the nurses' station?"

Susie shakes her head. "Where?"

"She can't see him, dear," pipes up Knitting Lady.

"Susie needs glasses," I sigh. "But that doctor does too because he's ignored me all morning."

Susie whips round. "What did you say?"

"I wasn't talking to you; I was talking to her," I say, nodding at my fellow patient.

"Who?"

Blimey, I hadn't realised just how bad Susie's eyes have got. Once I'm better I'm dragging her down to Specsavers because this is ridiculous.

"The lady next to me? Bloody hell, Suse, you need to sort your eyes out. Especially," I lower my voice, "if you can't see that bright yellow wool!"

"I can't see her, Cleo," says Susie slowly, "because there's nobody there. The bed's empty."

Click, click, click go the needles. Knitting Lady shrugs. "They can't all see us, dear. You must have the gift."

"I don't have a gift! I just have good eyesight!" I snap. "Stop messing about, Suse."

Susie is staring at me with eyes like saucers. "Shall I get a doctor, Cleo? Does your head hurt?"

"No!" I snap. "But you're doing it in! Stop winding me up; it isn't funny."

"Babes, I'm seriously not winding you up. You're scaring me." Susie plops herself onto the bed and lays the back of her hand against my forehead. "There's nobody in that bed. Honestly."

Shaking off her hand I open my mouth to apologise to Knitting Lady – and then close it abruptly.

The bed's empty. The skeins of eye-wateringly loud wool are nowhere to be seen and the overblown roses that have been dropping petals on the floor have gone. The sheets are tucked tightly against the bed and the pillows are plumped in readiness for the next poorly head.

Oh dear Lord. I've lost it.

"Head trauma is a serious thing." Susie is in nurse mode now. "You may well experience changes in smell and vision."

Changes in smell and vision I could handle. Having conversations with imaginary people I cannot.

"But she was knitting all night! She drove me mad!"

"Hallucinations," says Susie wisely. "It's not uncommon."

Hallucinations of knitting grannies? I work with mummies, for goodness' sake. Couldn't I hallucinate something a bit more exciting, like a chat with Tutankhamun? No, there has to be a rational explanation. There's *always* a rational explanation for these things, isn't there? Maybe she slipped out of bed and the nurses tidied up while I wasn't paying attention?

"Bollocks," says Susie bluntly when I offer this explanation. "Total bollocks. Your mind's playing tricks on you, babes. It's not unusual after a head injury."

"*My* mind doesn't play tricks," I say through gritted teeth. "*My* mind is rational. I have a PhD. I publish in academic journals. I *do not* imagine things. Ever."

Susie holds up her hands. "OK! OK! Don't get upset; it isn't good for you."

I swing my legs out of bed. "I'm going to settle this right now. Then we'll see whether or not I'm hallucinating."

My feet touch the floor – which is a little sticky actually, a detail that would send Tolly into orbit – and suddenly I feel very weird. The room rocks like a Tube train passing a bumpy bit of track and I sway before Susie clutches my elbow in alarm.

"Take it easy!"

"Yes, take it easy," echoes a nurse, shoes squeaking on the floor as she scuttles across the ward to propel me back into bed. "We're not ready to get up yet! What are we thinking?"

If I didn't feel so sick I'd tell her I'm twenty-nine, not nine, but unfortunately I'm too busy retching into a kidney bowl to say anything. Several doctors and bowls of vomit later, I'm safely back in bed and pinned beneath the stiff sheets like one of my mummies.

OK. Maybe I'm not as well as I thought I was.

"Be a good girl and stay in bed," says the nurse firmly, opening the curtains and revealing that the bed next door is indeed empty. "You need to rest."

I close my eyes in defeat. I'm seeing things – so it's a shrink I need, not rest. If, that is, I *was* seeing things? Maybe my accident has bumped the bit of my brain that processes space and time? That's likely, isn't it?

"What about the old lady in the bed next to me?" I ask. "Where's she gone?"

I open my eyes again, just in time to see Susie and the nurse exchange a look.

"Babes," Susie says gently, "I already told you: the bed was empty."

"But I saw her! I was talking to her!" I turn to the nurse in desperation. "You must know who I mean? She's an old lady? Talks a lot? And she knits non-stop? Those clicking needles were driving me mad, actually, because she knits all night."

The nurse looks surprised. "Why, that sounds just like Mrs Collins. She knitted all the time with the brightest yellow wool I'd ever seen."

"That's her! The wool was gross! I told you, Suse, I've been talking to her for days." Relieved beyond belief I turn back to the nurse. "Have you moved her? Where's she gone?"

"I don't know how to tell you this," the nurse says slowly. "It's going to be something of a shock."

I think I know what's coming but it won't shock me. I'm the girl who spends every working minute thinking about the deceased. OK, so they're thousands of years dead rather than minutes, but it's the same thing. A chemical process in the brain stops and the body ceases to function. It's all perfectly natural and, although unbearably sad for those left behind, nothing to be frightened of.

"She died, didn't she?" I say. I touch my stitches tentatively and smile. "I'm starting to realise just how much of an injury I've had. Don't worry, I won't freak out. I guess I just got a bit muddled with when things were happening."

But the nurse has turned very pale. "Mrs Collins did die but it wasn't today."

I must be more muddled than I thought. "Was it yesterday?"

She shakes her head. "Mrs Collins didn't die yesterday. She died three weeks ago and in that very bed. There's no way that you could have met her, no way at all."

Susie's mouth is hanging open. "A ghost?"

The nurse shrugs. "A lot of nurses see things in hospitals. The night staff often say they see old Dr Andrews. He gave a patient the wrong drugs and killed her by mistake. He couldn't cope with the guilt so he hanged himself in the locker room."

Susie's hand flies to her mouth. "How tragic!"

"They say he walks up and down the wards checking the charts, just to make sure no one makes the same mistakes that he did," finishes the nurse. "Poor man. Doomed to haunt the NHS for all eternity."

My hands are gripping the metal bed frame. If my stomach wasn't so empty I think I'd vomit again.

I don't believe in ghosts! It's all rubbish. Ghosts are for the credulous and the uneducated; they're just tales to add excitement to boring lives or add atmosphere to stately homes. Ghosts don't exist and I don't believe in spirits or spooks of any description. Full stop.

There's no such thing as ghosts!

So in that case what on earth is happening to me?

And who or what is Alex Thorne?

Chapter 7

"Are you sure you'll be all right?" worries Susie, tucking the duvet round me and handing over the remote control. "I don't like leaving you on your own when you've been so poorly."

I laugh. "I'll be fine. I'll just sit here and watch telly. I might even have a lovely hot bath."

Susie looks worried. "I'm not sure having a bath's a good idea. What if you pass out or something? You only came out of hospital this morning. Maybe I should cancel my shift and stay in with you?"

"Don't be silly. I was there for over two weeks. They wouldn't have let me out if there was anything to worry about, would they?"

The last thing I need is Susie flapping around like a mother hen. All I want to do is flip open my laptop, hook up to the Internet and get stuck in to some work, which definitely won't happen if Susie stays in. I'll be doomed to an evening goggling at drivel like *Totally Spooked* while she watches me carefully for signs of head trauma. As if anyone who watches and believes in *Totally Spooked* is in a position to comment on my head trauma!

"I suppose not," Susie says reluctantly. "It's really late notice for Giraffe Ward to get a bank nurse. Are you sure?"

"Of course I am." I nod like a creature deranged, which I suppose I am – deranged by everyone fussing over me, that is – and cross my fingers under the duvet. "I'll watch a bit of telly then have an early night."

"OK." Susie checks the thermostat and then blows me a kiss. "Everything's warm and toasty here, I've made you a flask of tea and the phone's on the arm of the chair. If you don't feel well call me straight away. Understood?"

"Yes, boss," I laugh.

"If anything," she pauses awkwardly, "if anything *strange* happens then call me at once. Promise?"

I roll my eyes. "Susie, we've been through this a hundred times. Nothing strange happened at the hospital. When I was floating in and out of consciousness I must have overheard the night staff telling ghost stories and chatting about their patients. That's all. I got all muddled."

"But you knew all that stuff about Mrs Collins!"

Poor Susie. She's so desperate to believe in the paranormal that she'll clutch any straw, however feeble. I've had a lot of time to mull over my strange experiences and to talk to the doctors about the side effects of head injuries, and of course there's a logical explanation for what I'd *thought* I'd seen. I just hadn't realised how bad my injuries were, that's all.

"I was concussed, Suse. You said I wasn't well enough to be discharged that day and you were right. It was all nonsense."

"Mmm," mutters Susie, still looking worried. "I guess so."

"I know so." I've got to be firm here or she'll be swinging crystals and dialling the telephone psychics before I know it. Thank goodness I didn't tell her about seeing a mystery man called Alex Thorne! She'd be trawling the hospital records at once and buying me a crystal ball. "Now get to work, Nurse Maxwell, or you'll be late."

Once I hear the door slam, followed by the thump, thump, thump of Susie thundering down the stairs, I count to twenty before slowly exhaling.

"Right, Freddie," I say to Freddie, Susie's fat white Birman cat. "Time for me to have some fun!"

I spend the next hour wallowing in a delicious milk-and-honey bath that wouldn't have been out of place in my namesake's palace. I slap on a face pack, deep condition my hair and shave my legs until they squeak. I'm going to go into work tomorrow and I'll probably see Simon, so it won't hurt to look my best. I need to try and make up for that last excruciating time he clapped eyes on me.

Feeling weak with mortification I try to distract myself by summoning up all the things I like so much about Simon – but for some reason every time I try to picture his face I see instead the face of my long-ago Christmas stranger, the young guy with the guitar who'd held me close, whose kisses had promised so much, and who'd vanished without a trace.

I must have hit my head extremely hard to be brooding over *him*. For years I've succeeded in blocking him out. I haven't wanted to think about him; I didn't want to remember how my limbs melted when I kissed him or how the hard contours of his body felt as he pulled me close. It sounds foolish, but in spite of all the time that's passed since that chance encounter my pulse still quickens at the memory and I can almost feel the coldness of the snowflakes on my upturned face. How can one stranger, one stranger who never got in touch, still have this effect on me? Why on earth am I thinking about him again after all this time, when I'm going to see Simon tomorrow?

I screw my eyes shut and try to focus on Simon, but no matter how hard I try to conjure it up his face just dissolves away like the snowfall in my memory and I see instead the wide violet eyes and sharp cheekbones of my Christmas stranger. All I can feel is the croissant softness of his mouth on mine and the way his hands cupped my face so tenderly…

I'm not dwelling on him. It's ancient history. Where have all these thoughts come from? Honestly, since I bumped my head I'm not myself at all. It was just a Christmas kiss between two total strangers on a deserted railway station. I never even found out his name because Dad arrived then and I was swept away into the horror of losing Mum. I scrawled my number onto an old till receipt but I never heard from my Christmas stranger again. It was as though he'd vanished into the snowstorm, and after the funeral was over there was nothing for me to stay in England for. I need to put him out of my head once and for all. A real guy can never measure up to a dream.

Wrapping myself in a snug bathrobe I make a detour into the kitchen, where I pour a large glass of white wine and tip Susie's flask of tea down the sink. Back in the sitting room I light a scented candle before curling up on the sofa with the cat and my duvet, and scrolling through the Sky menu. The room is warm and cosy, the wine is slipping down a treat and for the first time since I hurt myself I start to relax.

With one eye on the telly and the other on my computer I spend a happy half an hour deleting all the spam from my email folder, catching up with Facebook and browsing eBay. Then I open up my folder on Aamon and study the CT scans and notes until my eyes grow heavy in the warm vanilla-scented room and I end up typing nonsense. Yawning widely I click out of the folder and back to my home page, where I Google "head trauma" and terrify myself by reading about the horrendous side effects that I may soon be suffering from. Personality change, loss of sex drive, trouble with memory, delusions… The list is endless and very, very depressing.

Note to self: stay away from Wikipedia. My next search will involve some serious research papers on the subject.

I wander to the kitchen and slosh more wine into my glass. Is alcoholism another side effect? I don't seem to remember reading that as I worked my way down the list of doom. Then again, neither do I recall seeing that hallucinating about men called Alex Thorne is common either – and that certainly happened.

Settling down again on the sofa I balance the laptop on my knees and idly type *Alex Thorne* into the search engine. Without thinking twice I click on the first link and gasp when the screen fills with that achingly familiar face. Green eyes hold mine, dark floppy hair falling over them, and his head is thrown back as he laughs.

My hallucination is pictured large as life on the screen of my Mac. He exists. He really exists.

I lean away from the laptop. My heart's racing and for a moment I think I'm going to pass out. This isn't possible. There's no logical explanation; I've never heard of Alex Thorne before.

Reaching for my drink I lean forwards again and read the entire wiki page almost without breathing, not stopping until I've absorbed every detail about

Alex Thorne. Apparently he was in a band called Thorne and died a tragic death in a hit-and-run accident just outside Museum Tube station.

Hang on, that rings a bell. Museum Tube is where I was nearly attacked and where my would-be assailant claimed to see me with a young man. I laugh aloud at the absurdity of all this. It's clearly some head trauma I have, to be getting this confused. I must be mixing up all sorts of details and making myself believe them: that's it. The human brain is an incredibly sophisticated organ, after all. It contains tens of billions of neurons, so who knows what it can do when pushed or jolted?

OK, so I may *think* I haven't heard of Alex Thorne before but that could well be my brain playing tricks. Perhaps subconsciously I've caught sight of a headline or maybe heard a song. Maybe I even read about his death somewhere. That's plausible, given that he died only minutes away from where I work. Is that why I imagined seeing him in the hospital?

My head is really hurting now. I take my glasses off and rub my eyes. None of this makes any sense. I'd never even heard of Thorne before. I was in Egypt when they were taking Britpop by storm, and now that I have heard of them Alex is dead and the band is finished. Maybe I do need to see a head-trauma specialist.

My hands, resting on the computer keys, are chilly and stiff. The tip of my nose feels cold too and my breath is making clouds. The heating must have gone off or something. Maybe the electric's up the creek again? The TV seems to be on the blink too: ITV2 has vanished in a snowstorm of static. I burrow deeper under the duvet and stare at the computer screen, where a guy stands on stage, arms raised in salute as he grins at the camera. That's him. No doubt about it. Alex Thorne. The guy who saved my life.

Or rather, the guy I *imagined* saved my life, since Alex Thorne is nothing more than a figment of an imagination I never even knew I had.

Oh God. I am going mad; that's the only explanation. How can I conjure up someone I've never even heard of unless… unless…

"No way," I whisper. "It's impossible."

"No it isn't. It's perfectly possible."

Alex Thorne, dead rock star and invention of my troubled mind, is sitting in the armchair by the window, grinning at me. One leather-trousered leg is crossed over his knee, and hair as dark as molasses falls across his pale face. The cat leaps up from my lap, hissing and spitting at Alex before tearing from the room.

"I never really was a cat person," says Alex.

"You're just a figment of my imagination." I say slowly. "I bumped my head and this is a side effect. It says so on Wikipedia."

"Total bollocks," he says airily. "Besides, everyone knows wikis are a crap source of information. Someone as brainy as you really ought to know better."

I search frantically for a logical explanation. "This is my memory playing tricks on me because of the injury. There's no way I can see you because… because…"

I trail off miserably. There is no logical answer. For the first time in my life I'm well and truly at a loss. Thank goodness Susie isn't here.

"Go on, you can say it. You can't see me because I'm dead? It's OK. I'm over being upset about that now. I won't say it isn't annoying because it bloody well is, but I'm kind of used to being a ghost." Alex's eyes crinkle and a dimple dances in his cheek. "We have all kinds of fun."

"But ghosts don't exist!"

"Obviously they do, Cleo, otherwise you and I wouldn't be chatting now," says Alex reasonably. "Pinch yourself if you think you're dreaming."

Obediently I pinch myself very hard on the arm. "Ouch!"

"I'm still here," says Alex while I rub my arm. "Please don't self-harm any more on my account. Can't you just accept it?"

"No, I can't!" I snap. "It's impossible. When you're dead, you're dead. Life's just a chemical reaction."

He looks amazed. "Surely you don't really believe that? Life's far more than chemical reactions." He leans forward and fixes me with a bright emerald stare. "Why couldn't I have attached myself to some nice dippy hippy like your flatmate?"

"Yes, why me?" I ask, pulling my duvet up to my chin because the room's icy cold now. "Hypothetically speaking, of course, since I know this is just a hallucination."

Alex rubs his forehead with the heels of his hands and sighs. "If I told you, you'd never believe me."

"Try me," I say.

"Maybe you're a psychic? That'd explain it."

I laugh so hard at this that my head hurts even more. "Hardly. I don't believe in ghosts, remember?"

Alex shrugs. "And? That wouldn't matter if you were naturally psychic. Even if you didn't believe in us, you'd still have the ability to see ghosts."

I think about Mrs Collins in the hospital and that poor pacing doctor. How had I seen them? Me, a psychic like that lunatic Lilac Delaney? Surely not?

Alex's jade eyes narrow and he leans forward. "You *have* seen other ghosts, haven't you? I knew it! That bump on the head has woken you up to your psychic skills."

"Oh please," I say. "You sound like Susie. And anyway, *you* found *me*, remember?"

"I was drawn to you," Alex agrees. "And there's a reason for that. A really good reason." He stops, looks for a moment as though he wants to say more, and then just pulls a face. "Enough of that. Were you a Thorne fan?"

I take a sip of my wine. It's chilled now, a bit like the rest of me. "I hate to break it to you but I'd never heard of Thorne until this evening."

Alex places his hand over his heart. "Well, that puts my ego neatly in its place. Five Brit Awards and two Grammys, Cleo. We were a little bit famous?"

"Good for you," I say.

"Oh well, you don't look like the kind of girl who listens to pop music so I shouldn't really be surprised. Anyway, music isn't what links us. It goes back further than that. Cleo, I've been searching for you. How do you think I recognised you at Museum Tube station?"

"For me?" My head is a carousel of confusion. I wait for him to elaborate but Alex is suddenly quiet, as though he's already said enough.

"Go on," I say encouragingly, and he sighs.

"It's kind of complicated, so if it's all right with you I'll start with a Saturday night several weeks ago. Do you remember that evening when you were alone on the platform at Museum Tube and a strange man with a scar made his way towards you? He looked like he was going to sit down, didn't he? But then he started talking to thin air and moved on?"

"And later on he attacked a girl outside the station," I nod. "He claimed he left me alone because I had a man with me."

"You did," says Alex simply. "Me. I sat there and put my arm around you and I prayed with every fibre of my being that he'd see me. It must have worked."

"I smelt a citrusy scent," I recall. "And I can smell it now."

"CK One," says Alex proudly, with a wink. "Drives girls wild."

I'm intrigued. "How come a ghost can smell of aftershave?"

He grins. "What am I supposed to smell of, rotting flesh? It's eau de toilette, to be precise. And anyway, why does it matter to you? You don't believe in me, remember?"

I'd almost forgotten that minor detail. In fact I'm starting to forget a lot of things since Alex reminded me about the strange incident at Museum Tube station.

"This isn't possible," I protest.

"So you say, but here I am. I think you have a gift. That whack on the head has unlocked it."

"Oh please! You're not serious?"

"Think about it, Cleo. You can see me. I can manifest to you. Jesus, you have no idea how hard I've tried to reach my brother. It's impossible. There are some people who genuinely have the gift and you, Dr Carpenter, are one of them. You can really see me! Besides, ghosts love you. Your office is full of them. Can you find Aamon a proper football, by the way? That rubber-band one is crap. And get that bloody cat a basket."

I goggle at him. "You think you've seen Aamon?"

"I don't *think*, I know! We played a bit of footy together. He's a pretty cool kid and he wishes you'd talk to him rather than just thinking about his remains. He says you're right about his evil stepmother too."

"What?" There's a sensation like somebody's dropped a scoop of ice cream down my neck. I haven't shared this finding with anyone; it's far too early days and I was waiting for another CT scan to come back before I could verify my worst suspicions. "How on earth do you know that?"

"Because Aamon told me," says Alex patiently. "She sounds like a right bitch. Aamon says she wanted him out of the way so that her son, snotty Setau, could rule in his place. She stabbed him in cold blood, right between the neck and the top vertebra. The cat tried to claw her, so she killed that too. They were mummified very fast and the priests weren't happy at all. Not that his stepmother cared. She just wanted him written out of history."

I'm staring at Alex. He has just, in thirty seconds, confirmed several of my hypotheses.

"Don't look so surprised," he says. "That museum of yours is teeming with ghosts and we do talk. I don't know how you haven't noticed us."

My chin is practically in the basement flat. "You can find me at work? As well as here?"

"Pretty much anywhere. How do you think I managed to stop you from getting flattened on a busy road?"

"So you could appear at any time? Like when I'm in the bath or getting dressed?"

Alex raises an eyebrow. "I hadn't thought of that!"

A blush creeps over my face and my heartbeat increases. Obvious side effects of my injury, I suppose.

"Only kidding," he grins. "Not that I don't think you'd look lovely in the bath, of course. Not that I'm thinking about you in the bath! Oh shit." He buries his face in his hands. "Now I won't be able to think of much else!"

"If I believed in you I'd hit you."

"I wouldn't bother. You'd only go straight through me and it really tickles."

We grin at each other. Then Alex melts from the armchair and is next to me on the sofa.

"Cleo," he says, his breath like the north wind against my cheek. "I really need your help. I've tried and tried to reach Rafe on my own but I can't do it. You're the only one who can see me. I need you to talk to my brother for me. He's alone and he's in a really bad way. If he carries on the way he is then I don't think it'll be long before he joins me. I have to save Rafe from himself. That's the reason I'm still here."

Now my headache is really pounding. The wine sloshes in my stomach. "You actually think you had a choice?"

He nods. "Before I died Rafe and I said some terrible things to one another. Really awful, Cleo. I didn't mean any of it and I would have put things right, I really would, but I never got the chance. One moment I was jumping out of his car, the next there was nothing but noise and heat and metal crushing me. Then everything was over."

"And that was it? You were dead?"

"Yeah. I was dead and had no chance of making things up with Rafe. How can I find any peace knowing he's so grief-stricken? He's in a terrible way. You have no idea what happens to some people when they grieve."

I do actually. After Mum died we all crumbled in our individual ways.

But I don't ever think about that.

"Rafe and I are tight. When our parents died we would have gone into care if Nan hadn't taken us in. After she died we only had each other," Alex continues. "He's all the family I have, and I have to make sure he's OK. He's my brother. Cleo, I promised Nan we'd always look out for each other and look how it ended." He dashes his hands across his eyes, which are shimmering with tears. "Christ. Sorry."

Without thinking twice I move to put my arms around him, or rather I try to but my arms slip straight through his leather jacket. Goosebumps shimmy across my flesh.

"No way!" I gasp.

Alex gives me a watery smile. "Still think I'm a dream?"

I stare at him in shock. Did I really just put my arms through a ghost? The chill clings to my limbs and my breath clouds the air.

"This can't be happening," I murmur.

He pins me with big sad eyes. "It is. I promise you, it really is. Cleo, please help me make things right with Rafe. He's in such a bad way and I'm scared that unless I help him something terrible's going to happen. You can tell him how sorry I am and that I don't blame him."

"No way! Your brother will think I'm nuts! Or some kind of deranged stalker fan. Look, no matter what you may think, I'm really not the person for this job. Can't you find a medium?" I wrack my brains. "I know! What about that woman from *Totally Spooked*?"

He screws up his nose. "Lilac Delaney? You have to be kidding. She's a total phony."

"And I'm a total sceptic!"

"Who's talking to a ghost! Come on, Cleo! It'll be worth it just to get rid of me – and, believe me, I'm going nowhere until I've managed to make things right with Rafe."

We eyeball one another, both equally determined.

"I'm going see my consultant again," I decide. "I'll tell him all about these weird episodes and he'll give me some medication to make all this go away."

Alex smiles. "Go ahead; be my guest. Crank up the drugs. This isn't a dream. You really can see me and I'm not going anywhere."

"But I don't want to see you!" I cry, jumping to my feet and sending my wine and laptop flying. "Just go away! Go and annoy somebody else and leave me alone! Go on! Push off. I don't want you."

"Fine," says Alex coldly. "Be like that. But sending me away isn't going to help. Face it, if you can see me you'll see all the others too – and they might not be quite as obliging as I am. You know where to come when you need some help."

"Not to you!" I shriek. "You're nothing but a chemical reaction in my brain!"

A crazy chemical reaction in my brain, it seems, because I'm suddenly talking to thin air: the sofa's empty. A wine stain spreads across the duvet and my laptop lies upside down on the carpet. The television chatters to itself in the corner of the room, the fairy lights twinkle and the cat reappears to wind itself round my ankles. Even the warmth is back, although the sweat that trickles down my back is icicle cold.

I collapse onto the sofa. What's happening to me? Am I really going mad? Suffering from paranoid episodes? Having delusions?

But if Alex is just a delusion why do I now have two huge pinch marks on my arm?

Chapter 8

Five to nine the next morning finds me in the GP's surgery, playing dodge-the-virus with every snotty toddler and coughing pensioner in the vicinity. Normally I avoid such places, which is probably an overreaction to all the horror stories Susie tells me about MRSA and other killer superbugs. Seriously, if I listened to my best friend I'd never go near a hospital again and I'd only venture into the doctor's wearing a full nuclear decontamination suit. Already I've coated my hands with about eight squirts of hand gel and snorted half a vat of Vicks First Defence up my nose. I probably smell revolting but to be honest I don't care – I'm far too busy trying to avoid breathing too deeply. The man sitting opposite me is sneezing and spluttering everywhere and I can almost see the germs parachuting in my direction.

Great. I'm coming in with head trauma and probably leaving with pneumonia. Just what I need. Who exactly did I upset in my last life again?

Although it's only early, the waiting room is crammed to bursting point with patients balancing precariously on narrow plastic seats or being swallowed whole by enormous high-backed armchairs of the variety normally found in an old people's home. I've somehow managed to end up on one of these and I'm burrowing into it, my hands avoiding the worryingly tacky armrests, while I read all the posters and information leaflets on the walls in an attempt to distract myself from the germ warfare all around me. I've been sitting here for twenty minutes now and already I'm an expert in hand-washing techniques, understand the need to vaccinate my baby and have been well and truly warned that this practice will not tolerate violence and aggression towards its staff. I could also learn all about the importance of using condoms if I really felt like it – but on top of all my other problems right now, contemplating my lack of a sex life and how I made a complete fool of myself in front of Simon would probably push me over the edge.

I'm only here because I need help. After the events of last night, it's becoming clearer and clearer to me that either the doctors have missed something pretty major on my brain scan or I'm going crazy. There's no other logical explanation. I'm seeing visions of a dead rock star with whom I'm having imaginary arguments in my own sitting room. I mean, does that sound normal? If it hadn't been for the huge pinch marks on my arm I would have assumed I'd just fallen asleep and dreamed the whole episode.

My hallucinations of Alex Thorne had freaked me out so much that I'd been incapable of making further progress with my notes for the job application; nor had I felt able to re-examine my emailed scans of Aamon to see whether there was any truth in Alex's revelation. Or was it my own revelation, conveyed in a dream? My thoughts had been like tangled fishing twine, and no matter how hard I'd tried I just couldn't unravel them to make any sense of it all. Just as I'd followed one lead it had snagged and knotted itself up into another. Alex was merely a figment of my mind, I'd lectured myself sternly as I'd brewed some tea to warm myself up; the details I'd *thought* he'd told me I must have heard somewhere previously, that was all. The accident had just caused the part of my mind that processed memory and time to act a little differently. I'd cheered up significantly at this thought – until a small voice that I couldn't quite ignore pointed out that I'd been given the all-clear by my consultant. Besides, I knew that I'd never heard of Thorne before.

Still icy cold, I'd paced around the flat trying desperately to find an explanation. At one point I'd even raided Susie's pile of *Fate and Destiny* magazines just in case the articles on angels and guides and psychics could shed any light on the problem. Luckily I came to my senses halfway through an interview with the infamous Lilac Delaney, who was discussing how she'd first discovered her psychic gifts. No bumps on the head or dead rock stars for her; apparently she had always been able to see dead people, in true *Sixth Sense* style.

"It's my calling to help loved ones on the other side come through to share their messages of hope," she'd gushed. "Even pets that have passed over have something to say."

As Lilac had continued to communicate the innermost thoughts of a dear departed moggy, I'd put the magazine down in disgust, convinced that even reading it was sufficient evidence that I was losing my mind. Frustrated, I'd taken myself off to bed. I must admit I undressed as fast as I could, unable to shake the thought that Alex was lurking in the shadows hoping to catch a glimpse of my bra and pants. Honestly, the whole thing was ludicrous; there was no way I could carry on like this. If I was cracking up then I'd better find out why, and fast, before I started chatting to Elvis or something. It was always better to know the facts. If Mum had shown a doctor her lump sooner rather than spending weeks in denial, things might have been very different...

So, bearing all these factors in mind, when I woke up this morning the first thing I did was make an appointment to see my GP.

"There has to be a logical reason," I whisper to myself. "There has to be."

"Keep telling yourself that if you want," says an amused voice that's starting to become annoyingly familiar. "I've already told you the truth. You really can see me. No pills will make me go away"

Glancing to my left I groan out loud, causing several patients to look over in alarm. Alex Thorne is lolling in the chair next to me. His dark hair flops over his eyes but I can tell he's grinning at me.

"Go away," I hiss – or rather, I try to, but I don't want to look like a total lunatic addressing thin air. Quite a few other people are looking at me in a rather worried fashion now. I can't say I blame them. *I'm* looking at me in a rather worried fashion too.

"How can I if I don't exist?" says Alex reasonably.

It's a good point – not that I'm going to give him the satisfaction of conceding it. Instead I pointedly turn my back on him and pretend to be fascinated by a dog-earned copy of *Heat* magazine. Oh look! Katie Price has got married again. And who on earth are the Kardashians?

"Don't be like that," says Alex. "You're stuck with me so we might as well be friends."

"I am *not* stuck with you," I mutter out of the side of my mouth. "You're just a chemical imbalance in my brain."

The man on my right shifts down a seat. Thank God I don't know anybody here. Imagine if I started hallucinating at work? Walking down the staircase in my pants would look dignified by comparison. I really hope the doctor can give me something to sort this out – and soon, too, before I lose all credibility.

I focus my full attention on the magazine.

"I used to be in *Heat* loads," says Alex conversationally.

I try to ignore him, but he's very persistent, chatting away nineteen to the dozen and insisting on reading out all the posters describing infectious diseases. When the receptionist calls my name I leap to my feet in relief. Escape here I come! Very soon I'll have an explanation and some lovely pills, and life will go back to normal.

"Thank God!" cries Alex, jumping up and following me. "I couldn't take much more of that. I've already diagnosed myself with scabies, rubella and IBS."

"Whoa! Hold it right there!" I stop in my tracks and Alex cannons into me, or rather there's a whoosh of cold air just like you get when you leave the freezer door open. "Figment of my imagination or not, there's no way you're coming into the doctor's with me."

"Even if you're talking about me?" Alex looks put out, but I'm not falling for those sad puppy-dog eyes.

"Especially if I'm talking about you," I tell him, and then I'm inside the consulting room, shutting the door firmly behind me. Alex, hallucination or whatever strange chemical imbalance he represents, doesn't follow me.

"Cleopatra Carpenter? Please, take a seat." The GP, who must be about twelve, smiles at me from across the desk. Seriously? That's my doctor? I really must be getting old.

He's looking at me in a confused way. "Sorry, I thought you had somebody with you? I could hear you talking in the corridor?"

"Oh that? I was on my mobile," I improvise wildly. I know I'm here to talk about my hallucinations but I'm not intending to tell him quite the extent of them. I want to be cured, not committed. "It's switched off now."

While I take a seat, the doctor pulls up my records on the computer and regards them thoughtfully. When I explain that since my head injury I haven't felt quite myself and that I keep seeing things out of the corner of my eye, he nods sympathetically.

"That's perfectly normal and to be expected, after a head trauma. It's very common for patients to experience blurred or distorted vision."

I swallow. Blurred vision I could cope with, but being stalked by a dead rock star? I'm not so sure. For a second I'm tempted to tell him everything, but I stop myself just in time; the thought of what might be written on my medical records prevents me.

"All your test results seem fine," the doctor reassures me once he's shone a light in my eyes and checked my reflexes. "The CT scans are clear too. I think all you need is some rest. I'm more than happy to sign you off for a fortnight."

"Rest?" I almost laugh at the idea. "I haven't got time to rest. I'm flat out at work and so behind after being off. The last thing I can do is rest."

"So work is stressful?"

I want to bash my head on his desk in frustration. Work isn't stressing me out but seeing Alex Thorne everywhere I go will. But, of course, the moment I opened my mouth and mentioned work I sealed the deal. The doctor is now convinced that I'm suffering from a severe case of work-related anxiety, and I leave the surgery with a handful of prescriptions. Once outside I tear these up and stuff them in the nearest bin. Something tells me that medication isn't going to help one bit – and besides, there's no way I can risk dulling my mental faculties while I'm completing my research and preparing for the interviews. I'll just have to hope that the bit of my brain that's misbehaving sorts itself out soon.

But in the meantime I have the feeling that Alex Thorne won't be far away...

Chapter 9

OK, so my visit to the doctor wasn't quite the success I'd been hoping for; instead, it looks like I'm on my own with all this. According to the experts I'm fighting fit, my brain is looking fine and all I need is a rest. As if more than two weeks stuck in a hospital bed wasn't enough of a rest! It was having a *rest* that got me into this mess, if you ask me.

So what now? I stand outside the surgery and watch the early-morning world go by. It's a beautiful winter's day: the air feels like an ice blade across my cheeks and a round lemon-sherbet sun hovers in a bright cloudless sky. Overnight there was a sharp hoar frost and this morning London sparkles as though a child has tipped glitter all over the city. As I pause on the pavement my breath curls into smoke plumes and I feel my nose begin to tingle with the cold. All around life is teeming: couriers on bikes hiss by, buses rumble and confused tourists dither dangerously on the kerbside, only a heartbeat away from heavy wheels, while they attempt to interpret their maps.

They're off to explore the museum, of course. At just the thought of the Ancient World Gallery and the pools of silence in my office, my pulse starts to slow. Maybe, just maybe, if I can get back into my work and my routine, everything else will fall back into place too. I have my satchel with me, I'm officially cleared for action and there's a huge backlog to tackle – not to mention a very pressing job application to complete.

And, whispers a sneaky little voice, you might just bump into Simon as well...

I wind my scarf around my neck and shove my fingers deep into my gloves. This crush on Simon has got to stop. And soon. Along with the Alex Thorne hallucinations, it's taking up way too much headspace. Take getting dressed this morning, for instance. In the good old pre-Simon days, I would have put on some black trousers, a sweater and my trusty pumps without giving my outfit much thought. Today I devoted at least ten minutes to choosing a matching lingerie set; I don't intend to flash my knickers at all and sundry again, but from now on I'm making sure I'm prepared for any disaster. Then I spent another good quarter of an hour torn between a wrap dress in smoky teal and a cashmere jersey dress. Eventually, the teal dress won, and when I'd teamed it with a pair of boots and my black duffle coat I was just about ready. The whole exercise had only taken over an hour.

Over an hour to choose my clothes? Seriously? Maybe I'm more affected by this head injury than I'd realised.

As I turn left and walk back towards the museum, I reflect on the irony that I'm so devastated to have been given a clean bill of health. When I was stuck in my hospital bed I'd have given anything to be told I was absolutely fine. Today, though, this news fills me with despair, because if there isn't anything physically wrong with me then there's only one explanation: I really must be losing the plot. Either that, or I'm actually seeing ghosts – and that's not a notion I want to dwell on.

I pop into the museum café and order myself a latte. While I wait by the counter I text Susie and then check my emails. As I scan through them I suddenly become aware of the music that's playing on the radio, and the hairs on the back of my neck prickle.

> *Never thought love could feel like this*
> *I held her close*
> *One Christmas kiss...*

I can't believe it – it's that depressing Christmas song again. I swear that until the other day I'd never heard it; now it seems to be playing everywhere I go. It's like being stalked. I heard it on the radio in the cab that took me to the surgery, I heard it in the background on *Daybreak* while I was getting dressed and now it's even followed me into the museum coffee shop. I feel like covering my ears and singing "la la la".

Latte held in a shaking hand, I make my way up the main staircase. Several colleagues stop me to welcome me back, but I'm too wired to chat for long. Instead I mutter my excuses and even forgo a look at the latest additions to the gallery and a possible glimpse of Simon. I'm wishing I hadn't shredded that prescription. All I want to do is reach the sanctuary of my office, shut the door and slump at my desk. Then all I'll hear is the pulse of the museum around me: the soft footfalls, a slammed door maybe, distant voices. And no pop music.

My office is just as I left it. Everything is neatly stored in its place and all the papers are stacked in their files. My computer gathers dust on the desk and, as usual, the phone is off the hook. Comforted by this, I replace the receiver in the cradle, pick up the rubber-band ball that's mysteriously found its way to the far side of the room, and boot up my PC. The stillness of the place soothes me and little by little I feel the tension slide away. Coming to work was definitely the right thing to do.

I spend the next couple of hours catching up on paperwork and making phone calls. Once the contents of my in tray look a little less like Mount Sinai I take a breather, stretching out my cramped limbs by wandering around the office for a couple of minutes. Finally I pause by the replica sarcophagus cases and think about the mysteries that lie within the real ones, protected in the laboratory next door. One small boy and one cat. A pet or a deity? If Alex is right then this was a pet. It wasn't unusual for cats to be mummified too – our exhibitions are full of examples – but they were more often bred especially for pious burials than kept as pets.

Hold on. If Alex is right? What am I saying? He doesn't exist: this was just my mind using theories I already had and creating a narrative. Alex Thorne – who is a figment of my imagination – has not been helping me with my research. If I start thinking like that I may as well give up.

I force myself to focus on the facts and what I do know. Tests have revealed exactly the same materials, down to flakes of skin and strands of hair, which appear in Aamon's own cartonnage. That suggests the two were done at the same time. There could be a scientific link to the supposition.

Suddenly struck by this thought, I hurry back to my desk and pull open my files. I love it when ideas strike me like lightning. For a while there I'd been worried that because my brain was starting to play tricks on me it wouldn't be able to handle my work anymore, but I was wrong. I've got that wonderful fizzing feeling that tells me I'm onto something. Go, little grey cells, go!

I'm still thinking hard when there's a thud on the desk, followed by a loud yowl. Papers avalanche to the floor and I leap out of my seat with my heart hammering against my ribs. For a moment I can hardly breathe. In fact, I can hardly move. I'm rooted to the carpet with disbelief.

How on earth can there be a cat sitting on my desk?

While I stand staring, the cat purrs loudly and starts to make a big show of washing itself. This sounds crazy, but with its long legs, tabby coat, slanty green eyes and sharply pointed ears, it looks like some sort of Egyptian wildcat, even though it seems to be domesticated. Sleek and alert, this creature is certainly different from Susie's fat Birman.

I stare at it. This cat is no ordinary moggy. Far from it. In fact, in terms of its build, this feline bears some striking similarities to the mummified cat that I've been analysing.

Surely not...

It's a weird coincidence, that's all. Somehow a cat has found its way into the museum and wandered into my office. It's a bit out of the ordinary, of course, but that's what's happened. What other explanation could there possibly be?

"Here, puss." I reach forward to ruffle its fur, but the cat leaps down onto the floor with a loud meow and scampers across the office and out of the door. Without a second thought for my scattered papers and disrupted work, I follow it out into the corridor. Yet no matter how fast I run, I can't catch up with it: the cat remains several feet ahead of me as it bounds along. I'm not giving up, though. Apart from the fact that animals aren't allowed in the museum, catching it is the only way I can prove to myself that I'm not going crazy.

The cat turns a corner and I increase my pace, flying around the corner after it and running wallop into somebody coming in the opposite direction.

And wouldn't you just know it? That somebody only happens to be Dr Simon Welsh.

"Steady, Cleo!" His arms tighten around me and for a blissful second I sway against his firm chest like something from one of Susie's Mills and Boons. I can't help myself; I stay there just a little longer than I really need to.

"Where are you going in such a hurry? The staircase again?" he asks, those blue eyes twinkling down at me.

I feel my face flame. Is it my imagination, or are his arms holding me just a little tighter than is strictly necessary? Unable to cope with the way my knees are starting to turn into soggy wool, I break the contact and step away.

"Welcome back, by the way," says Simon. "We've missed you."

I stare at him. "Really?"

"Really. Now, why are you in such a hurry? I don't suppose you were on your way to my office?"

I'm still so spun out by the cat appearing out of thin air that Simon's words don't even register. Later on I'll torture myself with the cringeworthy memory that I don't make a witty retort but just come out with a garbled explanation about looking for a cat.

"A cat? In the museum?" Simon's brow pleats. "Are you sure?"

"Of course I'm sure! It was in my office and I've been trying to catch it. It must have run past you. Didn't you see it?"

He shakes his golden head. "I think I would have noticed if a cat had just wandered past me." His eyes narrow in concern. "Cleo, are you quite sure you're ready to be back at work? You've–"

"Had a nasty bang on the head," I finish. "Yes, yes, I know. And for the record, Simon, I'm absolutely fine. I'm just not a big fan of finding cats in my office, that's all. There are papers in there that I don't want disturbed."

Simon stares at me. "Right. Well, if I see it I'll let you know."

"Maybe you could ask one of the security guys to remove it," I say. "I don't want any more of my research notes messed up. And speaking of research, I'd better get back to mine."

"How about I lend you a hand with that?" Simon suggests. "You're looking really pale. Maybe you shouldn't be staring at a computer screen. I could help you transcribe things, if you like?"

He's smiling down at me and for a moment I'm seriously tempted. The only trouble is I don't think I'd be able to concentrate sufficiently to get anything done. Even now I'm distracted by the impossible thick sweep of his eyelashes and his strong forearms, sprinkled with golden hair.

I give myself a mental shake. This is not the time to start fantasising about my colleague. Anyway, I'm possessive about my research. Nobody's seen my findings on Aamon yet – and that's the way I'd like to keep it. The others can see them when I do my big reveal. Gorgeous as he is, even Simon isn't getting a sneak preview.

"Thanks, but I'll be fine," I tell him firmly. "Besides, I'm sure you've got quite enough on as it is. Just let me know if you see that cat. It really shouldn't be here."

And with this I return to my office, but I can feel Simon's gaze burning into my back. Great; now he probably thinks I'm even more of a lunatic than he did before. Nice work, and I've only been back here a morning. I can hardly wait to see what happens by this evening.

I'm about to open my office door when a noise stops me in my tracks. My fingers freeze as they close on the handle and my heart starts to race. I can hear laughter. Peals and peals of laughter – the high-pitched and infectious giggling of a child.

And it's coming from my office.

My empty office.

With a growing sense of terror I fling open the door, then stop abruptly when I see a small boy dressed in what can only be described as ancient

Egyptian clothing, playing with my ball of rubber bands; he's rolling it across the office for the cat that leaps after it. Seeing me at the door he looks up and beams at me, a delighted gap-toothed smile, which is followed by a gabble of sounds. Are these the long-lost words of an equally long-lost language? Did ancient dialect sound like this?

"Who are you?" I whisper.

Pointing to his chest the little boy smiles again broadly and then pronounces two syllables that floor me.

"Aamon!"

I'm clutching the doorframe, but even this isn't enough to anchor me in a world where everything is shifting. As the office dips and rolls and the light starts to dim, Alex Thorne's words echo through my memory and strike dread into my heart.

If you can see me, then you'll see all the others too — and they might not be quite as obliging as I am.

Maybe Alex isn't a figment of my imagination after all.

Chapter 10

"Right, one cup of tea with three sugars and a double chocolate-chip muffin. That should do the trick. We can't have you fainting like that again. I think you'll be responsible for my first grey hairs, finding you in a heap like that!"

Simon deposits the spoils of his trip to the museum café onto the desk and begins to unwrap the cake, crumbling it onto a plate, which he pushes in my direction.

"Thank goodness I needed to speak to you about the Assistant Director's position," he continues, his eyes brimming with concern. "Otherwise you might still be there lying on your office floor."

To be honest I wish he hadn't found me sprawled on my office floor, displaying today's knickers to the world. Then I could have come round slowly and on my own rather than to the shock of waking up and finding Simon looking down at me. Him and Aamon, the cat, two Roman soldiers and, to my even greater shock, Henry Wellby himself, every bit as whiskery and serious as he looks in his portrait.

It's a revelation. I never knew my office was so crowded. On the bright side, at least all the effort I put into choosing today's knickers hasn't been wasted.

"I know you're going to argue with me but I really don't think you're up to being back at work. You're still recovering from a head injury," Simon continues with a worried frown while stirring my tea vigorously.

He has no idea just *how* much I'm suffering from this head injury – and he's never going to know, either. At least, not if I have anything to do with it. I curl my hands around the hot teacup and try to ignore the crowds of unwanted visitors who've gathered around me. There're not really there anyway: all of this is in my imagination. I just wish they wouldn't talk quite so loudly.

"Still don't believe me?" Alex Thorne says. He's perched on the corner of my desk, his legs dangling in a carefree manner, and he's grinning at me like a Halloween pumpkin. "Still think ghosts don't exist?"

I ignore him; of course I do. Simon's chatting away and I'm trying to concentrate every scrap of my attention on him, although this is easier said than done while Aamon's playing football and Henry Wellby's leafing through today's notes. He looks impressed, which is good news even if he is just a figment of my imagination.

"Fine," shrugs Alex, scooping up the cat and caressing its bony head. "Be like that then. But don't say I didn't warn you, Cleo. It isn't just me, remember? You can see us all!"

"Shut up!" I hiss from out of the corner of my mouth.

"Cleo, are you sure you're all right?" Simon asks. His hand, warm and strong, closes around mine. His index finger skims across my palm and I shiver. God, he's even more beautiful close up. It's as if someone's drawn around his irises with an indigo fine liner.

"You're dreadfully pale and you're so cold," he adds, resting the back of his hand against my brow. "Shall I take you home?"

"He's hitting on you!" Alex teases. "Don't let us get in your way."

I turn my back on him. Whatever mad tricks my mind is playing on me, I'm going to rise above it all. I'll go back to the doctor and I swear to God I won't throw the next prescription away.

"I'm fine. I just skipped breakfast before I came to work," I fib. I don't think I've actually eaten breakfast since about 1998. I don't have time for breakfast: I'm far too busy.

Alex snorts with laughter. "Breakfast! That's a good one! It'll take more than a McMuffin to cure this!"

I shoot him a look that ought to be capable of laying him out dead at my feet – if he wasn't already dead, obviously.

Simon doesn't look convinced by my explanation. "I still think you're back here far too soon. It's all too much for you. Look, why don't you pass some of your workload over to me? I really don't mind helping out until you feel better."

Now there's one thing I never do, and that's share my research. The very thought fills me with horror. My work is so precious it feels as though he's asked me to hand over my child.

"I could take over the bits you've been doing on the boy pharaoh – Aamon, wasn't it – if that would help?" Simon continues, presumably mistaking my surprised silence for acquiescence. Although his tone is light and casual I notice that his index finger is busy squashing cake crumbs flat against the plate.

"That's a really kind offer, Simon, but I'm absolutely fine," I say firmly. There's no way I'm letting him get his mitts on Aamon. No way. The discovery of Aamon's secrets was always Mum's dream and I'm not giving it away to anyone else. Almost as though he knows what I'm thinking, the little Egyptian boy gives me a toothy grin and then turns a cartwheel before chattering away to Henry Wellby, who seems to understand every word and nods thoughtfully.

Oh Lord. I really should have taken the doctor up on that prescription.

"Are you sure? It wouldn't be any trouble for me," Simon insists, his denim-blue eyes wide and filled with concern. "I know the Aamonic period isn't especially significant but I really don't mind if it takes a load off you."

I nearly inhale a mouthful of my sweet tea. *Not particularly significant?* Does he have any idea just what I've uncovered here? How much this tells us about the course of history? It's immense! If it's true that Aamon was murdered and usurped it throws those who followed him into a whole new light.

It will change Egyptology forever.

Stung by his flippant dismissal of years of Carpenter family research, I feel my temper simmer. Step away from my work, buster!

"You don't have to thank me," says Simon gently, mistaking my gobsmacked silence for overwhelmed gratitude. "I'm more than happy to lend a hand. Shall I just copy your files to my hard drive? Or shall I take your laptop?"

Quite frankly I'd rather drown myself in my sugary tea than let anyone else near my research – however kind, well respected and good-looking they happen to be – let alone copy it. Resisting the urge to tell him to back the hell off, I simply say again that I'm absolutely fine and more than happy to resume normal service. I even force myself to eat the muffin, which suddenly tastes of cotton wool, and focus on him telling me all about his latest paper on the Ptolemaic period. Every now and then Simon asks me a question about my research, dropped into the conversation very subtly. My senses are heightened now. I can tell Simon's trying to get to some point, but I can't for the life of me work out what it is. He's been around the houses more than Phil and Kirstie.

"Do you know what?" Simon says suddenly, jumping to his feet and grabbing my hands. "I think we need a change of scene. How about you and I play truant for the afternoon?"

I glance at my desk. Papers are strewn all over it and my laptop screensaver blinks at me balefully. *Work*! it says, and I really should listen.

"I don't think so, Simon, fun as that sounds. I've missed quite enough time as it is."

"Then another hour or so won't hurt. Let me take you out for lunch. I know a super little place just off Covent Garden. They do the best moules. Come on, Cleo, humour me. I've been wanting to take you out for weeks."

He has? Wow. Funny though; a couple of weeks ago, pre bang on the head, the thought that Simon Welsh would be asking me out would have been enough to send my pulse sky high. I must really be off colour to be hesitating.

Now, what would Susie do in my position?

There's an easy answer to that question: she'd be sitting at a table in a low-cut top and putting in an order before you could say lunch date. Maybe it's time I loosened up a bit and took a leaf out of her well-thumbed book on dating. Besides, being in my office surrounded by all and sundry is starting to make me feel nervous. Who knows who'll appear next? Elvis? Henry VIII? Maybe a change of scene and some fresh air is exactly what I need.

"That sounds lovely," I say, deliberately turning my back on Alex et al as I reach for my satchel and start to gather up my papers. "Would you pass me my laptop, please, Simon?"

"Leave all that here," Simon says quickly. "Have some time off for an hour or two at least. Lock your office up; it'll all be fine until tomorrow."

For a moment I'm tempted. But then I think about the promotion and just how much work I have to do. Maybe I will take the afternoon off, but I'll work from home instead, and late into the night if I have to.

"Thanks, but I'd rather take it with me," I decide, as I snap the laptop lid down and scoop up the rest of my papers. "I need it all anyway to finish off the job application."

Simon's smooth brow crinkles. "You're still thinking of applying for the Assistant Director of the Department position?"

"I'm not *thinking* about it at all: I *am* applying," I tell him.

"After all you've been through? You seriously think taking on all that extra responsibility is a good idea?" He shakes his head and rakes a hand through his thick blond hair. "Cleo, as a friend – a friend who cares for you very much – I'm not sure that's such a good idea. I'm really concerned that the stress of it all might be too much for you."

I almost laugh out loud. Stress? From a job? He seriously has no idea. When Simon's experiencing the kind of crazy hallucinations that are bugging me right now, then he can talk about being stressed. Until then I think I'm the resident expert on that. Compared to seeing things that aren't there, running our department would be a walk in the park.

"I'm fine, honestly. The doctor says there's absolutely nothing wrong with me, so I'm still applying. Of course I am."

Simon shrugs in a defeated manner. "Well, good for you. I just think it's a shame that you're putting yourself under extra pressure unnecessarily."

I pause, holding my files in mid-air between desk and satchel. "What do you mean, unnecessarily?"

He looks a little embarrassed. "Come on, Cleo, don't make me spell it out."

"Go on, Cleo, do," says Alex, materialising at my elbow. "Take it from me, this guy's a creep. Good-looking bastard, but still a creep. Why do girls never see it?"

"Shut up!" I hiss. "I don't need you interfering! You make everything ten times worse."

"What's that supposed to mean?" Simon demands, looking hurt. "I'm only trying to help. I just want you to accept that you're not well enough to be here and that you need to rest. I want the best for *you*!"

"You want the competition out of the way, more like!" scoffs Alex. His green eyes glitter with dislike and he's bristling like one of Stephenie Meyer's werewolves. Goodness, he really is upset on my behalf, which is very sweet but completely unnecessary. I don't need a knight in shining armour, or in this case in a battered leather jacket and designer jeans.

"Can I handle this, please?" I say.

"Cleo, who are you talking to?" Simon steps closer, right through Alex, and puts his hands on my shoulders. He shivers. "Brrr. Your office is so damn cold. That's it; I'm taking you home. You're in no state to be here."

I shake him off impatiently. "I'm fine!"

"Sweetheart, you're not! You're talking to thin air!"

"He can't see me," says Alex, helpfully, just in case I don't get it.

I roll my eyes at him. "That's because you don't exist."

Alex rolls his eyes right back. "So why are you talking to me then?"

"Because you're a delusion!" I almost yell.

"Cleo, please," Simon pleads, now holding my hands tightly. I can see his breath in the air, and he's very pale. "Calm down. My God, just listen to yourself! There's no way you're up to even applying for this job, let alone doing it. You've been seriously ill; you're fragile and you need to rest. I'm begging you not to put yourself through the strain of it. Not when they've practically promised the position to me anyway."

"Practically promised isn't the same as *having* promised," Alex growls. "Tosser!"

"Go away!" I tell Alex furiously. "Leave me alone! This is all your fault."

Simon's face is grave. A muscle twitches in his cheek. "I'm sorry you feel like that, Cleo, really sorry. All I can say is, may the best man win. And right now I think we both know that person is me."

I stare at Simon. I know that he's as qualified as I am, but I've worked at the museum longer and I have far more experience in the field. I'm the better candidate, and that's not me being arrogant: it's just stating a fact. There's no way Simon's been promised anything. Our boss, Professor Hamilton, wouldn't do that.

Or at least, he wouldn't have done before my accident.

"I really do care about you, Cleo," Simon says, turning and heading for the door. "Just be kind to yourself and get well, please. Your career isn't nearly as important as your health."

My head's pounding. Alex, hands on hips, is looking at me expectantly while Aamon stands behind Simon pulling faces and sticking his tongue out. Suddenly all the anger and fight drains from me and I slump at my desk feeling dangerously close to tears. Oh God, what if Simon's right and I'm really not well? The evidence is right in front of me, isn't it? I'm seeing things that can't possibly exist. In despair, I bury my face in my hands.

"I'm still applying, Simon," I whisper, my eyes still closed and my temples thudding. "I'm still applying."

"Then it's up to you, Cleo. But you know how I feel. You're unwell and clearly not up to the job. And believe me, if Professor Hamilton and the board ask for my opinion, that's exactly what I shall be telling them."

The door clicks shut. When I raise my face again Simon has gone, our lunch date evidently off the agenda, and so have Alex and all the others. The office is suddenly very quiet.

I sit at my desk, all alone, and wonder whether Simon's right after all. Am I really going mad?

Chapter 11

When Dante was writing his "Inferno" he was careful to include only nine circles of hell. For his readers' sake, he decided to leave out the tenth and the most terrifying circle of all. Forget pits of fire and demons armed with pitchforks; those are nothing, absolutely nothing, compared to the hell that is shopping in the West End on a Saturday during the lead-up to Christmas.

Honestly, I must have had a bigger bump on the head than I realised to have agreed to go shopping in Oxford Street on a Saturday afternoon in early December. What was I thinking? I can't stand shopping at the best of times, and if I do have to buy something then it's preferably first thing in the morning and on a weekday. It just goes to show how persuasive Susie can be that I'm now squashed onto the Tube, roasting inside my thick duffle coat and with my face rammed into a stranger's armpit as we wait in the dark tunnel for the signal change. Down here in the city's intestines nobody can hear you scream; I've got no choice but to wait it out.

Susie was rather surprised when I called her earlier to say I was on my way. She wasn't the only one: I was just as astonished as she was. Normally I'd have made an excuse about being busy with work, so that I could keep myself hidden away in the museum – miles away from fairy lights, crowds and Slade telling me Christmas is here.

But these are not normal times and the problem is that my office isn't a peaceful haven anymore. Far from it. Since yesterday the delusions have only got worse. I could swear that there are people with me in my office all the time. I hear them and see them so vividly that I have to keep reminding myself that they aren't real. The place has been so busy that it's made Oxford Street look like a quieter option.

After Friday morning's events I'd gone home via the GP, picked up a new prescription, taken a couple of tablets and headed straight to bed. Before I'd drifted off to sleep everything had seemed fairly ordinary. Alex had vanished, the only feline following me was Susie's cat Freddie, and Aamon was nowhere to be seen. Simon was right: I was working too hard and the stresses of my job combined with my head injury were playing tricks on me. OK, so these weren't textbook episodes I'd been experiencing – my trawls of Google had yet to produce anything as crazy as seeing phantoms and having conversations with them – but every head trauma was different and individuals were affected in their own strange and unique ways. Still, unless I got a grip soon I would be jeopardising my career. That was not going to happen.

Anyway, I'd woken up early this morning – long before Susie, who was still sleeping off a heavy night's clubbing – and the world had still looked reassuringly normal. There were no signs of Alex, Egyptian cats or long-dead boy pharaohs, and in the bright winter sunshine I was able to laugh at myself. Of course there were no signs of these things, because they didn't exist! There was bound to be some medical explanation, I'd decided firmly as I'd left the flat. I'd probably watched a movie years ago and been replaying scenes in my mind. The brain was more powerful than any computer and capable of pulling all sorts of stunts. By the time I'd picked up a coffee from the little shop opposite the museum, crossed the road and made my way though the first wave of keen Saturday visitors, I'd been feeling even more optimistic. A good night's sleep had been all I'd needed.

I'd walked through the entrance hall, waving at a couple of the security guys and calling out a cheerful hello to the gift-shop crew before scooting through the Ancient World Gallery just to check on the new exhibits. Nobody else from the department was around, which was a relief; I wasn't sure I was up to facing Simon yet. Not only was he knicker-meltingly gorgeous (God, I was starting to sound like Susie), but he now thought I was a complete nutcase. I was also trying very hard to forget that he'd seen my underwear. Twice.

In any case, when I'd let myself into my office I'd been thinking of Simon and quite how I was going to redeem myself. I'd booted up my computer, fetched my notes and been about to sit down at my desk and get stuck in, when seemingly out of nowhere a cat had jumped right in front of me, purring loudly and spilling my latte all over my folder. Moments later Aamon had whizzed past with Henry Wellby hard on his heels and the rubber-band ball ricocheting off the walls. I'd clutched the desk in disbelief, shaking my head as though trying to clear water from my ears. Then I'd pinched myself so hard I'd yelped. If pain was proof that I was awake, then the livid marks on my arm were all I needed to tell me that this was not a hallucination. It wouldn't make any difference how many tablets I swallowed now: this was not going away. Alex's parting words were suddenly terrifying. "If you can see me," he'd said, "you'll see all the others too – and they might not be quite as obliging as I am."

Oh my God. What if it was only going to get worse? Apart from never being able to get any work done, I'd go mad. With a cry of despair I'd fled from the office and out of the museum. Suddenly I wanted nothing more than to be in the crowds of Oxford Street, listening to Susie natter on about her latest romantic adventure and with nothing more pressing to think about than what to eat for lunch. I'd fired off a frantic text to tell her I was on my way to Selfridges, and it was only when I'd found myself in the depths of Museum Tube station, crammed onto a platform with seemingly everybody else in London, that my heart had stopped racing.

Now, as I stand sweating in the fetid recycled Tube-train air and do that Londoner thing of avoiding eye contact with people only millimetres away from me, the panic starts to recede. I'm wondering again if I've been imagining everything. Is this some delayed nervous breakdown? Maybe Simon's right and I'm not up to going for the promotion. The thought of *not* applying is enough to give me a breakdown, though. I've been working for this for just about as long as I can remember. There's no way I can quit at the final hurdle. I have to find a way of dealing with this. There has to be an explanation.

"Busy, isn't it?" says Alex cheerfully. He's pressed up against the door and is grinning at me from beneath his floppy fringe.

What am I saying? Of course he isn't really leaning against the Tube-train door: *he doesn't exist.* Alex Thorne is no more present in this Underground train than the Tooth Fairy or Santa Claus. I ignore him. If I start talking to thin air that makes me the Tube nutter du jour and, as bad as things are, they're not quite that bad. Yet.

"Still ignoring me?" Alex's eyes are raised towards the curved ceiling of the train. "It's getting a bit boring to be honest, Cleo. I thought you were an academic? How much more evidence do I have to give you? I know: look at this poor girl here." He points at Emo-style student who's shivering in spite of the heat of the carriage. "Watch what happens!"

Alex steps closer and the girl's breath clouds as though, rather than being baked alive in an Underground train, she's out walking on a frosty day. She frowns and plunges her hands into the pockets of her shapeless coat. The man crammed into the space next to her winds his scarf more tightly around his neck and looks puzzled.

"How's that for physical evidence! Go me!" Alex crows. "Now, what shall I do next to convince you?"

I glare at him but he just grins. "Oh stop it, Cleo. If the wind changes you'll get stuck. You wanted proof; I'll give you proof."

I try to ignore him but I can't: he's dancing through the commuters, waving his hands in front of their unsuspecting faces, tweaking scarves and making copies of the *Metro* flutter to the floor. If he wasn't already dead I could throttle him.

"Tra-da! Only you can see me, Cleo! It's time you started believing your own eyes."

Now that he's finished showing off, Alex saunters back and stands next to me. Instantly the temperature plummets and my skin crawls with goosebumps, just like it did in the flat.

"Feeling chilly?" he says.

"Go away," I snarl. "I haven't asked for all this! I don't want it."

Alex shrugs. "I don't think you have any choice in the matter. Like it or not, you've got a gift. Look around, if you don't believe me. All the others know you can see us."

And just like one of those magic-eye paintings that you stare at for hours until another image takes shape, it becomes apparent to me now that the carriage contains the oddest mixture of people wearing outfits from times gone by. Thirties, forties, fifties, sixties and seventies fashions abound and, although I might be mistaken on this, there's even an eighties punk; I really don't think Mohicans are in anymore. All of a sudden the train is full of extra people, superimposed over the rest of the passengers like a bad Photoshop job or something from a Hollywood thriller. Bruce Willis will wander by in a moment with some weird kid who sees dead people.

"Why is an American GI winking at me from across the carriage?" I demand, giving the tall man with the roving eye my best killer glare.

"Oh that's just Hank," Alex says airily, following my gaze. "He was killed in a bombing raid in the forties. He could move on but he likes it here. He's pretty harmless but you do need to watch him. For all his sweet talk about stockings and cigarettes he loves to ride the Tube and perv at the girls. He reckons it's easier to peer down their tops when they can't see him." He smirks. "He could be right!"

I'm outraged. "That's disgusting! He's dead!"

Alex winks. "I think one vital part of Hank believes it's very much alive!"

"Well, he should know better," I say primly. "Whether or not they can see him is irrelevant. That's harassment!"

Alex's green eyes glitter with mirth. "Cut the guy some slack, Cleo. He's from the 1940s. Political correctness hadn't been invented then. Besides, it gets a bit boring down here sometimes too. He needs to get his fun somehow!"

"Well, *you* should know better," I huff, looking over at Hank, who's admiring the ample chest of an oblivious commuter. "You're from a post-feminist era and he isn't. Women aren't just objects, you know. We're doctors and scientists and lawyers and…"

"Egyptologists?" Alex offers, looking amused. "Anyway, who says we're all post-feminists? Tell that to the Thorne groupies when Rafe and I were fighting them off, or not! Oh come on, Cleo, lighten up. I'm kidding! Where's your sense of humour?"

"It vanished about the same time you showed up," I mutter.

We are not having this conversation for a second longer. I can't believe I'm on a Tube train having a discussion about equal rights with a figment of my imagination. Aware that people near me are starting to look edgy, I make a big show of pretending to be talking into my mobile, the effect of which is marred slightly by the fact that I'm goodness knows how many feet under London, where there's no signal. Marvellous. I probably look like even more of a lunatic now. Fortunately at this point the train starts to move; we all stagger forwards. Briefly, the lights flicker off – and when they come back up, Alex and all the others have vanished. If, of course, they were ever really there to start with.

By the time the train pulls in and everyone surges up the escalator I'm feeling utterly defeated. Emerging into the magic of the West End in the festive season doesn't improve my state of mind, no matter how much the shop windows glitter and promise Christmas day cuddled up in tartan pyjamas or fun evenings partying in a new sparkly frock. I take extra care crossing the road this time, because God only knows what damage a second bump on the head will do; I'll probably start seeing Godzilla or something. As I'm negotiating my way, I'm starting to think that meeting Susie for a coffee is a mistake. I could do with a real drink instead.

Great. Now Alex bloody Thorne is driving me to alcohol as well as round the twist.

Selfridges is brimming with shoppers. Tills ring, carols play and there's a sense of excitement in the air. Feeling about as full of festive cheer as Scrooge would if he were asked to stuff a turkey and then charged for the privilege, I elbow my way through the crowds of women gawking at handbags, stomp past the Jo Malone collection of fragranced products and slalom through the cosmetics before riding the escalator to the top floor. The stairwells have been transformed into a winter wonderland and on the second level a group of musicians dressed in silver and white are playing that miserable Christmas song again. Honestly, I swear I'd never heard it before and now it's everywhere I go, haunting me as much as Alex. If I weren't in a bad mood already then I definitely would be by the time I arrived on the top floor.

"Hey! Cleo! Over here! I've got you a latte!" Susie, surrounded by a heap of yellow carrier bags, is waving at me from the far side of the coffee shop. I'm impressed. It's only a quarter to eleven and already she's made serious inroads into her new credit card. Not that I'm going to nag her about that.

Well, not just yet, anyway…

"Looks like you've had a busy morning," I remark as I attempt to join her amidst her purchases. There are so many bags the army could pop up here and use them as an assault course.

Susie shoots me a warning look from beneath her matted fringe. "Don't start, Cleo. I have to buy Christmas presents."

I hold up my hands. "I haven't said a word. So, who's lucky enough to be receiving gifts from Selfridges then? And who did you raid the lingerie department for?"

She has the grace to look a bit abashed. "Bloody hell, Cleo. What are you, some sort of psychic?"

Unfortunately yes, that's exactly what I'm starting to think I am.

"It's only a few bits and pieces for the ward Christmas party," she continues, rummaging in one of her bags and pulling out what looks like two glittery gold napkins tied together with dental floss. "I got this too, from a little shop I found. The new doctors have just started their rotation and I want to make a good impression."

"You'll certainly make some kind of impression in that, although I'm not sure that *good* is quite the word I'd use," I say doubtfully. Even Katie Price would hesitate to wear such a revealing outfit.

"Any impression, babes, is what counts," Susie says happily, shoving the dress back into the bag. "One of the Second Years, Dave, is lush. He looks a bit like Harry Styles – well, sort of. I'm going to be the present he unwraps this Christmas, just you wait. Cougar Town, one-way ticket!"

Brilliant. There goes my peaceful Yule. Susie's bound to pull, she always does, and I'll have to listen to them doing their impression of the Discovery Channel right the way through from the Queen's Speech to the *EastEnders* special. Maybe I'll visit Dad after all.

"Are you all right, Cleo? You look ever so pale. Is your head hurting?" Susie is in nurse mode now and scalpel sharp. She frowns. "I must admit I was a bit alarmed when you texted to say you were joining me."

"So now my keeping to the promise of a girly shopping day is evidence of my brain injury?" I force a laugh, but it sounds a bit strange even to my own ears and Suse looks even more concerned. She knows me and I've never willingly joined her on a trawl around the West End.

"Honestly," I say quickly before she can leap in, "I'm fine. But you're right: I have been working too hard, so I've decided to take a day off."

My best friend stares at me as though I've just sprouted another head. "If I wasn't worried before, I'm really worried now. You've taken a whole day off work? To go shopping? What's going on here?"

I'm not surprised Suse is worried. I know I'm acting oddly.

"Absolutely nothing," I fib as I fix my attention on my coffee rather than on my best friend's inquisitive face. "I just felt like a change of scene and spending some time with you. There's nothing going on except me addressing my work–life balance."

"Hmm," says Susie, unconvinced.

We sip our lattes thoughtfully for a few moments. Once I'm sure she's stopped looking at me as though she's doing my obs and checking for signs of a brain injury (which, let's face it, for me would include taking days off work and going girly shopping in the West End), I say idly, "Suse, have you ever heard of a group called Thorne?"

"Like, duh! Of course I have! Everyone's heard of Thorne. They were supposed to be the next Coldplay but hotter, you know?"

No, I don't know. Besides, I can't say I find Alex Thorne hot anymore – not unless you count making my blood boil with annoyance.

"What's the sudden interest in them?" Susie wants to know. "Is it because their Christmas number one's being played everywhere?"

I wish. Wouldn't that make life simple? Much simpler than, say, *no, it's because I'm being haunted by a dead band member.*

"Yes, that's it." I nod like the insurance dog. Goodness, this head injury is certainly turning me into a dreadful liar. "I think I must have been on fieldwork in Egypt when they were on the scene. It was quite a few years ago, right?"

As if on cue, the music in the café changes from Bing Crosby dreaming about a white Christmas to the same miserable song that's already been played by the musicians in the stairwell. It's about as cheerful as a Goth convention for the extra depressed.

"Wow, spooky! Talk about weird timing. This is their Christmas song!" Eyes like saucers, Susie dives for her iPhone and starts tapping away.

"This is Thorne?"

"Yep. It's their Christmas number one. Honestly, Cleo, it's like you actually live in ancient Egypt sometimes! Everyone knows 'One Christmas Kiss'. It won gazillions of awards and it's got this amazing story behind it. Come on, you must know it? It plays at all the Christmas parties."

"Those will be the parties I don't go to," I point out, and Susie pulls a face.

"We are *so* changing that this Christmas! Hey! I know! Why don't I help you choose an outfit for the museum Christmas do? You could have one like mine – they were on sale. Sexy Si won't be able to resist."

I can't help laughing at this idea, even though Sexy Si will be giving me a very wide berth, if the look on his face when I last saw him is anything to go by. Besides, apart from the fact that the museum do is a fairly staid affair, I'd probably fit about half a boob into a tiny frock like that and end up getting arrested or giving Professor Hamilton a heart attack. All in all it would be about as good for my career as having delusional experiences on a daily basis.

Which leads me back to the subject in hand…

"So the song?" I prompt. Susie is a terror for getting distracted.

"It's the second-bestselling Christmas single of all time – according to Wiki, anyway," she reads. I can't help remembering how Alex told me I ought to know better than to trust wiki entries. Why this makes me smile I have no idea, given that he's the cause of all my problems.

"Go on," I say.

"It could just be made up, of course, but there's the most romantic story ever to the song. Rafe Thorne wrote it – I think he wrote all the songs – and it's about this girl he met one Christmas Eve. Apparently he was on a railway platform in the middle of nowhere – you know, travelling home with his guitar over his back and all that – when he met his soul mate. He knew straight away that she was the one for him. They were all alone, the snow was falling and he kissed her while the Christmas bells rang across the countryside. Isn't that just the most romantic thing ever?" She closes her eyes dreamily, which is just as well because she can't see the shock on my face. Then she starts to sing, "'*Falling in love with the drifting of snow, how could I ever have let her go? One perfect night, a love like this, an angel's touch, one Christmas kiss.*' And then he let her go and he never saw her again, the muppet!"

There's a rushing in my ears, as if a high-speed locomotive is tearing through my brain. The blood feels as though it's draining from my body and I'm cold from head to foot even without Alex being nearby. This isn't possible. It can't be true. But if I were to put on my logical head and start analysing the evidence, what would I say then? There seem to be quite a few coincidences…

"God, I wish something like that would happen to me," Susie is saying longingly. Her voice sounds as though it's coming from a thousand miles away. "If I'm lucky it's a snog by the photocopier or a grope under the mistletoe at Christmas. No one's going to write a song about that, are they?"

I shake my head, a response that's good enough for Suse because she's on a roll now.

"Can you imagine being immortalised in a song like that? Anyway, it's a bit sad really because he missed the one chance of being with the love of his life, his soul mate. Their paths only crossed for that one moment; it was love at first sight and then he lost her."

He didn't lose her. He never called! She waited and waited and waited but he never got in touch. Anyway, she wasn't lost. She was in Egypt doing her fieldwork, ironically enough trying to bury her unpleasant memories by digging up the past.

That's probably not quite so romantic.

There's a pause because Susie's waiting for me to say something.

"Err, Cleo? Isn't this the bit where you're supposed to tell me it's all bollocks, and there's no such thing as true love or soul mates? Love's just a chemical reaction to encourage the species to propagate?"

Wow. Don't I usually sound a right barrel of laughs? She's not wrong, though: normally this is *exactly* the sort of thing I would say, because once upon a time I did think I'd met my soul mate – only to be bitterly disappointed. But today my vocal cords have gone on strike, along with my logic, my reason and all the other things that keep me sane.

"It was so tragic what happened to Alex Thorne, too; he was gorgeous," Susie sighs.

Flipping annoying sums him up much better in my opinion. Still, whether I'm annoyed with Alex or not, I must admit I'm curious now.

"So the band broke up after Alex was killed in the car accident?"

"Pretty much. Alex was the lead singer but his brother, Rafe, was the one who wrote the music. He was supposed to be a genius. You never saw much of Rafe: he was in the background and he hardly ever did press stuff. The rumour was that he wanted to give up the band and just write."

"What happened to Rafe?" My mouth is so dry I'm amazed I can speak at all. This is really him, the brother that Alex is so keen I help him reach. Is it possible that his brother is also my Christmas stranger? This has to be one coincidence too far.

Then again, coincidences do happen. Maybe my Christmas stranger was someone else entirely.

Susie maximises the screen with her thumb and forefinger and squints at it. "Wiki doesn't say much more, but I read in *The Sun* that Rafe Thorne hasn't written a note for years. I think he's pretty much a recluse. Here, have a look."

The iPhone is scooted across the table – but I don't even need to look at it to know what I'm going to see. Staring up at me with those wide-spaced violet eyes and a serious expression is a face I've not seen for a very long time. Ten years, in fact.

It's impossible.

Rafe Thorne, Alex's brother and Britpop legend, is none other than my Christmas stranger.

Chapter 12

My shock at seeing the face of my Christmas Eve stranger again is so profound that Susie's able to drag me around Selfridges for another couple of hours. Usually I'm driven crazy by her disorganised approach to shopping – which entails zooming backwards and forwards to look at things over and over again, with not a list in sight – but right now I'm glad of an excuse not to have to think. It's far better to concentrate on glittery things and frocks than to try to figure out what's happening to me. While I'm being frogmarched in and out of changing rooms and giving my credit card a hammering, at least I can't be thinking about the way my life is beginning to fall apart at the seams.

The world around me looks absolutely normal, give or take all the Christmas paraphernalia. There are no shoppers dressed in the fashions of bygone eras and so far Alex hasn't peered at me over a rack of clothes or waved at me from across the designer section – but even so, I'm not sure I can trust my senses anymore. Everything in my world has shifted and all my certainties have turned to quicksand. It's the most terrifying thing that's ever happened to me and, try as I might, I'm struggling to come up with a logical explanation.

I'm starting to worry that there isn't one, which leads me to one very unwelcome conclusion: this is actually happening.

While Susie's been chatting away I've been so deep in thought that she's managed to draw me into Topshop in Oxford Circus, fill my arms with party dresses and goodness knows what else, and shove me into a changing room. If she thinks it weird that I'm not protesting or taking exception to her choice of outfits, she's far too busy taking advantage of my distractedness to say anything. After all, this is her chance to get me into some bright colours and funky Kate Moss designs, and Suse isn't going to look a gift horse in the mouth by questioning my state of mind. Why let a head injury get in the way of a makeover?

I lock the changing-room door and lean against it, exhaling slowly. Did I really kiss Rafe Thorne all those years ago? Was it his mouth, softer than the brush of butterfly wings, that had skimmed mine? And was it his fingers that had so tenderly wiped away my tears? As I pull off my boots and unpeel my wrap dress, I might be staring at a floor-length mirror and a pile of party outfits, but in my mind's eye it's a snowy railway platform that I'm seeing: a moment frozen in time, a perfect moment to which nothing before or since could ever compare. Every detail is as fresh as if we'd only met hours earlier rather than a decade before. Of course it was him. There was no mistaking those unusual eyes, almost violet in colour; they'd leapt out of the screen, every bit as compelling online as they'd been in real life. My perfect stranger is Rafe Thorne, rock legend and brother of the phantom who saved my life and has been following me ever since.

Hang on, that's a thought. Does Alex know who I am? Does he know I'm the girl from the song? And if so, why hasn't he said anything?

"Because I didn't want to freak you out."

I'm certainly freaking out now, because Alex is sitting on the floor looking up at me – and apart from the fact that he's made me jump out of my skin, I'm in my bra and knickers. At least today's are white but that's not the point! I've had quite enough of men seeing me in my underwear lately and, whether he's dead or not, I'm certainly not making an exception for Alex Thorne – he of the playboy reputation and dubious taste in pervy ghost friends.

"You can't come in here!" I screech snatching up my dress and shielding my body with it like a prudish Victorian sea bather. "I'm changing!"

"Oh chill out, Cleo," drawls Alex. "I've seen it all before. Besides, you don't believe in me, remember, so what's the problem? Nice knickers by the way, although I did prefer the spotty ones! Sexy! Woof!"

I am not amused. Can't a girl have some privacy? There's no way I'm going to stand here in my smalls with Alex Thorne about.

"Go away!" I order. "I'm not kidding, Alex!"

"Keep your hair on! Anyway, *you* called *me*, remember?"

I glower at him. "I did no such thing!"

Alex looks triumphant. "I'm afraid you did. Why else would I be in Topshop on a Saturday afternoon? Believe me, no guy – dead or alive – really wants to spend his spare time waiting outside the changing room–" His eyes take a road trip over my body. "Although I must admit, being inside is a whole lot more fun!"

There goes that annoying blush again. "You're as bad as Hank!"

"Ouch. That's harsh, even for you. Look, I'll close my eyes, how about that?" Alex makes a show of screwing his eyes tightly shut and then places his hands over them for good measure. "Ooo! It's dark! I'm scared. I hope there aren't any ghosts!"

I hug the dress tighter against my chest. I'm not sure I trust him not to peek. Ghost, hallucination, whatever; he's still a boy.

"What did you mean about me calling you?" I demand.

"Who said that?" he deadpans, but I'm not laughing. This is not a joking matter. This is my life that's being disrupted.

"Seriously, Alex, I need to know what you meant by that?"

"You were thinking about why I hadn't told you about Rafe, so it's your fault I'm here. You summoned me. Don't blame me if you're half undressed." The lips below the hands curve into a smile. "Anyway, you're not the first girl who's taken her kit off and called me over, and I'm really hoping you won't be the last."

I choose to ignore his teasing. "So you appear if I think about you?"

This is not good news. If Alex does exist, and unfortunately all the evidence I've gathered so far is pointing in favour of this alarming conclusion, then I can't have him popping up whenever I might randomly think of him. What if I'm in the bath? Or on the loo? Or naked?

"Now you're panicking that I'll appear when you're in the bath or something, aren't you?" he laughs. "Like I want to see you on the loo, Cleo Carpenter!"

I'm scarlet now; my cheeks feel like the core of Sellafield.

"I thought I was supposed to be the psychic one?"

"Aha! So you are starting to believe me? About bloody time. No, Cleo, give me some credit. I'm not Hank. Anyway, you weren't thinking: you were talking out loud, which, unless I'm very much mistaken, is one of the early signs of madness."

"The first one is believing in ghosts," I say bleakly.

"Or denying all the evidence to the contrary," he shoots back.

I'm still trying to think of a cutting retort, and failing miserably, when there's a sharp rap on the cubicle door, followed by a bout of nervous throat clearing.

"Is everything all right in there?" asks a shop assistant. "I thought I heard voices?"

"Yes! Yes! Fine! Just, err, FaceTiming my boyfriend to ask his opinion on the dresses!" I explain hastily. Lord only knows what the shop assistant thinks I've been up to.

"The long green velvet one," says Alex helpfully. "That'll look great with your hair. And anyway, just for the record, I normally like to be bought dinner before I see a girl without her clothes and have to go shopping with her!"

I consider the green dress. It's strapless and floor length with layers of netting under the skirt. You can tell Susie picked it. Maybe I should get this for the staff Christmas party? It's not that I'm trying to impress Simon or anything, but it might be fun to have a change…

"Look, I'm not going to lie to you," Alex is saying a little awkwardly, interrupting my train of thought. "I've always known you were the girl my brother wrote about. At least, I've known that ever since I found myself in this peculiar situation. You have no idea how long I'd been trying to get your attention. I couldn't believe my luck when you hit your head and could see me. It really was my lucky day!"

When it comes to lucky days, that one isn't top of my list. It's not even on my list.

Then a thought occurs to me. "You were stalking me?"

"How uncharitable! That's not quite how I'd have put it. Listen, my brother isn't like me. I'm a lot more outgoing and brash – maybe even a little tactless at times."

"No. Really?" I say, and Alex laughs.

"Yeah, hard to believe, I know. I loved fronting the band and all the attention and that kind of shit that came with it, but Rafe, well... He's really shy; he was happy to just write the music and stay in the background. To be honest he hated the fame, hence our huge row about signing a new contract. He always feels things deeply, which is why when he told me about that girl he'd met – you, Cleo – and how he knew she was the only one for him, I knew he meant every word."

"Yeah, right. Is that why he never got in touch?" As soon as the words dive off my tongue I could kick myself, and hard. Great, Cleo. Well done. Now you sound really pathetic, still stewing about a guy who never called ten years after the event! Why I'm worrying about what my hallucination thinks is something I don't want to dwell on. I have a horrible feeling that I'm starting to see Alex as a real person. And if that's the case then it means I've accepted that ghosts really do exist. I'm not sure I'm quite ready for that paradigm shift just yet. I may be standing in my knickers in the changing room of Topshop and talking to thin air, but I'm still clinging to the final remnants of my intellectual dignity.

"He lost your details," Alex is saying. "I know it sounds like a lame excuse but he really did. Seriously, Cleo! He went crazy trying to find you. It drove me insane too. We must have spent hours staking out that station. I swear to God I almost took up trainspotting just to pass the time. And why the bloody hell didn't you tell each other your names?"

"It just didn't seem important," I say, although it does sound bonkers now. He'd called me Christmas Girl. I guess we were far too busy kissing. Names, history, futures – none of that seemed to matter back then. But then it doesn't, does it, when you're nineteen? You live in the moment. It's only now that I'm older that I find myself living more and more in the past.

"Well it might have saved ten years of heartache and ten years of Rafe wishing he could find you," Alex says, raising his eyes to the ceiling. "Jesus. You two deserve each other."

I stare at him. Discovering that Rafe hadn't just ignored me is almost as much of a shock as learning his identity.

"I'm not making it up," Alex insists. "Rafe was sure if we gave it long enough you'd turn up eventually. He remembered that your family lived nearby. You never did show, though, and in the end he had to accept that you probably never would."

"I was back in Egypt by then," I explain. "My mum died and I took off pretty soon afterwards." There hadn't felt like much else to stay for. Let's face it: I've pretty much stayed away ever since.

Alex nods, still with his eyes closed. "That figures. Anyway, long story cut short, Thorne was signed shortly after that and it all got pretty crazy. Rafe never forgot you, though. Our biggest chart hit was written about you – they reckon it even outranks Wham! now – and I know that every Christmas Eve without fail he went back to the station just in case." He pauses. "At least, he used to. I don't think he goes anywhere now apart from the off-licence."

There's a lump in my throat at this. It's all water under the bridge now but I can't help wondering what might have happened if we'd met again.

"So why were you looking for me?" I ask. Surely the wrong brother is crouched on the floor here?

"It was Rafe who made Thorne great. It was his talent that drove the band," Alex explains. "His lyrics and his compositions made us famous; I was just the front man, the Robbie to his Gary, if you like. Rafe never wanted the fame, but he put up with it because it was what I wanted. I knew I owed everything to him and I always said if there was one thing I could ever do it would be to help him find you. When I found myself…" He pauses.

"Dead?"

"Why mince words? Yeah, when I found myself *dead* I was drawn to you straight away. I guess I have to fulfil my promise before I can go wherever it is I'm supposed to go next."

"To the light?" I suggest helpfully. Lilac Delaney, psychic to the stars, is always sending spirits into the light on *Totally Spooked*.

Alex splays his fingers to give me a pitying look through his hands. "I've said it before and I'll say it again: you watch far too much crap telly for somebody who's supposed to be intelligent. All I know is that I need to make sure my brother's safe before I can do anything else. Maybe it's my mission? I don't know! No old man with a beard has popped up to tell me."

I'm pulling my own clothes back on again. The mention of Lilac Delaney has given me a horrible jolt. At the back of my poor confused and injured brain I seem to recall that I made a very rash promise to Susie. A promise that I think I'm about to regret...

"Anyway, that's my story," Alex finishes, oblivious to the fact that I've just remembered I have an evening appointment with Britain's most famous psychic. "Now do you understand why I need you to find Rafe for me? It's important!"

I do understand, actually. Alex has to fulfil his promise to Rafe before he can rest. It's classic stuff. Don't all the best ghost stories go this way? My mind is working furiously because this isn't an uncommon myth in ancient cultures either. Tombs are filled with writings concerning the soul's journey through the afterlife, and customs the world over repeat this exact idea. Perhaps I just need to give in and go with it. Maybe this is my brain's very complicated way of healing itself.

"So if I help your brother you'll leave me alone?" I say slowly. "You'll go away? My life can go back to normal?"

He nods. "I think that's pretty much how it works. Hey, I'm sorry for not telling you the whole story before. I really wanted to but I didn't want to freak you out."

"In that case I dread to think what happens when you do want to freak people out," I retort wryly. "And just for the record I *am* totally freaked out on just about every level. If I go and see your brother – and it's a huge *if*, by the way – then he'll think I'm a lunatic. People don't tend to take kindly to this sort of thing. I'd be furious if a total stranger came along and tried to give me a message from my mother."

Alex is indignant. "No he won't! Rafe'll be thrilled to see the love of his life and you and he will get together and everything will be fine. You'll live happily ever after and I'll push off to the pearly gates. Tra-da!"

"Who's had the bash on the head here? Do you seriously think we'll take one look at each other and fall into each other's arms, get married and have babies? You are kidding?"

Alex looks shifty and I know at once that this is exactly what he thought.

"And you say *I* watch too much crap TV? That's rich coming from a man who seems to think life's a Richard Curtis movie!" I shake my head. "I promise you that a touching reunion is never going to happen, Alex. It was years ago. To be honest I'd forgotten all about it."

"You're such a bad liar," Alex says airily, "and I think–"

But I don't get to find out whatever it is that Alex thinks, because at this moment Susie starts hammering on the cubicle door, and when I next look he's gone. My head's spinning and I hold the changing-room door to steady myself. I'm not sure how much more of this I can take.

"Cleo? Are you OK in there? You've been ages," calls Susie from the other side of the door, sounding worried. She probably thinks I've passed out from the shock of trying on exciting clothes.

"Just coming," I chirp back. Shoving on my boots and scooping up the outfits, none of which actually made it off its hanger, I unlock the door and step into the communal changing room – which is thankfully devoid of dead pop stars. It's full of teenage girls with willowy bodies; they're all preening in front of mirrors and moaning about non-existent fat bits. I feel about as ancient as one of my mummies. What on earth am I doing in Topshop? To my mind, the only person over twenty-five who could blend in well here is Kate Moss, and she has the unfair advantage of being a supermodel.

"Any good?" Susie asks, looking at the clothes hopefully.

I glance down. To be honest, I have absolutely no idea, but I do know that I can't face having to repeat this experience in H&M and Monsoon and Mango and everywhere else she'll take me. Knowing that Alex could pop up at any time, whether I'm dressed or undressed, is very off-putting.

"They're all great! I loved them and I'll take the lot," I declare impulsively while my credit cards start to tremble in the depths of my purse.

Alex is right about me being a bad liar; Susie's looking alarmed.

"You liked everything? Seriously?"

I glance down at the clothes in my arms. There are scarlet leggings, skinny jeans, miniskirts, the green party dress, three sweaters in jewel hues, and not a black or grey garment in sight. A pair of butter-soft leather trousers has even made it into the collection. Leather trousers! I'd never try on clothes like this, let alone buy them, so no wonder Susie is surprised. If she knew the half of what's been happening to me she'd be more than surprised. Leather trousers I can just about handle; ghosts I can't.

She threads her arm through mine. "Who *are* you and what have you done with the real Cleo Carpenter? Oh, who cares! Quick, whoever you are, I'm going to get you to the till before the real Cleo comes back and decides she wants to wear sludge colours again and bottles out of seeing Lilac Delaney tonight."

As she drags me to the cashier and watches, arms folded and head nodding approvingly with every beep of the scanner, I can't help wishing that the real Cleo Carpenter, the one who was always so certain about everything, would come back.

Nobody misses her more than me.

Chapter 13

"This is so exciting!" Susie is dancing from foot to foot, hardly able to contain herself. "I can hardly believe we're doing this, can you?"

Since what we're doing is queuing outside the local theatre for *An Audience with Lilac Delaney* then my answer is a resounding no, I cannot believe we're doing this. I've already made several attempts to wiggle my way out of it but there's no way Susie's going to let that happen. It doesn't matter that I've spent the whole day out shopping, let her persuade me into buying an entire new wardrobe and put up with my personal kryptonite "One Christmas Kiss" now playing in every shop I step foot inside, because I've *promised* that I'll go with Susie to see Britain's favourite medium in action. And best friends don't back out of their promises.

Unfortunately.

"But we've had a great day out shopping," I'd pointed out as Susie had unpacked her purchases. Wasn't this enough?

"To make up for my birthday, you mean?" Susie had not been prepared to negotiate. Her face had had that determined look, which I'd already seen on several occasions today when she'd homed in on another item she simply couldn't live without. "Which you missed, remember? And you *promised* to come to this, Cleo. You promised. It's way too late for me to find somebody else and I really don't want to go by myself. Please don't let me down. I'll be so upset. I'll probably never get over it, but hey! Up to you."

When Susie had put it like that, I'd felt terrible. Mostly because I'd known there would be no escaping this latest hare-brained episode. Like it or not, it seemed that I was doomed to spend my evening watching Lilac Delaney ripping off the vulnerable – err, I mean giving comforting messages of a spiritual nature.

"I know this isn't your bag at all," Susie had added, "and you think it's all a load of total and utter nonsense, but can't you just treat it as a bit of a laugh?"

The problem was that I was beginning to fear that this was *exactly* my bag. And I really, really didn't want it to be; neither was I laughing. Quite the opposite.

I'd thought back to the conversation Susie and I had had all those weeks ago when I'd been so blissfully certain that I was right that there was no more to life than we can see, and I could have howled. Why did it all have to get so complicated?

"I know you're an academic; I get that," she'd continued, totally misreading my stricken expression, "and I know you're certain that there's no such thing as ghosts, so what have you got to lose? Why don't you call it research?"

And right then and there I'd had such a light-bulb moment that I'd felt like hugging Susie on the spot. Of course! Why on earth hadn't I thought of this myself? What would I do if I came up against a brick wall with my academic research? The answer was that I'd go and consult another expert in the field, maybe Simon or the Professor, bounce ideas around for a bit and get some feedback from them. So why not just treat this whole bizarre experience the same way? If Lilac Delaney was the top medium in the country – and judging by her countless columns in magazines, bestselling books, TV shows and sell-out tours this is *exactly* what she was – then who better to ask for advice? She would know how I could get rid of Alex bloody Thorne!

Susie was a genius! If Alex really was a ghost/spirit/deceased pain in the backside (delete as appropriate), then it stood to reason that going to see Lilac Delaney would be the proof I needed. If she could see him too then maybe she'd give Alex Thorne a big shove back into the light for me. And if she couldn't see him then at least I would know that I was slowly going mad.

There was, of course, one huge flaw in this plan: I was assuming that there was even the slightest possibility that Lilac Delaney was genuine. A few weeks ago I would have dismissed this notion instantly. It was a sign of my illness that I would even contemplate taking such a crank seriously now, but I was desperate to get my life back to normal. If going to see this woman was the only way to make that happen, then I would just have to swallow my pride and hope that nobody saw me.

If my colleagues do see me, I tell myself now as I stand in the queue, they'll never recognise me. Not when I'm dressed like a lost member of Little Mix.

They do say that life is full of new experiences – and being grateful for wearing leather trousers and a bright green jumper, teamed with one of Susie's purple-tasselled scarves, is certainly a first for me. When I looked in the mirror before we set out I hardly recognised myself. And since when has my hair got so long? It's about time I dug out the scissors again and hacked a bit off.

"I have such a good feeling about tonight," Susie confides as we shuffle forwards. "I was reading all about Lilac's live show in *Fate and Destiny* magazine and apparently her spirit guides wander through the audience and choose people they need to give messages to. One's a Native American Indian and the other's an Aztec High Priest. Maybe they'll choose me for a reading? How cool would that be?"

There's a rude snort from by my elbow. It's Alex, lolling against the wall and practically wetting himself with laughter.

"And one's a builder, and one's a cop and the other's a cowboy?" he scoffs. "Oh purlease!" And then, right under the oblivious Susie's nose, he starts singing "YMCA" by the Village People and dancing. I try to give him my best stern look, but it's really quite funny and my lips start twitching upwards.

"You don't have to laugh at me," says Susie, looking hurt. "I was just saying."

"I wasn't laughing at you; it was something I was thinking about," I say quickly. *Stop it!* I mouth at Alex when she isn't looking.

Alex carries on regardless. He has a great voice, all gravelly and sexy, and his actions are hilarious. The groin thrusting I could do without, though.

Honestly, I knew that having him tag along was going to be a liability. It wasn't as though he was invited either, but somehow he got wind of what I was up to and appeared just as we were setting off for the theatre, and nothing I hissed out of the corner of my mouth could put him off.

"This is actually my area of expertise, Cleo – and, anyway, since you don't believe in me I'm not sure what your problem is. I'm not here, according to you, so what is there to be annoyed about?" he'd said.

I couldn't think of an answer, so I've been trying to ignore him ever since – which hasn't been easy. Alex has spent most of the journey here trying to distract me by pulling faces and making droll comments; I'm almost at my wits' end. I can't wait for Lilac Delaney to send him packing.

"I know this is just a big joke to you," Susie says, totally oblivious to Alex still doing the YMCA dance next to me, "but for most of us here it's something we take very seriously. I mean, look around you. There must be over three hundred of us waiting to see Lilac. Doesn't that tell you something?"

"Yes, it tells me that there are a lot of deluded people in this city," I quip, but it's hard to sound like my old disbelieving self with a dead pop star singing and dancing next to me. Anyway, Susie's right: there are an awful lot of people here and they all have an air of hope about them, as though they've been holding out for tonight as the answer to something. Quite how Lilac Delaney is going to meet all their expectations is anyone's guess. She's only one woman and she'll only have two hours. The Native American Indian and the Aztec Priest are going to have their work cut out, that's for sure.

"You wait, Cleo. You'll be totally impressed. My friend from work saw Lilac last year and she said it was amazing. Lilac knew things about her that nobody could possibly have known. It was incredible."

"Amazing, my arse; she's a total fake," Alex says bluntly, grinding to a halt. "Come on, Cleo! You know this is a crock of shit! What on earth are you doing here?"

"Maybe she'll give me some proof," I say. I'm going to address any comments to both Alex and Susie from now on. That should work. There's no need to look crazier than I already feel, after all.

"*I'm* here talking to you! What more proof do you need? That charlatan cold reads: it's all lucky guesswork – whereas I really do know things about you and Rafe that you haven't told anyone else, ever." Alex is slapping his hand against his head in exaggerated despair. "Jesus, why did he have to fall for you? You're bloody hard work."

"I'm sure she will!" Susie's eyes are sparkling with excitement. "Cleo, I know you think this is all rubbish and that I'm barking mad but," she lowers her voice conspiratorially, "I've been told several times that I have psychic abilities myself. I've got the strongest feeling that something's going to happen this evening. In fact, I can sense that there are spirits nearby. Maybe even right next to us!"

"Wow, she's good, your mate," says Alex, waving at Susie, who of course hasn't a clue. "Yep, she's got the gift all right!"

"Stop it," I snap, annoyed with him for taking the mickey. Of course, Susie thinks I'm talking to her, and her crestfallen expression makes me feel terrible.

"Sorry, you're just making me nervous," I say lamely. I turn my back on Alex. With any luck he'll soon be exorcised and I'll never have to see his annoying face again.

"Oh babes, don't be worried. This is going to be fun!" Susie promises, giving me a hug. "Oh look! We're going in!"

Sure enough the queue is surging forward now. Susie fishes our tickets from her bag. "Nearly there!"

"It wasn't even this busy at our concerts," I hear Alex say, awed. "Bloody hell! Thirty quid a ticket? This woman is making a fortune! Hey, Cleo, maybe you could give up being an academic and make a killing doing this instead? You could probably buy yourself a pyramid!"

I ignore him and, following Susie into the crowded auditorium, prepare to say goodbye to several hours of my life that I'll never see again. The theatre is absolutely packed! The sensible side of me can't believe just how many people are fooled by all this. It's quite worrying actually, especially if Lilac Delaney really is a fake.

"It's very busy," I whisper to Susie, glancing around. "Is it legal to have several people sharing seats?"

Susie frowns. "Who's sharing? I can't see anyone sharing a seat. Brr, it's flipping cold in here; that I do know. Maybe the dead are already among us?"

"Susie can't see us," Alex whispers in my ear. He's settled into the seat next to me and has put his biker-booted feet up on the back of the chair in front. "Look around more carefully, Cleo. It's not quite as full as you think, is it? Lilac Delaney, psychic to the stars, doesn't just attract attention from the living. Lots of us have turned up hoping she might notice we're here."

"There are ghosts here?" I whisper.

"I'm sure there are!" Susie whispers back, her eyes big circles of excitement.

Alex nods. "Hippy chick's right. They're everywhere – and they're all hoping this woman's genuine, every bit as much as your mate hopes she is. Possibly even more. They all have messages they need to pass on, you see."

The lights are going down now and the audience is falling silent. Then a purple spotlight swoops onto the stage, mystical angel-harp music builds to a crescendo and, in a cloud of importance and dry ice, none other than Lilac Delaney steps forward to applause.

"Thank you, thank you, dear ones!" she says in her famous breathy tones, a bit like Marilyn Monroe with asthma, as she clasps her hands over her ample chest. Wind machines off stage make her lilac robes drift in an unearthly fashion. At least I assume it's the fans doing this and not the famous spirit guides. There's no sign of the Village People on the stage. To be honest I'm a bit disappointed. I'd been looking forward to them.

"Now, my dearest friends, it is time to be still and think about our dear departed," Lilac says, and the music and lighting drop as though in sympathy. "I am just a channel for their messages, a mouthpiece for spirits, if you will, and my beloved guides, Great Brown Bear and K'uc Mo, are joining with me today to make the link between the planes. They are either side of me now, sending love and blessings out to you all."

They are? I can't see them. Lilac seems to be able to, though, and is having quite an involved conversation with thin air. I'm confused. If I can see Alex and Aamon and all the others, you think I'd be able to spot a Native American Indian and an Aztec Priest in full garb. They're not exactly subtle guises, are they?

Still, even though I can't see them, Lilac's guides must be hard at work: within minutes she's delivering messages to people in the audience. Call me a cynic but these communications seem terribly vague. I mean, it's quite probable that a woman in her fifties will have a grandparent who's "passed over", isn't it? And Betty is quite a likely name for a grandmother…

"And your grandmother had a pet, didn't she, my love?" Lilac is saying, warmth and sincerity oozing from every pore.

There's a nod from the woman she's talking to, who was chosen by Great Brown Bear, apparently. I still haven't spotted him, even though I can see Alex as clearly as anything and also the gathering crowd of ghosts who've made their way up to Lilac and are asking her to pass on their messages. One even waves his hands in front of her face, but the world-famous medium doesn't turn a hair. They're literally queuing up to talk to her, which will render her spirit guides redundant – if they ever turn up, that is. Somebody needs to have a word with them about their timekeeping.

Then the penny drops.

"Oh my God," I murmur to Alex. "She really can't see them, can she?"

"Told you," he says smugly. "You're the real deal, Cleo, whereas she's just a con artist. Now watch the spirits. They're going to get really pissed off because she's a fake and has let them down big time. Just wait!"

"And this dog went everywhere with her, didn't it, my love?" continues Lilac, eyes brimming with emotion. "You gran is telling me she loved her dog."

The woman is nodding. "Oh yes! She adored Goldie! He meant the world to her!"

"I know, she's telling me that right now, my love. He's right here, too. Goldie – a beautiful… retriever!"

Her subject's face drops. "Oh no, no. Goldie was a cocker spaniel. Maybe it isn't him at all? Perhaps this is somebody else's dog?"

"Goldie has a retriever with him," Lilac says quickly. Is it me or is there an ugly look in her eye? Maybe I've imagined it; it's only fleeting and now the sympathy is back. "He has lots of doggy friends in spirit. He's not alone there and he loves his squeaky toy. He's a lovely little chap with his golden curly coat. Oh! He's gone! What a shame. My guides are showing me another message. Is there anyone here called Sue?"

"Oh my God! Yes! Me!" Susie springs to her feet and instantly the spotlight swings to her, highlighting me at the same time. I shrink into my seat.

"Susie, sit down!" I hiss. "You have never gone by the name of Sue! Not in twenty-nine years!"

"But my name's Susannah!" she hisses back. "It has to be me." She waves her hand in the air, like a keen student wanting to attract the teacher's attention. "Yes! I'm Sue! Here I am!"

"A Sue who has a grandfather called Billy?" Lilac continues. "Yes, it's a Billy I have with me, and I'm getting the name Sue."

"Your granddad Henry is alive and the other one was called Ron," I say desperately to my star-struck friend, yanking her arm. "Sit down, Susie!"

"Don't be a spoilsport, Cleo; this should be fun. She's making it all up anyway," grins Alex, giving me a nudge that makes me feel a bit like I'm leaning into a freezer cabinet. "Hey, here's an idea! Why don't you get up and give Lilac a hand?"

"Over your dead body," I say, tugging Susie back down into her seat and sighing with relief when a big woman, who looks as though she'd be better suited to *The Jeremy Kyle Show*, declares that she's called Sue and that Bethnal Billy was her granddad. As she does so, she looks about the room as though challenging any of us to say otherwise. She's got bigger biceps than The Rock and looks like she chomps on paediatric nurses and Egyptologists for breakfast. Susie sits down hastily.

"Sorry, not me then!" she apologises. "Wrong Sue!"

Susie might be out of the spotlight but now it's my turn to have all the attention – only mine isn't from Lilac and her lighting team. If only. No, unfortunately for me it seems that all the other ghosts, who've given up trying to get Lilac's attention, have spotted me talking to Alex.

"Hey! You can see us!" cries one. "Look! She can! She's talking to him! This girl can see us even, if that fraud on the stage can't!"

There's a scene in *The Lion King* where the wildebeest stampede, and this is what happens right now, except that I'm not trampled by hooves but surrounded by ghosts, young and old, modern and in period costume, all trying to get me to listen to them. It's like *The Sixth Sense* on steroids.

"Tell my husband I know he was cheating on me!"

"I need to let Sally know I love her!"

My ears are ringing and the room's starting to spin. They're crowding around me now, all frantic to speak. I feel drained, as though all my energy has been sucked away by some gigantic ghostly Dyson.

"Back off, you lot," warns Alex. "She's new to it!"

"But she can see us!" insists another. "Why should she only talk to you? That's not fair."

The room is starting to sway. I have to get out of here – and fast, before I faint.

"I'm going to get some air," I tell Susie. "It's too hot in here."

"Hot? Cleo, are you coming down with something? It's bloody freezing. Must be all the ghosts, ha ha!"

Do you see me laughing? Leaving her to listen to Lilac spinning a bigger work of fiction than even JK Rowling could come up with, I stumble over the toes of the people in my row, muttering my apologies as I bash into their shins, and shove my way through the doors into the foyer. But it's hopeless: no sooner am I there than I'm surrounded again by countless individuals all imploring me to listen to their stories. In desperation I cover my ears with my hands and sink to my knees. I'm going mad, I have to be. It's the only explanation. And if this doesn't stop soon then I don't know what I'm going to do. Beg my GP for more tablets? Then what? Kiss goodbye to my hard-earned career?

"Go away," I plead. "Just go away!"

"Leave her alone, you lot! Go on, get lost!" Alex is by my side and squaring up to the others. "This isn't fair and you know it! Go on! Sod off!"

There's a blast of cold air, and suddenly the place is deserted except for a worried-looking usherette.

"Pounding headache," I say weakly, rising to my feet and giving her a wobbly smile. "Sorry."

"Are you all right, love? You look like you've seen a ghost!"

That isn't even funny.

"I'm fine. It's just very noisy and hot in there," I say.

The usherette doesn't look convinced, which is fair enough. I can't even convince myself anymore. Somehow I manage to haul myself into the ladies, where I splash water onto my face and stare at the hollow-cheeked, wild-eyed woman in the mirror. Everything about her is a stranger, from the new clothes to the long hair tumbling loosely over her shoulders, to the illogical and quite frankly crazy way in which she's behaving.

"I know I promised I wouldn't follow you into the loo, but I wanted to check you were OK?"

It's Alex. He's standing near one of the other sinks, arms folded and looking at me through narrowed green eyes.

"Of course I'm not OK." Tears sting my eyes and my throat is tight. "I'm going mad, I'm seeing things and unless I sort it out soon I'll lose my job. No, Alex, I am not OK. I'm as far from OK as it's possible to be."

"Stupid question, sorry. I always was crap with crying girls."

He's next to me now and I'm taken aback to see him in the mirror.

"Hey. How come you have a reflection?"

"Duh! Because I'm not a vampire," Alex says, rolling his eyes. "This isn't *Twilight* you know. And, just for the record, I don't glitter either – or watch you sleeping, or any of that creepy stuff."

I laugh in spite of myself. "And no werewolves?"

He grins at me in the glass. "Now that would be telling! Seriously, Cleo, I'm sorry about what just happened but I did try to warn you that it might be the case. You're like a beacon to them once they know you can see."

"I can't go on like this," I say wearily. "It's going to ruin everything. How can I work like this?"

"I can help you keep them away but I need you to do something for me in return. I think you already know what that is, don't you?" His gaze searches for mine. "Don't you?"

Our eyes meet in the glass and I nod slowly. If I want to keep my academic reputation and what little sanity I still possess, then I need to take control of this hallucination. It doesn't really matter anymore whether this is my subconscious mind enjoying payback for all the years of hard work or, crazier still, it's all for real. I just know that I have to find a way to get this to stop. If not then I can kiss any hope of a promotion and my normal life goodbye.

"All right, Alex," I say slowly. "You win. Keep them away from me, make this stop and I'll do my very best to help you. I'll go and see your brother. I'll find Rafe."

Rafe, my Christmas stranger. My stomach cartwheels and I grip the sink tightly. If I was terrified before, it was nothing compared to the thought of seeing him again. Absolutely nothing.

Chapter 14

It's one of those beautiful December mornings when frost ices the pavements and glitters from the railings and trees. The rooftops are white, spiders' webs on the bushes have been turned into lace and, as I walk to work, my breath rises like clouds of the incense Susie loves to burn. Despite all this, the winter sun has some warmth in it yet, and London shimmers in its rays. Even the rumble of the morning traffic and the wailing of a siren don't detract from the scene. As I stride along the street and arrive at the museum I can't help feeling optimistic.

After I'd got home last night, totally exhausted and feeling as though I'd been drinking heavily all evening rather than watching Lilac Delaney's atrocious acting, I'd staggered to bed where I'd slept heavily and without any dreams. Or at least, I'd slept until half five: Susie's on a morning shift today. Although she thinks she's as quiet as a mouse when she gets ready, it's more like a whole mischief of mice clog-dancing around the place while playing thrash metal at top volume. Nonetheless, I'd felt oddly calm when I'd awoken, as though I'd weathered some huge storm and made it through to the harbour. Once the flat door had slammed, announcing Susie's departure, I'd slipped out of bed, made a coffee and then fetched my big rucksack down from the top of the wardrobe.

The flat was warm, Susie's cat Freddie was curled up on my bed and there was no sign of Alex or any other unworldly visitors anywhere – but I wasn't fooled. This was just a lull, the space that he'd promised me, and I needed to take advantage of it if I was going to put an end to all this insanity. Yesterday I'd promised Alex that I'd go and see Rafe for him, and this was exactly what I was going to do today. I was in no doubt that Rafe would think I was crazy; he'd probably get his security guards to throw me off his property. I had to admit I was a bit vague about that part, but since Rafe Thorne was rock royalty these days, rather than a scruffy guy with a guitar slung across his back, he was bound to have security guards, wasn't he? At any rate, at least I would have tried my best. Then Alex would push off to wherever he needed to go next (Alex was as hazy about this as I was about the security-guards issue) and life would go back to normal. Simples.

So earlier this morning I'd dusted off my rucksack, feeling a pang of nostalgia when I'd caught sight of the Cairo address on the luggage label still attached to the shoulder strap. Then I'd flung in all the bits and pieces I might need for a week or so away. My research and books had gone in first, followed by all the outlandish clothes I'd bought yesterday (proof of a bash on the head if there ever was one), and then my jeans, sweaters and wash kit. I'd shoved my purse and phone into the top and crammed my laptop into a separate shoulder bag. There. I was packed and good to go. All I had to do now was leave a note for Susie before phoning my father and telling him I was coming home for a few days.

Now *that* was going to be the hard bit. I never went home unless I really had to. Maybe I'd call him later, once I'd travelled to Buckinghamshire, located Rafe Thorne's house and come up with a plan?

There are some things that can't be put off, though. Handing in a job application I've slaved over is one thing; telling Professor Hamilton, the director of our department, that I need a few days off is another. I can't say I'm looking forward to that at all. I've had a lot of time off lately, which really doesn't look great, especially when I'm hoping he's going to persuade the board to appoint me as his assistant. Thankfully the hours I've spent poring over my research have paid off, and I know I have exactly what it takes to do this job justice.

It's early for visitors and it's Sunday too, so the Wellby Museum is eerily still, as though holding its breath in anticipation for the busy day ahead. I nod at the security guard and cross the foyer – my boots ringing out on the floor, horribly loud against the quiet as I head towards my boss's office. Still, at least there's no sign of anything out of the ordinary. Alex has kept his word about making certain I'm left in peace, that's for sure. I quite miss Aamon's gap-toothed smile, though; at least he and his cat were always pleased to see me, whereas most days Professor Hamilton just looks irked.

"Ah, Dr Carpenter," the Professor says when I enter his office, and with the same degree of enthusiasm that you might declare *Ah, a bout of sickness and diarrhoea!* "And what can I do for you so early on a blessed Sabbath?"

Professor Hamilton always appears as though he's been digging for artefacts all night. Today his grey hair is sticking upwards in all directions, making him look permanently startled. A Bic is shoved behind his ear and his glasses balance on the end of his nose. As usual his office looks as though it's been burgled. I have no idea how he operates like this, let alone produces some of the most groundbreaking research of the modern age; just looking at this chaos makes my inner neat freak start to sweat.

"Sorry to interrupt you," I say apologetically, because I have interrupted him. Anyone who knocks on the door is interrupting; that's just a given. "I needed to ask your permission for a few days' leave."

Professor Hamilton pushes his glasses up his nose and squints at me. I know he's still a few millennia away so I add helpfully, "I've got a couple of family issues that I really need to go home for."

He steeples his fingers under his chin and stares at me. "Are you sure this isn't because of the incident?"

"The incident?" My brain is whirling. Surely he's not about to mention the knickers episode?

The Professor clicks his tongue impatiently. "When you were knocked over? A few weeks ago? Are you quite certain that it's not because of the accident that you need some time off?"

I cross my fingers behind my back because, indirectly, I suppose I do need time off as a result of the accident.

"No, no. It really is family stuff."

"There isn't anything else that's been bothering you? Something else you're worried about?"

For one awful moment I think he knows that I've been seeing ghosts and that my academic career is about to implode. Who would ever take me seriously again if they knew I'd spoken to our museum's long-dead founder or played football with a pharaoh? I try to speak but my mouth feels like it's full of sand from an Egyptian desert, and all I can do is stare at him.

"The Assistant Director's job?" Professor Hamilton says eventually when I don't reply. "It hasn't escaped my notice that you haven't applied yet, Cleo – and I must say that I'm unpleasantly surprised, because it really is the next logical career move for you. You're more than ready for it, if that's what's worrying you. Dr Welsh did mention that you weren't feeling quite yourself last week and I do understand just how difficult the past few weeks must have been. Do you need extra time to put something together?"

He thinks I need to pull a sickie in order to finish the job application. How mortifying is this? I'm the girl who's never missed a deadline in her life and I'm not about to start now. No way.

"Actually I have the application with me," I tell him, patting my rucksack. "I just need to go to my office and pick up a couple of supporting documents. I really want the job, Paul, and I'm the right person for it. I know I am."

He nods slowly. "I'm very glad to hear it. In that case, why not work from home for a day or two? Just make sure you drop that application off before you leave. I need it in soon."

"I will. Thanks," I say. But the Professor isn't listening to me anymore: he's preoccupied with his work again, ancient civilisations being far more interesting than present-day staff. I back out quietly and leave him in peace.

To my great relief my office is quiet today. My papers remain neatly stacked on my desk, the rubber-band ball is exactly where I left it and the telephone receiver is sitting snugly in the cradle. It isn't until I breathe out slowly that I realise I've been holding my breath. Sunshine trickles through the blind and dust motes whirl and dance in the air, but apart from those everything is still.

There are no cats, little boys or dead archaeologists in sight: everything is exactly as it should be.

I unpack and boot up my laptop, then pull up the supporting documentation for my application and send it to the printer. While that buzzes away to itself I take advantage of this little chunk of normality to gather up a couple of books to take with me. To be honest my office looks and feels just as it always did before my unusual experiences started, and I start to wonder again if I've been imagining everything. This time, however, I'm not prepared to risk being proven wrong. I have far too much at stake. Putting all thoughts of the supernatural firmly to one side, I open my desk drawer and pull out the large dossier I've prepared to accompany the application.

Crikey. I must have been in a really bad way the last time I put this away. The front of it is all creased and the introductory pages are out of sequence too, which really isn't like me. Annoyed with myself for being uncharacteristically slack, I try my best to smooth out the title sheet before rearranging the pages in their correct order. Once the printer has finished I gather up all the documents and clip them neatly together. Then I hoist my rucksack onto my back, return my laptop to its bag and shoulder that too, and make my way to the Professor's office.

It's locked. Unfortunately while I've been faffing about with my printing he's wandered off, and I know from experience that locating him won't be easy. The Wellby isn't the biggest museum in London – it's nowhere near as vast as the British Museum or the V&A – but there are all sorts of winding passageways connecting a jumble of buildings together, and countless spaces and nooks where treasures are stored. He could be anywhere. I decide to find Dawn instead and leave my application with her.

It's ten to ten now and Dawn, who's scheduled to work on Sunday this week, should be at her desk – but there's no sign of her. Since Dawn is to timekeeping what Mr Spock is to emotional outpourings, she could roll in at any time between now and eleven, full of tales of car breakdowns, Tube strikes or forgotten packed lunches. She's so good at creating works of fiction she should be working for one of the publishing houses, not a museum.

I try the Prof's door again but there's still no answer. Hmm. What to do? I could pop down to the lab and see if any of my colleagues are about. Alternatively I could leave my application with Dusty Dave, the museum's librarian. The trouble is, some of my colleagues can be very vague at times and I daren't run the risk that they might forget. Dave is likely to bury it under a pile of manuscripts, which is not what I need. My hands tighten on my file. I've an idea written inside that I feel sure will clinch the job: a fantastic exhibition which has actually been inspired by Aamon and, in a weird way, Alex. It would be an exhibition showing the real lives of some of our mummies, with all the interactive features and human dramas our visitors love. Seeing the past colliding with the present, or more accurately chasing a rubber-band ball around my office with Alex, has truly made me think of my subjects as real people. Obviously I've always known that they were once alive and as full of their own hopes, dreams and fears as the rest of us – that's what makes my job so fascinating – but this has added a whole new dimension to my work.

Anyway, I can't bear the idea of somebody putting the file down and losing all its contents while I'm away. I think the bottom line is that I don't trust anyone to do this apart from me.

God, Susie's right: I am a control freak. Rafe Thorne should be very afraid.

I'm still dithering in the corridor when Simon comes striding towards me, his handsome face all smiles of delight. I glance over my shoulder to see who the lucky recipient of this greeting might be, but there's nobody there. Goodness. It seems it's *me* he's so pleased to see. I'm a bit taken aback. The last couple of times we've met we've hardly parted on good terms – and I still haven't forgiven him for insinuating that I'm not a viable candidate for the Assistant Director post. Still, it's hard to hold a grudge against somebody who beams at you as though you're the only woman in the world, and I find myself smiling back. If Dawn could see me now she'd be envious – as green as my new sweater, even – because Simon has pulled me into his arms and is dropping a kiss on my cheek. She'd probably burst.

"Hello, stranger," Simon says. With his hands on my shoulders and his deep blue eyes staring down into mine, he steps back slightly. "Hey! You look different. Nice, but different."

I'm in jeans and a duffle coat and my hair is loose. I look a wreck. Still, it's sweet of him to try.

"Where are you off to?" he continues, lifting the label on my rucksack. "Cairo? Seriously?"

I laugh. "Nothing quite as exciting as that. I've got to go and see my father for a few days, so I was just letting the Prof know."

"Nothing serious, I hope?" Simon's voice is feathered with concern and I can't help feeling bad for fibbing.

"Just family stuff," I tell him quickly. Well, this isn't exactly a lie. I am going to Bucks on family business; the family just happens to be Alex Thorne's and not mine.

"And how are you feeling?" His hands are still on my shoulders and he's so close that I can feel his minty breath on my cheeks. "I've been so worried about you."

Actually I'm not sure I like way his hands are clamped on my shoulders. Being this close to Simon isn't all it's cracked up to be after all. I feel odd. Trapped. Wiggling away and pretending that I need to adjust my rucksack straps, I say briskly, "I'm fine now, Simon. Honestly. Once I've sorted out this family stuff it will be back to work as per normal. In fact I'm just about to give Paul my job application. Or I would do if I could find him."

Simon whistles. "You are feeling better! I've just passed the Professor on his way to see the Principal Director, probably about this very matter."

I pull a face. "Great. No Dawn and no Professor Paul. I guess Dusty Dave it is."

"Dave? Christ! I wouldn't leave a shopping list with him," Simon shudders. "Look, don't waste time hanging about here. I can see you're in a hurry to get to see your family. Let me take it for you. I'll catch the Prof later on and make sure he gets it."

Simon holds out his hand for my folder. I pause.

"I'm not going to read it," he says softly. "My application went in several days ago. Don't leave it with me if you feel uncomfortable, but please don't leave it with Dawn. That girl has a brain like a Swiss cheese."

He looks so worried on my behalf that I'm touched. "OK, I promise I won't give it to Dawn."

"Phew!" Simon mimes mopping his brow. "The future of the Wellby's Egyptology Department is saved. How about you and I grab some breakfast to celebrate? We never did make it out for lunch, did we?"

I glance at my watch. It's almost ten o'clock already. If I'm going to find Rafe Thorne before dusk I'd better get going.

"I'd love to, but I really need to get to Marylebone."

"I'm starting to think you don't want to hang out with me," he sighs, pulling a mock sad face. "What do I have to do to persuade you? Look, I'll even buy. Come on Cleo, you know how much lattes cost in this place – and me on an academic's wages, too. What more can I do?"

How can I resist? Even the stone statues in the exhibition rooms would be moved. We make our way to the café by the stairs, where I sit and text Susie while Simon fetches the coffees. By the time we're drinking them and sharing a Danish pastry, I'm feeling much more relaxed. Bloody Alex; this is his paranoia about Simon, not mine. I really need to get a handle on this.

"I really must go," I say finally, once we're saturated with lattes and have covered our tray in flaky pastry crumbs. "I'll probably have caffeine shakes for the rest of the day."

"Spare a thought for those of us here," Simon sighs. "I've got a paper to finish before I get to enjoy my Sunday."

He helps me put my coat on and offers to accompany me to the station. Then, when I decline, he kisses me on the cheek and wishes me a good stay.

"If there's anything you need me to do," he says softly, "then just ask, Cleo. I'm only a phone call away."

I'm clutching the folder in my left hand, and both of us drop our gazes to look at it. Simon raises a quizzical eyebrow and shrugs.

"My offer to deliver that still stands," he says. "And leave your laptop with me too, just in case the Prof needs to see anything on it. It'll save him having to call you and ask. You know how that drives him wild – and he's useless at downloading files."

I do know this. But abandon my laptop? I'm not sure. I know my files are password protected and backed up on the office computer as well as on a USB stick but, even so, abandoning my laptop would feel a bit like losing an arm…

"I don't know," I say. I suddenly have an overwhelming urge to tighten my grip on the strap of my laptop bag. "What if I need it for work?"

Simon's chiselled face is a picture of concern and he shakes his golden head at me.

"Cleo Carpenter, what am I going to do with you? You're supposed to be going home for a rest and to spend time with your family, not to work. Besides, what is there left to do? The application is done, isn't it?"

"Yes," I say reluctantly.

"So what will you need your laptop for? Hacking into NASA? Or maybe your online poker habit? No, don't tell me, because I'll be devastated: you have countless online admirers on some dating site or other," Simon teases, and I can't help laughing in spite of the odd clawing sensation in my stomach. I'm being ridiculous. Simon just wants to help.

"Seriously, Cleo," he says gently, "you have your iPad for browsing and your Kindle for all that weighty reading or your secret chick lit! Don't lug anything more onto the train than you have to. I'll lock the laptop away for you and if there's anything that Paul needs he can always ask the techies for your password. Or guess it! *Rumplestiltskin*, right?"

Aamon actually. Not the most original choice, I guess, but I'm hardly the Pentagon. I glance at my laptop bag, torn between hanging onto it and leaving it safely locked away. My laptop isn't a bright and shiny MacBook Air almost light enough to float, but an ancient contraption that runs on steam and is the size of a small table. The department issued it when I first started at the museum and it's so heavy that when I have it slung over my shoulder and across my back I resemble one of the Ninja Turtles. I've kept it partly because it works and partly because I'd prefer that we spent money on my research rather than on gadgets. Simon does have a point: it weighs a tonne and, combined with my rucksack, will probably be responsible for a couple of trips to the chiropractor when I return.

"It's up to you," Simon says. He glances at his watch. "Christ! You'd better decide one way or another because your train's leaving in about half an hour."

"I'd no idea we'd been here so long! I'd better get going," I agree.

Simon nods and says nothing. Again I glance hesitantly at the folder containing my application, and then at my laptop bag. What is the matter with me? I never used to be this emotional. He's right: travelling light makes far more sense and I need to get to the station on time for my train.

Right. That clinches it. I'm being ridiculous. Come on, Cleo; just give this nice, sex-on-a-stick Egyptologist your job application and laptop. That way, rather than playing hunt the professor, you can just get on with your journey, see Rafe Thorne and get rid of Alex. Then your life goes back to normal.

I pass the folder and the bag containing my laptop to Simon and try to ignore the sense of panic tightening around my chest. I never, ever let anyone else handle my research; it's as though I'm parting with a baby. Once the folder is in his grasp and the laptop bag is slung over his shoulder, my heart starts to hammer against my ribcage and I have to stop myself from snatching them back. This is crazy behaviour, and yet it's how I feel. Even when I arrive at Marylebone half an hour later I'm still uneasy about the whole thing – but by then, of course, it's far too late.

The matter is literally and metaphorically out of my hands.

Chapter 15

The feeling of unease stays with me after I board the train at Marylebone; try as I might to tell myself I'm being irrational, I just can't shake it off. As the guard blows his whistle and the train begins to creep out of the station, I'm wondering whatever possessed me to leave my research and job application with Simon. I never leave my research with *anyone*. I'm realising now that my decision is more evidence that I'm not myself at the moment – as if seeing ghosts and having conversations with imaginary rock stars isn't enough proof of that already. I've never been one for gut instincts and intuition before, but having made such a rash choice, now every cell in my body is urging me to turn around and snatch my laptop back. I'm beyond irritated with myself.

Still, on the bright side, now that I'm committed to a wild goose chase across Buckinghamshire, everything around me seems remarkably ordinary. The carriage is almost empty apart from a handful of tourists and a few students, and so far today there's been no sign of Alex. Yes, the world is looking like its usual self, with not a dead rock star in sight – which is just the way I like it.

As I fiddle with my iPhone I can't help thinking that it's a supreme irony that Alex's absence confirms rather than makes me doubt his existence. He's promised to stay away if I play my part, and so far so good. Things are normal, if a little dull, but I'm determined this is just how they're going to stay once I've kept my word and made a prat of myself in front of Rafe Thorne. Dull is good if you ask me. Dull is *wonderful*. I've had enough excitement lately to last me for a lifetime.

The train gathers pace and before long the crammed terraces of the inner city start to smudge into the semis of suburbia. I haven't done this journey for a long time but I know that within the hour I'll be watching the green blur of the Chilterns pass by, threaded through with the silver ribbon of a young Thames, before I have to change at High Wycombe for the branch line. Trying my best to push away thoughts of the kind of reception I'm likely to get from Rafe Thorne – he'll think I'm mad at best and a lunatic stalker at worst – I send up a quick prayer of thanks to whatever genius invented on-train Wi-Fi, and tap Rafe's name into Google. I think the only way I can carry out my mission and keep some dignity is to treat it like a piece of research. I'll start digging through his history and find out exactly what it is I'm dealing with. Then, just like I would with my work, I'll start to examine the facts. Never mind the chance encounter we had all that time ago: I just need to find a way to let Rafe know that his brother doesn't hold him responsible for his death.

Alex might be full of bright ideas and good intentions, I think despairingly as I scroll through online newspaper stories about Rafe's latest stint in rehab, but he hasn't been an awful lot of help when it comes to how I might deliver his message. No, that minor detail of his master plan seems to have escaped his attention. Somehow I don't think turning up on Rafe's doorstep and saying that his dead brother sent me is going to work.

"Any ideas?" I say aloud, glancing around the carriage just in case Alex is about – but for once he's silent. Fat lot of help he is; it looks like I'm on my own with this. I sigh and return to my phone, scrolling through the Google search results and feeling more nervous by the minute. Rafe Thorne has had an eventful few years, that's for sure. The open-faced young man I met for that brief hour has vanished and in his place is a scowling Heathcliff type, shut away in his big house with only alcohol and memories for company. His face glowers at me from my laptop screen; it's a pap shot taken when he checked out of rehab for the latest time, and although the eyes are the same there's a darkness behind them now that was never there before. I shiver. This merging of the familiar with the unfamiliar makes me very uneasy, and I can't say I'm looking forward to knocking on his door. I really wish I had Alex with me.

Listen to me. I wish I had Alex with me? I'm seriously missing a dead guy I never knew in his lifetime? My imaginary friend?

Susie's right: I ought to get out more. But in the meantime I need all the help I can get. "Alex! I need a hand with this!" I murmur. I take a deep breath and try to quell the growing wave of panic that threatens to swamp me as I consider the insanity of what I'm planning to do when I reach my destination. "Come on, Alex! This isn't funny. I need some help."

But apart from the noise of the train speeding ever closer to what could well be my impending doom, there's silence. Alex does not materialise on the seat opposite; neither does he choose to whisper words of wisdom into my ear like something from a Hollywood movie. God. Whoopi Goldberg was so lucky to get Patrick Swayze. Here I am carrying out Alex's final wish, and probably making a right idiot of myself to boot, and he can't even be bothered to show up. He's probably riding the Circle Line right now and peering down girls' tops with Hank.

Men are useless. Dead or alive.

I raise my voice. "Alex! How on earth do I speak to Rafe? What do I say?"

There's no reply and I feel like thumping my head on the table in frustration. Only the fact that the last time I banged my head didn't work out too well stops me.

"Thanks a lot," I mutter, beyond caring now whether I look crazy. What does it matter when in an hour or two I'll be behaving like a lunatic anyway? Luckily most people in the carriage are wired into iPods and phones, and the bunch of teenagers at the far end are far too busy trying to look cool to notice me. My questions go unanswered. Defeated, I return my attention to Google, where I read all about Rafe's acrimonious relationship break-up, his heavy drinking and finally his reclusive life in his house on the River Thames. It doesn't make me feel much better.

By the time I change trains at High Wycombe and take my seat on the small branch line that winds its way through some of Buckinghamshire's prettiest countryside, I'm extremely nervous. No matter what Alex thinks, I know this isn't going to end well. I'm also dreading seeing my father and being back in a house that echoes with grief and memories. With every mile of track I'm coming closer to my own past and, believe me, I don't like digging about in that at all. Some things really are better off left buried. It's too late to back out now, though: the train's drawing into Riverside Halt and I know from experience that there won't be another back to the town for over an hour. Like it or not, I'm committed to this.

The small unmanned station that serves several scattered dwellings seven miles beyond Taply-on-Thames hasn't changed a bit, but then why would it? Just because everything in my world shifted and altered that long-ago Christmas doesn't mean it did for anyone else. That "Stop all the clocks" poem has it spot on; how is it possible that the day-to-day minutiae of life carry on when it feels as though your world has ended? We buried my mother, my lovely, clever, ambitious, beautiful mother, and then we all tried to return to our lives as normal. But of course nothing was ever normal again and our family was changed. Dad went to pieces, Tolly became obsessed with work and I fled to Egypt. Vicars could drone on about heaven as much as they liked, but I doubted its existence. Working with the remains of a culture who'd believed wholeheartedly in the afterlife, only to end up as dusty artefacts, had erased any lingering faith I might have had in life after death. Or at least, it had until a few weeks ago.

What a little ray of sunshine I am this morning. *Snap out of it Cleo*, I tell myself firmly as I shrug my rucksack on and wait patiently for the train to stop fully so that the doors will open. Maybe I ought to read one of those self-help books that Susie's always *accidentally* leaving on my desk or open on the arm of the sofa – books with covers showing ancient scrolls and which claim to unlock the secrets and mysteries of eternal happiness and abundance. What a load of hokum! Susie, who's permanently broke, really should ask for her money back. Besides, it's pretty hard to think positive when you're worried that you're going mad and that your entire life hangs in the balance. Somehow I don't think any of those books have a chapter on what to do when a ghost called Alex Thorne won't leave you in peace and makes you go and visit his brother to deliver a message from beyond the grave. I'm just going to have to figure it out for myself.

The winter's morning, which had made London glitter with frost, has iced the hills of Buckinghamshire too; when I step onto the platform I'm struck by just how pretty this part of the world is. Spiders' webs lace the railings, and the metal seat where Rafe Thorne and I once spent a Christmas Eve sparkles. There's nothing here but a handful of houses and a picturesque medieval Church where couples clamour to get married, so anyone who alights at Riverside Halt is soon driving away to the villages beyond. Nobody journeys to their destination on foot from here, except me.

The countryside is just as quiet as I remember. As I walk down the narrow lane the only sounds I can hear are the chirruping of a robin and the thudding of my own heartbeat. It always was an isolated spot. The fields around are white; cows stand in chilly huddles by the hedges and horses are wrapped up in blankets, smoke pluming from their nostrils as they canter across the frozen grass to the gate just in case I have treats. I don't know much about horses but I can tell these ones are worth a fortune. The station's in the middle of nowhere – a throwback to the golden age of branch lines – but beyond several fields and a muddy footpath is the Thames, a silver serpent winding its way through three counties. Here the cluster of houses beside the Thames forms some of the most expensive real estate in England: beautiful riverside properties owned by bankers and actors.

And rock stars.

Rafe Thorne lives in Mellisande, a thirteenth-century house right next to the river. I remember it from childhood walks along the riverbanks: a mellow grey-stone building smothered in deep green ivy and slumbering behind crumbling walls. Thanks to its status as a listed building, it's escaped being levelled and turned into a glass-and-chrome modernist creation like some of the other houses here. It's beautiful but hardly the kind of property I'd have expected a rock star to live in. It's a house for a poet rather than a pop star.

It's an interesting choice, and one that I can relate far more easily to the sweet guy I met all those years ago than to the brooding man with the dangerous edge that he's apparently turned into.

With my rucksack on my shoulders I continue up the lane and climb the stile leading me to a footpath skirting fields of furrowed earth. Crows fly upwards, caw-cawing as my feet crunch across the frost, and in spite of my nerves I enjoy the walk. Or at least, I enjoy it until I find myself in front of the big wrought-iron gates of Mellisande. Then my heart plops into my boots.

"This would be a great time for you to show up, Alex," I say hopefully, but there's no answer, only my breath clouding the air. It looks like I'm on my own.

The gate isn't locked and when I give it a shove it swings open soundlessly. The path beyond is overgrown; hedges straggle across it. I wind my way around them, through to the front door. There are no lights on and the whole place has the look of somewhere long shut up. A blackbird flies up with a cry of alarm and the gossamer threads of a spider's web stretch and break when I push my way through. Rafe Thorne hasn't been out today then, at least not along this path. It doesn't look as though anyone's been this way for a while.

I climb the three steps into the porch, treading stones smoothed by centuries of feet, and pause. The windows are small and diamond paned, and beyond them all I can see is darkness. Fat spiders scuttle into the corners but otherwise all is completely still. It doesn't look as though there's anyone at home. Maybe Rafe's back in rehab again? From what I read online this would hardly be surprising. I lift the heavy brass knocker and rap it against the door. The noise is shocking against the stillness. For a few seconds I wait, my heart hammering against my ribs, just in case the door swings open – but there's no response.

I could give up and walk back to the station, but I hate the thought of coming this far and quitting. Besides, I want my life back and a promise is a promise, isn't it? I can't risk Alex and pals never going away, so I'm going to have to find Rafe Thorne sooner or later. I may as well just get it over with. Maybe he's out in the garden or something?

There's a path leading around the side of the house to the lawns at the back. Crossing my fingers that I won't come across any dogs or security guards, I follow it right the way around until I come to the overgrown formal gardens that roll gently down to the river and the boathouse. There are no footprints on the frosty grass and apart from the chugging of a passing boat everything is still.

Is he inside? Should I knock on one of the French windows maybe? Or try to peer through? I release my rucksack from my shoulders and abandon it while I decide what to do next. This kind of thing always looks so straightforward on TV, but in real life it's not so easy gaining access to someone else's home, especially when the terrace is covered in empty plant pots – over which I trip and nearly go flying. Only grabbing the trellis and ending up with half a tonne of dead Virginia creeper on my head saves me from toppling over. I end up yanking half of the thing off the wall and almost skewering myself on a piece of the trellis. Fan-bloody-tastic. Now I'm not only trespassing but causing criminal damage as well. If only I was back in my office, absorbed in my work. Life was so simple before I had my accident. OK, so it was rather uneventful – boring, even – but at least it was uncomplicated.

I dust myself off and lean the damaged trellis back against the wall as best I can. I'm pretty certain that this kind of thing never happens in *CSI: Miami*. Windows are clean and sparkly there, and nobody nearly turns themselves into a human kebab on a chunk of broken trellis. Now I'm covered in leaves and bits of splintery wood and have wrecked the climbing plant as well. I should stick to being an academic; this detective lark is easier said than done, that's for certain.

I venture back to the French windows. One heavy brocade curtain has been dragged halfway across and the other has been abandoned as though whoever went to draw them lost heart mid task and gave up. I press my face against the glass but it's so gloomy inside that it's hard to discern anything at all at first. I shield my eyes against the glaring reflection of the river and squint; slowly, the room comes into focus. I can just about make out a sofa and a table and possibly the blank screen of a television, but beyond that the room swims in darkness. The house is empty. Wherever Rafe Thorne may be, it isn't here. There's a familiar feeling to this place, with its heavy furniture and fittings and its air of abandonment. It's as though the occupants have just slipped away, leaving behind only whispers and secrets. It may be a beautiful medieval manor house bathed in watery winter sunshine on the banks of the Thames, yet it feels exactly the same as one of the ancient tombs I've worked on back in Egypt. There's the same sense of stillness and expectancy, as though the occupants of the place have only just left…

I stop myself. Did I really feel like this in Egypt? It's hard to remember now, but I'm sure this isn't the way I would have described it at the time; this is far too flowery and fanciful. I'm really not myself – of course I'm not. I'm trying to peer into somebody else's house because a hallucination told me to.

What am I thinking? This is insanity. I should get out right now.

I'm poised to turn around and make my way back to the station, furious with myself for coming out here in the first place, when something in the room catches my eye. Years of looking for details in the strangest places have trained me well and the smallest clues rarely escape me. So when I spot a foot just visible in the pooling shadows in the furthest corner of the room, my stomach lurches. Suddenly all my thoughts of crime shows and CSI dramas aren't nearly as amusing. With my heart racing, I push my face to the grimy glass, squint into the gloom again and hope that I'm mistaken.

There's a body sprawled across the floor. Oh. My. God. There really is.

I blink just in case I'm having another hallucination, but there really is a man's body lying motionless on the carpet – and I don't need to look any closer to know exactly who this is. My every cell is on red alert.

Rafe Thorne, my Christmas stranger, is lying unconscious on the floor.

Chapter 16

"Alex! If there was ever a time I needed you around then this is it!" I cry. I bang my fist against the thick glass with all my might but the figure on the floor doesn't stir. I can't even see his chest rise and fall. Oh God, I'm too late. Alex was right all along: his brother really is in a terrible state. No wonder he was so frantic that I should help him.

"Hello! Rafe!" I hammer again with my fists but there's no answer. How can there be when he's motionless? Is he even alive?

OK, Cleo. Breathe. Think. Use your logical brain, not this emotional one you've developed recently. Think smart and think fast. What can you do now to help him? Break the window? Call an ambulance? Fetch the neighbours?

Ambulance. I need an ambulance. I pull out my phone but there's no signal. Of course there isn't: I'm in the sticks and miles from anywhere. Neighbours then? But this is a remote spot and I haven't got any time to waste. If I'm going to call an ambulance I'll need a landline. There's nothing for it. I'll have to break in.

Glancing around, I search for something, anything, tough enough to break the glass. Maybe that rusty shovel? Would that do it? Or what about that wooden bench? It looks a bit big for me to shift though. I pause. No! I've got it! The stone birdbath is perfect. That'll make short work of the French windows.

Just as I'm attempting to drag the deceptively heavy birdbath across the terrace, Alex appears in front of me. "What on earth are you doing?"

"Breaking the window," I gasp. "Rafe's collapsed. I'm going to have to smash the glass."

"You don't need to do that," Alex protests.

"I do," I pant. My hands scrabble against the rough stone, lichen gathering beneath my nails. My palms are already scratched, but I'm beyond caring about any of that. All I want to do is reach out to Rafe now he's all alone and needing help, just as he once reached out for me. "Your brother's on the floor, Alex! He needs help."

"Wait! Don't smash the window. There's a key," Alex says quickly. He steps in front of the birdbath and immediately there's a blast of icy air as though the sun has slipped behind a cloud. "By the back door there's a rotting window ledge. The top part will pull off and Rafe always kept a key hidden underneath. Crap place, I know, and bloody obvious–"

But I'm not waiting to listen to any more from Alex. Where's he been all morning when I needed his help anyway? Ignoring him I tear around the house to the small back porch where I locate a key exactly where Alex has said I'll find it. I guess if I was in the frame of mind to be thinking clearly then I'd be able to log this under Proof That Ghosts Exist, but right now I'm just relieved to be able to get inside without severing an artery. For a minute I struggle to get the key in the lock because my hands are shaking so much; then the key turns and I'm inside.

The house is still. The only sound is the rasping of my breathing. I've let myself into the kitchen, a large room with an ancient range cooker and an enormous scrubbed oak table flanked by countless chairs. The table is strewn with sheets of handwritten notes covered in crossings outs, and hundreds more screwed-up sheets litter the floor like angry snowballs. And either Rafe Thorne is running Taply's bottle-recycling facilities or he's a man who goes on serious and regular benders. Outside of the booze aisle in Tesco, I don't think I have ever seen so many bottles in my life.

So much for all the stints in rehab.

Beyond the kitchen is a gloomy passageway. Drawn curtains shut out the daylight and the place smells old, of things too long left shut – the smell of absences and despair. I shudder and then force myself to jog down the corridor in the direction of the room where I saw Rafe. Left, I think, then right and maybe through those double doors?

"This really isn't a good idea." Alex is now standing in front of the double doors and he looks alarmed. "Please don't go in. I'm sorry I ever involved you. Look, go home, Cleo. I'll leave you alone, I promise."

"It's a bit late for that now. Your brother's in trouble," I say impatiently. "He's on the floor and he needs help, Alex. I thought my helping him was what you wanted? He could be dead!"

Alex gives me a wry look. "I think I'd know if he was dead, don't you?"

It's a fair point. "So maybe he's not dead," I concede, "but he's certainly hurt and he needs help. Now get out the way, Alex!"

But he doesn't budge. "Look, this is bloody awkward and I know you're trying to help – which I totally appreciate, by the way – but take it from me, this is not a good idea. Really, I don't think that you should–"

Right. I've had enough. There's no way I'm going to stand here having a conversation with my imaginary friend when there's a man lying on the floor just the other side of these doors. What Alex Thorne thinks I should or shouldn't do is irrelevant to me as I charge straight through him, shove open the doors and race to the crumpled figure on the floor by the chair.

This room is dark and fuggy with the sour taint of sweat and whiskey, and as I crouch down beside the man on the floor alcohol fumes hit me in the face like a punch from a heavyweight boxer. There's even more paper here – piles and piles of it scrawled all over with notes, both words and music, and scored with furious crossings out. I reach to see if Rafe has a pulse, but my elbow catches several bottles that roll onto the stone flags with a clatter.

The formerly motionless figure and I both jump. A strong hand clamps down on my right shoulder and immediately I realise my mistake.

Rafe Thorne isn't dead or injured or even sleeping. He's just passed out after a particularly heavy bender and now he's been woken up, hung over and glowering, by a total stranger who has broken into his house.

"Who the hell are you?" he snarls. His other hand circles my wrist like a manacle; no matter how I pull and twist I can't break free. "What the fuck are you doing in my house?"

"This is a bit awkward," says Alex from the doorway. "I did try to warn you, Cleo. But you never listen to me."

I ignore him because right now I have more pressing matters to think about, namely explaining to Rafe Thorne how and why I'm in his house – before he flips. His left hand has tightened like a vice on my shoulder. His fingers bite through my coat and into my skin. The smell of stale alcohol makes me gag. Rafe sits up – wincing at the light, which streams in through the unopened curtain – and gives me such a shake my bones rattle.

"Just what the hell do you think you're doing?" he hisses, his dark brows meeting in a scowl. "This is private property. I said, how the fuck did you get in?"

It's as though a cobra is poised to strike. I shrink back, rifling through all the things I could say but finding that I'm suddenly unable to utter a word.

"If you're from the press you can fuck right off. I've nothing to say to any of you lot," Rafe continues angrily. A muscle in his cheek twitches. "I'll have you for breaking and entering. I'll sue your filthy little rag for everything it has."

His hand is still clamped onto my shoulder and it's starting to hurt, and I fear my wrist in his other hand will snap like a twig.

"I didn't break and enter: I had a key," I say quickly. "I know this sounds crazy but I saw you through the window and I thought you were hurt, so I let myself in with the key you keep hidden under that rotting window sill."

Rafe stares at me. His head is probably pounding and I expect he feels like death. If I drank that much I'd need hospitalising. He frowns, the violet eyes dark with anger. I try to pull away but he still has me in his grasp. There's a dangerous strength about him that was never there before, the strength that comes with not caring and having nothing left to lose.

"How the bloody hell did you know a key was there? Who told you that?"

"Don't tell him!" Alex pleads. "He'll freak! Honestly, Cleo! This is not the time to come clean. He'll never believe a word you say again if you blow it now."

For once I'm in agreement with Alex. Rafe looks like a man on the edge and I'm not inclined to be the one who makes him topple. I shrug.

"It's the first place anyone would look. You ought to be more careful."

The hands loosen their grip a little. Rafe leans forward and stares at me through narrowed eyes, and as he does so he sways.

"So let's rephrase. What the hell are you doing peering in my windows and snooping around the property, if you're not from the press?"

I'm tempted to tell him the unbelievable truth, but his hand is still holding my shoulder – and I have a nasty feeling that if I say his dead brother sent me, Rafe will lose the plot entirely and shake me like a terrier would a rat, until my neck snaps. Maybe it's time to divulge some of the truth, at least the part that won't make me sound like a lunatic. I'll just sound like a stalker instead, albeit one who's ten years late.

"I'm not from the press," I say quickly, finding my voice at last. "Honestly, I'm not. I've come to see you and when you didn't answer the door I looked through the window. When I saw you on the floor I thought…" I'm still trembling because I really had thought he was dead. It's one thing working with the dead of a long-gone culture, but quite another to think you're about to be faced with a recent corpse. I have a sudden insight into Susie's everyday working life and am humbled with admiration for her. Then I gather myself and press on because Rafe is still glaring at me as though he'd like to drown me in the icy river outside.

"When I saw you on the floor I thought something awful had happened," I say. My voice is as splintered as the wooden windowsills, my confidence flaking away like the paint. "I thought you were dead or hurt and I wanted to help."

A frown creases his brow. "Very noble, but that doesn't answer my question. Why were you snooping here in the first place? This is private property."

Alex is standing behind his brother, shaking his head like he's got water in his ears. It's very disconcerting. I ignore him. Alex wanted me here, and here I am. If he doesn't like it, well that's just tough.

"My name's Cleo Carpenter," I say softly, "but you won't know that, of course, because I never told you. We met a long time ago. At the station?"

Rafe Thorne doesn't say anything and I feel myself start to turn red. So much for writing the definitive Christmas love song about me, his one who got away. He hasn't a clue who I am.

"Take your hat off," Alex says hastily. "He's hung over to shit, it's bloody dark in here and you're all swaddled up. It looks like Scott of the Antarctic's rolled up and barged into his house. He'll remember you, I promise!"

I reach up and pull off my green bobble hat so that Rafe can see my hair. For nearly thirty years being a redhead has been one of the first things people notice about me. Surely he'll remember my hair? But there's still no response. I'd think he's passed out again if it wasn't for the fact that he's staring at me. I can see myself reflected in the dark eyes. I look petrified.

"You were waiting for a train?" I prompt hopefully. My stomach is twisting into knots under that intense violet gaze. "I was waiting for a lift? It was Christmas Eve. I was crying and you…" I can't speak for a minute because the memory still moves me, "you comforted me."

Rafe remains silent. How can he not remember? I'm floored with the disappointment. Now that he's just a heartbeat away from me the past ten years have evaporated – so how can it be that he doesn't feel the same? Was it all in my imagination?

"It was a while back," I say awkwardly. "Maybe you've forgotten?"

"He hasn't forgotten!" Alex insists. He looks distraught. "This is much worse than I thought. He's given up with everything. I've left it too late."

The room is still. I hear a clock ticking somewhere. The blood is rushing in my ears. Then Rafe's hand slips from my shoulder and reaches out to touch my cheek. His other hand loosens its grip on my wrist and slips down to weave my fingers with his. I hold my breath, everything in me poised to flee because he feels dangerous, as though he could combust at any moment. One forefinger skims over my face and down to my lips, where it brushes over my mouth as softly as his lips did all those years ago. In spite of all my layers and my fear, goosebumps ripple all over my body.

"It's you," Rafe says slowly, looking at me with those shadowed eyes. "The Christmas girl. Jesus. Just how strong was that whiskey?"

"It's not the whiskey," I whisper. "It's really me."

We stare at each other. The world seems to halt on its axis and beyond the window even the waters of the Thames slow their pace until I'm nineteen again. For the briefest of moments, I think he's going to pull me close, wrap his arms around me and kiss me like he did back then. I feel dizzy with longing. How could I ever have thought I was attracted to Simon? He's never made me feel like this. Nothing even close…

But Rafe exhales slowly, like a man who's come to the end of a long and exhausting journey. His hand slides away and falls to his side. It looks as though he's struggling to find the right words.

Then he shrugs. "It's too late, Christmas Girl. Way too late."

"No it isn't!" cries Alex, hopping up and down with impatience. "Come on, bro! I've brought her to you like I said I would. Of course it's not too late. Don't be a knob!"

"What's too late?" I ask Rafe.

"Everything. You. Me. You coming here now." Rafe's words are bleak, and the expression on his face is hard to read; it's oddly aggressive, as though he's fighting some huge internal battle. "If you came here hoping for a reunion then you've wasted your time."

I stare at him. Does he really think that?

He clambers to his feet, staggers to the mantelpiece and leans against it. He passes a hand over his red-rimmed eyes and the scans the room. "Christ. I need a drink."

"You bloody well don't," says Alex. As Rafe sways across the room, homing in on a half-empty bottle of Jack Daniel's like some kind of booze-seeking missile, his brother rounds on me. "This isn't what's meant to happen."

"What did you expect?" I say sadly. "That we'd fall into each other's arms and live happily ever after while you go into the light?"

Alex's face falls; of course this is what he'd hoped for, my poor, dead romantic.

From the look of him Rafe Thorne could teach Lord Byron a few things about being mad, bad and dangerous to know. He's certainly not about to declare undying love for me anytime soon. Not that I'd want him to in any case, I remind myself sharply. I'm only here to get Alex off my back and my life returned to normal.

"Great plan," I say to Alex. "Any more bright ideas?"

Fortunately Rafe is far too busy sloshing Jack Daniel's into a glass to take much notice of me talking to thin air. He's probably still drunk.

"Christ," he says again to himself before necking the shot and pouring another. "What's the point of anything now? It's all too late. It's all too fucking late."

"What is?" I ask him.

"Just about everything, Christmas Girl–"

"Cleo," I interrupt. Since I hate the festive season, Christmas Girl is not a moniker I wish to be saddled with. "My name is Cleo. Cleo Rose Carpenter."

Rafe swirls the amber liquid in his glass and raises it to me. His wide, sexy mouth curls into a sneer. "Well, to you, then, Cleo Rose Carpenter. To the millions and millions of pounds you made Thorne. That song makes a lot of people, including my accountants, very happy, even if it's way too late for me. Or you. Here's to our 'One Christmas Kiss'."

Alex is standing beside him. I can see Rafe's breath, but he's too busy downing his whiskey to notice the peculiar cold. Rafe Thorne, I'm fast discovering, doesn't pay attention to much apart from drink. His face is unshaven, the strong jaw sprinkled with several days' worth of stubble, and his thick dark hair falls over the collar of his shirt. He's too thin for his frame, which is made to be broad and strong; even his high-cheekboned face is gaunt. For once the British tabloids haven't been exaggerating.

"What do you mean, it's too late?" I ask. "I don't understand. Too late for what?"

Rafe fixes me with a long hard stare and in the depths of his eyes I see such raw pain that it takes my breath away.

"For everything, Cleo Rose Carpenter. It's too late for me. For you. For my brother. Everything's changed." He tips the drink down his throat and slams the glass onto the table before wiping his mouth with the back of his hand and pouring another. "The person you met back then, that boy with the guitar and the dreams? He doesn't exist anymore. He's not existed for years. He's gone for good, and if you've got any sense you'll get the hell out of here and forget all about him, because if you came here looking to find that person then you're in for a big disappointment. You need to go home, Christmas Girl. Some things are better left in the past. You're too late now. If you wanted to find me then you should have come before."

"I couldn't come before," I say softly. There's a tight knot deep inside me, which feels horribly like grief. But what am I grieving for? A lost chance? A life that never was? A *Sliding Doors* moment? I take a deep breath because I want to get this right and make him see. "Rafe, my mother died that night and afterwards I went abroad for ages. I didn't know who you were and I had no way of finding you again. In fact I've only just found out who you are."

Rafe laughs. It's a harsh, joyless sound that scrapes the quietness.

"Oh, I get it. And now you *do* know who I am it seems like a good idea to check me out, does it? What do you want? A share of the royalties? A cheque? Well, I've got news for you, sweetheart, there's no cash waiting here for you.

Thorne's legal team have got that all tied up. Jesus!" He shakes his head and his lips curl into an ugly sneer. "And to think I ate my fucking heart out over you for years. You're as bad as the rest of them. You just want cash. Well get in the queue, darling, because that's all everyone ever wants from me. That or a good story."

"I don't want your money!" I leap to my feet and, hands on hips, glare right back at him. Of all the cheek! He seriously thinks I've come here for money? "I'm only here because–"

I just manage to stop myself in time. If I tell him that I'm only here because his dead brother wants me to pass on a message, he'll go berserk. Rafe's wired with the kind of energy that speaks of too little sleep and too much booze, and he's teetering on the brink of desperation. One tiny shove will send him plummeting over – and then who knows what will happen? I don't know Rafe Thorne. I never knew Rafe Thorne. He could be violent. He could be dangerous. He could be all manner of things. I'm suddenly very aware of my own vulnerability being alone with this volatile man.

"He's drunk," says Alex bleakly. "There's no getting through to him when he's like this, and it's getting worse. He's nothing like this when he's sober. I promise."

I'm unconvinced. The Internet was brimming with lurid stories about Rafe Thorne's behaviour since his brother was killed. I need to leave.

"So, if you don't want money then what do you want?" Rafe demands when I don't rise to his insults. He glares at me; any earlier sympathy I may have felt between us has totally vanished. The violet eyes glitter dangerously. "Come on, *Cleo*. Don't hold back. Is it blackmail or have you been paid for a story? Is that it? Are the fucking red tops swarming again?"

He swallows the drink and reaches for the bottle again. It's empty, and with a savage and despairing cry, Rafe sweeps it from the table and onto the hearth where it shatters into thousands of lethal pieces. I step back in alarm. The stories of his drinking and black moods haven't been exaggerated.

"Get out," he hisses. "Get out and don't come back."

"I'm so sorry," says Alex, turning to me. His shoulders sag and he looks utterly defeated. "This was a stupid idea. I'm so sorry I ever involved you."

"I'm not sorry I came," I say.

"Well you should be," snarls Rafe. "You should have stayed in the past. I don't need you and your pity. I don't need anyone at all. Not anymore. So just remember that."

He turns his back on me and I can tell by the way his shoulders tremble that he's overcome with emotion. Alex stands helplessly beside him and my eyes fill with tears. I know all about grief and anger and shutting yourself away, but until today I never realised quite how much damage all that could do. Suddenly I can't wait to get away from this place and find my father.

"I want to help you," I whisper. And I do, I really do.

Rafe wheels around to face me. His eyes are colder than the frosty ground outside and his expression is taut. "Get out. I don't need you here. And help? Christ. How do you possibly think you could help me? You haven't got a fucking clue. Go on! Get out. You know where the door is."

The words are fierce and I flinch. Guilt is eating Rafe Thorne up, devouring him from the inside out like a powerful acid.

"Get out!" he hollers when I fail to move. "Get out!"

I don't wait to be told again. I turn on my heel and flee via the terrace, pausing only to retrieve my rucksack. It's only when I'm down the path and back on the lane that I realise I've left my hat inside the house – and, of course, I left Alex behind too. I'm shaking from head to toe.

"I did my best, Alex," I say out loud. My voice is trembling as well. "I tried, OK? So now will you please leave me alone?"

But there's no answer, only the calling of the crows in the skeletal trees edging the river; the only sign I've even spoken at all are clouds of my breath in the air. Blinking back tears I turn away from the house. I'm determined to leave Rafe Thorne firmly in the past where he belongs.

Chapter 17

"Cleo Rose! Come in, come in! What a wonderful surprise!"

I strongly suspect my father means "shock" rather than "surprise", as it's unprecedented for me to show up on his doorstep unannounced like this. To be fair I'm pretty surprised myself: since Mum died I can count on one hand the number of times I've made it back to the family home.

"Sorry to turn up on you at such short notice," I say, sliding my rucksack from my shoulders as I hop up the two steps into the porch and follow him inside. It smells the same as it always did and my stomach lurches because I still expect to see Mum come striding out of the study, glasses sliding down her nose and gabbling away excitedly about her latest research project. God, this feeling of barbed wire being dragged through my insides is unbearable. How is it that I still feel like this ten years on? Is this what Rafe Thorne feels like all the time?

No wonder he drinks.

"Sweetheart, you don't ever have to apologise. This is your home," my father says. He takes my rucksack and stows it under the stairs, exactly where I chucked my school bag every weekday afternoon for years. I don't even need to poke my head into the messy cupboard to know that it will still be full of ancient wellies, old coats hanging like weary bats from pegs, and even the skeleton of an elderly pram – just as I know there's a hole in the sitting-room carpet just out of sight beneath the hearthrug, and a creaky floorboard at the top of the stairs. This ordinary-looking Victorian terrace in genteel Taply-on-Thames is as much a part of my history as pyramids and grave goods are a part of ancient Egypt's.

Is it my home? It doesn't feel like it, but then nowhere really does. Is home the flat I share with Susie, or is it my office? That's certainly the place where I feel the knots in my shoulders loosen and where I can always breathe easily – but a home? No, not really. Maybe it's time to face the fact that at the grand old age of almost thirty I don't have a home as such. I have letters after my name and I've written papers that academics refer to, but apart from those I don't have much at all. Who would want to drown their sorrows in Jack Daniel's if Cleo Carpenter fell off the face of the earth?

Visiting Rafe Thorne has had a very bad effect on me, that's for sure. Where has all this introspection come from all of a sudden? I have a strong urge to flip my laptop open and get stuck into some work, or maybe call the museum and have a chat with the Prof about my application – Simon should have delivered it by now. If only I'd brought my laptop with me rather than left it behind. While Dad chats away about Tolly's latest flash car and what antics his GCSE history class have been up to, I sneak a glance at my watch. Four o'clock on a Sunday afternoon. Hmm. Even the Professor will have gone home by now. Drat. It'll have to wait.

"So what brings you here?" My father is asking as, bag and coat safely deposited, we head for the kitchen. "Not that I'm not thrilled to see you," he adds hastily, just in case I might feel unwanted and take flight. "I'm delighted to see you, darling, but it's a little out of the blue. I know how busy you've been at work."

"I'm being haunted by a dead pop star and he wanted me to bring a message to his brother, which I've just cocked up in spectacular style. And by the way, this brother just so happens to be a guy I once kissed on a railway platform and have never forgotten," I say.

Except I don't say this. How can I? It would sound totally deranged. It *is* totally deranged; Dad would think I'd got an even more serious head injury than anyone had realised, and I'd be whipped into the nearest shrink's office before you could say straightjacket.

"No reason really," I shrug, as he fills the kettle. "It was a bit of a last-minute decision."

Abruptly, my father stops what he's doing and spins around to look at me. Water sprays everywhere.

"What's going on? Is there something you haven't told me?" Concern twists his lined face. "Are you sick? Has something happened? Is it the accident?"

He looks so stricken, and I feel awful. Of course Dad's alarmed. I never, ever do things on the spur of the moment, do I? Or rather, the old Cleo Rose Carpenter never used to. The new me, however, is a little *too* fond of being impulsive.

"I'm fine," I promise him. "I was just in the mood for some time off work."

Now my father looks even more worried. It's fair enough. After all, I am the girl who lay in her hospital bed and demanded her laptop.

"I've just finished the Aamon project and applied for the position of Assistant Director of the department, so things will be pretty quiet for a few days," I explain as I fetch a tea towel and steer him to a seat at the kitchen table. While I mop up the water and busy myself with making tea, I explain that I was owed a couple of days off work and wanted to catch up with some old friends. If my father is stunned to learn that I have any old friends in Taply then he keeps it to himself, but the look on his face speaks volumes. I'd bet all my qualifications that the minute I'm out of earshot he'll be on the phone to my brother to discuss my weird behaviour. Thank goodness he doesn't know the half of it.

The PG tips still live in the tartan tin in the cupboard above the sink, and it's frightening how easily the old routines return to me. I locate the mugs, teaspoons and biscuits as though my brain is on autopilot. Any minute now my mother will emerge from her study, screw up her nose at the builder's tea and start hunting for the Earl Grey. Despite being a woman who could find long-lost artefacts, she was regularly defeated by the layout of her own kitchen. It was just as well she had Dad on hand. Suddenly her absence feels as ragged and as raw as it did the day she died, and panic starts to claw at my chest. My God, I really do understand why Rafe Thorne is drinking. If somebody came along and offered me a whiskey right now I think I'd down it in one.

Since my earlier flight from Mellisande, Rafe Thorne has been haunting my thoughts every bit as effectively as his brother has been haunting my day-to-day existence. I'd sprinted up the lane with Rafe's bitter words still ringing in my ears, humiliated by the way he'd spoken to me and for mistakenly thinking he was hurt. Had there been a part of me that had been secretly hoping he'd be over the moon to see me again? Was that what had come of sharing a flat with a girl who owned a mountain of pink novels? I must have absorbed Susie's romantic streak by osmosis or something.

Alex, with his crazy dream of happily-ever-after, hasn't helped either. I only need to look at my sad and lonely father to see that there aren't any happy endings. I'm glad I'm single: it's easier this way.

Rafe Thorne was just a stranger, I'd told myself firmly as I'd stomped back to Riverside Halt. He was just somebody I'd accidentally bumped into a lifetime ago – a fleeting dream, nothing more. I felt like an idiot now, that was for sure, but what had I really expected? Thank God I hadn't told him that his dead brother wanted me to pass on a message. The thought of his reaction to that little gem made me feel hot with horror, and as the small train had carried me back towards High Wycombe, where I could catch a bus to Taply, I'd comforted myself with the knowledge that I would never, ever have to lay eyes on him again. I'd vowed that when I got back to my flat in London I would try my very hardest to forget this whole sorry episode.

Unfortunately, though, my brain – always brilliant at remembering every minute detail – had insisted on replaying the encounter over and over again, and with every mile I'd travelled I'd felt worse rather than better. Whatever had I been thinking, barging into the house of a total stranger? He'd probably thought I was a deranged fan. And I'd as good as broken in, too. I hoped he wasn't inclined to complain to the police…

Feeling as though a swarm of scarab beetles were chomping on my innards, I'd tortured myself for the entire bus journey from High Wycombe to Taply. Then, still lost in thought, I'd wandered around the shops for an hour. The town had been looking beautiful in the winter sunshine, the Thames flowing slowly beneath the stately arches of Taply Bridge and carrying flotillas of swans down river. The Christmas tree was up in the town centre and festive white lights were strung through the streets; as the afternoon had begun to fade they'd flickered on, turning the place into a magical warren of medieval houses and lamplit windows. I'd bought a takeout coffee and sat with it on the riverbank, my hands wrapped around the paper cup, staring at the ever-changing water until my drink had grown cold. I'd half hoped and half dreaded that Alex might appear. At least he'd have understood.

And he could have told me whether Rafe was all right…

No matter how hard I'd tried, I hadn't been able to put Rafe out of my thoughts. His haunted eyes and the bleak twist of his mouth were etched on my mind's eye. He'd been every bit as tortured by guilt and regrets as Alex had told me he was.

Even now, as I sit with my worried father, Rafe hovers on the edge of my thoughts; it takes a big effort to push him away.

"You're just like her, you know."

My father's words pull me back to the small kitchen. The cosy lamplight and the warmth from the Rayburn are a world away from the cold neglect of Mellisande.

"Sorry?"

"You. You're just like your mother." My father's voice is sad but he's smiling a wistful half-smile. "You get more like her all the time."

"Because of the Egypt thing, right?" I know I got this from my mother, along with my single-mindedness. That used to drive Dad crazy; Mum would vanish into her study for hours and he'd practically have to drag her away from her work to eat. I've been known to do exactly the same, except there's nobody to drag me out of my office – other than maybe an exasperated security guard. My eyesight and skinny body are down to Dad's genes, although thank God I didn't inherit the beard.

I sip my tea. "I guess when I talk about my work, especially the Aamon stuff, it must remind you of her?"

"You certainly got the archaeology bug from her – but, no, that wasn't really what I meant." My father leans back in his seat and considers me thoughtfully.

"Claudia might have gone but she lives on in you, Cleo Rose, and not just in your work. It was more the expression on your face just a moment ago, that dreamy faraway look: that reminded me of her."

This is a bit of a surprise. My thoughts were miles away – about six miles away as the crow flies – but I can't say I ever thought of my mother as being a dreamer. No, I remember her being focused on her work or gathering lecture notes together. She was always busy.

"You don't believe me, do you?" My father shakes his head and reaches out to take my hand. "She wasn't always a mum and a professor, you know. And we met in the seventies. It was a different age. People behaved differently."

I laugh. "I know! I've seen the pictures! Kipper ties, flares and tank tops. There were no fashion police, that was for sure – and don't think that Tolly and I never noticed your special *herbal* cigarettes."

"Ah, yes. Well, the less said about those the better, I think. But it's true that Mum was a bit of a daydreamer; she always had the most vivid imagination. Your granny used to say she was fey."

My maternal grandmother, Granny Rose, always seemed as ancient as anything she and my mother were studying, and when she died it was after a long and happy life. She'd been a great storyteller and I'd loved hearing about her adventures on digs. It was Granny Rose who first discovered Aamon's tomb and who had begun the family tradition of loving all things Egyptian.

"When Claudia was younger she was always daydreaming," my father continues, his own eyes now adopting a faraway expression. "I used to tease her about it. She'd have these conversations with thin air – talking to herself, she called it – and she'd often know things about people that would surprise them. Granny Rose used to say she had the sight."

"What?"

"I know, I know! It's crazy, isn't it?" Dad laughs. "Utter nonsense, of course, although it was quite uncanny the way Granny Rose found that boy pharaoh's tomb. I'll never forget that story; she used to say it was almost as though somebody led her to it, but to be honest that was probably your grandmother's instinct. Apparently she could practically sniff the artefacts out. And she'd have insights into things that had never occurred to anyone else. It was definitely some kind of gift – and your mother certainly inherited it."

I stare at him. This is true, but it's not how I remember my mother, not in the slightest.

"This doesn't sound at all like Mum. Are you sure?"

"Long before she was your mum, Claudia was my wife," Dad reminds me. "I used to tell Mum she could always get a job predicting the lottery! She said second sight ran in the family but it didn't do to make too much of it, especially since she had her heart set on being a don. She mentioned it less and less as she grew older, but I often wondered whether you or Tolly might take after her. Still, it seems you've just inherited my sensible, if slightly dull, genes."

I wish. As my father wanders down memory lane, recounting some long and involved story about something Ptolemy once did, I'm far too busy trying to reconcile the mother I knew with the person my father's just described. The Claudia Carpenter I remember was an academic who wrote for serious journals and who lectured at Oxford. She was professional and focused and intellectual. In other words, my mother was everything I admire and everything I've always wanted to become. To discover that she may have had experiences similar to mine is both comforting and alarming at the same time. If only she was still alive so that I could talk to her. I know Mum would have been able to help me.

Silence falls between us – but for once it's companionable one rather than an awkward one. We sip our tea and listen to the ticking of the grandfather clock in the hall and the distant sounds of traffic.

"I'm sorry I didn't tell you sooner that Mum was so sick," my father says suddenly. His shoulders sag and he looks exhausted, worn out from ten years of not broaching the subject. I almost choke on my tea because this is the most taboo topic in the Carpenter family. Never mind Harry Potter's He Who Must Not Be Named: this was the Carpenters' That Which Must Never Be Discussed. I couldn't have been more taken aback if my father had painted himself blue and started tap-dancing across the table.

"We thought we were doing the right thing for you and for Tolly by not burdening you with it, but I can see now that we couldn't have got it more wrong. Parents don't have all the answers." My father looks wistful. "I wish to God we did, but the truth is we're just as clueless as anyone else. There's no magic knowledge that appears the moment you become a parent. You just have to do the best you can. And sometimes you get it wrong. Very wrong."

It's the first time we've ever talked about this. I mean properly talked about what happened, rather than skirting around the elephant in the room.

"If I'd have known how sick she was, I would have come back much earlier," I say. My throat feels tight and my eyes prickle. "I wouldn't have stayed in Cairo. I'd have spent time with her."

"And don't you think Mum knew that?" My father shakes his head. "Oh, Cleo, she was so proud of everything you achieved. To drag you away just to sit at her bedside was the last thing she wanted."

"But what about what *I* wanted?"

"It doesn't work like that. We didn't get to choose what *we* wanted because this wasn't anyone's decision to make except Mum's. Not mine, not Tolly's and not yours either, Cleo Rose. Claudia wanted everything to be as normal as possible and I had to respect that. Do you really think it was what I wanted?" His eyes are bright now. "It would have really helped me to have had you both here too. There were times when all I wanted to do was pick up the phone and share it. Being alone with it all was almost as bad as watching her slip away from me, day by day, hour by hour."

I look at my father and suddenly I see him. I *really* see him. I see beyond the familiar things – the wire-framed glasses, faded grey sweater and hands ink-stained from marking mountains of GCSE coursework – to the tired and lonely man underneath. There's grey in his once dark hair and lines fan out from his eyes, giving a sad droop to his expression. It tugs at my heart. Nursing somebody in the final stages of cancer must be hell on earth, and to do it all alone an even deeper Hades. I'm skewered by shame that I've never once thought about how it must have been for him. I've been like Rafe Thorne, haven't I? I've been so immersed in my own grief that I haven't been able to think of anyone else. I was far too busy blaming my father for keeping me away. Not once did it occur to me that this might not have been his decision.

"I'm so sorry, Dad. I had no idea. I thought–"

"I know what you thought, sweetheart, and it's what I decided I wanted you to believe. It was bad enough for you losing Mum without being angry with her too. What would that have achieved?"

I open my mouth to reply – but then I think of Rafe Thorne, so resentful towards Alex for dying in the first place, and eaten up with guilt and grief. I decide to keep quiet, because I know Dad has a point. Would it have helped to know that Mum had chosen to shut me out during those final months? Probably not. It would just have been another hurt.

"I didn't want you to blame Mum, not when you were already so upset, so it seemed far better that I took the blame instead." He gives me a rueful smile. "I guess I just didn't think you'd still be quite so angry with me almost a decade on."

"I'm sorry," I whisper.

His ink-stained hand closes around mine and even though I'm almost thirty it still feels as big and as safe as it did when I was a child. Once upon a time I used to clamber onto my father's lap and he would make everything better by giving me a hug and telling me that everything would be OK. I'm not about to try this now, but I have a very similar feeling.

"No, I'm sorry." He squeezes my fingers. "It wasn't the right decision and I shouldn't have let Claudia have her way. But you know what your mother was like. She could be pretty determined!"

I laugh because I don't think "determined" really covers it. "Bloody-minded" and "stubborn" are probably more accurate. Then I realise that this is the first time my father and I have talked about Mum since she died. It still hurts, but not nearly as much as I've always been afraid it would; in fact, it feels good to open up about it at last. As the afternoon seeps into evening and the sun casts shadows into the kitchen, we share memories, and rather than feeling sad my heart feels lighter with every word.

"I'm so glad you came over today," my father says finally.

I nod. "Me too. I just wish we'd talked about this before."

"No regrets, sweetheart. That's the past – and if there's one thing that being a historian's taught me, it's that no matter what we may think, there's no way we can change that. We just have to come to terms with it, learn the lessons and then move on as best we can. And if we can't…" His voice tails off.

"And if we can't?" I echo.

My father gives me a sad smile. "Then I guess we're more stuck in the past than anything you might find in a pharaoh's tomb, and just as dead inside."

For some reason an image of Rafe Thorne, passed out on the floor in his cold empty house, flashes across my mind and I shiver. I wish I could have helped him.

"I'm so thankful that we've been able to talk today." My father takes off his glasses and pinches the bridge of his nose between his thumb and forefinger before replacing them and giving me a rueful smile. "Mum would have hated to think that the way she chose to die drove a wedge between us all. We used to be such a close family. You'll think me a silly old fool for saying this, but I've always felt that she just wouldn't be at rest until she knew we were on our way back to that." He pauses and looks at me with tired eyes, once bright blue but now as faded as stonewashed denim. "Is that ridiculous?"

No, I think, not ridiculous at all. Since I walloped my head there are many things that make far more sense than they did before.

But I won't tell Alex Thorne this. No way. It'll make him far too smug.

"And I really feel that today we've started to find our way back, don't you?" Dad adds hopefully. "I know things can never be the same – but you, me and Tolly, we're still a family. Mum wouldn't have wanted us to become strangers because of a choice she made. She'd have hated that."

Dad's right. There was once a time when the Carpenter family was a tight unit. We travelled together and played together, and Mum and I had even tentatively started working together on the Aamonic period. As I sit at the table, the tired sunshine squeezing its last hopeful rays through the ragged net curtains, memories flicker through my mind like faded snapshots in an old album: Dad and Tolly in the garden; Mum and I wielding spades and grinning like loons on our first dig; the flat we rented in Cairo with its cracked tiles where lizards basked before we chased them; a lonely railway station at Christmas…

I exhale slowly. Some memories are best left buried and others are bittersweet. Are we finding our way back? I look at my father's hopeful face and suddenly it's as though I've just shrugged off my biggest rucksack, packed to the brim with my heaviest textbooks. A rucksack I hadn't even known I was carrying.

"Yes, I think so too," I agree.

Dad smiles and silence falls, along with the evening.

"I'll make us both a nice cup of tea, shall I?" he says finally, and then winks at me. "Thank goodness for tea, eh? Where would the British be without it when emotions run high?"

While he bustles with chipped mugs and hunts out the same tartan biscuit tin I remember from childhood, the oddest feeling comes over me. It's a bit like pins and needles, but in my head. Dad's still speaking – something about how Tolly might be taking his latest girlfriend to the Caribbean for Christmas – but I can't take it in.

As my oblivious father chats away, Mum is standing right next to him as clear in every detail as though she were really in the room. The peachy light of the sun's last rays bathe her and she looks exactly as I remember her, tall and slim and with her thick red hair loose in ringlets to her shoulders. As I watch her she's looking at Dad with such love that my eyes fill with tears, and when she turns and smiles at me they spill over and the whole room becomes a kaleidoscope of shimmering light. By the time I've dashed them away she's gone.

Was that another trick played on me by my damaged cerebral cortex, I wonder as I sip the tea, or was she really there? I know what the former, logical Dr Cleo Carpenter would say, but the new me – the one who talks to dead rock stars and breaks into houses – thinks very differently. I feel as though my mother has put her arms around me and given me a hug, the hug she couldn't give me on her last Christmas Eve. I close my eyes and allow myself just to be for a moment or two, to enjoy that sense of love and acceptance. I have the strongest conviction that now she knows I've made my peace with Dad I won't be seeing her again, but rather than being sad about this I'm calm. It feels right.

I feel right.

And maybe it's a coincidence – maybe it is my injured brain playing tricks – but when I go to bed that evening in my old bedroom, the sense of peace stays with me. I lie in my single bed and burrow under my duvet, feeling warm and as safe. If I did see Mum then she's happy and at peace. And even if I didn't, I've still taken the first steps towards making things right with my father. Whether the vision was my imagination or not, I can't remember when I last felt so calm. Nothing else matters right now. Not the museum, the research, the job or even Simon Welsh.

Alex had been right all along: making peace with your loved ones does help to make sense of it all. Now all I need to do is figure out a way that I can do the same for Rafe. That won't be easy. If he sees me again he'll probably call the police.

Hmm. That's a problem for another day. Right now I can hardly keep my eyes open.

I click off my bedside light.

"I love you, Mum," I whisper, and although she doesn't say it back I feel it. Moments later I tumble into the deepest sleep I've had for a very, very long time.

Chapter 18

You know that wonderful feeling you get when the school summer holidays start and you lie in bed knowing that you don't have to get up and have nothing to do for ages and ages? Well, this is exactly how I feel when I wake up the next morning. I have nowhere to go and nothing to do today. That makes a huge change!

For a moment I'm a little disorientated to find myself back in my old single bed listening to the rumble of traffic outside as Taply-on-Thames wakes up for the day, rather than being in my flat and hearing Susie crashing about in the kitchen – but seconds later I remember the events of the day before, and everything falls into place again.

I really ought to be at the museum getting ready for my interview and helping my team with the latest exhibits, not lying here in my teenage bedroom. I glance at the digital clock on the bedside table, the very same clock whose insistent beeping and flashing neon display drove me out from under the covers every morning until I left home, and I'm taken aback to see it's almost midday.

Midday? Seriously? I'm staggered at this, because I never sleep late nowadays. Since adulthood, my internal body clock has always prompted me to be out of bed and bustling around by six at the latest. It's one of the (numerous) things about me that have driven many ex-boyfriends absolutely crazy – not to mention Susie, who could give Rip Van Winkle a run for his money.

"For God's sake, Cleo!" she'll complain, appearing in the sitting room bleary-eyed on a Saturday morning, while I'm dashing around with the vacuum cleaner trying to do some chores before I nip into work for a few extra hours. "Why can't you just chillax for a bit? It's Saturday! It's the sodding weekend!"

But I'm not very good at "chillaxing". I'm normally about as relaxed as a coiled spring, and I can't stand the thought of lazing in bed. I'm a busy person with lots to do. I can't afford to waste time snoozing.

"There are other things to do in bed, besides sleep," Suse will grumble, rubbing her eyes. "Read a book? Eat breakfast? Shag a gorgeous man's brains out?"

Since most of the gorgeous men Suse brings home have the same IQ as a particularly dim cabbage, I can't believe shagging their brains out would take very long at all. And as for eating breakfast in bed? I had quite enough of that during my enforced stay in hospital. So, no. Cleo Carpenter likes to be up with the lark, getting things done and moving on with her day – unlike Susie, who's right up there with John and Yoko for staging a bed-in.

Anyway, my having slept for most of the morning is yet another unprecedented event to add to the growing list.

Sunshine slips through the curtains and warms the ancient carpet. I stretch my arms above my head and yawn. The long sleep has done me good; maybe Susie was onto something after all. I feel as though I've exhaled after holding my breath for a long, long time. Everything seems lighter – even my psyche's refreshed. I don't know what today will bring, but whatever happens I feel more than ready to face it.

Let's be honest, I decide as I jump out of bed and pad downstairs, nothing could be worse than yesterday's meeting with Rafe Thorne. As I boil the kettle to make tea I relive the entire episode and my face feels hotter than the water I slosh onto my tea bag. I can hardly bear to think about the impression he has of me right now. I've gone from being the muse of his most famous hit to a housebreaker and possible kiss-and-tell girl in one easy move. Nice work.

Try as I might I can't stop my skin prickling with embarrassment when I recall the moment Rafe opened his eyes and found me in his house. Next to displaying my red spotty knickers to all and sundry in the Wellby Museum, this has to be the single most mortifying moment of my life.

"Don't feel bad. Rafe's bloody difficult these days," remarks Alex. He's leaning against the oven and regarding me from beneath his floppy dark fringe. "You tried."

"Shit!" I practically leap out of my ancient Snoopy tee shirt, and boiling water sloshes all over the kitchen table. "Will you stop creeping up on me like that?"

"Sorry," says Alex. He doesn't look it though. In fact he seems rather pleased with himself. "I just wanted to make sure you were all right after yesterday?"

I grab some kitchen roll and do my best to staunch the flow of water now surrounding a pile of my father's marking like a moat around a castle of exercise books. Ink is already starting to bleed across the pages and my frantic dabbing isn't helping.

"I'm fine," I tell him. "Totally embarrassed and humiliated, but otherwise fine."

"Don't take it personally," Alex says kindly. "Rafe's like that with everyone. No wonder his girlfriend dumped him. Not that she's much loss."

I pause in my dabbing. "Wasn't he dating some model?"

Alex nods. "You've been doing your homework, I see. Well, I guess research is your thing. Yeah, Rafe was dating Natasha Lacey."

Even I've heard of Natasha Lacey. She's a model who's plastered over billboards everywhere, wearing bras that would fit Barbie and tossing her mane of honey-coloured hair. With legs as long as a racehorse's, a bee-stung pout and teeth that would give dentists orgasms, she's absolutely stunning. I bet Natasha Lacey never wears spotty knickers or sleeps in a tee shirt she bought in 1998.

Come on, Cleo. Who cares what Rafe's girlfriend looks like? He's a rock star; of course he dates gorgeous models. It's practically obligatory. Anyway, I bet Natasha Lacey can't decipher hieroglyphics.

Alex grimaces. "Natasha might look good, but her head's as empty as a Ming vase. God knows what Rafe found to say to her." Then he grins at me and shrugs. "I guess they weren't about *talking*? Anyway, Rafe didn't see much of her after the accident. She wasn't into sticking around once the good times stopped and, much as it pains me to say it, I can see why. He isn't easy to be with these days."

"That's an understatement." I lob the wad of soggy kitchen roll into the bin and pick up my tea. "Look, Alex, I'm really sorry about yesterday and I'm really sorry about Rafe too, but I don't think there's much I can do to help."

"So could I please push off and leave you in peace? Let everything go back to the way it was?"

Actually, this was exactly what I'd been thinking.

"It's nothing personal," I say. "It's just that I'd like to stop seeing things now and get back to normal."

"Sorry to disappoint you, but as I've said before I don't think it works like that. I can go away and leave you alone, but that won't stop you seeing things. That hasn't come from me: it's in you."

I'm about to correct him when I recall the conversation I had at this very same table with my father only hours earlier. He'd told me that my mother had a gift. What if he's right? What if the bang to my head has unlocked something that was lying dormant within me? If that's true then life will never return to how it was before. Is that really such a bad thing? Yesterday I saw my mother in this kitchen, I know I did, and I know that she's at peace now. I can feel it. Last night I slept the best sleep I've had for years, which has to be a positive. I look at Alex and wonder if maybe there's a way I can come to balance these two parts of my life.

Or maybe I could just find a bloody good shrink?

"Anyway, aren't you going to get dressed?" Alex is asking. He points to the kitchen clock. "Look at the time. It's a lovely day outside. I thought it might be fun to go for a walk and, sexy as you look in that fetching nightie, you'll probably freeze."

It's gone midday, and I had been quite content just to stay indoors and enjoy the quiet while my father was at work, have a bath, catch a bit of afternoon telly and call the Prof to chat about when they'll schedule my interview. I was quite inclined to stay in my tee shirt too, even if it is stretched out of shape and keeps slipping off my shoulder. I can't remember the last time I had a duvet day. Actually, I don't think I've ever had one: I've never wanted to bunk off work.

It's official. I'm weird.

"Don't look like that." Alex folds his arms and fixes me with a determined look. "Go and get dressed and then come for a walk. It'll blow the cobwebs away."

"Why are you so determined to make me get up?" I grumble. "What are you up to?"

"I'm hurt," Alex says, placing a hand over his heart and adopting a wounded expression – but he can't quite meet my eyes. He looks shifty to me. "What must it be like to be so distrusting? I just thought a walk would be nice."

I don't believe him for a minute. I'm starting to get to know him, after all, and he's definitely up to something. Still, the world outside the kitchen window does look all bright and glittery, and the thought of getting some fresh air is quite appealing. Maybe I'll wander along the Thames as far as the lock and then grab a coffee? I could even visit Mum's grave and have a quick tidy-up. Normally the thought of visiting the little churchyard fills me with dread, but today I'm rather looking forward to it. Perhaps I'll even pop into the florists and buy some flowers.

"Fine," I say, putting my mug down with a thud. "I'll go for a walk."

"Brilliant!" Alex looks pleased. "Wear something warm!" he calls after me as I stomp out of the kitchen and up the stairs. "And put some make-up on too. You don't want to scare anyone!"

I ignore that comment; although when I venture into the bathroom I must admit that my white face and deep red hair do make a bit of a scary contrast.

Dumping the Snoopy tee shirt into the old wicker laundry bin that's been unravelling for as long as I can remember, I jump into the shower and wake myself up with a blast of cold water. A good dollop of some faded-looking pineapple body wash – which I'm pretty certain was discontinued sometime in the nineties – and one hair wash later, I'm back in my bedroom. The world outside looks bright but chilly, and bearing this in mind I pull on my new skinny jeans, my soft green sweater and a thick pair of socks. A quick slick of lip-gloss, some mascara across my lashes and a brush pulled through my hair, and I'm good to go. My reflection doesn't shatter the mirror, so Alex has nothing to be worried about; the good people of Taply won't be terrified.

I'm just checking my mobile in case Professor Hamilton has sent a message when there's a hammering of knuckles on the front door. Grabbing my bag I fly down the stairs to answer it – and then almost fall down in shock when I see who's on the doorstep.

Now I understand why Alex was so desperate for me to get dressed and put some make-up on.

"Hello, Cleo Rose Carpenter," says Rafe Thorne softly. "Can we start again?"

Chapter 19

"What are *you* doing here?"

OK, so this isn't the most gracious way to greet a visitor but I can't help myself. The last person I'm expecting to find on the doorstep is Rafe Thorne. For a split second I'm tempted to slam the door in his handsome face and bolt back upstairs and burrow under the duvet.

"Don't be mean," says Alex bossily over my shoulder. "He's made an effort to come all this way to see you. The least you can do is be polite."

Rafe has made an effort; it's true. Yesterday's stubble has been shaved away and his black hair is freshly washed and glossy as it brushes the shoulders of his battered leather jacket. He smells good too, of something citrusy and sharp, which is a distinct improvement on Eau de Stale Booze. A scarlet scarf is wound around his neck, and he's wearing faded blue Levis and brown biker boots; the obligatory shades complete the casual rock-star-about-town look. When he pushes these back onto his head and stares down at me I notice that his striking violet eyes are no longer bright with anger but thoughtful.

I guess that's an improvement.

"I hope I haven't disturbed you? I thought about breaking in and creeping around but there's no way I can compete with your cat-burglary skills," Rafe teases. As he speaks his eyes crinkle at the corners, lines starring out towards his temples – reminders that there was once a time when he probably smiled a lot. "Catherine Zeta Jones in *Entrapment* has got nothing on you. By the way, why didn't you wear the leather suit?"

I ignore his teasing and fold my arms across my chest. Rafe might be amused and Alex is laughing like a drain, but I'm not finding it funny. When I think about yesterday's meeting I feel hot all over. "I didn't break in. I used a key."

"Of course. Forgive me. You used a key to *let yourself in totally uninvited.* I'm slightly more old-fashioned. I like to be asked in, or at the very least ring the doorbell."

"He's just kidding," Alex says hastily. "Rafe's got a very dry sense of humour."

"Do you see me laughing?" I shoot back.

Luckily Rafe assumes I'm talking to him.

"Look, I'm ever so grateful really. Even though you were *trespassing.*"

See. You try to do somebody a good turn and what do you get? Grief and hassle. No wonder I prefer being left alone in the museum.

"Sorry," I say stiffly. "I apologise for thinking you might have been in trouble and in need of help. I should have left you there."

Rafe raises his eyes to heaven. "Cleo, I'm teasing you!"

"Don't bother, fam," sighs Alex. "She's got no sense of humour some days."

Yep. And this day is one of them.

"Look," Rafe continues, stepping forwards and smiling at me, a slow smile that makes my insides knot even though I'm annoyed with him after yesterday. "I'm grateful, I really am. Nobody's been bothered about whether I'm all right for so long now that I guess I'm out of practice. I don't understand why you were there or how you've suddenly reappeared after all these years, but I'm touched you wanted to help. And I'm sorry I was less than receptive. I've come to thank you."

Yesterday's embarrassing episode is now spooling through my mental cinema on a loop and I'm cringing more with every second that passes. I just want to draw a line under all this.

"And I brought this back," he adds, reaching into his pocket and pulling out my green hat. He holds it out at me hopefully. "You left it behind. I had to return it."

Thanks a lot, bobble hat. If it wasn't for you I could still be slobbing around in my Snoopy tee shirt and doing my best to forget yesterday. Or maybe booking myself in for some intensive psychotherapy? Anything but standing face to face with Rafe Thorne.

"Thanks," I mumble, rather ungraciously. "You really shouldn't have bothered though. It's only from Primark."

Rafe grins. "Hey, don't knock Primarni. Our stylist used to swear by the place." He pauses and his brow furrows thoughtfully. "I have to ask, did you leave the hat behind on purpose?"

I snatch it back. "Don't be ridiculous. Of course I didn't. Why would I?"

Rafe shrugs. "So that you had an excuse to come back? Fans do the weirdest things."

Fans? He thinks I'm a fan? Of all the bloody nerve! I'm not even going to dignify this comment with an answer, so instead I just glower at him. My glower has made the undergraduates I teach quail and ex-boyfriends quake, and is just about the only thing that makes Susie give in and clean the flat, so it's generally very effective. Unfortunately though, it doesn't seem to work on Rafe Thorne, who's lolling against the doorframe with irritating insouciance.

"You wanted to see me again." It isn't a question. "So you left your hat. I must admit a hat makes a pleasant change. It's normally knickers or bras I have thrown at me, not bobble hats." The smile widens into a grin. "Although I wouldn't have complained if you'd felt the urge."

For some reason I now have a vivid mental image of me in Rafe's drawing room peeling off my underwear and whirling it around my head like something from the Moulin Rouge, and my face is even hotter.

"Don't be embarrassed," Rafe says kindly. "I'm flattered. You went to a lot of trouble to find me."

The fact that he's taking pity on me is the final straw. There's only so much humiliation a girl can stand.

"You actually think I'd want to see you again after your behaviour yesterday?" I say incredulously. "Have you been drinking again? What on earth makes you think I'd want you to come here?"

Rafe winks. "Maybe because you typed your address onto my computer? I have to say that's original, even though I could have done without having my lyrics messed with. I'm having enough bloody trouble writing as it is." He shakes his head. "I must have been more drunk than I realised not to have seen you do it. Or did you type the address while I was asleep?"

I stare at him. "What? Don't be ridiculous! Of course I didn't do that!"

His dark brows lift. "You're denying it?"

"Of course I'm denying it. *Because I didn't do it.*"

There's an awkward throat-clearing noise behind me.

"Err, sorry," says Alex somewhere behind me, sounding anything but. "That *may* have been me. It took an awful lot of energy. That's why I didn't come and find you last night. I was spent."

Oh great. So now I look completely deranged and there's no way I can explain myself without sounding even more bonkers.

Rafe pushes a lock of dark hair back from his well-defined face and regards me thoughtfully while I pray for the floor to open up and swallow me, which of course it refuses to do. His lithe body fills the door, his shoulders and chest tapering into a lean waist and hips. I look away.

"OK, of course you didn't, then," says Rafe kindly when I fail to reply. He's acting as if he's taking pity on a deluded fan, which is pretty galling. "I must have just imagined it and found your address by magic. Yes. It must have appeared by magic."

"Maybe a ghost typed it?" suggests Alex. Not helpful.

"Well?" Rafe is still waiting for an explanation. I have the feeling that unless I can come up with one I'll be standing in the doorway for a while. "What's your suggestion?"

"Oh! My address!" I force a laugh. "Oh yes! Of course! I remember now. I… err… I typed that in while we were talking, remember?"

"No, actually, I can't say I do." Rafe doesn't look convinced. "But then I was very drunk. Look, Cleo, I'm really sorry about yesterday. You didn't catch me at my best. I'd had some bad news and, what can I say? I hit the Jack Daniel's."

"And the Stella and the wine," I shoot back. I won't forget that scene in a hurry. The drawing room had looked as though somebody had ransacked Oddbins.

He nods. "I drink too much. I know that and believe me I have tried not to, but sometimes things just get too much, you know? And that's the only thing that helps."

"No it isn't!" Alex yells. He leaps up from the stairs where he's been slouched listening to our conversation and shoves past me until he's staring right in his brother's face. "Drinking isn't helping, you stupid bastard! It's making it worse!"

"Brr, it's chilly here." Rafe pulls his scarf more tightly around his neck and buries his hands in his pockets. Then he smiles at me, a slow sexy smile that lifts one corner of his mouth. Goosebumps rise on my arms – and not from the cold, either. Suddenly I'm nineteen again and on that railway platform. It's the oddest feeling.

"I'm doing this all wrong, aren't I?" he says softly. "Listen, Christmas Girl, I'm really glad you left your address because it's given me the chance to return your hat and apologise for behaving so appallingly yesterday. I was kicking myself once you'd left. I've waited years to find you again and when I do I turn into a tit."

"I found *you*," I point out, and in my head I hear Susie groan. If my best friend were here now, apart from having a meltdown because a bona fide rock star was at my house, she'd be telling me to bat my eyelids and enjoy every minute because Rafe Thorne is "sex on a stick".

Well, sex on a stick or not, he can flipping well grovel. He *did* behave appallingly.

"Of course; you found me." His lips twitch as though he's laughing, but then a more serious expression settles across that sharp-cheekboned face and he exhales slowly. "I'm so sorry, Christmas Girl, if it wasn't the reunion you'd expected or hoped for. But I'm not that boy any more than you're that same girl. Things have happened to me since then. I've changed–"

I nod. "Yeah, me too."

He holds up a hand. "I've changed, but there's one thing that has remained the same for all this time, one thing that I've always trusted, and that's my memory of meeting you. It's never altered."

Well that's just great, given that Rafe's totally shattered my memory of that snowy Christmas meeting. Seeing him again has only proven to me what a load of twaddle love and romance really are. He's no romantic hero after all: he's just a guy with a guitar, a dead brother and more baggage than Heathrow's Terminal Five. Thank goodness I've not been wasting my time dreaming about him but have been busy building a career. A career that I can't wait to get back to once this lunacy is over. Mental note to self: ring Professor Hamilton as soon as possible and find out when the interviews are.

"Do you still think about it?" Rafe asks softly when I don't reply.

I do, but I'm starting to wish I didn't. Some things, unlike artefacts from ancient Egypt, are better left buried in the past.

"It was a very long time ago," I hedge.

Rafe stares at me and then shrugs. "Yeah, yeah. You're right. It was."

An awkward silence falls. We're both a decade away on the station. Snow is falling like soft feather kisses on my cheeks, and he's just a heartbeat away. I don't think I've ever felt as close to anyone as I did to him that night. Isn't it funny how things can change? Funny and so very sad.

"Well, thanks for returning the hat," I manage eventually.

"That's no problem. Look, let me at least buy you a drink to make up for yesterday – a coffee, obviously," Rafe suggests swiftly when he sees my dubious expression. "Please, Cleo? I'm sorry I was so ungentlemanly. I know you were only trying to help."

Rafe has no idea just how much I've been trying to help. My entire life is falling to bits because of it.

"Go on," urges Alex. "This could be the one chance we get."

"Please?" Rafe blows on his fingers and pulls a pleading face. "It's freezing standing here, and if these fingers drop off my career as a musician really is over. Let me at least warm up while you make me grovel."

I laugh in spite of myself. "You haven't grovelled nearly enough."

Rafe plummets to his knees and looks up at me hopefully.

"Come for a coffee with me, Christmas Girl. Please? Look, I'm grovelling!"

"Please go for a coffee with him," pleads Alex, dancing from foot to foot in a blur of red ghostly Converse boots. "Go on. Where's the harm? And you promised you'd do your best to help."

There's a man kneeling on my father's doorstep and a ghost begging me to take pity on him. Mrs Lewis from across the road is practically tugging her net curtains down in an attempt to see what's going on. Even a couple of passersby are looking. "Say 'yes', love!" one of them calls. "The poor man's bloody freezing!"

Oh great. Now it'll be all round Taply in a nanosecond, and before teatime I'll be engaged/pregnant/dumped depending on what juicy titbit takes the neighbours' fancy. No wonder I live in lovely London where you can be completely anonymous.

"The man's right. Please say *yes*," Rafe continues, gazing up at me with beseeching violet eyes. "And say it soon!"

"You must be really desperate for a coffee," I comment.

"No, it's my knees! They're killing me," Rafe winces. "James Brown's patellas must have been knackered. Come on, Christmas Girl, I'll be stuck here until spring if you don't give in soon."

I can't help it: I'm starting to laugh at him with this clowning around.

"Stop it, you idiot! OK, I'll have a coffee with you. Just get off the step."

Rafe springs to his feet with the lean, powerful grace of a panther. So much for bad knees.

He grins. "Phew, that was touch and go for a moment! I thought my caffeine fix hung in the balance."

"Why do I feel I've been conned?" I grumble as I unhook my jacket from the newel post at the end of the banister. As I put it on I turn my back on Rafe and mouth at Alex, "*You are not invited.*"

He shrugs and winks. "Have fun. Don't do anything I wouldn't!" and when I look up from fastening my zip, he's gone. Now it really is just me and Rafe and I feel oddly shy, which is crazy. It's one coffee, in broad daylight and with a guy I once knew. There's absolutely nothing whatsoever to feel nervous about. It's not as though this is a date or anything. As if. Rafe Thorne dates blonde-bombshell models, not ginger Egyptologists.

While he waits patiently, I lock the house and hide the key in Dad's usual place under the plant pot by the front door.

"And you told me off for my hiding place," Rafe teases when he see this. "Fancy popping into the greenhouse and lobbing some stones about?"

"Believe me, if burglars try to rob Dad's house they'll think somebody got there first," I promise him as we turn left at the end of the garden gate and head into the town. "I think he's the only person I know who still has a cathode-ray telly and prefers the VCR to his DVD player."

He laughs. "VCRs! My God, my brother and I used to drive our Nan wild taping bits of *Baywatch* over her *EastEnders* collection. In the end she hid her videotapes inside the piano cabinet. We only found them when my brother decided that he wanted to learn to play. The keys made the weirdest sound."

"They played the *Baywatch* theme and then everybody started running down the street in slow motion?" I deadpan.

"Hmm, not quite Nan's style, but Alex might have been tempted. He was always one for showing off."

You have no idea quite how right you are, I think wryly as we cross the main road and join the path that follows the river towards the centre of town.

It's a cold December afternoon and the sun has given up now, wrapping itself in layers of grey cloud; the river looks leaden. A group of ducks bobs hopefully by the bank just in case we have crusts, and a rowing four scoots past, the rowers' breath rising upwards in clouds. Rafe slips his shades back down to cover his eyes, pulls a beanie hat out from his pocket and shoves it onto his head.

"I don't want to be recognised," he explains when he sees me looking. "I don't go out much these days and when I do there's normally some pap lurking to catch me at my worst. I've lost count of the times I've been splashed all across some scummy red top, so if it's all right with you I'll go incognito. Unless you want to be my new mystery redhead in tomorrow's *Sun*?"

I shake my head, thinking of the lurid headlines I've read about Rafe Thorne while trawling the Internet to catch up on ten years of Thorne history. I think I'll give the tabloids a miss. I don't think it would do my academic credibility any good to be featured in them.

"So that's why you were so angry with me and thought I was from the press?" I ask. "You really thought I'd come to get a story I could sell? Seriously? Do people really do that?"

Rafe sighs. "You are young in the ways of the tabloids," he says. Then the smile slides from his face and he looks bleak. "God, Cleo, you'd be amazed what people will do for a story or fifteen minutes of fame. Forget humiliating yourself on *Big Brother*; it's far easier to sleep with a rock star and do a kiss and tell, or take a compromising picture on a mobile. I can't trust anyone."

"You can trust me," I say. I glance up at him and when his eyes meet mine I get such a jolt it's a miracle I don't topple off the path and splash into the Thames. "You didn't have to get so angry."

"Cleo, I'll be honest. I'd sunk the best part of a bottle of Jack Daniel's the night before. I've felt better." He gives me that crooked smile again. "Then again, I've felt worse. Much worse."

"I'm sorry about your brother." There. I've said it. I've mentioned the unmentionable. Maybe this is the part where I tell him Alex's message, Alex whizzes off in a white glow and life goes back to normal? I can only hope.

"Hey, thanks, but it wasn't because of Ally that I was drinking. Well, not directly anyway." He pauses and fixes his attention on the water lapping at the riverbank, seeming suddenly fascinated by the river. "After Alex died I lost it, big time. It was my fault, you see."

"No, that's not true–" I interrupt, because hasn't Alex told me enough times himself that it was just a silly row and an accident?

But Rafe doesn't want to hear this.

"It was my fault. Please don't insult me by pretending you know the facts. It was my fault my brother died and I have to live with that every day. That's my punishment, Cleo, and that's why I'm still here rather than at the bottom of that river. I deserve to be miserable after what I did to him." His mouth sets in a tight line and his chiselled face is rigid. "I'm not excusing my behaviour yesterday but I am trying to explain it. I don't suppose I was easy to live with either after the accident. My girlfriend soon had enough and I can't really blame her. I was a bloody mess."

I nod. I was the same when Mum died. If I'm honest it's only been since last night that I've realised just how much of a mess.

"Natasha left," Rafe says flatly. "Packed her bags and walked out without even saying goodbye. I lost it then and before long I was in rehab."

I don't say anything because I sense that there's still more he wants to tell me. Instead, I watch the river flow by.

"I did OK. I managed to pull it back together. I poured the booze down the sink. I carried on. Then a couple of days ago I read that Tasha's hooked up with some new boy-band lead singer. You know the ones: the latest talent show wonders, who all look about twelve despite being in their twenties? Apparently it's love, or so they've been busy telling *OK!* – in between giving interviews to all the newspapers, of course, and being papped non-stop. Natasha says she's never felt like this before. It's the best sex of her life too, apparently, which is a big dent in my fragile male pride. She's also sold a big story on what life with me was really like. Shit, apparently."

"Ouch."

"Ouch indeed."

As though by some unspoken mutual agreement we turn away from the river and into Taply. The town is well and truly prepared for the festive season. Brightly coloured lights are threaded like beads through the High Street, and the Christmas tree is up in the square. The shop windows have been sprayed with fake snow and rammed full of sparkly wares to draw shoppers in like mesmerised magpies. The coffee shop has a chalkboard outside boasting its seasonal menu, and Boots is crammed full of gift ideas and shimmering party make-up. The charity shops are in on the act too, with their Christmas cards and fair-trade gifts.

I have to admit defeat. I cannot escape Christmas. Oddly, though, I don't feel quite as twitchy about all this as I usually do…

At the far end of the High Street stands the River Man Inn, Taply's oldest pub and a magnet for tourists. With its late-sixteenth-century beams, tiny lead-paned windows and walls bulging as though they too have indulged on the ale and become paunchy over the centuries, this pub is ideal for smothering in Christmas decorations. Usually I find baubles and tinsel garish, but in here the decorations are tasteful and soothing. Greenery swathes the lintels and crowns the bar, white fairy lights flicker and a log fire crackles in the grate. Perhaps before I head back to London I could do something similar for Dad's house.

While Rafe fetches the coffees I settle down in a snug window seat and watch the river as it flows towards London. I can hardly wait to go back there myself, but rather than wanting to flee as I have in the past I feel a lot more serene about being here. Maybe I'm even starting to make my peace with Christmas too.

"The coffee machine isn't on, so I got you a mulled wine and a Coke for me." Rafe deposits the spoils of his trip to the bar onto the table and lowers his lean frame into the sofa opposite me. "Diet Coke, that is, not the powdery rock-star variety, just in case you were wondering."

I hadn't been wondering, but then as an Egyptologist I struggle to afford the dark-brown bubbly type of Coke, never mind anything else.

"I also got us some crisps." He rips open a packet of salt and vinegar and smiles across at me. "Food of the gods."

"Wow," I say, reaching for my drink. "You certainly know how to show a girl a good time."

It's the wrong thing to say. A shadow flickers over Rafe's face. "Apparently not."

"Sorry," I say hastily. "That was tactless."

He shakes his head. "Hey, don't apologise. It's stupid; it's not as though Tash and I were serious in any way, but when I read that interview it just felt like another kick to the guts. It wasn't even about her, if I'm really honest." He picks up his Coke and swirls it thoughtfully as though it's a whiskey. "What can I say? All my good intentions were forgotten in an instant."

"And so you drank."

"And so I drank," he agrees. "And when you broke in—"

"*Let* myself in," I correct swiftly; I'm nipping this version of events in the bud. "I had a key."

"Sorry, when you *let yourself in*, I wasn't quite at my best."

He pauses and as I sip my warm and citrusy mulled wine, I know we're both seeing the same scene: the fusty drawing room, the empty bottles, and the figure slumped on the floor. Rafe runs a hand through his thick hair and shrugs.

"Look, I am grateful you cared enough to try and help, I really am, but what I actually want to know is what the hell you were doing there in the first place. I haven't laid eyes on you in ten years, so why come back now? Why ignore all the interviews I gave and all the lyrics I wrote about you, only to reappear at that particular point? What's going on?"

This is it, the moment when I could take a chance and tell him everything. I'd be keeping my promise to Alex and setting myself free. It would be a win-win situation. Rafe would probably think I was a lunatic and want nothing more to do with me, but at least I could then walk away from the Thorne brothers, catch a train to London and slip right back into my usual life. It's very tempting.

I glance across the table at Rafe, who's observing me with the kind of intensity I usually adopt when I'm focused on my research, and my heart does a somersault and then starts thudding like a Samba beat.

What's happening here? Why can't I just tell him? I want life to go back to normal, don't I?

"It's complicated," I whisper.

Rafe pulls a rueful face. "Isn't everything?"

I teeter on the brink of telling him – sway a little, almost topple over the edge – but something holds me back. I take another mouthful of mulled wine. *If in doubt, try Dutch courage* is Susie's motto, so maybe I should try it?

"I heard the song," I say eventually, because this is true. "And I realised who you are."

"Who I *was*, you mean." He downs the Coke and I can tell he wishes it were a shot. "God, I'm a mess, Cleo, a bloody liability. What you saw yesterday? That drunken prick? The guy who drowns his sorrows in whiskey and passes out on the floor? That's me now. I'm not the man you met all those years ago. He was young and full of hopes and dreams. He had everything ahead of him." He thumps the glass down as though trying to slam his thoughts away. "*He* didn't kill his brother."

"You didn't kill Alex. It was an accident."

Rafe laughs, but it's a bleak sound. "Yeah, on a technicality, maybe, but it was my going on at him about the band that made Ally jump out without looking. He was keen to sign a new deal and I wanted to take some time out. The fame thing? It's not all it's cracked up to be. Ally couldn't believe it. He said we were on the brink of breaking the USA. I told him that I didn't care. I wanted to stop. Jesus, Cleo, I was so tired. We'd been on the road for six months with the tour. I was sick of living out of suitcases. I just wanted a rest. Ally was furious. He said that I was throwing everything away and if I didn't sign, he'd never forgive me." He pauses, passes a hand over his face, and then carries on. "I told him that if he did sign the deal then it was over between the two of us; we were no longer brothers. He died believing that I meant that. So, you can say what you like but I know the truth. I may as well have been driving the car that hit him."

I open my mouth to tell him that Alex doesn't see it like this, but then shut it swiftly. How will I explain how I know what his dead brother would think? I'll sound like Lilac Delaney.

"I have to live with this every day," Rafe says softly. "Every bloody day. Some days it hurts more than others, so I think to myself what harm does one little drink do? Except that it's never one. It's never, ever one because one drink doesn't blot it out, and neither does another or even the whole bottle. I killed my brother, Cleo, and nothing that happens now will change that."

What can I say to this? He's wrong about the guilt but he's spot on when he points out that nothing can change the past. Look at how I've spent ten years feeling so angry and so betrayed about never having the chance to say goodbye to Mum. Did that bring her back or make me feel any better? Of course it didn't: it just cast a huge shadow over the time I've been lucky enough to have since. Our lives are so fleeting – my work has taught me that much – and we try everything we can to create a sense of permanence for ourselves, but at the end of the day it's a vain task, isn't it? All that's left behind of us is the love we once had, and I'm starting to understand now that this never goes away.

I'm wrestling with how to express this without sounding like a cross between a gushing agony aunt and Lilac Delaney, when Rafe exhales and gives me a rueful smile.

"Aren't I cheerful company? I invited you out to say sorry and to buy you a drink, and I end up dumping on you. Still, while I'm doing deep and meaningful, there is something else I wanted to ask you."

I look up at him questioningly. I hope he doesn't want me to explain again how I just so happened to be meandering past his house, because I'm struggling to think of a plausible excuse.

"Listen, I know it sounds crazy and more water has gone under our bridge than the one over there—" he nods in the direction of Taply Bridge, with its golden honeyed stone and intricate carved arches, underneath which the river flows and swans drift gently past, "but that Christmas Eve really meant something to me. I was devastated when I realised that I couldn't find you. Why didn't you get in touch? I'm not bragging – well, only a little bit – but the song I wrote for you was huge. Every interview I gave I talked about you."

The river flows by. Light is already starting to seep from the sky; the naked trees, stark against grey clouds, look as bleak as I remember feeling that long ago Christmas Eve.

"I wasn't in the country." I close my eyes and see again the coffin, the graveyard and then my bags packed and labelled for Cairo with no return ticket booked. "My mum was ill, do you remember?"

He nods. "Of course I remember. You were breaking your heart."

"Well, she died that night, before I could even get home to see her. I was too late." There's a massive lump in my throat. "I never got to say goodbye."

Rafe looks appalled. "Cleo, I'm sorry. That must have been fucking awful."

"Yeah, I think 'fucking awful' just about sums it up," I agree. "I didn't stick around for long afterwards. I went back to study in Egypt and I ended up staying there for six years. I'm afraid I'd never even heard of Thorne until Alex—"

Whoa! Careful Cleo!

"Until a friend told me about Alex," I correct myself swiftly. "I wasn't in the country. Besides, you never got in touch either. I gave you my number."

Rafe is staring at me. His eyes are dark with an emotion I can't quite fathom.

"I lost your number and I couldn't contact you. I was frantic about it. Christ, I drove Alex mad. He wanted to concentrate on the band and suddenly I was obsessed with hanging out at railway stations on the off chance that I might find you. I couldn't believe I never even asked your name."

Our eyes lock. We both know why we'd been distracted. Then the train had arrived and time had been kicked into a gallop.

"And by the time you came home," Rafe finishes, "Alex was dead and Thorne was over."

I push my hair back from my face. "That's about it. I'd never heard 'One Christmas Kiss' until recently."

Rafe reaches across the table and takes my hand. "All the effort I put in to writing a message for you was in vain, then? Talk about being star-crossed! Yet now here you are, as though not a day has passed, looking just like I remember you. The beautiful Christmas Girl I wrote my song for."

I'm shivering. Rafe's still holding my hand, and the thrill of feeling his skin against mine is every bit as intense as I remember. This makes no sense. I don't know Rafe. He's damaged and angry and a total stranger, but my heart is telling me that none of this matters because somehow I understand him anyway, and in the most meaningful way a person can.

I gasp. What's happening to me? Is this my head trauma or something even more frightening?

Rafe mistakes my surprise for outrage and his fingers slide from mine.

"Sorry. I probably shouldn't have done that but I just couldn't help it."

"Were you nineteen again?" I tease. "I know I am. It's almost a shock to find myself sitting in a pub rather than on a deserted railway platform."

He gives me that crooked smile again. "I think maybe I was."

Butterflies flutter in my stomach.

This isn't the in-control version of me that I'm used to. Alarmed, I turn my attention to my wine and the moment is broken. The conversation diverts to other topics, including my job and Rafe's futile attempts to write again, and before long we're parting by the River Thames – Rafe to catch a cab and me to go home and cook supper for Dad.

"It's been good to see you again, Christmas Girl," Rafe says softly. He pulls his shades back on and I see myself in them, a pale shadow reflected in the darkness of the lenses.

"You too," I nod. It has been good to see him. And terrifying. And wonderful.

An entire kaleidoscope of emotions is turning and shifting within me. Maybe that mulled wine was stronger than I thought.

When Rafe stoops to kiss me goodbye I'm almost holding my breath, wondering whether he'll brush my mouth with his and if the kick to my senses will be every bit as powerful now as it was ten years ago. As his lips touch my cheek – a kiss as soft as a butterfly's wing, just millimetres from my mouth – it takes all the strength I have not to turn my head.

"Take care, Christmas Girl," Rafe says. And then he's gone, dissolving into the late-afternoon shopping crowds, a tall rangy figure with midnight hair and the weight of the world on his shoulders. I watch him until I can't make him out any longer from the press of bodies all fatly wrapped against the cold in their thick coats and scarves. Once again Rafe Thorne vanishes from my life just as swiftly as he's entered it.

I dig my numb hands into my pockets and turn for home. I'm feeling unsettled and edgy and strangely lost. As I walk back past the town square a busker is strumming a guitar and singing a bittersweet song in a minor key that tugs on my heartstrings and echoes through my mind. The words float towards me on the chilly air, mingling with the chatter and the growl of traffic. With a pang I recognise the song Rafe wrote for me, and my eyes fill with tears for the people we once were and the people we could have been.

I blink them away impatiently. I've done my best. I've met up with Rafe and tried my very hardest to tell him that Alex's death wasn't his fault, but of course it was pointless. No matter what Alex may have hoped for, I can't help his brother find peace and forgiveness.

Only Rafe can do that now.

Chapter 20

It's beyond me how people cope with having time off. What on earth do they find to do with themselves? By Thursday morning I've run out of things to do and am slowly starting to go stir crazy. So far this week I've cleaned the house from top to bottom, organised my father's desk (he wasn't best pleased about that but I've no idea how he functions in such utter chaos), emptied the fridge of all the rotting veg and the salad bags full of brown slime, restocked the cupboards after a visit to Waitrose, and become hooked on *Game of Thrones*.

Hmm, the *Game of Thrones* addiction is a worrying development. I discovered the DVD buried down the back of the sofa – along with my father's long-lost reading glasses and two crumpled A-level essays – while I was on a tidying spree. Because I was trying anything I could to distract myself from phoning work, I made the fatal mistake of popping the disc into Dad's much neglected DVD player and ended up binge-watching the entire first season. Alex has also become hooked; he nagged and nagged until I caved in and downloaded Season Two. Now we're both feeling a little queasy from all the bloodshed, but weirdly desperate to watch the next season. So far I've managed to resist – but it's like TV crack. Watching semi-naked hunks sword fighting in furs is not the usual activity of Dr Cleo Carpenter – and it's yet another unwelcome development that I'm putting down to my bash on the head. Goodness knows how I'll ever get to watch the rest of the shows without Susie discovering my guilty secret. She'd laugh her head off at the thought of serious academic me choosing to watch such nonsense.

So anyway, I've banned myself from iTunes today – which has annoyed Alex immensely – and have been spending the morning tidying up the small corner of St Jude's churchyard where Mum rests beneath the soft green grass. It's funny, but until recently this is a place I've avoided like the proverbial plague, yet all of a sudden it doesn't hold any horrors for me at all. Quite the opposite, in fact. This morning's been a frosty one and the graveyard still sparkles and glitters in the early sunshine. As I weed around the headstone and arrange my small posy of white roses, the birds sing and the noise of Taply-on-Thames going about its daily life drifts on the wind. My mother isn't here, that's for sure – and neither is anyone else. It's a bit ironic that one of the only places where I don't see anything out of the ordinary is the graveyard; my ghost-loving flatmate would be most disappointed.

Once Mum's area is neat and tidy, the roses softening the stark marble headstone, I head into town. Today the Christmas paraphernalia doesn't seem nearly as intrusive as usual and I find myself humming along to Slade while I push my trolley through the supermarket, food shopping being my latest method for entertaining myself. I even catch myself adding fairy lights and a couple of candles to my haul. At this rate I'll be dragging a tree home and donning a Santa suit. Susie's right: head injuries are not to be taken lightly.

The walk home from town takes me along the river, following in reverse the journey I'd taken with Rafe. The water glitters in the sunshine and although it's winter the beer garden at the River Man Inn is busy as office workers take advantage of the patio heaters and mulled wine and enjoy their lunch beside the Thames. Maybe Dad and I could go there for a meal at some point before I head back to London? My father hasn't said as much, but I can tell he doesn't get out and about very often. In between his school preparation and academic research I suppose there isn't a huge amount of time for socialising, but he doesn't seem to have many friends and the phone hasn't rung at all since I arrived. He must be lonely, I realise with a stab of guilt, but he's never once said anything or complained. Tolly and I may have lost our mother, but he'd lost his wife – and, in effect, his two children, whose grief and anger had kept them away.

The sun dips behind the leaden clouds and a chilly wind whips along the riverbank, scattering leaves and sending ripples scudding across to the other side. I shiver and wish I'd worn gloves. The handles of my carrier bags cut into my fingers and as I walk they twist and tighten, making the flesh glow and tingle. Spotting a bench, I treat myself to a few minutes' rest and watch a family of ducks sail by and a couple of keen runners pounding the path, plumes of breath rising like smoke in the chilly air. Life is going on all around me. Across the Thames a little girl wobbles past on a pink bicycle, her father running behind her to rest a hand on her back and steady her, and I whiz back through the years to a long-ago December when Dad spend all of Christmas Day and Boxing Day doing exactly the same for me. There were so many happy times, and now that I'm starting to dig away at the top layers of my grief it's comforting to rediscover them.

Here and now, I make up my mind to stay in Taply until Sunday. I have a fair bit of making up to do and, besides, they seem to be doing just fine without me at the museum. Nobody's called to ask my advice or to let me know when the interviews are being held. There's not even been so much as a text message from Simon, who'd claimed to think so much of me. I may be less than fifty miles away, but with him it really seems to be a case of out of sight and out of mind.

Am I bothered about this? I dig my hands into my pockets, uncurling my frozen fingers and gazing thoughtfully at a couple who've paused near the water's edge, arms wrapped around one another and lost in their own world as they kiss the cold away. Do I wish that Simon and I could be like this couple? How would I feel if he were to pull me close and lower his lips onto mine? I try my hardest to picture it but instead all I see is a snowy railway platform, snowflakes whirling silently down from an inky sky, and Rafe's violet eyes holding mine…

I shake my head, irritated with myself. That was another lifetime. Didn't Rafe say himself that he wasn't the same person anymore? And I'm certainly not that starry-eyed girl either.

So why am I thinking about Rafe rather than Simon? I know the past is my profession but I need to spend slightly more time in the present.

Fishing my iPhone out of my pocket I dial Simon, feeling annoyed when the call goes straight to answerphone. That's the third time now it's done that, and he hasn't called me back either.

"Simon, hi, it's Cleo, again," I say, hoping that he'll pick up on my sharp tone. "Hope all's well with you. Just wondering if there's been any news about the interviews yet? And did you lock the laptop away? Give me a call when you get this message. Thanks."

I press the call-end button and frown. There's an uneasy seesawing sensation in the pit of my stomach and for a minute I toy with the idea of calling Professor Hamilton. But what would I say? Simon isn't talking to me? Where's my new job? I know the Prof and he wouldn't be impressed at all with being interrupted to answer those kinds of questions. Dawn will call me when there's something I need to know; until then I just need to be patient and enjoy my time off.

Decision made, I heave my shopping bags up again. I can't help feeling very glad I haven't become too involved with Simon Welsh. It would only complicate things, and to be honest it's easier to just be colleagues.

At the corner of my father's road a white van has pulled up and two men in donkey jackets and rigger boots are selling Christmas trees, threading them through a machine and wrestling them into nets. Excited children are bouncing up and down next to their parents, pointing out the trees they want and hardly able to wait to go home to decorate them. I watch for a few minutes, remembering doing exactly the same myself while Tolly pretended he was far too cool and grown up to care. Dad would carry the tree home and then Mum and I would decorate it with whatever baubles we could find, and normally far too much tinsel. Until recently these memories would have stung, but today they make me smile because they're happy ones.

Maybe I'll come home this Christmas rather than staying away as I usually do. I could help Dad pick a tree, and book us in for Christmas lunch at the River Man Inn. Tolly's in the Caribbean with his latest blonde, but at least one of us will be here to keep Dad company. Christmas can't be a great time for him.

Isn't it funny how I've never seen it like this before? I guess I've always been too caught up in my own loss to think about anyone else's. If I come back maybe it will help us both.

And maybe, says a small voice that I'm trying very hard to ignore, *you'll see Rafe Thorne again if you do?*

I squash the voice with the knowledge that this seems highly unlikely. I haven't heard from Rafe since our last meeting and I don't expect to either, but I sincerely hope he's staying away from the booze and holding it together.

Deep in my pocket my phone vibrates. Simon, I think with relief, and about time too! Lowering my bags onto the pavement I pull out my phone, only to be disappointed when I see that it's Susie. No disrespect to my best friend, but I'm yearning to know what's happening at work.

"Suse, hi!" Tucking the phone between my chin and shoulder, I scoop up the bags and continue on my way. "How are things?"

"All good here." There's a clatter in the background, followed by a thud. "That's the plumber," Susie tells me. "I had him come in to check the heating because it's been so cold in here lately, but he can't find anything wrong. I must admit it's been better the last few days though."

I bet it has – since I left, to be accurate. Dad's house is chilly though. He was wearing two sweaters last night, until I told Alex to leave. Then the room was like a sauna.

"Is the telly working now too?" I ask innocently.

"How did you know? Are you psychic?" Susie giggles. "Yeah, it's really funny but that fuzzy thing the screen kept doing's totally stopped. It must have been atmospherics or something."

"Mmm," I say. Alex does have a very bad habit of upsetting a girl's viewing experience. We were both getting frustrated watching *Game of Thrones* through a snowstorm of static, until we figured out that sitting him miles away from the screen worked a treat.

"The cat's back too," Susie says. "I've no idea where he's been but he's hardly moved from the sofa now."

"And how's the flat looking?" I tease. "Neat and tidy?"

"Err…" Susie pauses. "Sort of."

I laugh, knowing full well that the place will look like a bomb's gone off. There'll be a washing-up mountain in the sink, the bathroom will be spattered with pink hair dye and the fridge will be growing mould that will soon be an alternative life form. It will look like something from one of those TV shows about hoarders, only even messier.

"When are you back?" Susie asks casually, but I'm not fooled. She'll be panicking that I'm about to return before she can fumigate the place.

"Not until Sunday evening."

"Err, sorry?" Susie sounds shocked. "I think I heard that wrong? I thought you said you'd be home on Sunday? Which means you've been away a week? Who are you and what have you done with the real Cleo Carpenter? Haven't you heard? The Wellby Museum is in chaos!"

"Very funny. I just reckoned that I needed some time off. It's been a tough couple of months. Besides, it's Christmas and Dad could do with a bit of company."

"Now I'm *really* scared," says Susie, actually sounding worried – and not just because she thinks I'm going to tell her off about the state of the flat. "You're still not quite yourself, are you?"

Luckily Susie has no idea just how "not quite myself" I am these days.

"It will be back to business as usual next week," I say, with a great deal more conviction than I feel. "It's just that I've been figuring a few things out lately. The museum has been really good about giving me some time off."

"They must owe you about two years in untaken holiday," Susie points out. "Anyway talking about the museum, I meant to tell you: I gave that gorgeous guy the artefact he needed, like you said?"

As we've been chatting I've kept the phone tucked between my chin and collar bone so that I can continue to walk home. I'm just about to cross the road and turn into our street as Susie says this. Her words stop me in my tracks. There's no way I can cope with negotiating the traffic and comprehending what she's telling me.

"Sorry, Suse, I don't think I've heard you right. What gorgeous man? What artefact?"

There's a heavy sigh at the end of the line. "Please, please go back and see the specialist. Short-term memory loss is often an indication that there's a bigger problem."

Susie is back in medic mode now, which would be fine if I actually thought there was a medical issue here. I may be seeing ghosts – and watching box sets with them – but I am not losing my memory.

"What man?" I repeat.

"That one you've been on about?" I can almost see her rolling her eyes. "Girlfriend, I take it all back. He is *way* hot! I totally get it now, why you spend so much time at work. That Dr Simon is hot."

"You've met Simon?" I'm confused. Has Susie flipped and visited the museum? I can't quite imagine it. The last time I looked the gift shop didn't sell funky boots.

"He came round here to pick up that funny little statue that you had in your room? The one your grandmother gave you? You'd said he could take it for the exhibition. Didn't you?"

I'm horrified because this statue is the key to my research. The symbols on the base, meaning *not the gods' will*, are the biggest clue that Aamon was murdered. Carved by a daring priest, they were the starting point for my grandmother's search to find the young pharaoh's body and discover the truth. Along with her work, she left the statue to my mother – who in turn left it to me. I would never, ever lend it to anyone. I don't even keep it in the museum, although I plan to donate it to the nation once my research is finished. I'd never hand it to Simon, bump on the head or not. Never!

I open my mouth but no words come out. Simon went to my house and took the statue of Aamon? I wrack my brains and I cannot remember a time when I ever offered to lend him my statue. It means the world to me, just as completing the research on the Aamonic period is my final gift to her. There's no way I would ever part with that statue, bump on the head or not. Never! There's a horrible sensation breaking over me, as though all the blood in my body is being pushed to the tips of my fingers and toes, turning icy as it does so.

"When was this?" I manage to say.

Susie is quiet for a second. "Blimey, it was a day ago. Two days, maybe? No, I know: it was the day you left. Simon was so sorry to have missed you." She pauses and then adds excitedly, "I think he really likes you!"

A cold finger of unease traces a path down my spine. I saw Simon the day I left. I gave him my application. He knew I was on my way to Buckinghamshire. He even offered to accompany me to the station. He knew one hundred percent that I wouldn't be in the flat when he turned up.

What's going on?

Making my excuses to Susie, I end the call and then try Simon again. There's no answer so I leave a swift message asking him to call me as soon as possible. For a moment I contemplate calling the Professor and asking him what the hell Simon's up to, but I manage to stop myself just as my finger is poised over the call button.

Something tells me that Simon will already have a plausible explanation and my anger and shock will count against me. I'll be seen as a hysterical woman and, worse than that, an irrational and unreliable one – one whose mental health is in question thanks to her unfortunate head injury. Simon will insist I said he could borrow the statue and then make some sad-eyed reference to my accident, probably suggesting that I'm not well. My skin crawls with dread as I recall the numerous times Simon has so caringly brought up my health, under the guise of being solicitous. *You're forgetting things* – that's what he'll say, and what is the Professor to think? It'll certainly look as though I've lost the plot. Let's face it; my behaviour recently has been out of character in so many ways. Rumours start easily in institutions like ours and spread like wildfire.

As an academic I need to be seen to be rational. I've got to take a deep breath, compose myself and calculate what to do next. Simon's made a move in our game of career chess and I need to work out how to counter it. Making accusations and charging back to London right now, which is what I feel like doing, won't help. Instinct tells me that turning up ranting and raging will be playing right into Simon's beautifully manicured hands. I need to be cool, calm and collected. Level-headed and cerebral Cleo, not this shaking and fuming version of me.

I have no idea what Simon is playing at. Trying to force my heartbeat to slow, I shove my phone into my bag and attempt to formulate a plan.

Maybe I should have a tee shirt or a mug emblazoned with *Keep Calm and Deal with Your Thieving Colleague*, I think as I cross the road and turn towards my father's house.

Then I decide that tomorrow morning I'll take the first train to London. There's nothing I can do from here. I'll catch the quarter-to-seven train and be in the museum before Simon. I'll fetch my statue back from his office and afterwards I'll quietly but firmly insist on an explanation. If I'm not satisfied then I'll speak to the Prof. I'm sure he'll view this incident in a very dim light.

Yes, this is what I'll do. I shall be dignified and firm and the antithesis of hysterical – in other words, I shall be the opposite of what Simon is expecting.

Feeling slightly calmer now that I have a strategy, I kick open our front gate, prepared for tomorrow and the psychological battle that lies ahead. I think I see Simon's game now. He wants to use my head injury to discredit me so that he can have the job. He tried to win me around with gentle flirting and sweet talk about his concern for me, and by inviting me on dates, but when that didn't come up with the results he was hoping for he moved on to the next tactic.

Well, bring it on, buster! I'm fighting fit and once I get back to London I'm going to prove it.

In the meantime, I'll try to unwind with a cup of tea and maybe treat myself to another episode of *Game of Thrones*. Maybe I can use it to inspire me.

Picturing myself wielding a broadsword and hacking Simon to ribbons could be very cathartic.

At least, that's the plan – but like most of my plans lately it very quickly goes pear-shaped. All thoughts of TV and tea vanish in an instant when a figure uncoils himself from the doorstep and strides down the path towards me as though his life depends upon it.

"You're back at last!" says Rafe Thorne, staring down at me from behind his aviators. He holds out his hand. "Come on, Cleo Rose! There's something I need to show you."

I'm still clutching my shopping. Rafe steps forward and gently untangles the heavy bags from my fingers before swinging them into his grasp as easily as though they were made of air. I'm not sure how many shocks I can take in one day. After our conversation in the River Man Inn, where he'd told me that he was no longer the same person as the one I'd met all those years ago, I'd been certain I'd never see him again.

I'm overwhelmingly pleased to be proven wrong.

Chapter 21

"Where are we going?" I ask Rafe as he tows me up the path, out of the garden gate and towards a sleek red car parked at a crazy angle and with one wheel up on the kerb.

"My place," Rafe replies. He hasn't paused to ask if I want to come or stopped to explain why he's appeared out of the blue to whisk me and my carrier bags away, but he's supremely confident that I'll follow him. So far he's right. I'm practically falling over my feet as he pulls me behind him, too astonished to protest. I'm still reeling from the Simon business and haven't really got the energy to fight being kidnapped by a determined rock star.

"We're going to your place?" I'm bewildered. Until about thirty seconds ago I didn't think I'd ever see Rafe Thorne again, but now he's taking me to his riverside rock-star mansion in a car that looks very much like a Ferrari? Whatever happened to the tortured goodbyes, the "I'm not the same person I was" speech and the whole tragic artist drinking himself into oblivion thing?

It's official: men are weird.

Rafe pushes his sunglasses back from his face. His eyes, although shadowed, are burning excitement.

"Yes, yes, my place. A house on the river where strange girls like to break in?" he teases. "I need to show you something."

"What? Please don't say your etchings," I warn.

Rafe grins, a delighted grin that seems to light him up from the inside and completely transforms his face. Suddenly the planes and angles are less sharp, laughter lines fan out from the violet eyes and two deep dimples appear in his cheeks. This is the Rafe who must have been present before Alex died, the Rafe Thorne who made girls swoon with his heartbreaking lyrics and dark good looks; in other words, the very same Rafe Thorne I met all those years ago. All at once I'm lost. I'll be in that car and off before you can say *Cleo Carpenter has lost the plot.*

Rafe tugs my hand impatiently. "Etchings later! This is a surprise."

"I don't like surprises," I say grudgingly. "They're more normally known as shocks."

He rolls his eyes and looks so much like Alex that I start to laugh in spite of myself. That's the exact expression Alex pulled when I first told him that ghosts didn't exist.

"This is a *nice* surprise – or at least, I think it is," he says. "Come on! Live dangerously."

Living dangerously is not something I like to do. I like to be measured and methodical, but there's something about Rafe's enthusiasm that's contagious. I glance around, hoping Alex might put in an appearance and explain what's going on here, but I'm not in luck. Alex, I'm fast learning, has a habit of never being about when I actually need him – but he's guaranteed to show up when I could really do with being left in peace.

Come on, Alex, I plead silently. I could do with some backup here. This change in Rafe from taciturn and maudlin to having more energy than the National Grid is rather unsettling. What if he's taking drugs? Has my reappearance pushed Rafe Thorne over the edge? Have I unwittingly made things a million times worse? I knew I should never have let myself get involved…

"Don't look so worried," Rafe says gently. "This is something good, I promise." He squeezes my hand. "I'm not over the limit either, I promise. I haven't touched a drop of booze since you walked into my house last Sunday. I'm not proud of the state I was in that day, Cleo, or how I behaved – and I'm going to do my very best to make sure that never happens again. You were the wake-up call I needed."

"Yes!" At last, Alex has arrived; he's jumping up and down as though on an invisible pogo stick, and beaming at me. "I knew you'd be good for him, Cleo! I knew it! Aren't you glad you listened to me?"

I think of all the disruption to my neat and ordered world and am about to shake my head, but suddenly I'm struck by how happy the brothers look. Alex has lost the haunted expression, which is rather ironic, and Rafe's no longer the brooding Byronic figure from the tabloids. Then I see again the image of Mum smiling at me, and I recall how much I've enjoyed spending time with my father. To my surprise, I realise that the answer is a resounding *yes*.

A high-pitched beep rouses me from these thoughts. Lights flash on the Ferrari and Rafe opens the door. "Hop in. Your chariot awaits."

The red Ferrari is Rafe's. Of course it is; it's all textbook rock-star stuff. As are drugs and rock 'n' roll and sex. Not that I'm thinking about sex – no matter how gorgeous he looks in his battered leather jacket, torn 501s and chunky Timberland boots. No, I'm more concerned about whether or not he's fit to drive. His parking looks as though Mr Bean was behind the wheel.

"I'm shit at parking," Rafe adds, reading my mind so easily that I blush. I hope he can't read the part about me thinking he's gorgeous, although I have a horrible feeling he can already tell how I feel. I try to comfort myself with the idea that he's probably used to girls hurling themselves at him, but this makes me feel even worse.

"I honestly haven't had a drink since Sunday," Rafe assures me. "And before you ask, I never touch drugs, no matter what the papers might have you believe. If I'm acting strangely then it's because I'm so excited, and if I'm jumpy it's because I'm exhausted, but that's all, Christmas Girl. I promise."

I believe him. Although he's still as unshaven and as scruffy as he was when I so rudely awakened him, his hair falling across his face and his clothes definitely crumpled and slept in, there's a different kind of energy about Rafe today. I can feel it fizzing through his fingertips and imagine it crackling with his every movement as he clasps my hand in his.

"So, will you come with me?" Rafe asks softly. "Let me show you what it is that's kept me up for hours on end?"

He's looking at me so hopefully that there's no way I can say no, even though I know I really should unpack the shopping and make my plans to travel back to London ready to confront Simon. I guess my curiosity is piqued: I want to see what's changed him.

"I'll come," I agree.

"Great! Hop in!" Rafe opens the door and I swing myself into the low-slung leather seat. Thank goodness I wore thick black tights with my denim skirt and knee-high boots; otherwise our neighbours, busy watching from behind their net curtains, would be treated to a view of my knickers – and I've flashed those quite enough for one lifetime.

"Good luck," says Alex over my shoulder. "Rafe's a horrible driver. Cling on and pray that you don't end up with me!"

He isn't kidding. Rafe drives like something out of *Wacky Races*, only you don't see me laughing. I know he's a guy who feels he has nothing to lose, but does he have to take the bends so fast, or stand on the brakes quite so often? Taply-on-Thames flies by in a blur of river and stone before blending with the green lanes of Buckinghamshire, as though someone's tossed the car into a giant food processor and pressed the high-speed button. Insects splatter against the windscreen, and the Ferrari feels so low to the road that I can practically touch the tarmac. I would ask him to slow down, but G-force and terror render me speechless. Rafe probably mistakes my open-mouthed horror for excitement. My hands grip the seat so tightly that my knuckles glow through my skin and the cream leather is scored with nail marks. But never mind the car; I'm equally scared by the racing line he takes through the lanes and the speed at which the world flies by. No wonder Alex leapt out that fateful day. By the time Rafe pulls up outside his house with a flourish of gravel and tyres, my head is spinning around more than Kylie in gold hot pants, and my life has flashed before my eyes. Actually, it was rather dull except for the last couple of months...

Rafe jumps out of the driver's seat and opens the door for me, catching me when I stagger forth on legs that feel as strong as boiled wool. I will never, ever, moan about playing sardines on the Tube again.

"Hey, are you OK?" he asks, tightening his grasp on the tops of my arms. "You've gone ever such a funny colour."

I glance in the wing mirror and a wide-eyed reflection stares back at me. My face is so white that my freckles stand out like bruises.

"You look like you've seen a ghost," Rafe continues, still holding onto me. Ironically, Alex is standing next to him as he says his, his cheeky ghostly grin far less scary than his brother's driving. "Didn't you enjoy the drive? That car's not been out for months. I only used it because I wanted to get to you quickly."

"Put it away again," I suggest. "Maybe get a push bike?"

"Is this a clever way of saying you don't like my driving? Look, I'm safe. I did a track day at Silverstone with an F1 coach. He said I had talent."

"Lewis Hamilton must be shaking in his boots," I say drily. "All you need is a Pussycat Doll in the passenger seat and we wouldn't be able to tell you apart. Look, don't let me get in the way; go ahead and call Bernie Ecclestone."

Rafe's wide eyes, those unusual violet irises ringed with black as though an artist has lovingly traced them with a fine liner, twinkle at me.

"For your information I have driven a member of a girl band in that car, and she shrieked all the way to the O2. Maybe not a Pussycat Doll, but still. You, Cleo Carpenter, are much harder to impress."

Rafe wants to impress me?

"Don't look so taken aback. I'm not a completely lost case," he says, hands still on my shoulders. "I'm mortified by how I behaved on Sunday and I've been kicking myself. I mean, what kind of moron waits ten years to see a woman and then balls it up in such style when she finally arrives? I wanted to make it up to you."

"By driving like a maniac in a red phallic symbol?"

He releases my shoulders and raises his hands in surrender. "Put like that, it sounds bloody ridiculous."

I smile at him. I can't help it. Behind the hair he's pushing away from his face, he's blushing. That's really endearing.

"Hey, you're a pop star. It comes with the territory," I tell him.

Rafe raises his eyebrows. "What? Behaving like a knob? I think I've been in the industry too long. I knew I'd turn into tosser if I didn't get out." He pauses and the smile slides from his face. It feels a bit like the sun has slipped behind a cloud.

"I should have listened to you," Alex interrupts, at his brother's side now and sounding frantic. "You were right," he continues, even though Rafe can't hear him. "We did need to have some time out, and we were behaving like spoilt brats. Jesus, I even did that spoilt rock-star thing where I could only have certain candles and linen in my fucking dressing room! Me! A kid from a council estate in Hayes! You were right, Rafe, and I was wrong!" He turns to me, wide eyed. "Tell, him, Cleo! Tell him that I don't blame him for any of it and I want him to carry on writing. I want him to have his life back – we shouldn't have both stopped living that day."

But how can I say all this? I'll sound like a maniac. Somehow I will broach the subject, but it will be when I think the time is right.

"Anyway, it's getting chilly out here." Rafe turns the collar of his coat up and gestures towards the house. "Let's warm up inside and I'll show you why I wanted you to come over."

Leaving Alex shaking his head in despair, I follow Rafe up the worn stone steps and into an entrance hall with a high vaulted roof crisscrossed with huge beams. There's a tense atmosphere, as though the building is holding its breath to see what kind of mood its owner is in today.

Rafe lobs his keys onto a table; the rattle echoes around the empty space. Dust falls through the air, dancing in the beams of sunshine that filter through the leaded windows. And yet I know we're not alone. Up in the minstrels' gallery there's a swish of velvet skirts, and from the corner of my eye I spot a portly figure in a ruff, who waves at me cheerily.

"Ignore them," says Alex, now at my shoulder. "They don't need you. They like it here – that's why they've stayed. That's Sir Henry. He built the place, and he's always about. He's as sick of Rafe's moping as I am; says the house is going to rack and ruin."

"It's too big and dusty in here." Rafe gives me an apologetic look as I follow him through the hall and down a passageway. The house is freezing and the doors to most of the rooms are closed. It doesn't feel at all like a home. This is a house built to hold a large and noisy family, a house where voices should ring, fires should blaze and wonderful parties should be held for guests to dance until midnight. It's no place for a grieving man to live alone, and I'm not surprised Rafe's hit the bottle.

"I bought it as an investment," he continues as we progress towards what looks like a dead end. "Thorne were making a fortune and I knew I had to do something with the money."

"There are only so many phallic symbols a guy can drive," I agree, and he laughs.

Rafe has a nice laugh; it's warm and infectious. It's a shame he doesn't use it more often. I guess he hasn't had much to laugh about lately.

"Yeah, and hot tubs full of famous models soon get so boring! I know it isn't very rock and roll, but our Nan always said that bricks and mortar never let you down. I wanted to buy her council house for her, but Nan wouldn't hear of it – she was a dyed-in-the-wool socialist – so instead I splurged on this place." Rafe shrugs. "Aren't Thames-side mansions the stuff of rock-star dreams? Jagger had one in Richmond and a couple of Beatles have had places near here too, or so the estate agent told me. So here I am, although I rattle around in it a bit. Natasha had big design plans for it, but those vanished about the same time she did. I haven't had the inclination to do much with it since I bought it."

We're at the end of the corridor now and the gloom is so deep that even though it's a sunny day outside the thick stone walls, it feels as though it's the middle of the night. I try to imagine living here alone, and fail. Suddenly I have a real longing to be back in the flat and surrounded by Susie's clutter and noise.

"This is the one room I did do up," Rafe announces as he throws open a door at the end of the corridor. "It's one of the few rooms I use, although until Monday I hadn't been in here for over a year."

He stands back and beckons me to step past. I follow him into a long room with tall windows that open onto the green banks of the Thames and the glittering river beyond; they're curtained outside by ivy, which blows gently in the wind. As Rafe steps aside and I cross the threshold I can't help gasping, not because of the stunning view but because I've been abruptly transported from a neglected medieval manor house to a state-of-the-art studio that wouldn't be out of place in the nerve centre of an LA recording company. There's a huge sound booth, complete with giant microphones dangling from the ceiling, banks and banks of computers and complex-looking switches, and all kinds of instruments lined up in readiness for somebody to pick them up and play. There are also several squashy black sofas, dotted with sheets of manuscript paper that are scrawled with notes and lyrics in a sloping spidery hand. Half-empty coffee cups are lined up on the low-slung coffee table and there's an overflowing ashtray balanced on the arm of one of the leather sofas.

"Horrible habit," Rafe sighs, seeing me look at this. Striding across the room, he picks up the ashtray and tips the contents into a bin. "It's weird, but I only ever smoke when I'm writing. Half the time I don't even notice I'm doing it. Alex always said it was a throwback to being a teenager and hanging out in the garage with the gang."

I glance across the room at Alex, who's been checking out the mixing desk.

"He's been writing!" Alex cries, punching the air and in his excitement sending a sheaf of papers fluttering to the ground. "Yes!"

"I'll shut the door. It's bloody cold in here," Rafe says, scooping up the music and then kicking the door closed with his scuffed Timberland boot. "That's some draught, too. Have a seat, Cleo. There's something I have to show you, or rather play you."

Rafe seats himself in a swivel chair and begins switching on the computers, opening programs and sliding dials on the mixing desk. Intrigued, I sink into the nearest sofa and curl my legs under me, while Alex perches on the arm and rests his ankle over his knee.

"After we had coffee I came straight here," Rafe tells me. His face is bright with the glow of the monitors and that barely contained excitement from earlier. "I didn't leave the studio for three days. I've slept here, drunk gallons of coffee and spent the whole time working." As he sets up whatever it is that he's doing, there's an intensity to him that makes the hairs stir on my forearms. His dark hair falls across his face and he pushes it back impatiently, his attention trained on the recording equipment. "I had a line of music running through my mind and I had to get it down. First of all I picked it out on the keyboard, then I added in a guitar rift and finally I started to hear the lyrics. I played and I wrote and I added and then suddenly nearly three days had gone by. It was like being in a dream."

Wow. I'm a girl who's often accused of being obsessed with her work, but even I haven't stayed in the office for almost seventy-two hours. I'm impressed.

"That's amazing," I say.

Rafe spins around on his chair with such speed it's a miracle he doesn't get whiplash.

"Cleo, it's more than amazing. It's mind-blowing. I haven't written a decent word since Alex died. I've wanted to – Christ, I've tried enough times – but it was like my ability to write had died with him. That was my punishment for what happened."

"Rafe, what happened to Alex wasn't your fault. It was an accident: a horrible, senseless accident. You didn't deserve to be punished for it."

A muscle tightens in his cheek. "You really think so?"

"Yes, that's exactly what I think!"

"Yeah, you and my shrinks, but that wasn't how it bloody felt. Every time I closed my eyes I saw the accident play out over and over again. In my dreams I try to get out of the car and pull him back to safety but I'm always a fraction too late. My fingertips slip from his jacket or I trip, or he's just too goddamn far away. Then I hear the screaming of brakes and the thud of a body against metal and I wake up. I can never, ever save him."

"You couldn't save me, fam," Alex says. "It was impossible. Nobody could have. It was an accident."

But of course Rafe can't hear his brother. "I wanted to write about it," he continues. "That's always been my way of working things through, but it was like a tap had been turned off. No matter how hard I tried the words wouldn't come and I couldn't hear the music anymore. So I started to drink."

He pauses and I don't say anything. What can I say? I lost Mum and I coped with it by working. How would I have managed if even solace that had been taken away?

"I went a bit crazy maybe," Rafe continues. His voice is low and filled with sadness. "I even started travelling up to where he died and just sitting there, outside the Tube station, trying to feel close to him. I haunted that place for days. Shit, months even. I was obsessed."

I don't know what to say so I sit quietly and attentively, sensing that he wants to talk now. Maybe he's wanted to talk for a long time but has never found anyone who'll just listen.

Rafe exhales. "It was pointless. I didn't get any message from him so I hit the bottle even harder – and the rest, well, the rest you probably know. I'm not proud of it. One stint in rehab followed by a phase of spilling my guts to the press, and the next thing I know my agent's on the phone saying they want me to be a mentor on one of the big TV talent shows. Cleo, I was in such a state I couldn't even tell you what one it was or what country it was based in. It could have been *The X Factor* on bloody Mars for all I knew."

I don't watch reality TV but even I've heard of *The X Factor*. Susie's normally glued to it; last year she ran up a monstrous phone bill voting for her favourite act. I think she'd have said something if Rafe Thorne had been a mentor on the show though, so I'm presuming he didn't take the job.

"What happened?"

"I turned it down. I'd lost my brother and I'd lost my gift." His voice cracks. "What use would I have been? I couldn't play. I couldn't write a word. I couldn't hear a note. I was finished in every way a person could be. Knowing Alex died hating me is unbearable. How could I ever write again knowing that?"

Alex turns to me, urgency etched into his face. "Cleo, please! You have to speak to Rafe," he begs. "I know this isn't easy for you but, please, you've got to tell him I never once hated him. I thought he was being a total cock and I was furious, but I never hated him."

I can't refuse. No matter what it may cost me in terms of looking sane, I know that this message is more important than my own feelings. Gathering up my courage, I take the plunge.

"Your brother didn't die hating you, Rafe," I say gently. "I'm sure he'd be upset to think you believed that."

"Too right," agrees Alex. He's standing next to his brother now and Rafe shivers.

"I think somebody just walked over my grave," Rafe says with a bleak half-smile.

I don't smile back. "What happened to your brother was an accident. It wasn't your fault, Rafe. People argue all the time; it was just really bad luck. I'm sure if Alex was in the room with us right now he'd say exactly the same thing."

"Please listen to her," Alex insists, so close to his brother that their eyeballs are practically touching.

But Rafe can't hear him. "Much as I'd love to think you're right, you weren't there. We said some pretty ugly things to one another. I told him if he stepped out of the car then he could forget that we were brothers. I said–" His voice breaks. "I said he'd be dead to me."

What can I add to this? Any comfort I try to offer will just sound like a platitude.

"I couldn't write, I couldn't think, I could hardly get out of bed in the morning," Rafe finishes quietly. "Sometimes I had the bleakest thoughts – so bleak that they scared me. There didn't seem to be any point in going on. Alex was dead, Nan was dead and I couldn't write, so why bother?"

I'd felt like this after Mum died. Often I'd lain in my narrow bed in the university accommodation block watching the ceiling fan whirling round and round in endless circles, wondering how I would ever summon the energy to drag myself into a sitting position, let alone get showered and dressed and off to the dig. The traffic would buzz outside the thin walls and the sunlight coming through the blinds would tiger the walls, glancing off the white plaster and making my eyes ache. The lightweight cotton sheet had felt leaden across my legs, and the effort required to move it had seemed too much to contemplate, let alone execute. Only knowing that somewhere out beyond the city, buried deep beneath the shifting desert sands, slumbered secrets that my grandmother had longed to uncover had prompted me to move. If it hadn't been for my work, who knows what might have happened?

Our eyes meet and there's a jolt of mutual understanding.

"I've been there," I whisper.

Rafe leans into the leather back of his chair, which creaks in sympathy.

"I haven't written a note, haven't composed a lyric, since Ally died," he continues quietly. Then, rising to his feet, he fetches a guitar. He hesitates for a moment. His hands stroke the instrument tentatively, before he glances at me, smiles shyly and starts to strum. A flurry of melodies fills the room.

Eventually, the music ceases and he lifts his gaze back to my face.

"Then I meet you again," Rafe says, "and it's like something in me has been unlocked. I can't explain it but suddenly there was this tune in my head, where before there'd been nothing but silence. Almost before I knew what I was doing I was opening up this room and picking up instruments I hadn't touched for ages."

He's smiling as he speaks, but as much as this lights his face it also highlights the exhaustion and strain he's been under.

"And once you started you found that you couldn't step away," I finish, because I understand completely. After all, how many times have I worked into the small hours or been chased out of my office by the morning cleaners?

Rafe nods slowly. "You've got it. I *had* to write. I couldn't *not* write, and I certainly couldn't stop until I'd nailed the final note and scrawled the last word onto the manuscript." He looks down at his notes and then back at me, bashfully and through the thick locks of hair that fall across his face. "This probably sounds crazy, but I think it's been meeting you again that's been the key."

"Of course it is!" Alex cries, but I'm not convinced. I met Rafe Thorne a long, long time ago and when we were two very different people. I'm not into music and I can't really see myself as some kind of muse.

"I'm sure it's nothing to do with me," I say.

But Rafe shakes his head. "It has everything to do with meeting you again."

"It certainly does," Alex agrees. Turning to me he adds, "See, Cleo? I told you that you were the key to it all."

I'm totally confused. None of this makes any sense. Actually, nothing's made any sense since I hurt my head all those weeks ago. If this were one of Susie's chick-lit books I'd wake up in hospital soon and find that it had all been a dream.

"You've made me realise that maybe, just maybe, my brother could forgive me after all," Rafe says quietly. "I know it's a cliché, like something from one of those stupid psychic shows, but I think meeting you is a message from Ally."

"Eureka! Now I know how Archimedes felt!" cries Alex, slapping his forehead and leaping around the studio like a demented creature. Sheaves of notes and manuscript paper flutter to the floor, but Rafe is far too busy studying my face for a reaction to notice the strange breeze that's come from nowhere.

"You probably think that sounds insane, don't you?" he asks.

Prior to my accident this is definitely what I would have thought. Today, though, life has a very different complexion.

"This will probably sound absolutely crazy," Rafe continues, putting the guitar down and sitting back in his chair. "Cleo, you have every right to get up and walk out of here and write me off as a lunatic, but there was an interview a few years ago in *Music Mad* where I was talking about the song I wrote about you."

"The Christmas one?" My heart does a crazy fluttery thing. It seems I no longer find that song as mournful or as irritating as I once did.

Rafe scoots his chair across the room until he's facing me. Leaning forward, he takes my hands in his. "That's the one. I poured my heart and soul into that one, Christmas Girl."

His hands are cool and strong, and his long musician's fingers lace with mine. Has the drum machine got a life of its own, or is that my heartbeat thrumming in my ears?

"So what was the interview about?" I ask, desperate to try and sound normal. I fail: I sound like Orville.

"You." Rafe is still holding my hands in his. "I can't remember it all exactly, but at the end Alex said something about finding you for me if he could." He shrugs. "Do you know, I haven't thought about that interview for years, but that afternoon when you and I had coffee I came home and found that exact issue lying face up in the kitchen. I can't understand how it came to be there. I didn't even know I still had it."

"It took me ages to find," Alex says with a grimace. "Rafe hoards heaps of shit in this house. You should see it, Cleo. It'd bring your neat-freak self out in hives."

"Isn't that weird?" Rafe presses when I don't reply. "I can't explain it at all, except that maybe meeting you after all this time is a message from my brother."

"Couldn't be any clearer even if I appeared right now and sang it," laughs Alex – and then, when he sees my face, "Oh lighten up, Cleo! This is a good thing! Look at him; he's writing again and he hasn't had a drink in days. This is fantastic."

It is fantastic and I'm thrilled to see the light in Rafe's eyes. I just wish I could tell him that yes, this is a message from his brother – who's sitting right opposite me and looking as though he's about to pop.

"It is strange," I agree, although strange hardly comes close to describing some of the events in my life lately.

"Once I saw that article again it was as though a jigsaw piece had fallen into place. God knows where it is now, though; I can't find it for the life of me. Maybe I dreamed it?"

"Or maybe I hid it again just in case you got pissed and lost it?" says Alex. "It took me ages to find it amongst all your crap, bro!"

Rafe's eyes meet mine. I can't look away. "Anyway, it doesn't matter if I saw it or if I dreamed it. Just remembering it was enough."

"Enough for what?" I don't understand.

Releasing my hands, Rafe leaps to his feet and turns his full attention to the bank of recording equipment. "Enough for this! Once I'd seen the magazine piece I came in here and I started writing, and once I started I just couldn't stop. And this is it! This is what I wrote."

The room fills with the most beautiful guitar chords, simple and in a minor key, yet rich and almost unbearably haunting. Then Rafe's voice begins to sing, a deep voice as warm and as smooth as melting chocolate, and the hairs on my forearms stir.

The song is about loss and grief and waking up with your cheeks wet with tears, your loved one always a dream away with each sunrise. With each line and each breath he takes, Rafe pours his heartbreak and pain into the notes rippling through the room. Then, several bars in, a piano melody begins, picking out the same notes – now transposed into a major key – chasing the rift over and over and filling the melody with warmth, like splashes of sunlight flickering across the landscape.

Then I saw her
The girl with the sunrise hair
Her smile lets in the light
Drying tears with her laughter
Chasing away the night

The music crescendos and then diminishes. Long after the final notes tremble into stillness the imagery remains with me: grief fades but love never leaves. Instead, love grows and sustains the memories until they soothe rather than sting. I'm thinking of Mum and the love she had for her family, and when I raise my hand I find that my own cheeks are wet.

"I wrote it for you," says Rafe quietly. "The you of now, not of ten years ago."

He's left his chair and sits next to me on the sofa. I feel his energy and it makes me quiver.

"Cleo, you've opened the blinds for me and you've let the first rays of light back in. I don't know why and I don't think I'll ever understand how you've reappeared again, but it's the truth and I'm so thankful for it."

"Time I left," says Alex, but I hardly hear him or even notice him vanish, because Rafe is tenderly wiping my tears away with his thumb. Before I have time to think he's cupping my face and kissing me so softly that I almost wonder whether I'm dreaming. Afterwards, my fingers rise to my lips and I stare at him. Rafe's lips on mine have sent a shockwave through me. When he takes my hand and pulls me to my feet I don't resist. Then he kisses me again, longer and deeper this time, and there's no chance of any coherent thought. The museum, my job, Simon's deceptions, paranormal experiences – none of these things seems important.

Right now I'm nineteen again and on a snowy railway platform with a boy who turns my bones to water. To be quite honest, nothing else seems to matter very much anymore.

Chapter 22

"Cleo! What on earth are you doing here?"

Susie couldn't look more horrified to see me. Although it's late morning she's still wearing the bum-skimming Playboy tee shirt that doubles as her nightgown, and she has the remains of last night's make-up sliding down her face. Her pink dreds are even more dishevelled than normal and right now they're several shades lighter than her face. I don't need to see the large pair of trainers discarded in the middle of the sitting-room carpet or the trail of clothes leading to her bedroom to gather that my best friend has been entertaining in my absence.

"I live here, remember?" I point out helpfully, plonking my rucksack down by the door and heading for the kitchen. After my journey back from Taply I'm looking forward to a cup of coffee and maybe even a piece of toast before I head to the museum. I'm not confronting Simon on an empty stomach – and after a very late night with Rafe I need several shots of caffeine to keep my eyes open.

Rafe. Just the thought of him is enough to make my stomach flutter and my lips curl into a smile. Even discovering a young man dressed in nothing but his boxers and sitting at the kitchen table eating Cornflakes out of the packet because the milk has all been used can't chase away my good mood.

"I didn't think you were coming back until after the weekend!" Susie squeaks, shooting past me and lobbing jeans and a shirt at our masticating guest. "Put some clothes on, Dave, for heaven's sake! Don't just sit there."

Normally I'd be narked to find the milk gone, the place looking as though a bomb had gone off and Susie's latest conquest ensconced in the flat, but this morning I feel as though I'm drifting along on a cloud of marshmallow. Nothing can upset me today. As the train had clattered through the frosty countryside I'd been unable to stop smiling. Even alighting at Marylebone and being confronted with Christmas in all its garish consumerist glory hadn't managed to take the edge off my good mood.

After Rafe had kissed me we'd stared at one another.

"I hadn't expected to do that," he'd said finally, tracing the curve of my cheek with his hand, "but I'm very glad I did."

I'd been too alarmed by the racing of my pulse to speak. If it was going at this speed after just one kiss, what on earth would have happened if we hadn't paused?

Instead, my hand had stolen out to echo his gesture. The rough graze of his stubble against my fingers and the brush of his lips on my palm when he'd turned his head and kissed it had taken my breath away. In an all-too-rapid heartbeat, sensible Cleo had vanished – and when Rafe's arms had slipped around my waist and pulled me close I'd been unable to think straight. I'd wound my fingers into his hair and touched my lips to his again, our kisses growing ever more urgent until we'd finally broken apart, laughing and breathless. Then Rafe had drawn me close again, slowly and tenderly this time, murmuring that he'd been waiting for me ever since that long-ago snowy Christmas. At that point I'd melted, just like the snowflakes had when they'd landed on our cheeks. Perhaps it was all nonsense springing from the euphoria of Rafe writing again – according to the press Rafe had been far from lonely during the past decade – but I was past caring. It was like being a teenager all over again.

Or, more accurately, it was like being a nineteen-year-old on a lonely railway platform…

Much later on, as I'd lain in Rafe's arms, bathed in the blushed light of the rising sun, I hadn't regretted a moment. It was as though I'd slipped out of myself, level-headed Cleo with her research and her well-organised life, and become somebody else. Who this new Cleo was I had no idea. She saw ghosts, took time off work and slept with rock stars. That really had been one big bang on the head: my world was now inside out and upside down. Did I wish it had never happened? That I had never seen Alex, or been drawn into a world that was about as far removed from my sensible existence as possible? Life before my accident had been so safe and ordered; that was how I'd liked it. My father had been miles away, my attraction to Simon had mostly been an intellectual one – or so I keep telling myself – and my work had kept me busy. Aamon had been a research project rather than a gap-toothed boy who constantly wanted to play football, and I'd been able to walk down the street without seeing people who weren't really there. There had been no danger of being hurt because I had kept myself so safe. Then again, there had been very little chance of taking a risk either.

When Rafe had tightened his arms around me and pulled me closer, grazing my temple with his lips, I'd known instantly that whatever the cost was, I couldn't regret a second that had led me to this moment. I could feel his heart thrumming against my own, beating together with mine, beating the same, and I never wanted to move. It had been almost painful to tear myself away from him, hence my late arrival back in London. Saying goodbye to him outside my father's house had taken a supreme effort of will.

"I've got to go," I'd said finally. "I'm already really late. I should have been at the museum for opening time. That would have made finding Simon a whole lot easier."

"Do you want me to come with you?" Rafe had offered, his hands holding mind as we sat in the car. "This Simon sounds like a total prick." His fingers had strengthened their grip and his eyes had narrowed dangerously. We'd talked late into the night, him excitedly about putting his new song out as a free download, me less excitedly about Simon taking my statue and generally behaving oddly.

"If he's prepared to steal your belongings, who knows what else he might do," Rafe had warned.

I'd smiled at this, unused to having a knight in shining armour. "Simon's an academic, Rafe, not a Bond villain. He's just got a bit carried away, that's all." I wink at him. "Professional academia can be pretty cut-throat, you know!"

He'd whistled. "So I'm learning. And there was I just thinking you all dug about in holes and looked at relics! I didn't think academic espionage went on."

"Haven't you seen *Indiana Jones*?" I'd joked, and Rafe had grinned.

"Now I have all sorts of exciting images of you cracking whips!" He'd leaned forwards and kissed me. "Now get out of this car and go to work before I kidnap you and drag you back to bed. No more playing hooky."

I'd watched him drive off, and only when the bright red car had turned the corner had I let myself into the house. Would I see him again? Or was this it?

Calm down, I'd told myself firmly while I'd packed my things. You're behaving like a teenager. Focus on work. The Assistant Director's job. Your research. Simon's unacceptable behaviour. But try as I might I couldn't rip my thoughts away from Rafe Thorne. His scent, the texture of his skin next to mine, the warmth of his lips against the hollow of my throat, the weight of his body pressing into mine…

"Cleo? Hello? I just said I'm really sorry about the mess and Dave is on his way out. Aren't you, Dave?" Susie waves her hand in front of my nose and with a jolt I realise I'm in our kitchen rather than curled up on the sofa in Rafe's studio with his arms around me and my mouth swollen from his kisses.

Susie stares at me hard for a moment and then her eyes widen. "Oh my God! I don't believe it! Cleo Rose Carpenter! You've been with a guy!"

Have I got the word *slapper* written across my head or something?

"I don't know what you're on about," I bluff. "I'm just running late, that's all, and I popped back here because I needed to change into my work clothes."

Susie puts her hands on my shoulders and gazes up at me, her brow crinkling for a moment as she stands on her tiptoes. "You've got a soppy look on your face that I've never seen before, your hair's wild and *you're running late*! You don't fool me, Cleo Carpenter. Normally I can set my clock by you. And you're not worried about the mess or my… err… friend? Something's up and for once I don't think it's work."

"It's fine about Dave," I assure her. "I'm not your mum. How's it going on Giraffe Ward?"

"Don't you dare try and change the subject! Dave, be useful: get dressed and fetch us some more milk. Cleo and I need tea."

Dave stretches and yawns widely, and once he's dispatched Susie does her best to drag details, any details, out of me. There's no way I'm telling her anything, though. She'll be unbearable enough if she thinks there's something going on; if she finds out it's Rafe Thorne I've been seeing there'll be no stopping her.

And am I? Seeing Rafe, I mean? It's not as though we've made any plans to see one another again. Maybe this was a one-off? A blip in our otherwise separate lives? Perhaps rock stars do this all the time.

Duh. Of course they do. Sex and drugs and rock 'n' roll, right?

It's shocking how this thought makes my heart lurch, and as much as I'd love to pour my woes out to my best friend I don't dare because I don't think I'll ever stop. So no matter how much tea she brews or how many probing questions she asks, I still don't give anything away.

Eventually Susie gives up and when Dave returns, bearing milk, croissants and a big bunch of flowers, she's sufficiently distracted for me to escape into my room and change. Ten minutes later I return in a black trouser suit, my satchel over my shoulder and with my curls tamed into a bun.

The same curls that last night Rafe wound around his fingers, so that he could pull me closer and closer until we melted into one another...

"Penny for them!" Alex chirps, at my side as I walk to work and matching me stride for stride. He gives me a cheeky sideways look. "Hmm, you look tired, Dr Carpenter. Didn't you get any sleep last night?"

"Not you as well. Can't I get any privacy?" Then a dreadful thought occurs to me. "You weren't–"

"Ew! Of course not! Who do you think I am? Hank? Of course I wasn't there! Give me some credit. I made myself scarce, don't you worry."

I *was* worried. Having a ghost following me around is starting to make me paranoid.

"So, is it on? You and Rafe?" Alex continues. He dances in front of me now, scooting backwards and grinning like a loon.

"I don't know," I say. The sun is shining and above the grey rooftops the sky is bright blue. Hey, I'm smiling again. What's up with me?

"Well, I do." Alex beams at me. "You were the key. I knew it. I always knew it and I can't thank you enough. I know it hasn't been easy for you and I know I've disrupted your life but," he pauses and gives me a hopeful look, "maybe it hasn't been all bad?"

An image flashes through my mind, of Rafe's eyes holding mine, his mouth just a kiss away and the moonlight silvering his hair. I know that just for this memory alone every disruptive second has been worth it a million times over.

"No," I say softly, "not all bad by any means, Alex."

I'm at the foot of the museum steps now. A steady stream of visitors moves up and down them. I pause at the bottom and let the human tide flow round me. The sun shines brightly, glancing off the glass doors and bouncing over the pavement. Yet its light trickles right through Alex, and my breath still clouds the air around me as goosebumps ripple across my arms.

"Rafe's writing again," I say slowly. "He seems to be starting to accept that he isn't to blame for what happened to you. You've succeeded, Alex."

Alex nods. "So why am I still here? Why haven't I drifted into the light with an angelic chorus singing me to my eternal rest?"

"I have no idea," I say.

I glance about and, when I focus, I know I'm seeing all kinds of things that aren't really there, or at least that aren't really there in the conventional sense. Take that Victorian gent doffing his hat to me, for instance. I guess in a weird way I've just started to get used to all of it.

"Do you stay?" I ask. "Or do we need to get somebody to, I don't know, move you on?"

Alex frowns. "I honestly haven't a clue. Maybe it isn't the right time yet? I have a feeling my journey isn't over yet. Maybe there's something else I have to do?"

I sincerely hope not. I dread to think what other hare-brained schemes Alex might dream up. I'll be a laughing stock by the time he's finished.

"And what about the others?" I wave my hand in the direction of a man on a penny-farthing who's bowling merrily along, followed by a soldier on a horse. "Will I stop seeing them when you go?"

"I have no idea," says Alex. "But to be honest, Cleo, I don't think you seeing ghosts has anything to do with me being about. Maybe this is something you have to deal with from now on?"

"Great. Just wonderful."

"I think you had a dormant psychic ability and that wallop on the bonce awoke it. Didn't your old man say that your mum and your grandmother both had the gift?"

"It's a gift I want to give back," I grumble, but Alex has vanished and since there's no point talking to thin air I mount the steps and enter the museum.

Oh, it's good to be back! Once in the foyer I feel like myself again, the confident and in-control Dr Carpenter. I nod hello to various colleagues, take a detour through the exhibitions just to check everything is in order, and then leave the public areas for the peace of the offices – if there can be such a thing as peace when Aamon is shrieking and cartwheeling down the corridor, followed by the yowling cat. I'm surprised just how pleased I am to see them both. Absence really does make the heart grow fonder, at least in their case.

I don't hold the same sentiment for Dr Simon Welsh, however. As I rap my knuckles on his office door I psyche myself up to ask him what the hell he thought he was playing at when he took my statue. How dare he help himself to my personal belongings?

I knock loudly but there's no answer, so I knock again, twice as hard just in case he hasn't heard or is hiding. I call out too. There's no escaping from me, Sneaky Simon. Come on out and give me back my statue. Or else.

"Simon? Are you there? It's Cleo."

There's still silence, which is frustrating because I was ready to charge in and read him the riot act. It's quite an anti-climax to be all geared up for a confrontation, only to discover that the person you need to have it out with has gone AWOL. There are quite a few other bones I have to pick with Simon, too. He's lucky this isn't the Natural History Museum: their entire dinosaur exhibition probably wouldn't contain enough bones for all the picking I intend to do. What did I ever see in him?

I check my watch. It's just gone noon, and he doesn't usually take lunch this early. Where on earth is he?

"Hello Cleo! Welcome back. You look better!"

It's Dawn and today must be one her days for escorting school kids around: she's in full Egyptian garb, complete with rubber asp and half of the Maybelline counter plastered over her face. It's a bit drag-queen-meets-*Carry on Cleo* for my taste, but who am I to spoil the fun? Besides, I hardly made a great success of the exercise myself. At least Dawn's Cleopatra doesn't flash her backside at people.

"Thanks, but I haven't actually been ill. I was spending some time with my father," I say patiently. Our junior is well known for getting the wrong end of the stick. She once typed up a private collector's name as Crispy Cock rather than Chris Peacock; although it made all of us howl with mirth, it nearly resulted in the offended elderly gentleman withdrawing the artefact he'd loaned us. Only some careful sweet-talking on my part prevented him from making an official complaint.

Beneath her make-up, Dawn looks even more perplexed than usual.

"Oh, sorry. I thought Simon said you weren't very well. I must have got confused. You know what I'm like. I'm such a butterfly brain! I was worried when you were off because of your accident. Simon was saying at the meeting yesterday how head injuries can be really dangerous."

I hold my breath and count to ten while Dawn rabbits on and on. Simon, it seems, has been very busy telling all and sundry just how unwell I've been and laying it on not so much with a trowel as with an entire lorry load of cement and a team of builders too. The more Dawn tells me just how upset they've all been and how concerned Simon is, the more I seethe – because now I know exactly what his devious little game has been and, like an idiot, I've played right into his hands. When Dawn tells me that they were even going to have a collection and send me some flowers, I think that Simon's very lucky he's not in his office, otherwise I'd burst in and batter him to death with the stolen statue. Then he could try a head injury on for size.

"So where is Simon?" I ask when Dawn finally runs out of steam. "Polishing his halo somewhere?"

She gawps at me. "Eh?"

"Never mind," I say. "He's clearly not in his office. You carry on; I'll find him." *Or die in the attempt,* I add silently.

"He is in his office," Dawn says, looking confused. Then her eyes widen, two white islands floating in a sea of kohl. "Oh! You don't know!"

"Don't know what?" I ask. But Dawn isn't listening: she's far too busy grabbing my hand and towing me down the corridor towards Professor Hamilton's office. To my surprise she stops at the one before it, traditionally the Assistant Director's office, and beams from ear to ear.

"Wrong office, silly!" Dawn giggles. "Tra-da! Here he is! I bet you're dying to see him and say well done!"

And stepping aside she points proudly to the nameplate on the door. I can hardly believe what I'm looking at. I even rub my eyes until I see stars. Unfortunately this doesn't make the slightest bit of difference: the words remain exactly the same.

Dr S Welsh – Assistant Director, Egyptology Department

"Isn't it exciting!" squeals Dawn. "Simon's been promoted!"

Exciting isn't the adjective that springs to mind. *Underhand, thieving* and *totally bloody unfair* seem far more appropriate in my opinion. All of a sudden everything makes complete and utter sense. While I've been caught up with Alex and Rafe, Simon has stolen the job from right under my nose.

And I have a nasty feeling that I know exactly how he's done it.

Chapter 23

I don't have red hair for nothing and although I seldom lose my temper, when I do it's pretty spectacular. Before I know what I'm doing, I'm flying into Simon's new office like a tornado, only to be greeted by an empty desk.

"Where is he?" I snarl, scanning the place like Robocop just in case Simon's cowering behind a pot plant – and believe me, he ought to be cowering after what he's done. "I thought you said he was in here?"

Dawn dithers on the threshold, one hand pressed theatrically to her large bosom. Her mouth swings on its hinges.

"I don't think he's here after all, Cleo."

I clench my fists and force myself to count to ten. "I think I've worked that one out for myself, Dawn." The statue of Aamon is perched on the desk, which feels like the ultimate V sign. Hardly able to contain my rage, I snatch it up and clutch it to my chest. Then, spinning on my heel, I fix Dawn with my famous steely glare.

"Where is Dr Welsh supposed to be, according to his schedule?"

Dawn takes a nervous step back. "I haven't checked the diary but think he's working on the new exhibition."

"What new exhibition?" It's the first time I've heard of this and I've only been away a week. Have I been pitched into a parallel universe? If so, it's a pretty crappy one.

"It's a really exciting idea he's had," Dawn tells me, looking relieved that I'm changing the subject. "It's very cool, actually Cleo. Simon's had this idea that we could have everyday ancient Egypt as an exhibition with all sorts of interactive stuff and even actors in role. The Prof is dead excited about it. Well, we all are. It's going to be huge. It's featuring the life of a boy pharaoh, Aamon something or other, and there's this brilliant story too. Simon's found out loads of cool stuff and he told us all about it when he delivered his paper at the last department meeting. Seriously, Cleo, you'll love it! This is going to be huge!"

I'm cold from head to foot. Of all the devious, sneaky, underhand gits!

"That was my idea! He's stolen it and presented it as his own!"

The cat hisses and Aamon stamps his foot furiously, scattering papers everywhere.

Dawn bites her lip. "Maybe you should talk to him?"

"Oh, I intend to; don't you worry about that," I promise her. I cast a quick glance around the room in case there's anything else of mine lying around, then storm out of Simon's new office and blast down the corridor to find the Professor. He needs to know exactly what's happened. This time I'm not holding back. I don't care if he thinks I'm crazy. I'm telling him the truth.

"Come in," calls the Professor when I rap on his door. "Ah, Cleo! Welcome back. We weren't expecting to see you this week, but always a pleasure." He pushes his glasses up his nose with a forefinger and smiles at me. "Are you feeling up to coming back to work? I was sorry to hear that you'd decided not to apply for the Assistant Director's job. My dear, you didn't have to pretend you had family business to attend to. You could have told me the truth. I know you've been unwell and I would have understood."

I goggle at him. What?

"I did spend some time with my family. I told you that before I left. I thought I'd explained it all?"

His brow pleats in confusion. "Ah. I see. My apologies in that case, Cleo. I'd naturally assumed ill health was the real reason why you didn't apply for the Assistant Directorship. I can't say that I'm not disappointed – you were a very strong candidate – but I do understand. You've had a great deal on your plate recently. Having family issues so soon after your accident must have compounded everything."

"But I did apply!" I stare at him in horror, hardly able to take in what I'm hearing. "I left the application here. Simon was going to take care of it and pass it to you."

A shadow flickers across his face. "Ah yes, about that, Cleo. Maybe we should discuss it alone?" The Professor motions to me to sit down but I ignore him. There's no way I can sit still while I'm fizzing with agitation.

"Paul! You have to talk to Simon. He's stolen my application and my research! He's used everything I'd prepared, to win the job for himself." I'm shaking with anger. "Paul, he even went to my house and took this statue of Aamon so that he could pass my work off as his own. You have to believe me! Simon Welsh is nothing more than a fraud and a thief! I left my laptop here too. He's used it to steal my work!"

"Be careful," warns the Professor. "You're making some very serious allegations here – allegations which would end up with you receiving a written warning if it wasn't for the fact I know you've been unwell. I'm prepared to make allowances for that, Dr Carpenter, but only once. Not indefinitely."

"I'm as fit and healthy as you," I protest. "Paul, that's all part of it! Simon's been telling you all I'm unwell and exploiting my accident to further himself at my expense. He's bloody good, I'll give you that. I can't believe I didn't see it sooner myself. No wonder he was always trying to encourage me to go home and offering to help with my research. He even tried to get me to go on dates with him. Good old Simon's been playing the long game."

"Bloody hell!" breathes Dawn, still at the door and agog to hear all this. "What a bastard!"

"Thank you, Dawn. You can carry on with your tour now," the Professor says swiftly. There's steel in his voice now, too. "Not a word of this conversation is to be repeated. Not a word. Do I make myself plain?"

Dawn nods, looking disappointed. She was probably dying to spill the details of this juicy conversation to everyone from the tea ladies to the security guards. Once the door has closed behind her the Prof exhales and gives me a piercing look.

"Dr Carpenter, please take a seat and try to calm yourself down. This is no place for hysterics."

Reluctantly, I sit down. Or rather, I perch one buttock on the chair; I'm too on edge to relax. I'm still clutching the statue while Aamon slips his small chilly hand into my left one. The cat leaps onto the Prof's desk, stalking backwards and forwards and whisking papers with its tail.

"I have no idea where this dreadful breeze is coming from. I thought I'd asked the maintenance people to investigate it," the Prof sighs, anchoring some documents with a pink pyramid paperweight. "My wife's idea of a joke," he explains when he sees me looking at this. "Naff, I know, but these offices are so draughty – and cold, too. Is your office cold?"

"My office is fine, thanks," I say shortly. What are we doing wasting time talking about our rooms when there are far more important issues to discuss?

"Paul, I'm not here to talk about my office. I'm telling you that Simon Welsh has stolen my research and my application. He's cheated his way into the Assistant Director's job and he deliberately withheld my application from you." My voice is shaking with anger. "I want to know what are you, as director of this department, going to do about it?"

Professor Hamilton looks at me for a moment, then rises from his chair and fetches a file from the cabinet at the far side of the office.

"Cleo, I did receive your partially completed application. Simon handed it to me the day you left for Buckinghamshire." Returning to his seat, he puts the file in front of me, pushing it across the desk with his forefinger. "Do you recognise this?"

I stare at it. This is the foolscap folder in which I placed my application. With an icy sense of dread I release Aamon's hand and flip open the folder. Even before I read its contents, I know exactly what I'm going to find.

"This isn't mine," I whisper. The application is in my name but none of this is my work. It's on the Ptolemaic period, for a start. Simon must have switched the applications.

Professor Hamilton shakes his head. "Can we please stop this? Your incomplete application is there right in front of us. It's disappointing but I understand why you would call and ask to withdraw it. There's potential, and you have put forward some excellent arguments – but Simon's work on Aamon is groundbreaking. It gave him the edge and I think he also has his finger right on the pulse of the zeitgeist. You were right to entrust your mother's findings to an academic of his calibre. His Egyptian Life idea is superb too; it's exactly what we need."

"That was my research and my idea!" I jump to my feet. "I was researching Aamon. You know I was! It was my mother's life work – and my grandmother's too!"

"And you passed the project to Dr Welsh when you had your head injury." The Professor looks at me with pity. "Don't you remember, Cleo? Simon has everything on his laptop. The dates all tally up from that time too."

"Because he copied it from me!" I'm desperate now. "I never gave him my laptop then! He only took it last weekend. He was going to lock it away for me so I didn't have to carry it on the train."

"Cleo, you gave him your laptop. You even emailed me to say so." Professor Hamilton turns to his own laptop, opens his email and spins the computer around to face me. Sure enough, there's a message from me granting Simon total access to my work. I'm horrified. Did Simon somehow manage to glimpse my password? That would have enabled him to see all my files, access my email and even look at my personal accounts, including Facebook. It would serve me right for using the same password for everything. He was my office too that first day I saw Aamon and the cat. Did he see something while I was passed out on the floor? Would he really be so callous as to take advantage of my ill health like that?

Of course he would. It's all coming back to me now: I remember that he was trying very hard to persuade me to let him take over my work.

My mouth is drier than the desert where Grandmother Rose found Aamon's tomb. No wonder he knew all my movements. Like a spider weaving a web around a fly, Simon has been carefully trapping me for months. Of course the Prof is convinced. It looks as though I've authorised everything. Even I'm starting to wonder…

Panic clenches my heart and sweat trickles down my back. This is impossible. The more I protest the madder I look. It was a lucky day for Simon Welsh when I had my head injury. I've been so preoccupied with Alex and Rafe since then that my eye has been well and truly off the ball.

And, to my utter shame and humiliation, I was also blinded and flattered that somebody as good-looking and popular as Simon might be interested in me. How he must have laughed. I really was a sitting target. Tears fill my eyes and I blink them away frantically. I'm not beaten yet. There has to be a way to prove that I'm not crazy or jealous, or any of the other things Simon has made me appear to be. He's plausible and devious and clever, but I know I'm the better academic. I just need to find a way to make the Prof realise this.

"Cleo, you've had a tough few months and you've been working so hard here. Maybe it's time you took a sabbatical? Perhaps you could go back into the field for a year?" He leans forward and pats my shaking hands awkwardly. "I blame myself for pushing you so hard. You do seem to have been a bit unsettled lately. Simon mentioned that you thought there were cats in your office. My dear, stress does strange things to us all. There's no need to be embarrassed. Simon was concerned about you; we all were. After a serious head injury it's hardly surprising you can't recall certain events and have struggled to keep up with your work. You are a gifted academic, there's no doubt about that, but as the director of this department I have to put the needs of the museum first – and I don't think this is the right time for you to take on any extra responsibility. Simon is the obvious and, in my opinion, the right choice."

It's so unfair. I have kept on top of my work. Better than that: I've excelled myself *and* managed to cope with a sudden psychic gift I never asked for or wanted.

I'm racking my brains to think of a way that I can prove what Simon has done, when the man himself breezes into the office as though he hasn't a care in the world. With his golden hair swept back from his smiling face, and in his spotless cream cords, sky-blue shirt and newly acquired wire-framed glasses, he looks every inch the cultured academic. If he's surprised to see me sitting here holding the statue he's stolen, Simon doesn't show it. There's not even so much as a flicker of unease. He's certainly very sure of himself.

The cat arches its back and hisses, leaping off the table and toppling the heavy pyramid paperweight. Aamon sticks out his tongue and I glower, but Simon doesn't turn a hair.

"Ah, Simon, here you are," says Professor Hamilton awkwardly. "Dr Carpenter and I have just been having a little chat about you."

Simon plasters a smile across his insincere face. "No wonder my ears were burning while I was chatting to the guys at the Ashmolean. They've agreed, by the way, Paul. I'll get Dawn onto organising the shipping. Sorry, Cleo. I'm getting carried away. How lovely to see you back. Are you feeling better?"

"You know full well I haven't been ill," I say, so coldly his gonads should have frostbite. "I've been visiting my father."

Simon nods sympathetically but I see him slide his gaze to Paul's and lift an eyebrow in resignation. "Of course, of course. Look, this is a little embarrassing, but I totally forgot that you wanted to keep those headaches of yours between us. How long are you back for?"

"Back? I'm not going anywhere," I say through gritted teeth.

"But what about the sabbatical you wanted so much?" Simon's eyes are big circles of innocence. "You were so keen to get back into the field again. I even spoke to Paul about it, although I know you didn't want me to try and pull any strings on your behalf."

My mouth falls open. He's unbelievable.

"I never said I wanted a sabbatical!" I exclaim. Turning to the Professor, I say desperately, "This is all nonsense, Paul! He's totally making this up. You have to believe me! He even stole my grandmother's statue of Aamon."

Simon shakes his head sadly. His blue eyes shine with candour. "Cleo, I did no such thing. I borrowed it as part of my research, just as we agreed I could. Don't you remember arranging it?"

"Of course I don't, because it never happened!"

Those blue eyes widen. "So you really think I went to your flat under false pretences and stole the statue? Cleo, your flatmate made me a cup of tea and gave me some biscuits. Would she have done that if I was stealing it?"

His hair gleams as winter sunshine trickles through the blinds and dances across his smooth face. Of course Susie welcomed him into the flat. Simon makes Ryan Gosling look plain, and I'm amazed she only gobbled up the biscuits rather than eating him alive.

"She had no idea what you were up to. You conned her too," I say bleakly.

He sighs wearily. "Yes, Cleo. Of course I did."

There's a taut silence.

"You left me with your application too and your laptop," he continues eventually. "Hardly what you'd do if you thought I was so untrustworthy."

I have no answer for this. He has me well and truly cornered. Besides, I did still trust him at that point – sort of. Simon could teach Machiavelli a thing or two about duplicitous behaviour.

Knowing that he's just moved his king into checkmate, Simon now changes strategy and plays the injured friend.

"Cleo, I'm very fond of you but I honestly can't put up with much more of this character assassination. I've tried to be a good colleague and friend, I've saved you from doing some crazy things on more than one occasion, and I really appreciate the heads-up you gave me with the Aamon research, but this has got to stop." He shakes his head sadly, the very picture of a man wronged. "If it carries on then I'm really sorry but I'll have to take advice. I can't have my reputation, professional or otherwise, ripped to pieces like this."

"You're threatening *me*? After what you've done?"

"And exactly what have I done?" Simon shoots back. His blue eyes bore into mine, gas-flame bright. They're actually far too close together. Now that I look at him in detail I can see that the pieces don't fit that well at all; he just does a great job of dazzling people so much that they don't notice. He folds his arms and stares at me. "You're accusing me of all sorts but where's your proof?"

"On my laptop! The one you stole the research from!"

With slumped shoulders and a defeated expression, Simon turns to the Professor. "You asked me to lock the laptop away, Cleo. It's in your office. Go and check it if you don't believe me." He passes a despairing hand across his face. It's Oscar-winning stuff, that's for sure. Johnny Depp should be very afraid. "I can't win here, Paul. It's Cleo's word against mine, isn't it? I know she's had a head injury, but this has got to stop. My academic reputation will be wrecked."

I know he's copied the files from my laptop. Of course he has – but I have no idea how I'm going to prove this. Simon's been planning this for months. No wonder he always seemed so solicitous and kept wanting to check on me in my office. He was on the rob.

"What academic reputation?" I ask incredulously. "You've stolen my work!

"Where's your proof, Cleo?" Simon repeats softly. "Or is it fair to say there isn't any? That this is all in your head?"

The proof would have been on my laptop, of course – the same laptop that I was stupid enough to let Simon take from me last week. I bet he was thrilled when I did that. I already know, without even looking, that he'll have copied my work and wiped it, using my own passwords so that it looks as though I had a mad moment. He'll have done this within minutes of my handing it to him, so that I can never prove he did it.

"You know I can't prove it," I say bitterly. "You've made sure of that."

The Professor, who's been listening intently to our exchange, runs his hand through his unkempt grey hair and clears his throat.

"Dr Carpenter, I know you've been unwell lately so this one time I'm prepared to overlook your erratic behaviour, but be assured I won't continue to be so tolerant. Consider this a verbal warning. I don't want any more accusations flung around the department. Is that clear?"

"Yes," I mutter. Resentment and anger threaten to choke me.

"Maybe you should think about that sabbatical," he adds. "You could leave after Christmas. It might be a good idea all round."

I stare at him, horrified. "You want me to leave?"

"Not leave, just take some time out. Recover from your injury and take the pressure off," he suggests kindly. "Think about it, and see what you might be interested in doing. I'll have a word with contact in Luxor and see what they've got coming up in the field. Now, if you would please excuse us, I need talk to Simon about a few matters."

He's dismissing me, making it abundantly clear that he doesn't believe a word I've said. Stunned, I haul myself to my feet and head back to my office, with Aamon and the cat trailing after me. I'd have hoped that the Prof would have known me well enough to trust me after working with me for almost three years, but it seems that he too has been hoodwinked.

Am I really taking a sabbatical after Christmas? There was a time when I would have leapt at this idea, but not now. I don't want to depart under a cloud and I don't want to leave my father either – or, more terrifyingly, Rafe. But unless I think of something pretty fast, it doesn't look as though I'll have much choice.

Right, think hard, Cleo. It's December now. There's less than two weeks to Christmas. Under two weeks for you to find a way of proving what Simon did. That should be long enough, surely? Then I have a brainwave. Of course! The office computer! Everything was backed up on that, and if it's mysteriously deleted itself the backup copies are saved on the USB stick I keep in my desk. All I have to do is produce that and it will prove everything. Suddenly elated, I sprint along the corridor – nearly knocking Dawn flying, and wanting to whoop and cheer every bit as loudly as Aamon, who's ahead of me.

As I enter my office I'm filled with determination. There's no way I'm letting Simon get away with this. No way at all. He's a cheat and a liar and I'm not going to be bullied by him out of a job I love. I boot up my trusty old PC and while it beeps and whirs into life I spin around on the office chair, much to Aamon's delight.

"You'll make yourself dizzy, young lady," Henry Wellby remarks disapprovingly from his telephone corner – but I ignore him, spinning faster and faster when Aamon leaps onto my lap. "And you should have a little more dignity, Your Highness," Mr Wellby adds.

I'm not in the mood to be nagged by ghosts in my own office. In fact, I'm through with being bossed about today.

"Chill out, Henry," I say. "We're just having some fun."

He shakes his head and tuts. "You used to be such a sensible girl, Cleo Carpenter. Don't think I haven't been keeping an eye on your career since you've worked here. That young Alex has been a very bad influence on you."

I'm starting to think Alex has actually been a very good influence on me, and that his brother has been an even better one. My lips still tingle from Rafe's kisses, and every time I think of him my stomach tangles itself up in the most delicious knots. It's probably best not to share this information with Mr Wellby though. He's from another era, after all.

The computer is up and running now so I tip Aamon off my lap and squiggle the mouse about to open my files. The desktop is empty – I'd expected that – but I also save my files on the network. Maybe, just maybe, Simon has overlooked them? The seconds that it takes me to log into our network are painfully slow, and then I'm into the system, clicking through the levels of security required until finally I'm in my own area and opening up my personal folder. Any minute now…

"No!" I stare at the screen in dismay. Rather than seeing hundreds of beautifully indexed documents charting all my hard work for the last twelve months, I'm staring at a screen blanker than Dawn's brain. Everything has gone.

"Bastard," I breathe. Somehow Simon has got into the computer system and deleted everything. I click the mouse frantically but there's still nothing. Everything has been well and truly wiped. "Total and utter bastard."

"Language," reproves the eminent Egyptologist in the corner, tutting at me again through his moustache. "There's a child present."

"Sorry," I say hastily, "but I think you'd resort to bad language too if every single piece of your research had been stolen."

"My dear! That's appalling." Abandoning the phone, Henry Wellby joins me at my desk and peers at the blank screen. "Were the papers inside this magical knowledge box?"

"Something like that," I say. There's a lump in my throat. Aamon's chilly hand creeps into mine and the cat winds itself around my ankles. It says it all when the dead are nicer company than some of the living around here.

"Your young gentleman colleague was in here on many occasions. He spends a great deal of time examining the magical box," Mr Wellby tells me. He takes off his top hat and scratches his head thoughtfully. "My dear, I fear he may be the culprit. He even locked the door while he was in here."

"I bet he did," I say grimly. It's frustrating in the extreme that my only witness to Simon's theft is a ghost. I suppose I could demand that the IT department look into the issue, but what will they find except that I'll appear to have had a mad five minutes and deleted all my own files? Simon's bound to have logged on as me last Sunday, so this is only going to confirm all the Professor's fears that I'm not of sound mind.

There's only one hope left: that the USB stick is still in my drawer. But as I open the drawer and slide my fingers in, I have a horrible feeling that I'm not going to find the memory stick. Simon's been far too clever to let a little detail like that wreck his plan. With a growing sense of dread, I recall how I'd noticed before that the contents of my desk had been disturbed. I'd thought it was the antics of Aamon and his pals, but no: Simon had been rummaging. Sure enough, the memory stick has vanished too – and along with it my last hope of proving beyond all doubt that Simon's stolen my work.

"He's taken everything." I place my head in my hands. My temples are throbbing. "It's all gone."

Aamon wails, the cat yowls and Henry Wellby paces the room furiously, tugging at his moustache.

"You can't let him get away with this," he says finally.

"He's already got away with it." I feel utterly defeated. I have no idea what on earth I can do now, except pack my bags and push off to Egypt. At the thought of this my heart lurches – and not with the excitement that the idea of a dig would normally bring, but with the dread of having to leave. If I'm on sabbatical in Egypt how will I see Rafe again?

What? That's ridiculous. There's nothing between me and Rafe – nothing agreed and permanent, anyway. Maybe we've had our moment, and that's the end of it. He never mentioned seeing me again and he hasn't got my number. He's a rock star, for heaven's sake; he probably does this kind of thing all the time. This idea is even more painful than the loss of my research, and I close my eyes despairingly. How is this even possible? What's happening to me?

"You can't just give up!" Wellby barks, ripping me out of my misery. "Show some backbone, young lady! Would Howard Carter have discovered Tutankhamun's burial chamber if he'd adopted that kind of defeatist attitude? 'Give up,' they all said. 'It's not there.' Lord Carnarvon even considered pulling the funding, but Howard never let people's doubts grind him down. And what about me? I kept going, held my head up when it looked as though I would never find the lost city of Nephet. And what happened? I persevered and I found it in the end. I'm famous for my finds there. Stiff upper lip, Cleo my dear! That's the spirit on which the Empire was built."

I listen patiently even though I've heard these stories a million times. They're the stuff of every Egyptologist's dreams, after all – and besides, I don't have the heart to tell him the Empire is long gone. Anyway, a stiff upper lip in twenty-first century Britain? Thank goodness he's not seen people caterwauling on *The X Factor* or airing their very dirty linen on *The Jeremy Kyle Show*.

"There'll be a way to prove what that scoundrel has done. You just have to find it," Henry Wellby continues firmly. "Come on, girl. You're supposed to be brilliant. That's what they all say here, and now's the time to prove it. All you have to do is think hard and it will come to you. We'll help too if we can."

Aamon nods and the cat leaps onto the desk, rubbing its bony head against the computer monitor. In spite of my despair I can't help smiling. I have a world-famous Egyptologist on my side and a pharaoh, and maybe even Rafe too.

That's some team. Simon Welsh should be very afraid.

"You're right," I say slowly and with a growing sense of determination. "He can't get away with this. We need a plan."

I pick up my pencil and gnaw the end thoughtfully. There has to be a way. All I need to do now is figure it out.

Chapter 24

"He did what?" Susie is so shocked that her fork, laden with cheesy lasagne, is frozen halfway between the plate and her lips. Gloopy meat sauce splashes onto the white tablecloth, but for once I don't move to mop it up. What are a few splashes of lasagne in the general scheme of things? Let's face it: I've got a far bigger mess to clean up.

It's early evening and, after a fruitless day spent mostly pacing up and down my office muttering *bastard* at regular intervals, I've left work and met Susie for supper in a pretty little Italian restaurant just off Covent Garden. My head is still spinning and so far I've not touched my seafood risotto, but a fair amount of red wine seems to have slipped down my neck.

"He stole all my research and passed it off as his own," I repeat. "And then he swapped my application with his and now he's the Assistant Director of our department."

Susie's jaw falls open. More lasagne splatters onto the tablecloth. "No way! Seriously?"

"Seriously. I know it sounds far-fetched, and believe me he's done a great job of making me look like a brain-injured lunatic at work, but that's exactly what's happened." I slosh some more wine into my glass and swirl it about miserably. "Simon stole my passwords and copied everything that was on my laptop, and now I haven't got any proof that it was my work to begin with. And before you ask, no, I haven't got my work saved anywhere else. He's wiped the backup files and stolen my USB stick."

"Bloody hell. What a mess. Can't you tell somebody at work?"

I laugh bitterly. "I did try but Simon's managed to twist everything so that it looks as though I'm the one out to wreck his career."

Susie lowers her fork. "I take it this is the same Simon who came round to the flat and took the statue? Tallish? Stocky?"

I nod.

"Bastard!" Susie's fork clatters onto her plate. "He walked in as cool as anything and chatted away. He was so convincing. I really thought you'd said he could borrow it. Cleo, I'm so sorry. He had me totally fooled. I even made him a cup of tea. I wish I'd spat in it now."

She looks distraught and I reach forward and lay a hand on her arm. "Hey, don't blame yourself; he's totally plausible. Even I was sucked in for a while. And of course the whole head-injury thing has been a gift for him. He's passing off any objections I make as evidence that I'm not up to being at work."

I rip off a chunk of garlic ciabatta, wishing that it had voodoo powers and that somewhere Simon was writhing around in agony. It's only when my mouth is too crammed with bread for me to speak that Susie says carefully, "You must admit though, you have been acting a little bit strangely lately: not quite yourself."

Over Susie's shoulder I see an elderly gentleman in eighteenth-century dress; meanwhile, Aamon and the cat are squashed up next to me on the red velvet banquette. They've stuck to me like glue since the incident in the Professor's office. To be honest, I'm finding it rather comforting to have them around. At least Aamon still believes in me. There's no sign of Alex, so maybe he's managed to drift off to wherever it is he's supposed to be. Who knows? Certainly not me. I don't feel like I know anything anymore. My world has been turned upside down, so yes, it's safe to say I'm not quite myself. But still, I think I might remember if I'd donated a whole year's work to Wanker Welsh. I'm not *that* deranged.

"Not that I'm doubting you at all," Susie adds hastily. "No way. It's just that you do seem a bit different – in a good way, of course! I'm thrilled you're not so bothered about mess these days, and Dave thinks you're totally great."

I gulp down the garlic bread. "Stop trying to dig yourself out of a hole. For your information, I still care about mess and I'd rather not bump into semi-naked junior doctors over the Cornflakes. And before you ask, no, I'm not about to lend you the rent."

Susie pulls a hurt face. "I wasn't going to say that. I just think you seem happier since you hurt your head, which probably sounds crazy given what's been going on, but you've been less obsessed with work. And you've spent some time with your dad. These are good changes."

"Now look where they've got me," I say gloomily. Susie does have a point: work hasn't been my number-one priority lately. Getting shot of Alex has been.

"Talking of work," I continue, spearing a fat pink prawn on my fork, "unless I can think of a way to clear my name in the next week or so you'll be able to make as much mess as you like and keep a male harem if you feel the urge. The Professor wants me to go on a year's sabbatical to Luxor. They want rid of me."

"Can they do that?"

I put my fork down. My appetite has vanished because, yes, it seems that they can. "It will be under the guise of career development, but in effect it's a handy way to smooth over an awkward situation. I guess I either take the sabbatical or I could go and work elsewhere."

"Leave the museum? But you love your work!" Susie looks shocked. "But, then again, you love Egypt too."

I nod. "I do, and normally I'd be there like a shot – but this is different, Suse. It's leaving under a cloud and there's no way I want to do that. I have to clear my name and get my work back. I just need to figure out how."

We return to our food for a bit, both deep in thought. Susie puts forward a couple of ideas about being a honeytrap and getting Simon to confess, but since he's already met her the plan soon gets derailed. She even offers to speak to the Professor and tell him that I never authorised her to part with the statue, but what would that prove? It's still Simon's word against mine.

"Egypt it is, then," Susie says gloomily as we scrape up the final smears of tiramisu.

The sweet pudding curdles in my stomach. A whole year in Egypt. Once upon a time you wouldn't have seen me for dust, but now I'm reluctant to leave England. There's my father, for one thing. I don't want to leave him behind just when we've started to rebuild our relationship. And then there's Rafe…

I've tried hard not to think about him today – I've needed my wits about me – but I just haven't been able to stop myself. Even in the middle of a full-on career meltdown I've caught myself drifting away into thoughts of him: the way he held my face between his hands and kissed me as though he'd never let me go again, his mouth soft and full on mine. My fingers steal to my lips. It feels as if I've always known Rafe Thorne – which is ridiculous, given that we've probably spent less than twenty-four hours in each other's company. But what if there is a person you're meant to be with? How many of us ever get to recognise that person or be with them? It might be a fleeting encounter on a train or perhaps passing each other in a crowd; your eyes meet and you know with every fibre of your being that that person is the other part of you. That's how I felt about Rafe on the snowy railway platform all those years ago, and that's exactly how I felt about him last night.

"Out with it." Pudding finished and wine glass drained, Susie gives me a stern look. "Who is he?"

"Who is who?" I try to bluff, but I'm a redhead so now I'm the colour of the velvet seat.

Susie gives a cry of triumph. "The guy who's put that soppy look on your face. Don't try and deny it! I know you, Cleo Carpenter, and I've never once seen you look like this. *And* you rolled in this morning with a daft smile, your hair in a tangle and looking like you hadn't slept all night. Don't hold back on me! Spill!"

My hair had been tangled because Rafe had spent hours threading my curls around his fingers and pressing kisses into them. I hadn't slept all night either.

And the daft smile? Everything to do with what we'd been doing while the rest of the world was sleeping. If I close my eyes I can still see his face silvered by the moonlight and feel his lips tracing the curve of my throat. Even all these hours on I can still sense his skin against mine and the rasp of his stubble against my neck, and shivers dance across my limbs.

"Just somebody I used to know a long time ago," I say.

She rubs her hands together in glee. "I knew it! I am never wrong! So, Dr Oh-So-Secretive-Carpenter, when are you seeing him again?"

"I don't know. We haven't made any plans."

Aamon is under the table playing some involved game with the cat, and an icy draught whisks around us. At least I think that's caused by Aamon. It might be the thought of not seeing Rafe again that chills me.

"Well, duh! Call him and make some," says Susie. "Honestly, Cleo, you are hopeless. If he's the reason you've started to relax then he's got my vote."

I suppose that in a roundabout way Rafe is the reason I've changed. Alex is certainly the reason my life has been totally disrupted.

I pull a face. "You're right, Suse, I am hopeless. I don't even have his number."

"You're going to wait for him to call you? Babe, we don't have to sit by the phone anymore! We're all equal now. Don't play text chess; life's far too short. Find his number and call him!"

While Susie gives me the benefit of her wide and varied love life, filling me in on how to tell if a guy is *into me*, I pay the bill and then we stroll arm in arm along Floral Street and into the piazza. It's bitterly cold tonight and everyone is wrapped up in thick coats and big scarves, but even the biting north wind can't whip the smiles from the faces of the late-night shoppers. Before I can protest, Susie's grabbing my hand and tugging me into various shops, where we end up buying all sorts of odds and ends that she thinks will be great presents, but which we both know she'll end up keeping.

We're just leaving the covered market and heading for the Underground station when two buskers break into a rendition of "One Christmas Kiss".

Usually I run for the hills as soon as I hear those opening chords, but this time I stop and listen to every word until Covent Garden melts away and I'm standing back on the empty platform, circled by Rafe's arms and with the snow silently drifting down. When the buskers finish to enthusiastic applause I find that my cheeks are wet.

"Blimey," says Susie, handing me a crumpled bit of tissue. "You have got it bad."

I dash the tears away. "Sorry. Bit of a weird day." Week. Month. Delete as appropriate.

"That song reminds me of something I saw trending on Twitter earlier," she tells me as, arm in arm, we thread our way through the crowds. "It's by a band called Thorne. I think I told you about them once? They came to an end when the lead singer died, remember?"

I nod. How could I ever forget?

"Apparently the lead singer's brother, Rafe Thorne, who's been pretty much a recluse since then, has just put a new song out as a free download. Everyone's going mad for it and the press have freaked." Susie fishes out her iPhone and scrolls to her Twitter feed. "It's like Elvis popping back into the building and recording again. People are going crazy because Rafe Thorne is gorgeous!"

I close my eyes and picture Rafe's slow, stomach-flipping smile. Even when I open them again I can still see him.

"Apparently it's the fastest downloaded track this year. Everyone's talking about it." Her expression grows dreamy. "It's a beautiful song, Cleo. It's called 'Sunrise Girl'. She saved him from despair and every day the sun rises in her smile. God, I'm happy if Dave puts the loo seat down. Whoever she is and wherever she is, she's a lucky cow. He's crazy about her."

Susie dives into the Underground station, but I'm rooted to the pavement with her words echoing round and round in my head. People and ghosts – I can hardly tell them apart these days – swirl past me, but I barely notice them any more than I notice the wind slicing into my face or feel the jostling elbows of the other commuters. Suddenly Simon, the museum and even all those months of lost research don't seem to matter nearly as much as they did earlier. My heart is rising like a helium balloon. The message in this song couldn't be any clearer: Rafe feels about me the same way that I feel about him. I'm tingling from head to foot. The twinkling lights and Christmas decorations don't seem out of place now. I realise that the world is full of wonder and magic. How have I ever doubted this?

"You did it, Alex," I whisper into the cold night. "You really did it! Rafe Thorne is back on the music scene!"

Chapter 25

It's no good. No matter how hard I try I just can't seem to come up with a foolproof way to prove that Simon Welsh has lied, cheated and thieved his way to the Assistant Director's job. Everything I think of falls at the first hurdle because there's no evidence —anything I might say will just be interpreted as sour grapes. I spend the next four days alternately racking my brains for a solution and then wondering why I haven't heard from Rafe. At night I lie awake in the flat, watching the shadows swish across the ceilings when cars pass by, and reliving the night we spent together. Then, just to torture myself a little bit more, I listen to "Sunrise Girl". Like practically everyone else in Britain, I've downloaded it. Unlike everyone else, though, I pore over the lyrics as a miser might pore over his gold; I analyse each line and every piece of imagery until my head spins. When I was in Covent Garden with Susie I was so sure there was a message in that song for me. Almost a week later and with no sign of Rafe, I'm not so certain. My judgment recently hasn't been particularly great, has it?

It's late afternoon now and outside my office window London is swathed in gloom. The weather is still bitter and snow has been forecast, but as I try to focus on a paper I'm due to deliver, I feel even colder than the average person, since the cat insists on sitting on my feet while Aamon weaves rubber bands into his interpretation of a loom band. Sleet begins to patter against the windowpanes and in the public areas our visitors will be trailing damply across the foyer, steaming up the exhibits and crowding the coffee shop.

I push the paper aside. It's a lecture on Hatshepsut that I've delivered before, but I've had to rewrite it because my original is a victim of Simon's trawl through the hard drive. Before I can help myself, I'm opening up Google and typing *Rafe Thorne* into the search engine. Honestly, I'm not sure what's wrong with me. It's like I've got an addiction to typing his name: this must be at least the fifth time today that I've abandoned my work to do this. I'll never think of a way to catch Simon out while I'm mooning over Rafe like a lovesick fan.

Hang on. Did I just say *lovesick*?

I'm on the brink of minimising the screen, aghast at the workings of my subconscious mind, when I spot Alex, cross-legged on the floor and helping Aamon with his loom band.

"You ought to at least get him some colourful ones," he remarks, looping the rubber over his fingers with surprising skill. "I know you like sludge colours but these are dead boring – aren't they, Aamon?"

Aamon nods and says something that makes Alex laugh. Lord, it's infuriating when people have secrets from you – and even more infuriating when it's in a language that you've no hope of being able to understand.

"What?" I say.

"Nothing, nothing." Still grinning like a loon, Alex looks very pleased with himself. "Well, nothing other than he says you're far too busy looking at pictures of my brother to pay attention to much else."

I blush to the roots of my hair. "That's total rubbish!"

Alex raises an eyebrow. "Oh really? So if I looked at the history on your computer I wouldn't see any searches related to Rafe? None at all?"

"Certainly not," I fib. Well, none apart from the search relating to the sky-high sales of the new single, the pieces in the online tabloids speculating as to the identity of the girl in the song, the ITV press release discussing the possibility of Rafe's appearance on the next series of *The X Factor*, and the countless pictures of his brooding sharp-cheekboned face, that is. I've hardly searched for him at all.

"You're such a hopeless liar," says Alex fondly. "You go bright red. Don't ever play poker, for heaven's sake. Still, if it's any consolation, he's been Googling you too."

"Really?" My heart cartwheels at this. Every night I've fallen asleep with an image of his face in my mind. It's nice to think the feeling may be reciprocated.

"Yes, really. I thought about typing your mobile number into his to help out, but it seemed a bit freaky."

I'm horrified. "Please don't."

"I guess I'll just have to leave it to fate then. God, it's hard work playing Cupid," Alex sighs. Loom band completed, he appears at the side of my desk and glances over my shoulder. A chill breeze ruffles my neatly stacked documents and scatters the paper clips.

"Hey! What's this?" Leaning over my shoulder, Alex points at the letter that now lies on the top of the pile. I'd tried my best to bury it in a fine attempt at reverse archaeology, but some things just won't be hidden. "*Faculty of Archaeology, Luxor University – Research Fellow Sabbatical, Dr C Carpenter,*" he reads. "What's all this? Are you leaving? Were you going to tell Rafe or just push off again?"

He shoots me a furious look.

"I never pushed off, as you so nicely put it, the first time around," I point out hotly.

"So what's all this about then? The tomb of Senneferi? At the end of the Northern Line, is it? God, Cleo, you really haven't learned anything at all, have you? It's still career first and sod the rest of us – your dad, Pink Dreds, me, Rafe."

My head starts to pound. A headache has been dancing around my skull all day, or more accurately ever since the Prof knocked on my door earlier on to discuss my sabbatical.

"It's a wonderful opportunity, Cleo," he'd said gently, placing the information on my desk. "I've had a chat with Professor Ikram and he's very keen indeed to have you on board. They don't often have somebody of your calibre on the team. This will open doors for you, I promise."

I hadn't replied. I was seething because I knew exactly what this was: a convenient means of getting rid of a problem. However much the Professor might try to dress it up as a fantastic career move, he was effectively and firmly slamming shut the one door I'd been carefully inching open for months.

"You've got such potential. You'd bring in research grants and you're a wonderful lecturer. Maybe one day you'll even be head of your own department," he'd said. "This would only enhance your CV."

"That's the reason you've suggested it? Or is it because you've decided I'm a head-injured liability?" I'd asked bitterly. "Simon stole my work, Paul. I know I can't prove it – he's clever enough to make sure of that – but I would hope you know me well enough to believe me."

The Prof had looked away, dug his hands into his pockets and shivered. "Goodness, this office is even colder than mine."

I'd said nothing. Henry Wellby had been standing practically nose-to-nose with the Prof yelling, "Listen to her, man! How on earth did an imbecile like you get to work in my museum?" but it wasn't going to help.

"I must see the maintenance department," the Prof had said, half to himself, before turning back to me. "Cleo, try to view this sabbatical in the spirit it's offered. You've had a very difficult time, you've been badly injured, and I really think some warmth and a change of scene are exactly what you need. Still, it's your choice. Nobody's forcing you to do anything, but in my opinion this is the best course of action."

I tuck the details of my banishment back into a neat pile and then – sneaky deed by sneaky deed – I tell Alex exactly what's been going on. By the time I've finished, quite a crowd of ghosts have gathered around the desk, I'm wearing my coat to keep warm and there's a great deal of outrage on my behalf.

"So that's it," I finish bleakly. "Unless I can find a way to clear my name I'll have to leave." As I speak I picture my father all alone and Rafe struggling to piece himself back together, and grief tightens its vice around my chest.

Alex's eyes are dark with fury. "What a snake! I never liked him, Cleo, and now I know why. He's been planning this for months and I distracted you so much that it gave him the perfect way in." He starts to pace furiously. "There has to be a way to show him up for what he is."

"If there is I've yet to come up with it," I sigh. "I'm going round and round in circles but he's been far too devious. The Professor has well and truly been taken in. I think he'd only believe me if he heard it from Simon himself – and that's never going to happen."

There's a general discussion at this point. Henry Wellby is all for frightening Simon into a confession, a couple of Egyptian guards suggest torture, and even Aamon is chipping in with great excitement. I appreciate their concern but there's no point trying to fight this. The Prof has already made his mind up.

I'm about to give up for the day when the old phone rings. Leaving the animated discussion to carry on without me, I pick it up. I'm expecting a summons to the Prof or one of Dawn's dilemmas ("Cleo, I've put the wrong dates in the press release. Do you think it matters?"), so to discover that Rafe Thorne is my caller is a wonderful surprise.

"Rafe! How on earth did you get this number?" I say, astonished. I probably sound like a fifteen-year-old, but right now I couldn't care less. And anyway, when I was fifteen I was far too busy swotting for my GCSEs to talk to boys on the phone. I glance around to see if the others are listening in, but the room is totally empty. Even Alex has gone. How very tactful. And obvious.

"I know you're the one with the brains and the degrees, but even I can figure out that there can't be too many Cleo Carpenters working at the Wellby Museum," laughs Rafe. Although I can't see him I know that the dimples are dancing in his cheeks and that a smile lights his eyes. My heart crumbles like vanilla sponge. "Anyway, the girl on the switchboard was ever so helpful."

I bet she was, I think to myself.

"Congratulations on the new song," I say. "Even a musical Philistine like me knows it's doing brilliantly. It seems that you're well and truly back on the music scene."

"Hmm, be careful what you wish for," says Rafe thoughtfully.

There's a pause and then he adds, "You know I wrote it for you, don't you?"

My pulse skitters like stones skimmed across a pond, creating ripples of longing and excitement – and fear too.

"Yes," I say softly.

The sleet has turned to snow now, whirling dizzyingly outside – swirling and spinning in perfect time with my hopes and fears. I watch it and know that something in me is spinning away too, out of control and out of sight.

"Can I see you again?"

I coil the telephone flex around my finger. My heart is hammering so hard that I'm amazed he doesn't hear it.

"Cleo?" Rafe says. He sounds uncertain now. "Is that OK with you?"

"Yes. Yes. Of course." I take a deep breath. "When?"

"I'm going to totally blow my cool now and probably break all the rules, but I really don't care," Rafe tells me. "I've tried to do the whole giving-you-space thing – I know how busy you are – but it's driving me crazy. How does now suit you?"

"Now?" My eyes widen. "Right now? Seriously?"

"I don't think I've ever been more serious in my life. Or possibly any crazier! Yes, right now! I'm standing on the steps outside the museum. You can't miss me, Cleo: I'm the man in a far-too-thin leather jacket wearing a stupid beanie hat, sprinkled in snow and slowly turning into an icicle while he waits for the most amazing woman he's ever met. Don't take too long, though; I think frostbite's setting in."

He rings off but his laughter stays with me as I tear around the office, shutting down the computer, shrugging on my coat and ramming my hat onto my head. If my colleagues are surprised to see me fly past them, curls escaping from my hat as I leap down the main staircase and dodge the visitors, then they don't say anything – but I feel their stares and I know that the moment I'm out of sight the gossip will be spreading. If they had any suspicions before that I've gone mad, then I've surely confirmed them now.

And maybe I *am* mad? I'm certainly not behaving like myself: all I know is that I can't wait a second longer to see Rafe Thorne again. Knowing he's only moments away only makes the urgency sharper. I dash across the concourse, gasping my apologies to the visitors I'm bashing with my bag, and then I'm pushing my way through the door and out into the snowy London night. Car headlights and taillights bejewel the street and for a moment I'm dazzled and stand blinking in the cold.

The air is sharp and the snow's already settling on the steps, but I don't feel the biting wind or the flurries of flakes that brush against my cheeks. I don't notice anything except the man who's waiting for me beneath the ornate lamppost. He's dark haired, square jawed and unmistakably Rafe Thorne, my Christmas stranger. His battered leather jacket, bright red scarf, scuffed Timberlands and beanie hat might disguise him from the rest of the world, but I'd know him anywhere. For a few frozen moments in time we stare at one another, the world around fading away until all I can see is him. The soft lamplight warms his face, turning his violet eyes to deepest indigo and shadowing the high cheekbones and strong jaw. My breath catches in my throat. It's as though the ten years since we first met have stood completely still.

Rafe holds out his hand to me. I walk down the steps and he slips his arms around my waist, pulling me into him as gentle kisses fall onto my lips, my eyes and my throat. Then he unwinds his scarf and, looping it around my neck, draws me closer still, until our snow-dusted eyelashes are almost touching.

"Let's get out of here," he says.

Chapter 26

"You seem very happy this morning," Dawn remarks, breezing into my office with a mug of coffee and a pile of folders. Her nose is still pink and her breath is rising in little clouds – which is hardly surprising, since the room is full of ghosts. I barely notice them anymore: I'm becoming used to the extra faces I see as I walk around the museum or the city. I think I might even miss Aamon and the cat now if they left.

Now there's something I never thought I'd say.

"Mind you," Dawn continues, putting the coffee on the desk and sloshing it everywhere, "I'd be happy too if I was being sent on a year's paid holiday to the sun. You're so lucky, Cleo! I'm well jel!"

"Hmm," I say. There's no point telling Dawn this is a banishment rather than a reward, and there's even less point telling her that I have absolutely no intention whatsoever of going to Luxor. The smile that's remained on my lips ever since I saw Rafe waiting for me last night has nothing to do with my career.

No, I decide firmly as I sip my drink and Dawn settles down on the edge on my desk, I'm going to find a way to clear my name. There's no way I'm leaving a job I love, just because of Simon. If I was determined before, spending time with Rafe has hardened my resolve. There's far too much to play for now. While Dawn rabbits on about where she may or may not book for next year's holiday (Magaluf being *so* over, apparently), I let my mind drift back to yesterday…

Rafe had curled my fingers snugly inside his and tucked our hands into the pocket of his jacket. His scarf had been soft against my skin and as we'd walked away from the museum I'd turned my face into the fabric, inhaling his scent. As though by an unspoken understanding, we'd walked through the streets matching footstep for footstep. Neither of us had said a word, but the gentle caress off his finger against my gloved palm and the way his gaze had never broken mine had been more eloquent than any speech. Rafe Thorne could have led me right across the city and I wouldn't have protested; I'd been happy just to be close to him.

Was happy the right word? As we'd turned into New Oxford Street, I'd decided that "happy" was far too simple an adjective to describe this deep contentment and ease. But how was it possible? What did I actually know about Rafe? Of course I knew the same things that anybody with access to the Internet could discover. I knew that he was thirty-one and one of the most talented songwriters on the planet. I knew he'd dated models (although I was trying not to think about them), and I knew he had the dark good looks of a fallen angel. But I felt that I knew *more* than this. I'd felt exactly the same ten years ago and nothing had changed. Was this the once-in-a-lifetime connection that people talk about – finding a soul mate, if you like? As Rafe had smiled down at me, a smile laced with both danger and promises, I'd been sure it was exactly that. None of it made sense or could be measured or tested or proven.

Which was why I trusted it entirely.

We'd walked like this until we'd finally reached Covent Garden. Strains of music had drifted with the snowflakes and applause had rippled as jugglers thrilled the crowd. A flower girl had run up to Rafe and offered him a posy, but of course he hadn't seen her, any more than he'd seen the tall man in white gloves and grey suit who was always here too. At least Alex wasn't about, I'd thought, feeling rather disloyal; two was company, after all.

At that point Rafe had stopped so abruptly that I'd cannoned into him.

"Sorry!" His hands had slipped to my waist and he'd pulled me tightly against him before dropping a kiss onto my temple. "I was just trying to get my bearings. It's been a while since I was last here, but can you smell that? Isn't it wonderful! I knew if we walked far enough we'd find it!"

He'd sniffed the air hungrily and I'd laughed. The night air had been laced with the tang of malt vinegar, sharp enough to make my mouth water, and the unmistakable aroma of frying had beckoned us towards a chip shop, where warm buttery light spilled onto the pavement and picnic tables were crammed with customers – testament to the good food within.

"Chips?"

Rafe had nodded. "Of course chips! There's nothing better than being outside and eating chips out of the paper." Then he'd paused thoughtfully, giving me a slow sexy smile that had made my stomach flip. "Well, maybe there is *one* other thing that's better, but eating chips in the fresh air comes a very close second. It's the food of the gods!"

"And hungry rock gods?" I'd teased.

His arms had tightened around me. "Cleo, I'm not a rock god. I'm just an ordinary bloke who got lucky. I just wrote the songs. Alex was the star of the show."

"That's not what Alex thinks: he says he was the Robbie to your Gary," I'd said without thinking, and Rafe had stared at me, a frown furrowing his brow. I could have kicked myself. Rafe had no idea that I knew his brother. "I mean, that was what I read somewhere," I'd added hastily, wanting to smooth the gaffe over but also knowing that this was an opportunity to pass on Alex's words. "I'm sure he'd be thrilled to think you were writing again."

But Rafe had still been gazing down at me, his brows meeting in a puzzled expression. "That was word for word what Ally used to say. What interview did you say you saw that in?"

I'd shrugged. "I can't remember. Hey! Don't make me confess that I've been Googling you! How uncool does that make me look?"

"I don't care about cool," Rafe had said quietly. We'd been standing in the middle of the pavement while pedestrians flowed around us like the sea. He'd pulled me closer, his violet eyes holding mine. "Cleo, I'm not even sure I care about the music business any more. I love writing but I hate all the crap that comes with it: the pretentious bullshit and the false people. This is what I want. This is real, being here with you, right now. Not the big house and the silly car and all the rest of it. I'm not a rock god, Cleo, I'm just a man, standing in a bloody cold street and asking the most wonderful girl I've ever met to share some chips with him."

He'd taken my face in his hands and pressed our foreheads together.

"The new song is doing so well," I'd whispered. "The papers have been full of how you're back again and how excited your management is."

"Would they be the same papers who loved writing about my spiral into despair?" Rafe had asked wryly. "And the same management company who didn't want to know me two weeks ago?"

He'd brushed his mouth against mine. Our breath had mingled and my heartbeat had broken into a gallop.

"The past couple of weeks have been the most amazing of my life, Cleo, but not because of any of that; it's because somehow life has brought you back to me again. I know it sounds crazy – you can laugh all you like – but I feel as though we were meant to meet again." He'd paused and then added softly, "I have the strongest feeling that it's what my brother wanted, too. I know that must sound insane and I can't explain it, but I suddenly have the biggest sense of peace."

I'd thought of all the times Alex must have been so desperate to attract his brother's attention, and I'd recalled his utter despair when we first met. I didn't understand his journey but I was starting to see why he had to make it.

I'd reached up onto my tiptoes to wind my arms around Rafe's neck, then curled my fingers into his scarf and pulled him closer until we were just a kiss apart. Even in the shadows I'd seen a lightness in his eyes that wasn't there the day I found him passed out at Mellisande.

'I don't think it's crazy at all," I'd told him. "In fact, I think you're probably more right than you'll ever know."

"Oi, you two! Stop snogging! Get a room!" This good-humoured remark from the juggler across the way had been enough to tug us both back into the real world.

"Will getting chips do instead, mate?" Rafe had asked, putting his arm around me and pulling me tightly into his side. I'd had the feeling that if he could have zipped me into his coat he would have done.

"If my missus was as pretty as her, I'd forget the chips and just get the room!" the juggler had called back, and Rafe had raised his eyebrows at me.

"I fully intend to," he'd said huskily and with an expression in his eyes that had made something delicious uncoil deep inside me. Then the corners of his mouth had twitched. "But chips first!"

Rafe and I had eaten chips – piles of golden treasure, crunchy on the outside and piping hot and fluffy when we'd bitten into them – until our tongues had been sore from vinegar and our stomachs so full we could hardly move. As we'd eaten, we'd chatted about everything under the sun. For a moment I'd been tempted to tell Rafe about Simon and my problems at work, but not wanting to spoil the mood I'd held back. There would be plenty of time to talk about that; why should I give Simon a second more of my time? Once the chips had been devoured we'd strolled back to the piazza to watch the jugglers and the fire-eaters. When Rafe had kissed me as the snow began to fall again, I'd known I was in trouble...

"So what are you wearing?"

Dawn's question, asked through a mouthful of soggy Rich Tea biscuits, rips me out of these thoughts and back into the present. I stare at her absent-mindedly, watching the crumbs fall to her cleavage; then I return to last night in the piazza, where I'd been kissing Rafe and a busker had been playing "One Christmas Kiss" in the background.

"This time I won't lose your number," Rafe had promised once we were back outside my flat. He'd tapped it into his mobile. "There. It's saved and when I call it you'll have mine too. I'm not letting you slip away for a second time, Cleo Rose."

I'd glanced up at the flat. The sitting-room light was on, which meant Susie was at home.

"Do you want to come up for…" I'd faltered because it had sounded too cheesy for words. "Coffee?"

Rafe had laughed. "I'd rather come up for something far more exciting than coffee but I know you've an early start tomorrow. Anyhow, from what you've told me about your flatmate, we won't get a minute to ourselves."

"That's true. Susie's a huge Thorne fan. She'll probably mob you before you've even made it through the front door."

He'd grimaced. "My days of fighting off groupies are well and truly over. I'll take the last train back to Bucks and save the battle for another day."

Then Rafe had tilted my chin up and kissed me so softly that I'd melted just like the snowflakes landing on the pavement.

"There's no rush, Cleo," he'd murmured. "I'm not letting you go again. We've got all the time in the world."

All the time in the world. I shiver at this delicious thought and then remember that I'm about to be banished to Egypt. Time is actually running out for us, unless I can find a way to make Simon confess. There has to be something…

"Cleo! Hello! I asked you what you're going to wear!"

"Wear?" I echo. I've got no idea what she's on about.

"The museum Christmas party on Friday night!" She raises her eyes to heaven. "Even you can't have forgotten that!"

"What's that supposed to mean, *even me?*" I say. "On second thoughts, don't answer that; I don't think I want to know."

"I've got this gorgeous pink wrap dress," Dawn is telling me excitedly. "I found it in Primark, but you'd never know. I'm going to Oxford Street later to find some shoes, if you want to come."

I don't, but it's kind of her to ask. If shopping with Susie was traumatic then a session in Oxford Street with the Primarni Queen will cost me years in therapy, and I'll probably end up dressed like Katie Price's less tasteful twin.

"Thanks, Dawn, but I'm pretty busy tonight," I say.

"Well, the offer's there if you change your mind." Dawn slides from the desk. "Just don't go forgetting to turn up to the party like you did last year. You missed a really good night. Security Bill passed out in the punch."

Ah, the good old traditional office Christmas party. Even crusty academics get excited at the thought of free booze and Pringles, and the department's Christmas bash is one of the highlights of the year. Booze flows, there's a tonne of food and everybody dresses up in their glad rags and behaves badly, or as badly as a bunch of academics can. Put it this way: nobody's ever photocopied their backside as far as I know, but one year there was a massive argument between Simon's predecessor and one of the junior staff over the interpretation of some hieroglyphics. Insults were thrown and quite a bit of food too. Yep, that's about as exciting as it gets. Last year I did actually make the effort to dress up and attend, but I was sidetracked by a fascinating twist in my research and by the time I finally made it to the party everybody was plastered and getting ready to leave. Dawn was clutching the mistletoe and crying in a corner, Bill the punch-soaked security guard was snogging the Ancient Greece Department's PA, and the Prof was dancing happily to "Walk Like an Egyptian".

I cannot wait.

"I'll be there," I promise, already thinking that I might live to regret this. Unless I can clear my name, the last thing I'll feel like doing is partying or pretending to be excited about my sudden sabbatical. I'll be more likely to take a leaf out of Security Bill's book and throw myself in the punch. Or, even better, try to drown Simon in it.

I rest my elbows on the desk and place my chin in my hands. I really don't want to go away to Egypt, but neither do I want to stay here and watch Simon gloating. The Professor thinks I'm nuttier than the fruitcake in the museum tearoom. Everything I say and do only reinforces his opinion, and these paranormal experiences make me doubt myself too. If I carry on like this I'm scared that I really will start to go crazy.

I bite my lip. There's only one decision I can really make. It's the hardest and most painful option, but one that at least means I'll leave with my professional reputation intact. There's no point in waiting to see what might happen next, because I'll be in Egypt before you can say pyramid.

My vision blurring, I open Word and start to type. Even though I can barely see, my fingers fly over the keys and before long a letter starts to take form. It's simple and polite and it does the job.

"My dear," says Henry Wellby, reading over my shoulder (which I have to say is one very annoying habit), "are you certain this is the right decision? You surely can't mean to let that scoundrel get away with it?"

"I can't prove what he did," I say bleakly. "Unless you have an idea?"

There's the deathly sound of silence, apart from the whir of the printer as it spits the letter out. Henry Wellby has gone. See, I'm right. If one of the sharpest academic minds of the twentieth century is stumped then there really is no hope. I hunt high and low for a pen so that I can sign the letter – and then I discover that Aamon has hidden them all in the wastepaper basket.

"No!" he wails when I fish one out and scrawl my signature across the page. His big brown eyes are wide and sad. "No!"

Even spectral children learn the word *no*. I try to ruffle his ghostly hair apologetically, but Aamon isn't having this and storms across the office, sending documents, books and paper clips flying around the room.

I do my best to ignore his protest – ducking a few times, it has to be said – and I still manage to place the letter in an envelope. I seal it straight away, before I can change my mind. With a shaking hand, I write the Professor's name on the front; then I deliver the envelope to his secretary. There's no going back now. Even before I'm back in my office tears are rolling down my cheeks and splashing onto the carpet.

I've resigned and Simon's won.

Chapter 27

I've never resigned from a job before so I've absolutely no idea what the etiquette is in these situations. For an hour or so I continue to work on my lecture notes, jumping every time I hear footsteps or voices outside my door in case it's the Prof wanting to discuss my decision, but eventually I admit I'm far too jittery to concentrate. For once my office is deserted, which puts me even more on edge; everything feels off-key and wrong. When I type the same sentence twice I know it's time to acknowledge defeat. I can't concentrate at all. I'd be better off getting out of here and working somewhere else where I won't need to listen to everyone chatting excitedly about Christmas parties or have to watch Simon gloating.

This afternoon is my designated research time, so I'm even more cheesed off when an email pops up from Simon regarding the Everyday Egyptians exhibition, complete with a great long list of jobs he needs me to do. I stare at it in disbelief. These are the kind of tasks you'd usually assign to a very junior member of the department; my experience and expertise are far more useful applied elsewhere, and it's more than clear that Simon isn't so much sticking the boot in as the entire Hunter welly factory.

By the time I reach the third bullet point on his list I'm fuming. I know exactly what he's trying to do here – provoke me until I snap, so that he has further evidence that I'm unstable and not fit to be doing his job, yada yada – but, even so, it's quite an insult.

I fire back a quick email saying that I'll be doing my research off-site and suggesting that Dawn takes charge of these jobs. Then I shut down the computer and pull on my coat. Down the back stairs I go, mobile in hand, and out of the door that leads onto the street.

I feel like I'm playing truant! This is so completely out of character for me. As I stride along the pavement, the wind slicing my cheeks and blowing my hair into wild tangles, I find that I'm smiling. Yesterday's snow has melted to grey mush and the sun is shining. The streets are full of people meandering along with their noses buried in guidebooks or sitting under heaters at pavement cafés, tucking into huge plates of pasta and sipping white wine. My pace slows and with every footstep that puts Simon further behind me I start to feel better. Why haven't I done this before?

I walk for another fifteen minutes. I'm warm now so I unwind my scarf, enjoying the cold air against my skin and the noise and bustle of the city before ducking into a coffee shop to top up my caffeine levels. I order a skinny latte and then settle into a faux leather sofa, brushing aside the muffin wrappers and crumbs to make a space for my cup. The windows have steamed up, the coffee machine hisses away, and the murmur of voices and clatter of spoons against china rise and fall in a tide of sound. The place is swathed in Christmas decorations. They make me nostalgic for the tree Mum always used to dress so beautifully before Tolly and I smothered it with clumsy homemade adornments. I sip my coffee thoughtfully, surprised and pleased that these memories no longer sting quite so much as they once did.

I smile when the seasonal track playing in the background changes from John and Yoko singing about war being over to the instantly recognisable tones of Alex Thorne and "One Christmas Kiss". It's odd but even though he's been such a pain in the neck, I'm actually quite missing having Alex about. I guess maybe the urgency has left him now, so he doesn't need me anymore.

Well, either that or he's off eyeing up girls with Hank.

Rafe's lyrics bring a lump to my throat. Ignoring the old lady in eighteenth-century dress who's complaining bitterly that this was her coffee shop and that she made a much better job of clearing the tables, I unlock the screen on my iPhone and send Rafe a message.

Bad day at the office! How are you? I type, then struggle with the age-old conundrum of whether or not to add an *x* at the end of my message. Leaving it off looks unfriendly; more than one seems a little too keen, stalkerish even. But will putting a kiss on my text be giving too much away? I swear my PhD didn't take this much thought.

In the end I add the *x* then let the text fly. After that I sit and stress until the phone pings with his reply.

Missing you! When can I see you again? X

He sent an *X* back! That has to mean something, surely? It's ridiculous just how delighted I am. Life was certainly simpler when all I thought about was work, that's for sure.

Left work early so am free this afternoon… x

While I wait for a reply the song reaches its conclusion, with Alex singing sadly about how he never knew love could hurt like this. I hope that isn't an omen.

Been busy day - can't get into town tonight : (x

Oh. I stare at the screen, crestfallen. I hadn't realised until this point just how keen I was to see Rafe again. While I'm thinking of what to say next, the text alert pings again.

Really want to see you and soon x

My coffee is cool now and I finish it quickly. An idea starts to take shape in my mind. So Rafe is busy, writing songs I guess, but he says he really wants to see me and I *know* I really want to see him. I've just been listening to the song he wrote about me and it's made me realise that there's no point in wasting time anymore. We've squandered far too much already. If I get moving now I could make the three o'clock train to Riverside Halt and surprise him. I know this behaviour is unlike me, but today is my day for being impulsive.

we'll catch up very soon, I type, *talk later x*

I shove the phone in my bag and gather up my coat. Moments later I'm hailing a taxi to Marylebone. For once the traffic is on my side and the cab sails through the streets with ease. Before long I'm sitting on the 3.18 to High

Wycombe as it winds its way out of London and I'm glimpsing snapshots of people's lifestyles: some of their back gardens are filled with toys, some are strung with washing, and others are weed-strewn and piled with old furniture. All these people and all these lives, I think to myself. In thousands of years' time will people like me study them and conjecture about them? Will researchers sift through the detritus of these people's everyday existence to pose hypotheses and theories, without ever understanding their hopes and dreams, fears and passions? That's what I've done for years, after all. I studied my mummies, discussed their possible ages and speculated over the causes of death – but I never really got it, the fact that they'd once been as alive as me, that they'd cried and laughed and loved. Then it dawns on me that this is exactly why the Prof and so many others are so dedicated to what they do and, of course, the very reason why my family have been so passionate about Aamon.

Alex has enabled me to appreciate this, and getting to know Aamon has taken me even further away from the person I used to be. When he was just a historical figure, an obscure pharaoh from a forgotten time, I'd been able to explore my theories happily. Did his stepmother have him killed in order to rule in his place through her son? It had seemed a possibility and the injuries to poor Aamon's body had certainly been strong evidence in favour of this idea; I can remember how excited I'd been when I'd discovered those. Excited? My skin crawls with shame. Now Aamon isn't a relic but a cheeky little boy who likes playing football, keeps me company and has a dreadful habit of knocking my phone off the hook. The idea of anyone wanting to hurt him turns me cold. His stepmother's crime needs to go down in history – and not because it's an interesting detail, but because it was evil and wrong and people need to know about it.

And this is the point when I finally realise that I've changed. I'm not the person I was a few months ago. My certainties about life, and death, have crumbled away and now everything looks different. It's not just that I've developed the ability to see those who've long since passed away: my behaviour has altered too. Would the old me have left my job in the middle of the day and raced back to the Home Counties to be with a man I've only known for a couple of weeks? Or forgiven my father and chosen to spend Christmas with him? Or cared about Aamon the child rather than the artefact I've been studying? I think I know the answers to these questions, and they make me very grateful indeed that I had my accident. The things I've lost have been more than compensated for by everything I've gained.

While I mull these thoughts over the train tears through Buckinghamshire, the landscape falling into shadow as the sun puts her head down for a nap on the pillowy hills. My stomach folds with excitement at the thought of seeing Rafe again.

Dusk is falling by the time I reach High Wycombe, so I treat myself to another cab rather than waiting for the branch-line train. As the journey takes me through the winding lanes, I grow more excited with every mile that brings me closer to Rafe. At last the car pulls up outside the gates of Mellisande, after steering around a white BMW parked by the kerb at a careless angle. I jump out and call to the cabbie to keep the change. Shoving the gates open, I sprint up the pathway, skirt Rafe's red Ferrari and leap the three steps up to the front door.

"Rafe!" I call, hammering my fist against the ancient wood. "Hello! Rafe! It's me, Cleo!"

I pause, expecting to hear the approach of his footsteps, but there's nothing.

"Rafe?" I thump the door again and then jangle the old bell too, but there's still no response. I frown for a moment, the romantic reunion that I'd envisaged with such delicious anticipation thwarted – although it has to be said that Rafe doesn't have a great track record when it comes to answering his front door to me. Now what?

I knock again; still nothing. Then a thought occurs to me and I laugh aloud because the answer is glaringly obvious. Of course Rafe can't hear me! He's bound to be in the recording studio, which I know is soundproofed. Buoyed by this realisation I abandon the porch and retrace the path I took the last time I was here. The garden is shrouded in shadows and the Thames beyond is invisible as it flows silently back towards the city I've just left. The sky is clotted with heavy clouds, heralding more snow perhaps, and my eyes strain to pick out the route. When I turn the corner and head for the back of the house I'm relieved to see fingers of yellow light stretching into the creeping darkness. That's the recording studio, so I was right: Rafe is busy working and couldn't hear me knocking.

The curtains of the studio haven't been drawn. Rafe must have been so absorbed in what he's doing that he hasn't noticed the night falling. I smile because this is exactly how it is for me when I'm working. Hours can pass and I won't have noticed. Sometimes I even go an entire day without eating – something Susie can't understand at all, but that I know Rafe will relate to. Moving against the outside wall I slide along the perimeter of a flowerbed, taking care not to stumble, until I reach the window. Then I slowly peer around the edge.

My eyes take a moment to adapt to the brightness in the room, a brightness that illuminates the couple deep in conversation behind the glass. The man, midnight haired, lean hipped and with his back to me, is Rafe; I'd know him anywhere. The slender golden-haired woman opposite him is equally recognisable from billboards and magazines.

My eyes widen because this woman is none other than Natasha Lacey, the model ex who broke his heart. She's here? No wonder he told me he was busy. I can hardly believe it. This is like a scene from one of Susie's novels, the kind where the heroine sees her man kissing another woman and is heartbroken.

"It's all utter nonsense," Susie had laughed, when she'd caught me leafing through her latest romcom. "As if things like that ever happen in real life! And if it did, she'd go and confront him, wouldn't she? Not just slink away and cry. As if!"

I turn on my heel and melt back into the darkness. I don't need to see any more. As it turns out, Susie's wrong. In real life there's no need to confront anyone. Natasha and Rafe may only be talking, but that isn't the point: Rafe has lied to me and that's all I need to know. The rest is just detail.

Chapter 28

How I make it up the path, through the gate and across the dark fields to Riverside Halt, I will never know. My chest is tight and I hurl myself, gasping, along the footpath until the lights of the small railway platform begin to glow their welcome through the night.

My breath is coming in painful sobs. This station, where Rafe and I first met, is the very last place I want to be right now. Dashing the tears from my eyes I push through the small gate and walk along the deserted platform. It's a lonely spot to be on a late December evening; anyone sensible is indoors by the fire. Shadows loom across the platform, while litter blows along the tracks. An owl hoots from the trees and I shiver. I hope a train arrives soon. I want to be as far from this place and Rafe Thorne as possible.

The small bench is still there, stranded in the middle of the platform and looking as forlorn as I feel. Reaching it, I sink down onto it and close my eyes. How is it possible that I've swung from such delicious excitement to crushing despair in a heartbeat? One moment I'm giddy with anticipation because I'm only seconds away from Rafe, the next I'm racing away as fast as I can with sobs tightening my throat. I can't believe Natasha was there with him. Why didn't he tell me he was seeing her this evening? Thank God I left when I did.

Rafe and Natasha. Natasha and Rafe.

There was no mistaking what I'd glimpsed through the window. Rafe is spending time with his beautiful ex, the woman whose rejection he as good as told me had sent him plummeting into despair just weeks ago. And who can blame him? She's gorgeous and understands the world of celebrity and supercars and wealth; just seeing them together tells me that she belongs there with him. Where I belong I have no idea. I thought it was with Rafe, but I realise now that was nothing but an illusion, a lovely dream – a product of my head injury, perhaps. I used to feel at home working in the Wellby, but Simon has destroyed that sanctuary now. I belong nowhere.

I bury my face in my hands and allow the hot tears to flow. How could he have written those words, immortalising our long-ago snowy meeting so beautifully – and even held me against his heart only hours before – if he was planning to meet up with Natasha? How is it possible that what meant so much to me meant so little to him?

How did I allow Rafe Thorne to get so close?

By deluding myself that our chance meeting meant more than it really did, that's how. I let myself believe in soul mates and fate and ghosts, and by doing so I opened the floodgates. Was I crazy? I know all this is nonsense, but for a while it felt real, more real than anything I've ever known.

I wipe my eyes on my sleeve and take a deep, shuddering breath. I know I have to take control of myself. The train will be here in a moment and I can't get on looking like a hobgoblin; I'll scare the other commuters. I can't sit here blubbing in public.

But it's no good. No matter how many pep talks the logical part of me comes up with, none of them makes any difference. This feels a million, million times worse than having my ideas stolen or resigning from the job I adore. I love Rafe Thorne far more than any of these things.

There's an abrupt screeching of brakes in my mind and I sit bolt upright with shock. What did I just say? That I love Rafe? I'm horrified that my heart skips a beat just at the thought of him. A montage of images flickers through my mind: his lips, the silky texture of his hair when I run my hands through it, the rasp of his stubble against my throat, the scent of him when I bury my face in his neck, the teasing eyes and one-cornered smile, the way he'd once wiped my tears away with his thumb…

Rafe Thorne. My past, my present and, I'd started to hope, my future too. Dig deep enough in the archaeology of my heart and you'll find Rafe right there, as much a part of me as my curly red hair or my freckles. I'd just never realised it until a bang on the head brought me to my senses.

I'm in love with Rafe Thorne, and knowing this makes me cry even harder. I saw him just now with Natasha, and whatever strange game he's been playing I want no more part in it. I just want to be left alone to piece myself together. Maybe I'm overreacting but I don't think so. He hasn't been straight with me and that isn't merely my opinion – it's a fact. As I dab my eyes I bitterly regret handing in my resignation: I should have taken the sabbatical instead. A year in Egypt no longer feels long enough or far away enough for me.

Snow-pregnant clouds have been building slowly, billowing in from the north, and now fat flakes begin to fall softly. The colour has leached out of the world and I watch mesmerised as the snowflakes whirl and spin in the beam of the lamplight. My fingers and toes are numb with cold, but I hardly notice because I want to be frozen. I don't want to feel anything ever again.

"What's the matter?" The voice comes out of nowhere, making me jump. In the gloom it's hard to make out the tall figure standing next to me, and for a moment I think it's Rafe. My treacherous heart leaps gladly, only to plummet again when I see that this is Alex. The same lean frame, strong wide shoulders and long dark hair, of course, but these are green eyes looking at me with huge concern, rather than those thrilling violet ones. He steps forward.

"Cleo? Are you crying?"

I turn my face into the shadows. I don't want to talk to Alex now, let alone explain myself to him.

"Go away."

"You *are* crying." He's sitting next to me now and I'm not sure what's colder – the flurries of snowflakes landing on my face and hands, or being close to him. "What's wrong?"

I round on Alex, the stresses and strains and disappointments of the last few weeks rising up inside me like an emotional Vesuvius. When I erupt it's with such force that he recoils.

"Everything! Absolutely everything! You've lost me my job, my sanity, my professional reputation–" My voice cracks because there's one more thing I'm not adding to the list: my heart. "My life's in a mess because of *you*!"

Alex stares at me – one beat, two beats, three beats – then I look away. I hate myself for lying to him. My life's not a mess because of Alex: my life's tumbling down around my ears because I was stupid enough to fall in love with Rafe Thorne. That happened long before I ever met Alex and I know I'm being unfair, but right now I just want to lash out at somebody. Besides, until Alex showed up and turned my world upside down I was happy, wasn't I? I had everything on an even keel and beautifully ordered, and if it wasn't always exciting at least it was safe. I went on dates, I wrote papers, I delivered lectures and I rarely cried. Now I'm afraid that I'll never stop.

"Cleo, I'm sorry," Alex says helplessly. "I thought everything was going so well." He rakes a hand through his hair. "That was why I stayed away. I can't explain it but everything felt good. You were happy. Rafe was happy–"

"Of course Rafe's happy! He's back with Natasha!" I can't help myself; the words fly from my mouth to land a verbal double whammy and Alex reels.

"What? That's absurd," he says, looking utterly astonished. "Of course he isn't! Rafe's crazy about you. He's always been crazy about you."

"So crazy about me that he's with his ex right now," I tell him bitterly. "Don't look at me like that, Alex. It's true. I've just seen them together."

Bemusement is written across his face. "No way. You're wrong, Cleo. I know my brother. He loved you from the minute he first saw you. There's no way he'd get back with Natasha. She was never important."

"She's with him now. I saw them, Alex. He told me he was busy and now I know why!"

There's a whispering along the tracks and in the far distance two lights shine, throwing beams of brightness into the night. My train is coming. Thank goodness. I'll step back on it and return to London and Rafe Thorne will never be any the wiser. I might go home and weep until I look like a frog, but at least I'll have kept my dignity. Imagine if I'd told him how I felt about him. Just thinking about this makes me feel sick.

"There's got to have been a mistake," Alex is saying desperately. I rise from the bench to walk to the far end of the halt, where the single-carriage train will pull in; Alex tries to grab my arm, but his fingers slide straight through me. "He's loved you for ten years. Why would he risk everything now by seeing Natasha? It doesn't make any sense."

"There's no mistake." I shoulder my bag and raise my chin. Ten years of missed opportunities tighten my throat with loss. The memories Rafe and I might have shared, the adventures we could have enjoyed, the children we could have had... All are gone now, along with the chance of ever making up for that lost time.

The train draws into the station. Brakes squeal and the signal turns red.

"There has to have been a misunderstanding," Alex insists. "Let me find out what's really happened. Cleo, please!"

"Just go away, Alex," I say, pressing the button to open the carriage doors. I can't even summon the energy to be angry any longer. "You've destroyed my career; isn't that enough for you? Rafe is writing again, he's not drinking and he's back with his girlfriend. He's sorted. Isn't that what you wanted?"

"No!" Alex cries as I board the train. "I wanted him to be with you! That's what I promised him and that's what needed to happen." His face is anguished and he's starting to fade, melting into the shadows with every second that passes. "Tell me what I can do to put it right."

So I tell him. "You can leave me alone if you really want to help. If you want to do the right thing you'll go away. You've done enough damage. I wish you'd never come looking for me in the first place."

"You don't mean that. I know you don't."

"I do! Just go away, Alex! I never want to see or hear from you or Rafe again, do you hear me? Leave me alone!"

The signal turns green and the doors hiss closed. As the train winds its way out of the small station I close my eyes to stop the tears from falling again, but even though I can't see him I know that Alex is watching. I sense his despair in every rattle of the vehicle and in every whistle of cold air that blows through the carriage, but as the miles stretch out between me and Rafe, Alex's grief is nothing to my own. I turn my face to the window and watch the snowflakes waltzing by in an endless dance, and then my tears hide them for the rest of the journey.

It's feels as though I'm drowning in misery here in my London bedroom. I lie on my bed staring at the ceiling and listening to Susie moving around the flat. No matter how hard I try, I can't seem to summon the energy to sit up, have a shower and rejoin the real world. My mobile's been ringing at regular intervals and beeping with text messages, which I've ignored. I've texted Dawn to say I'm working from home today. I really don't have the will to talk to anyone else.

I hardly know what I'm crying about anymore. The tears just won't stop. Is it Rafe's betrayal? Or my row with Alex? Simon's theft of my work? Mum's death? My accident? Everything has rolled into one big knot of grief and I can't seem to find a way of unpicking it. It's ridiculous! Until recently I'd prided myself that I hadn't cried for years, but suddenly I've lost control and nothing seems able to pull me back from the chasm of despair I've toppled into.

My logical part of my brain is patiently telling me that this is an overreaction, that Rafe's somebody I barely know and that these feelings for him are just another manifestation of my head trauma. There's an illogical part of me though, which is saying quietly that I've always been in love with Rafe Thorne and have been since the day I first met him – even though I did my best to put him firmly out of my mind.

I turn my head to the wall. I want the old me back again, the Cleo Carpenter whose life was full of certainties and who was supremely confident she had all the answers. Without any warning I've jumped from having life neatly figured out to being lost in the pitch dark without even a single match to strike a light and guide me. It's terrifying. For the first time since my accident I'm truly scared that I've done myself serious damage. Paranormal experiences? Falling in love with strangers? Handing in my resignation? These things don't belong to my real life. What if they're symptoms of something far worse?

I sit up and reach for my iPhone. By the time I've finished Googling *signs of serious brain injury* I've convinced myself I'm ill. I'm behaving extremely out of character – one of the indicators on the checklist, apparently – and I need help.

Just as I'm reaching this conclusion, the bedroom door flies open and Susie sails in, armed with a mug of tea and with the biscuit tin wedged between her chin and chest. She places these down on my bedside table and then rips open the curtains, flooding the room with bright wintery light, while I recoil like something from *Twilight*.

"It's snowed!" she exclaims excitedly. "Have a look. It's really pretty."

I know it's snowed. My train journey home was delayed for ages thanks to the white floaty stuff, and I had to walk back in it too because the buses weren't running properly. By the time I finally arrived home I was a Cleo ice pop and feeling even more wretched, if that was possible. I think I can be forgiven for not being in raptures about the snow.

She tugs at my duvet. "Come and have a look, lazybones. Up you get!"

I pity Susie's patients if this is an example of her bedside manner. Can't I just be left alone to be maudlin in peace?

"I'm not feeling well," I croak in a hopefully genuine way. My throat is sore from crying and I do have a headache too, so I'm not exactly faking.

"Bollocks." Susie hurls herself down on the bed and fixes me with a knowing look. "I'm a medic, remember? I know when somebody's genuinely ill and you, Cleo Carpenter, are as fit as a fiddle. Granted, you look like shit, but you're not ill. I know a bad case of *man trouble* when I see it."

"What?"

"You heard me. I've spent more hours than I care to think about bawling my eyes out over some tosser who didn't deserve a nanosecond of my time and I'm telling you, girl friend, that lying in bed is not the answer!"

It isn't? It had seemed like a pretty good solution to me. Still, Susie is an expert on these things and in spite of myself I'm intrigued.

"So what is the answer?" I ask curiously. "Not that I'm having man trouble, of course. I'm just wondering."

"Getting out there and showing him what he's missing! Victorian melodrama is so over!" She looks worried. "This really isn't like you, Cleo. In fact, I've never known you lie in bed this long. He must be somebody really special."

I'd thought so too. As it turns out I couldn't have been more wrong. I try to conjure up Rafe's face, but all I can see is him deep in conversation with the gorgeous Natasha. Did he kiss her? I feel the urge to be sick. I can't share any of this with Susie though. It's too painful – and we'll still be talking about the fact that I've slept with a rock star when we're sucking our suppers through straws in a care home.

"It's not man trouble anyway," I fib, crossing my fingers under the duvet. "It's work stuff."

Susie's hand flies to her mouth. "I'm such a dimwit. Of course it is! That bloody Simon! Oh babes, there has to be a way you can prove what he did. Come on, Cleo. Use your giant brain!"

"My giant brain isn't working so well lately," I confess sadly. "I'm starting to wonder if I really did myself some harm when I was knocked down."

"Double vision? Loss in taste or smell? Problems with balance? Headaches?" Susie demands and I shake my head to each of her suggestions, but if she adds *seeing ghosts* or *falling in love with damaged unsuitable men* I'll be off to the hospital before you can say poorly.

"You're probably okay then. In fact I think your bang on the head did you some good," Susie says thoughtfully. "You certainly seem to have had a lot more fun since, and your taste in clothes has improved too. You'll be out clubbing with me before you know it! No, babes, I think you're fine."

Even though I'm miserable I can't help laughing. My life is in ruins but as far as Susie's concerned wearing Topshop fashions more than makes up for this. It's one way of seeing the world, I suppose.

"I'm emotional, I'm losing sight of my priorities, I have feelings for unsuitable men and my work's gone pear-shaped. I'm hardly fine!" I point out.

"Real life's just caught up with you, that's all," Susie concludes. "It had to happen sooner or later, Cleo. You've been hiding away in your work for far too long." Then I see a sudden spark of excitement illuminate her face. "And anyway, who are these unsuitable men?"

"It's just a figure of speech. There was somebody I liked but it was never going to happen. He wasn't for me."

"That's not a head injury, Cleo: that's dating. You are one hundred percent fine."

Satisfied with her diagnosis, my best friend flips open the biscuit tin and hands me a digestive. "I prescribe you eat this, take a hot shower and then get ready for your Christmas party. Go to the museum and hold your head high. You've done nothing wrong. Show that Simon that you're not defeated. He's messed with the wrong person this time and now it's war. It's only a matter of time before he gives himself away. Then you can wear his balls as earrings."

"Blimey," I say, taken aback. "Remind me not to annoy you."

She winks. "You don't spend ten years in the NHS without learning to toughen up. There's a way to prove he's a cheating lowlife; you just have to find it, that's all."

We munch our biscuits in companionable silence. The thought of Rafe is still painful but I know I'm going to have to get used to this. Simon Welsh, however, is a different matter entirely. Dare I hope that there's still a chance I can expose him? If I can tell Aamon's story – drawing my mother and grandmother's lifelong work to the ultimate conclusion – and manage to salvage my career, it might soothe the ache in my heart. My work has always been a great panacea.

Tea drunk, biscuit eaten and one funny story about Susie's love life later, I'm feeling a little more human. I delete the six texts from Rafe without reading them, clear the call register and then swing my legs over the side of the bed. Bambi-like, I walk to the window and gaze out at the snowy city. It's only the slightest dusting but enough to make the street look magical. Over there, hidden behind the rooftops and iced treetops, is the museum and the work that I love, as well as a cheating colleague. I need to be there. I can't give in without at least trying.

"You're right, Susie," I say. "I've got a party to go to."

Chapter 29

If Susie hadn't chosen nursing as a career then she would have made a fantastic make-up artist. By the time I arrive at the museum there's no sign of my earlier sob fest. Armed with her brushes and lotions and tubes of goo, my best friend has smoothed away my tearstains beautifully. I catch a glimpse of my reflection in the glass of the door and think that if she could restore the same glow and sparkle to the way I feel, she might be really onto something.

"Wow! You look amazing!" Dawn, squeezed into a tiny pink frock that's trying valiantly to contain her boobs, joins me in the museum café, which this evening has been turned into the venue for the party. The place is packed with the museum staff and chatter flows as easily as the cava.

"You too," I tell her, and I'm not joking. She does look amazing. She's channelling her inner WAG tonight and I can't help being mesmerised by her giant false eyelashes the size of tarantulas. The hairpiece too is a feat of engineering, piled high and topped with a sprig of emergency mistletoe. In my floor-length green velvet dress and with my hair in loose curls over my shoulders I'm feeling a little underdressed in comparison.

"Thanks! My Gary said I look like I'm off to a lap-dance bar, cheeky git," she giggles, swiping a handful of canapés from a plate and cramming them into her lipsticked mouth. "Mmm! Yummy! You should try those, Cleo. They're lush!"

I don't think I can eat. My stomach is churning like a washing machine on spin and it's as much as I can do to sip my drink rather than hurl it down my neck. I'm ill at ease here; the place is full partying people, both living and dead, and I'm starting to feel crowded. Maybe this was a mistake.

"I said to Gary, if I can't dress up and let my hair down on Christmas Eve, then when can I?" Dawn grins. "Ooo! Talking of letting my hair down, there's

Simon and he's coming over! Doesn't he look gorgeous! I wonder if he'll let me try out my mistletoe?" One tarantula-like row of eyelashes winks at me. "Or maybe you'd like to give it a go?"

I'd rather mummify my head than kiss Simon. Sure enough though, he's making a beeline straight for me. He looks ridiculously handsome in a black tux, with his blond hair hanging to his shoulders and his blue eyes bright in his fine-boned face. The look he gives me is glacial but Dawn doesn't notice.

"I'll let you into a secret." She nudges me. "I think Simon really likes you. He's always talking about you. He'll be gutted when you go to Egypt."

"Who says I'm going to Egypt?" I mutter. The closer Simon gets the angrier I feel. When he finally weaves his way through the crowd to join us it's all I can do to resist kicking him in the shins.

"Dawn, looking beautiful as always!" Simon leans forward, has a good gawp down her Cheddar Gorge cleavage and then kisses her cheek, while Dawn simpers and turns the same colour as her frock. Afterwards, he smiles down at me. "And the lovely Cleo too. I didn't expect to see you here tonight."

I glower at him. "Really? Why not?"

He shrugs. "You've been unwell lately and I know that my promotion has been difficult for you. Nobody would have thought ill of you if you'd stayed at home and rested."

"That's very thoughtful of you," I reply, so acidly that I'm amazed my tongue doesn't shrivel.

He laughs. "I'm always thinking of you, Cleo. Did you like idea of the secondment in Egypt, by the way? Paul thought you'd be happy staying here but I managed to persuade him that you're far too ambitious for that."

I keep my face impassive but I'm clutching my champagne flute so hard it must be close to shattering. He doesn't know that I've resigned, which means the Prof hasn't told him. Is this because the Prof doesn't want to accept my resignation or because he's starting to have doubts about Simon?

Simon reaches forward and brushes a curl from my face. "I'm loving seeing your hair like that, by the way. It's wild and out of control. Is that a side of you that we'll see here this evening?"

I snap my head away. Much as I'd love to slap him I have to bite back my anger. I'm still searching for a suitable retort when a voice calls to me across the party. Henry Wellby and Aamon are waving frantically from the staircase.

"Dr Carpenter! Come up to your office! Bring the scoundrel with you!" Wellby calls. He's brandishing his hat excitedly while Aamon bounces beside him. "We have a plan!"

We do? It's a sign of the times that I'm willing to go along with figments of my imagination, but what do I have to lose? It's not as though I've managed to figure out a solution of my own. I catch Simon's elbow and look up at him.

"There's something we need to talk about," I say. "In private."

"Oh! Don't mind me!" Dawn's eyes widen. She drains her glass and grins. "I need another one of these anyway."

"We can talk here," Simon insists as Dawn wiggles away, the dress doing a sterling job of containing her rear end. "Besides, you must realise there's no point going over it all again."

"Appeal to his academic curiosity," Wellby urges. "He won't be able to resist."

I keep my hand on Simon's elbow. "There's one thing you didn't manage to find. It's the key to everything."

His eyes light up. "I knew there had to be more. What is it?"

"It's text on the base of the statue," I say. I bet he never even thought to check underneath it. Simon's lazy like that.

"And why would you share this with me?"

His interest is piqued. Time to reel him in.

I shrug. "Because I'm an academic and I want the full story on the record. But up to you, I guess." I make a show of glancing around the crowded room. "Where's the Prof? He may be more use anyway."

"Paul's still in his office. He had a last-minute funding meeting to chair. All right, Cleo, you have my full attention. Let's go."

We edge our way through the party, nodding and saying hello to various colleagues and acquaintances. Simon collects another drink on the way. His cheeks are flushed and he's clearly had a few already. Will alcohol make him careless?

As we mount the staircase and then head for the departmental area, the chatter and chinking of glasses start to fade. All I can hear when I turn my key and let us into the office is the ratcheting up of my pulse.

"Let me guess," drawls Simon, looking around idly while I flick on the light. "You've actually linked the death of Aamon with the succession of his stepmother, Sehepne? But hard rather than circumstantial evidence?"

I nod. "Yes, I have proof that Sehepne murdered him. The injuries to the body are inconclusive, but my mother had evidence that confirms the crime."

"You'd better pass that to me then." Simon folds his arms across his chest. "This is my area of expertise now, not your pet project."

Pet project? For a second I'm robbed of speech. The cat is hissing like crazy, Aamon blows raspberries and even Henry Wellby uses a few choice words, but of course none of this bothers my colleague. Water finds it harder to slide off a duck's back. My fingers are itching to slap his smug face. How did I ever find him attractive?

"Goad him!" Henry Wellby barks. "Make him say something! And for God's sake, don't give him that evidence."

I can't because it's on the bottom of my statue, which is safely hidden in my bedroom. Not that I'd give it to him anyway. I'm determined that I'll get my research back and tell Aamon's story properly rather than allow Simon's half-baked tabloid-style retelling.

"I'll have to dig it out," I say through clenched teeth. "It'll take a while."

"Well, get a move on. God, this is a chilly office." Simon is looking around disdainfully. "Poky too, and dark. I don't suppose you'll miss it that much. I bet you're looking forward to Luxor, aren't you? It'll be a darn sight warmer than here."

I bristle like the cat. "I don't know how you've even got the gall to speak to me after everything you've done."

"And what exactly have I done?" Simon takes a large swig of his wine and widens his blue eyes.

"Stolen my research!"

There's a rattle from the corner of the room. Aamon is playing with the phone again but unusually Henry Wellby is helping him. They appear to be trying to figure out how to dial. Knowing my luck they're probably onto Domino's by now. So much for a great plan. That pesky phone is one thing I won't miss.

Simon shakes his head sadly. "So dramatic, Cleo. That head injury really hasn't helped you, has it?"

"It's helped *you*," I say bitterly.

"I can't deny it." The satisfaction in his voice sets my teeth on edge. Simon's face is bright with victory and as he settles himself onto my desk I know he's just dying to twist the knife. The alcohol has loosened his tongue and, like a *Scooby-Doo* villain, he simply can't resist telling me how clever he's been.

"I'll grant you it's been useful," he agrees. "You really are far too naïve, Dr Carpenter, and far too trusting."

"Honest and trustworthy are how I'd describe myself," I shoot back. "Simon, I trusted you! I thought we were friends. Why else would I have left my application with you and given my laptop into your keeping?"

Simon smirks. "Yes, I must admit that was a bit of luck I hadn't anticipated."

"And my documents on the network? I take it that it was you who wiped them?"

"Of course that was me. You'd been so helpful too, labelling all the folders so beautifully. It only took me minutes. You'd chosen a blindingly obvious password and used the same one for everything, which helped. It's disappointing really, Cleo. I thought you were smarter than that."

I begin to open my mouth to tell him exactly what I think of this, but Simon's still gloating, enjoying every minute of his triumph. He finishes his drink and starts to laugh.

"Of course, all this would have been a great deal harder had you not suffered your unfortunate head injury. Not much usually gets past Dr Carpenter, the department's golden girl, does it? Jesus, Cleo, have you any idea how bloody nauseating it is for the rest of us to always be compared to you and have to listen to the Prof drivelling on about how brilliant you are?" His teeth are bared in a sneer. "He probably just wants to get in your knickers, but you're a frigid bitch, aren't you? Even I never managed that. He's got more hope of shagging one of the mummies."

"You're disgusting," I say, sickened. To be confronted with such venom is shocking. How did I not notice that Simon hated me so much?

He shrugs. "Maybe, but I'm the Associate Director of our department and you're being shipped out all the way to Egypt, so call me whatever you like. The truth is, Cleo, you've lost. Your research is mine, your job is mine – and your reputation? Well, let's be honest, I wouldn't want that because it's in tatters. You've been flaky lately, head injury or not, and you're not on top of your game. It's disappointing. I'd expected more of you. This has all been rather too easy."

In a haze of rage I watch him hop off the desk and saunter around the office, picking up my belongings and rifling through my documents as though he has every right to do so.

"You won't get away with this," I promise him, but Simon gives me a pitying look.

"I already have, many times, Cleo. I'm good at what I do. Make all the fuss you want. Nobody will believe you; they'll just think you're jealous. Which you are, and I totally understand. Of course the job was going to be yours – we all knew that – which was why I needed to level the playing field a little."

"Level the playing field? With what? A wrecking ball? Simon, you cheated!"

Simon smiles at me. "I do hope they're an understanding faculty in Luxor. I'd hate any rumours of your instability to reach them out there. That could cause all kinds of problems."

"Are you threatening me?"

"Are you threatening me?" he mimics. "God, for such an intelligent woman you can be very stupid at times. Yes, Cleo, I'm threatening you, or maybe more accurately I'm giving you a promise. If you continue trying to tell everyone that I've stolen your research I'll make it my personal mission to ensure that what academic reputation you do have is left in such tatters you'll be lucky to get a job teaching GCSE history in a sink school." He leans forward until his face is inches from mine. "Do I make myself clear?"

"Very," I say bitterly.

"Good." Business completed, Simon meanders to the window, beams at his reflection in the glass and smooths his hair. "Now where's that evidence you promised me?"

"It's at home."

"At home? What was this wild goose chase in aid of then? I thought you had it here?" He looks at me with great irritation, straightens his tie and picks a bit of dill from between his teeth. "Go and get it then, and make sure you drop it in to me on the first working day back after Christmas."

And with this parting shot Simon strides out of my office.

"Well, that went well," I begin to say to Henry Wellby – but it seems that Simon isn't the only one who's left: my office is deserted. Even the dead have given up. Deflated, I switch off the light, lock the door and make my way back to the party. I've tried my hardest to fight Simon but he's too cunning and his trap has well and truly sprung on me. The more I protest the crazier I'll look.

Back in the museum café the party is in full swing, but I'm in no mood to celebrate. Collecting my coat and bag I leave the action just as "One Christmas Kiss" begins to play. Couples peel away from the throng and begin to sway together as Alex's unmistakable voice begins to sing and another little piece of my heart crumbles.

I push through the crowd and stumble outside into the cold air. I want nothing more than to be as far away from here as possible. I pull my phone from my pocket, frowning when I see three more missed calls from Rafe and a text from Simon demanding that I bring him the evidence I mentioned or he'll have to speak to Paul. I feel sick with dread.

I'm still staring at the screen, trying to work out what on earth to do next, when the phone begins to ring, vibrating in my palm like an angry wasp. *Prof H*, says the caller display, and with a shaking finger I swipe it to the off setting. It didn't take Simon long to go telling tales. The phone rings again instantly and this time I turn it off completely. Whatever it is the Prof has to say, it can wait.

It's cold outside and I walk away from the museum, pulling my thin jacket tightly around my shoulders and trying to marshal my thoughts. The snow is starting to fall again, spiralling down in dizzying whirls and dusting the pavements and the railings. The windows of the shops twinkle with fairy lights and from the café on the corner "One Christmas Kiss" is playing on the radio. I don't think I've ever felt so alone in my life. What do I do? Where do I go? I wander aimlessly, my teeth chattering with both the cold and the realisation that for probably the first time in my life I have no plan at all. When a cab swishes along beside me I jump because I've been so lost in thought.

"Are you all right, love?" The window hisses down and the cabbie, a man in his mid fifties, bald and pink faced, leans across, giving me a concerned look. "It's a bit parky to be out in your evening dress."

He's right. I'm freezing. I've been so lost in my misery that I've hardly noticed the cold. The sky is thick with ominous clouds. More snow is coming.

"I'm fine, thanks," I say. "Honestly."

"You're blue, love! Come on, hop in," he says. "You'll catch your death wandering about like that and I can't have that on my conscience."

As though in a dream, I clamber in. The warm fug inside is almost shocking.

"Where to, love?" asks the cabbie. He has an elderly woman in the front seat beside him but is totally oblivious to her. Well, of course he is. She's yet another ghost. They're everywhere. I may have told Alex to leave me alone but the others are still there, superimposed on the real world like a clumsy Photoshop effect, and I have a nasty feeling they always will be.

"Hello, dear," she says. "Could you tell my son he needs to drive more slowly? And why isn't he wearing a vest in this weather? He needs a vest!"

The cabbie is waiting for my response. Where do I want to go? Back to a time before this whole mess began, that's where.

In that case the answer's obvious. I'll go back to where it all began, my love of Egypt, Aamon, Mum and, most painfully of all, Rafe Thorne. Maybe there I can start to make sense of everything.

"Marylebone station, please," I say. "As soon as possible."

The cabbie lets the clutch up and the car glides back into the traffic.

"Going anywhere nice, love?" he asks.

"Yes," I say, and for the first time in ages I feel the tension begin to slide away. "I'm going home."

Chapter 30

The station is dark and deserted, veiled by the falling snow and seeming to materialise from nowhere when the train rounds the final curve in the tracks. The carriage is empty and I've travelled in thoughtful silence ever since changing trains at High Wycombe.

My iPhone lies loosely in my palm. When I turn it on again there are two more missed calls from Rafe, logged since I left London, and a text from Susie telling me she's staying with Dave tonight. There's nothing more from Simon, thank goodness, although the Prof has tried again and appears to have left a voicemail. I stare at the screen for a few moments, toying with the idea of listening to it, before exhaling slowly. There's plenty of time for this later on. I've had more than enough of Simon's games for one evening and, anyway, the battery's very low. I turn the phone off again, wanting to conserve what little power remains. My father's at a school play and has promised to come and collect me as soon as he's able, but his timekeeping has always been dreadful and I'll probably need enough battery to call a taxi before I freeze to death.

The train slows and then shudders to a halt. I press the button to open the doors and step out onto the platform, which is every bit as snowy and as empty as it was all those years ago. The place is dark and utterly silent, the snow spiralling down onto the motionless world without a whisper. Behind me the doors hiss shut. The train accelerates with a growl, then rounds the track and vanishes into the darkness.

I pull my jacket tighter around my shoulders. In the orangey light of the lamps I watch the snowflakes tumbling to earth, dancing and waltzing before silently disappearing. The world beyond Riverside Halt is muffled, and as I walk along the platform I notice that my footsteps are left in the light dusting.

The waiting room is in darkness. I rattle the door but it's locked, so I hug myself against the cold and shiver. There's no sign of my father. What do I do now?

Litter rustles on the tracks, whisked up by the wind, and the station clock ticks the minutes away. I wander further along the platform, exhaustion prickling my eyes. There's the bench, hard metal with a curved back – the same bench where Rafe held me all those years ago. Tears make the scene swim. I wish so much that I could rewind the years. He'll appear then, with his guitar slung across his back and his black hair falling over his face; he'll brush it away as he smiles and holds out his hand.

"You're sad and it's Christmas," he'll say. "Nobody should be sad at Christmas."

I sigh. I don't think sad even comes close to how I'm feeling. Maybe the word for this biting sense of loss hasn't even been invented yet. Regret, loneliness, confusion… These are the emotions that chase through me, and of all the things that have hurt me I know that Rafe seeing Natasha behind my back is the most painful. He's been a part of me for so long, and for a few heady days I thought he was the future too. The future is wide open now in every possible way.

I lower myself onto the bench, flinching as the icy metal chills my skin even through my dress. The snow is thicker now, obliterating the world beyond. The station clock seems to tick slower and slower as though time, too, is freezing. Maybe it is. Perhaps only moments rather than years have passed since Rafe and I first met here? Or maybe I've slipped back in time and we haven't even met yet? Imagine that. All the opportunities and chances are still out there for the taking, just waiting for me to reach for them.

That makes me smile. It's a lovely fantasy but that's all it will ever be. I know now that life doesn't offer any second chances. Alex tried his best to make me believe otherwise, but Alex, if he ever existed at all, was wrong. We get one shot and if we mess it up, then tough. We have to learn to deal with our mistakes and live with them as best we can. My father knows this, Rafe knows this and, after the past couple of months, I know it too. All my certainties have melted away, just as the snow has dissolved in patches where the platform's been gritted.

A tear slips down my cheek and I dash it away impatiently. It's too cold to cry and my face feels raw with the clawing wind. Across the fields church bells sound as the ringers begin their practice, chimes echoing and trembling across the still world, taking me back to that long-ago Christmas Eve. Memories roll over me with each peal. Weary of fighting them, I close my eyes and dream that I'm nineteen again, just a girl alone on a railway platform waiting for life and love to write a footnote in her own history, an aside she'll remember until the day she dies.

There's growl of a car engine, followed by the slamming of a door. I gulp my misery back and wipe my eyes on my sleeve. This has to be my dad at last, miraculously on time for once. Footsteps crunch on snow, keys jangle and through the dancing flakes I see a man at the far end of the platform, striding towards me through the darkness.

Wait. He's tall. Taller than my father and wide shouldered, lean hipped and with such presence that my every cell wants to cry out in recognition. I don't need to see the crimson scarf, the stubble-shadowed jaw, the dark hair or the mouth set in a determined expression to know who this is. My heart is already telling me.

"You're sad and it's Christmas," Rafe calls softly, holding out his hand. "Nobody should be sad at Christmas."

Rafe is here. I don't know why and I don't know how, but none of that matters anymore. I leap up from my seat and now I'm running towards him, the snow stinging my face and the wind whipping any words from my lips. My feet in my heels slither and skid, but I feel as though I could fly. In my haste to reach Rafe I'm not bothered about practicalities – and when I catch my heel in my long skirt and pitch forwards I'm too taken by surprise to even cry out. I hear him shout a warning, but it's way too late for me to stop. My hands claw helplessly at the thin air and then I'm slammed onto the platform, the snow a useless cushion as my head hits the concrete.

Blackness. Dark and velvet soft. Spinning, falling, floating. Hands touching my face, voices whispering, somebody smoothing hair away from my cheeks. Traffic rushing by? Or is that the roaring of my own blood I can hear? Traffic was before, wasn't it? Or was that was another time?

"Cleo! Cleo! Wake up. Look at me."

The voice is insistent. I try to open my eyes but the glaring light hurts and renders the face gazing down at me little more than a shadow. I put my hand over my eyes to shield them, but cool fingers peel my hand away again.

"Cleo, it's me, Alex."

I blink and, sure enough, there Alex is. Rafe is cradling my head in his lap, raining kisses onto my cheeks and my lips, and doesn't see his brother crouched by my side. I groan and raise my fingers to my head; they come away sticky with blood. The sky is whirling like a roundabout. Rafe. Alex. Rafe. Alex. It's hard to see which Thorne brother is which; they're moving so fast.

"Rafe?" I whisper. "Alex?"

Alex brushes my face with icicle fingers. "Cleo, listen, I don't have much time. I think my journey here is done. You need to get in touch with the Professor. He's been desperate to speak to you. He wants to offer you the Assistant Director's job."

I've hit my head; no wonder this makes no sense. "No, no. He gave the job to Simon."

"Not anymore. He knows everything and he heard it all from Simon. He won't doubt you ever again."

I struggle to sit up. "That's impossible. Simon would never tell him."

Alex grins. "Not on purpose, but imagine if the phone in your office had *somehow* managed to dial the Professor and he'd heard everything when he'd picked up? Do we know a little pharaoh who likes playing with telephones and an Egyptologist who's incensed by Simon's disgusting behaviour and the disrepute this might bring to the museum? Can you imagine how a phone call to the Professor might have happened just at the same time Simon was bragging about what he's done?"

"Aamon and Henry Wellby? They did that? And the Professor knows that Simon stole my research? He believes me?"

Alex nods. "Simon can't deny it either. The Professor heard him gloat about everything he'd done. He's condemned himself out of his own mouth."

"Aamon loves playing with that phone," I recall.

"And he loves you too," Alex says softly. "You've uncovered his story, Cleo, and set him free. He won't forget that."

I close my eyes again. The darkness is so restful…

"Cleo, sweetheart," Rafe's lips are only inches from mine. I feel his warm breath on my cheek. "Who are you talking to?"

I open my eyes again. Rafe's face swims into focus, his violet eyes brimming with concern. I'm poised to tell him everything at last but Alex puts his finger on his lips and shakes his head. He's starting to fade in front of my eyes.

"Where are you going?" I say. "Don't go!"

"I'll never leave you," Rafe promises. "Never."

But my attention is fixed on Alex, who's becoming more and more translucent with every passing second.

"I don't know," he says. "But I do know that I'm done here. I've completed my journey and it feels good. It's all going to be OK. Neither of you need me anymore."

"That's not true!" I whisper.

"It is, I swear," says Rafe. "I'm never letting you out of my sight again, Cleo Rose Carpenter."

Alex smiles. "See? You really don't need me now. You're going to be a huge success and I know you'll both be happy. Cleo, trust me on this. I have to go now. It's my time."

"Don't go!" I cry. I try to sit up but the world revolves in a sickening blur and only Rafe's arms stop me from falling back onto the platform. I want to tell Alex I'm sorry we argued, that I don't blame him for anything that happened, that I'm glad I had the chance to get to know him – but it's already too late. Alex has gone. I close my eyes and there's his face again, gazing down at me in amazement as I lie in my hospital bed, laughing at Lilac Delaney's shenanigans, his green eyes furious when I ignored him. I see his cheeky grin when I made him put his fingers over his eyes in the changing room, and I hear his teasing voice. There's an ache in my head, as though my skull is going to split. I open my mouth in a cry of pain but only silence rushes in. My heart begins to race and panic swamps me. Everything goes dark.

"Cleo, please wake up. Please."

Rafe is holding in me in his arms. I feel his warmth at my side, the weight of his leather jacket slung over my body, the heat of his mouth pressed against my temple. The snow is still falling softly, brushing my face in an angel's kiss, and when I open my eyes I see that it's even settled on his shoulders. I blink before reaching out to touch his face wonderingly. Is this real? Or is it another dream? Or maybe I'm still in my hospital bed and none of this ever happened at all? The world looks as it always did; yet it feels different. Sharper and brighter, somehow, and when Rafe brushes my tears away with his fingers my nerve endings crackle with longing.

I feel alive. Violently and excitedly and utterly alive.

I glance around for Alex but he's not here. Usually I can feel him. Him and all the others. When they're about I have a sensation like an ice cube slithering down my spine and all my nerve endings tingle – but there's nothing now, no residual trace that he was ever here. Instead there's just the empty platform, the sickly orange lamplight and the snow falling softly while the church bells ring in the distance.

"Can you stand up?" Rafe is asking gently. "Try and hold onto me. You hit your head pretty hard. It's grazed."

"Seems to be a habit." I grip his arms and together we manage to haul me upright. The world rotates in a giddy rush, so I clutch him tightly – although when Rafe's arms close around me I'm no longer sure if it's the blow to my head that's making everything spin.

He leans closer; his words are warm against my ear. "I've been driving around like a maniac trying to find you. I even went to the museum – all hell was breaking loose with that blond colleague of yours – and I even gatecrashed your father's school production. He strikes a hard bargain, your old man; he made me sign autographs for the school raffle before he told me you'd be here." He wiggles his fingers and grimaces. "I've probably got RSI. See what happens when you don't answer my calls?"

"See what happens when you get back with your ex."

"My ex? Natasha?"

"Yes, Natasha." My head aches too much to waste time arguing. "I saw you with her, Rafe. You were in the studio together. You don't have to deny it. I came to see you and when you didn't answer I walked to the back of the house."

He raises an eyebrow. "Ah, that old trick of yours."

I ignore his teasing. The hurt of earlier is flooding back. "I know what I saw and I saw you together."

But Rafe is laughing. "Oh, really? You did, did you?"

"What's so funny?" I'm offended and try to pull away but his arms just tighten.

"You," says Rafe simply. He tilts my chin skywards with his forefinger so that I'm looking up at him. His violet eyes are crinkling with amusement. "For such a clever woman you certainly jump to some hasty conclusions. I thought you were supposed to be good at weighing up evidence and then analysing it? Yes, Natasha came to see me and yes she was at my house. Do you know why?"

I shrug. I don't want to know.

"Because she came to say she was sorry about how she treated me," Rafe says. "I'm not fooled. She's read the papers, I suppose, and seen how well the new song has done – and Tasha loves publicity. I turned her down, Cleo, and

I told her about you. She cried then. Her latest boyfriend has dumped her, as it turns out, and she's in a bad way. She sobbed; I gave her a tissue and then sent her packing. But I never once contemplated getting back with her. Shall I tell you why?"

I reach up and touch his face. "Why?"

He traces the curve of my cheek with a tender finger. "Because, Cleo Rose Carpenter, there's only one person I have ever loved and ever wanted, and she's standing here with me right now in the snow, in the exact place where I first fell in love with her."

Then he leans in to kiss me and I melt. Never mind the cold or my aching head; all other thoughts vanish in a heartbeat.

We break apart and smile wonderingly at one another. Rafe winds one of my curls around his finger and then shakes his head.

"I really can't explain how I came to find you again," he says quietly. "I don't think it's something I'll ever be able to understand."

I rest my thudding head against his chest. Rafe has no idea just how inexplicable this has all been.

"This probably sounds crazy," he continues, "but I have the strongest feeling that if my brother could see us now he'd be very pleased. Ally always wanted a happy ending for my Christmas Eve story."

I nod but say nothing. Alex has gone, I can feel that, but I also know that Rafe is right too in a way. Love never leaves us. We live and we die but the love we have is forever.

"This isn't the end," I say, and as I speak I'm not just thinking about us but also about my family, and Aamon and all the strange and wonderful things that have happened to me lately. I rise onto my tiptoes and brush his mouth with my own. "This, Rafe Thorne, is a very happy beginning."

He wraps me in his arms and together we walk along the platform and towards the snowy world beyond, a world that's suddenly brimful of hope and wonder. I know that in life I won't have all the answers, but I'm fine with this now.

Still, as Rafe and I head homewards, smiling into the snowfall, there's one thing that I'm absolutely certain of: wherever he is now, I know that Alex Thorne is smiling too.

Christmas

One year on

"This is it; the last box is down from the attic. There's nothing else left now from Mellisande."

Rafe deposits a large cardboard box onto the floor with a thud and wipes his brow with his sleeve. Puffs of dust shimmy in the lamplight and a spider scuttles away hastily.

Although it's only mid afternoon the light is already fading from the snow-laden sky, throwing our small courtyard garden into blue and purple shadows. The spires and rooftops beyond are silhouettes, a classic view that I've quickly come to love every bit as much as I used to love the rooftops and chimneypots of London.

Inside our cosy red sitting room, the wood burner is doing a sterling job of keeping the December cold at bay and the two big lamps flood the place with pools of golden light. A Christmas tree stands to attention in the far corner, with a single row of twinkling coloured lights and topped with an angel (who has the tip of the tree in a very interesting place). I did start to tell Rafe that angels may have originated with the Egyptian winged goddess Isis, but he stopped me mid lecture with a kiss that led to a very happy hour or so – after which you could have told me it was the Tooth Fairy perched up there and I wouldn't have given a hoot.

Right now I'm sitting on the rug with my back against the sofa, keeping my toes warm by the wood burner and leaving the organisation of our first Christmas in the new house entirely up to him. After all, everybody knows that a) I don't do Christmas and b) I've got far more important things to occupy me than the location of a few baubles. There's a c) as well actually.

Rafe Thorne, I've come to learn, is a complete Christmas junkie. He's already invited everyone for Christmas dinner: my father, Susie and Dave (he was useful for far more than fetching milk, as it turns out), and Tolly and his latest arm candy. He's also wound fairy lights around all the trees in the garden and wrapped the gifts. I guess I shouldn't have expected any less from a man who's written two of Britain's bestselling Christmas hits and, according to the download chart, is about to make it a hat-trick.

I'll have to keep a close eye on him. He'll be illuminating the whole house like Oxford Street if I'm not careful...

Rafe looks up from the box thoughtfully. "The rest of the Christmas-tree decorations are in here, aren't they?"

I abandon the book I'm in the middle of reading and, as always, my stomach does a delicious cartwheel just at the sight of him. Will this ever wear off? Somehow I don't think so. Even covered in cobwebs and wearing his scruffiest ripped jeans and sweater, Rafe Thorne is heart-stoppingly gorgeous.

"If you'd allowed me to be in charge of packing up Mellisande we'd know for sure," I tease. "The boxes would have been labelled and I'd have made an inventory too. We'd know where everything was and the tree would be long decorated by now."

"There was no way I was letting you crawl about in the attics back then. You'd have got wedged in the hatch anyway," grins Rafe. Box abandoned for the moment, he crouches down on the rug beside me and picks up my book, turning it over in his hands.

"*Spot's Christmas*. Very intellectual, Dr Carpenter. Do your students enjoy this?"

I laugh. "There's a waiting list for it in the Bodleian, I'll have you know! Anyway, Ally seems to like it. There's plenty of time for me to wean her onto Howard Carter's excavation papers."

"Over my dead body," says Rafe, grimacing. "She's going to be a musician." He gives me a searching look. "You *did* play Mozart to her while she was in the womb, right?"

We both glance down tenderly at the chubby baby lying next to me on the rug and gurgling away happily to herself. Alexandra Claudia Thorne. Reader of *Spot*, in-the-womb listener to lectures on the ancient world, and the biggest and best surprise I've ever had.

I cross my fingers behind my back. "Of course."

"Fibber," says Rafe, scooping up the baby and dancing around the room with her. "Mummy can't fool me. Never mind. Daddy will just have to take you to the studio when you're bigger. Would you like a guitar?"

Baby Alexandra gurgles up at her father delightedly. Like me, she adores absolutely everything about Rafe and now her violet eyes are huge with amazement as he waltzes her past the Christmas tree and shows her the fairy-grotto garden. I uncurl myself from the rug and place *Spot* on the coffee table, next to the proofs of my new book, *Aamon: Egypt's Lost Pharaoh*. Once Ally's fed and asleep I'll get back to going through them. I glance across the room to the small statue in pride of place on the mantelpiece and it seems to me that he's smiling, which is ridiculous, I know; it's the sort of nonsense I would have come out with during the very weird time of my head injury. Of course the statue's not smiling! It's an inanimate object, and there was never a small sloe-eyed boy either, or a cat. It was all my cerebral cortex playing tricks on me.

As I watch Rafe dancing around the house with our beaming daughter I wonder how it's possible that life can change so much in a year. If you'd told me twelve months ago that one year later I'd be living with my Christmas stranger and lecturing at Oxford, and that I'd have the most delicious violet-eyed baby, I'd have called for the men in white coats. It's funny too that it was a total breakdown and my own near miss with the men in white coats that brought all this about.

Of course, I'm confident now that it was my head injury that had caused me to think I was seeing and hearing things. My brain had obviously sustained more damage than I'd realised, and the only way my mind could deal with it was to construct a narrative, linking together a chain of coincidences and attempting to weave meaning from them. Ghosts coming back to make sure their families are happy are the stuff of Hollywood movies, not the real world. I've not seen or heard anything unusual since I slipped and fell on the snowy platform; fortunately the second bump on the head didn't do any more damage. My consultant says there's nothing wrong with me at all now, which is why life is back to normal – or, in this case, better than normal.

I do often think of Alex though, or rather the Alex I imagined. I think if he could see his brother now he'd be very happy. The drunken, blame-crippled Rafe has long gone and in his place is a talented, handsome man who quietly writes top-ten hits for Britain's biggest pop stars and looks after our daughter while I teach my students. Our narrow Oxford house with its uneven floors, wiggly stairs and sloping ceilings might not have the kudos of a rock-star pad on the banks of the Thames, but it's a stone's throw from my college and the Cherwell's waters are just a splash away. There's not a ghost in sight either. Ally often watches something I can't see and laughs merrily, but all babies do that. It doesn't mean anything.

I watch as Rafe pairs his iPod with the Bluetooth speaker and starts bopping to "One Christmas Kiss" with Ally. She's laughing.

"She really likes that one," I remark.

"Of course she does." Rafe stretches out his hand and the three of us dance together. "She knows that her uncle's singing about Mummy."

We sway and spin by the tree. The sharp scent of pine needles fills the room. How funny that exactly a year ago I was at the museum party feeling as though my world was in tatters. Simon Welsh certainly got his comeuppance. He was summoned to the disciplinary panel and he resigned before he could be sacked. The last I heard he was working as a history teacher somewhere, although that could have been just a rumour started by Dawn. The Prof was mortified by what had happened and offered me the Assistant Director's job and anything else I wanted to persuade me to stay, but oddly the one thing I'd craved so badly no longer appealed. To his and my own great surprise, I turned the job down to focus on writing Aamon's story – and, to my even greater surprise, being pregnant. The last thing I did before I left London was to arrange an exhibition about Aamon, which told his forgotten story for the first time. I'd almost burst with pride when it became one of the museum's biggest attractions. Now the whole world knows that there was once a boy pharaoh who loved cats and who was killed in cold blood by his ambitious stepmother. Lecturing undergraduates about the Aamonic period, my specialism, is something I adore too – and when I was offered a fellowship at my mother's old college I couldn't say no. Rafe has his studio in the basement and writes and looks after Ally while I work. It's pretty much perfect.

Isn't it funny? Life seems to have come round in a full circle, everything slotting neatly into place as though it was all meant to be. Not that I believe in fate, but just sometimes I can't help but wonder.

The track finishes and now Raymond Brigg's Snowman is "walking in the air". Rafe turns the music down and passes Ally back to me.

"Time to unpack this box," he says. "Let's hope it's the decorations, otherwise it's a trolley dash round Homebase for this family."

I perch on the arm of the sofa with the baby and watch Rafe unpeel the parcel tape that holds the lid down. Oh the anticipation! Will there be tinsel and baubles? Or more junk? That's another thing I've discovered about Rafe Thorne: he's a terrible hoarder. When he moved out of Mellisande he was practically dragging stuff back out of the skip.

Then Rafe's face crumples.

"What is it?" I ask, alarmed. He has a dreadful haunted look and my stomach lurches. The last time I saw that expression he was sprawled on the floor of Mellisande clutching a whiskey bottle.

"This isn't my box." Rafe passes a hand across his eyes. They're brighter than usual and he swallows hard. "This is Alex's stuff. I must have missed it."

He reaches in and rummages about. "I remember now. I had to clear the drawer in his bedside table after the accident. I couldn't bear to look at it then so I just scooped the lot into this box and bunged it in the attic."

"Put the lid back on and we'll keep this safe." I drop a kiss onto Ally's head, inhaling the warm baby scent of her. "When she's older you can tell Ally all about her uncle."

"Hmm, there's magazine in here. I'm not sure I want my daughter reading *Playboy* or worse." Rafe pulls out a magazine. "Oh! *Music Mad.* That's totally acceptable, seeing as she's going to be a muso."

"Egyptologist," I correct, and we laugh.

"God, this is really old," says Rafe, looking at the cover. "December 2009. Oh–" He sinks down onto the sofa beside me. The magazine is shaking in his hands and, wide eyed, he turns to me. "Cleo, this is the issue I told you about, remember? The one where Alex promised he'd find you? The one I thought I'd seen?"

The iPod has finished the track. The room is suddenly very still, as though somebody somewhere is holding their breath. Sensing that Rafe needs my full attention I lay the baby in her basket, where she sucks her toes and gurgles to herself. Then I sit next to Rafe and place my hands over his trembling fingers.

"Show me," I say.

The magazine falls open to the article – it's been well thumbed – and at once I recognise Alex grinning out at me across time. His grin is as wide as I remember, or rather his grin is just the way I imagined it. Obviously I don't remember it, because I never met Alex Thorne. Rafe is in the background, looking far more intense than his sibling and simmering with emotion. He looks so much younger and it hurts me to see afresh just how the loss of his brother changed him.

We scan the piece together and in silence. My eyes fill with tears when I read what Rafe said. I lace my fingers tightly with his. His love for me is there in black and white and for the entire world to see, or at least for the readers of *Music Mad* December 2009 to see. Yet this is nothing compared to what comes next.

"*She'll find him and they can live happily ever after!*" Alex had said, and it's as though I've been jolted by mains electricity. In an instant I'm whisked away, back to that Topshop changing room with Alex sitting on the floor, eyes tightly shut, while I tease him about being a closet romantic. He'd wanted me and Rafe to meet again, fall in love and live happily ever after, and I'd laughed at him.

I swallow. Who's had the last laugh?

Rafe's fingers clutch mine so tightly that I wince.

"Read the last line, Cleo," he whispers. "Read it out loud."

My throat feels tight, my tongue dry. The last line closed the interview; the journalist was obviously struck by an aside he'd overheard after Alex had teased his brother about living happily ever after with his mystery girl. Me. The journalist had surmised that Rafe would probably do just fine with a supermodel but had written down Alex's final comment anyway.

"'But if I could,' Alex says quietly to his brother," I read aloud, "'I'd move heaven and earth to find her for you.'"

Rafe and I stare at one another. My heart is hammering against my ribcage. *Move heaven and earth*, Alex had said. Oh my God. Was that exactly what he'd done?

Rafe raises my hand to his lips and brushes a kiss across my fingertips.

"Alex found you for me, didn't he?" he whispers.

"I'm sure of it," I say, and this time I really am. I don't need any more proof or evidence. My heart is telling me that this is the truth. Alex did exactly what he'd promised he would do. He moved heaven and earth to help his brother.

I'm toying with telling Rafe my very strange story, hoping he won't think I'm nuts, when a peal of happy giggles draws our attention to the baby.

Rafe's sudden intake of breath and tightening grasp on my hand tells me all I need to know. I'm not hallucinating or imagining things – not if Rafe can see this too. This is as real as the love in my heart for my family. As real as my mum's love for me. As real as Alex's love for Rafe. Because this is what love is: doing everything you can for those you care about. I know that now. I get it. I really get it.

In silence and by the flickering shadows thrown by the fairy lights we watch Alex bending over the Moses basket and pulling faces at Ally, who gurgles delightedly. Then he looks up, smiles at us and vanishes.

THE END

Dear Reader,

Sometimes an idea for a book pops into your head and just won't go away. The characters stick around, nagging you until finally you give in and agree to write their story. It's the weirdest thing and it sounds absolutely bonkers, but as a writer you can literally hear them chattering away. This was certainly the case with the characters from *Dead Romantic*. This book was the one I had no choice but to write and, quirky as it is, I loved every minute of telling it.

I was on the London Underground, on my way back from a meeting at Orion Towers, when Cleo Carpenter popped into my head and demanded that I told her story. She was determined, bossy and very single-minded. I knew instantly that there would be no getting away from her until I'd listened and done my job. Cleo was an Egyptologist and this was in no way an area of expertise for me. I asked her if she could be a science teacher instead but she wasn't having that! It seemed I would have to do some serious research.

Living in Cornwall made researching Cleo's job rather tricky. I visited the British Museum and the Ashmolean a couple of times and spent hours trawling the Internet, reading up on the subject of Egyptology and making notes. I was soon hooked on the History Channel too. Then, quite by chance, my mother told me that my granny had always been fascinated by ancient Egypt – something of which I'd had no idea – and had claimed she had an Egyptian spirit guide too. It had always been her dream to see the pyramids. I shivered. Maybe her guide was now with me, egging Cleo on? I must admit that I was a little unnerved by all of this...

At around this time a friend's husband was busy fitting a big lift to service the Egyptian Rooms in the British Museum, and he told me how the place terrified him and his team at night – this being the time when it was quiet enough for the men to do their work. He claimed that there was a very eerie atmosphere and that they all felt as though they were being watched. They were tough men, not given to being spooked, and he said they were very relieved when the job was completed. This was great material for me as a writer. My no-nonsense, sceptical heroine who spent many nights in her museum without turning a hair would laugh at this idea. It is in this exact kind of creepy setting, which unnerves tough builders, that Cleo feels most at home. That told me a lot about her. It was great fun to write about how someone so analytically minded and totally convinced that she has life figured out would react to suddenly seeing ghosts.

Although the characters were raring to go, I was still stumped by the Egyptology side of things. I could use my imagination, of course, but I owed it to my readers to get as many of the facts right as I possibly could. Belief can only be suspended so far. It was at this point that one of my colleagues at Bodmin College asked whether I had ever visited the Egyptian Museum in a nearby village. I hadn't, but I phoned them straight away and booked a trip. The place was a gem, a fantastic 1930s-style museum, filled with the couple's private collection of artefacts and replicas. I was lucky enough to be granted an exclusive tour. When I drove away my mind was racing with new ideas and I could hardly wait to start writing. I could also picture vividly the Aamon statue and artefacts that play such a central part of the story.

In the novel Cleo goes to see a celebrity psychic at a local theatre. She's hoping that this will be a way of proving once and for all that ghosts don't exist – but ends up with more proof to the contrary than she ever expects. As part of my research for this book I also booked tickets to see a celebrity medium in action. I won't name who this was but I was horrified by the mistakes they made – from getting the breeds of dogs wrong to telling a gay man all about his girlfriend! I'm not saying that I don't believe – far from it – but like Alex says to Cleo, there are many vulnerable people who could be misled by unscrupulous folk. It was all great novel fodder though.

Sometimes books just write themselves and this has been one of those times. Cleo, Rafe and Alex were vivid presences as I wrote. When I typed

"The End" I felt truly bereft. *Dead Romantic* accompanied me through some very tough times in my own life and it felt odd to walk away from it.

Dead Romantic is really a story about love in all its guises. Love for a partner, a sibling, a child, a job – as well as the agonising pain of losing a loved one. The Egyptians had a strong belief in the afterlife but Cleo, although she has studied their ancient culture, has learned to close her mind and her heart to anything other than her work. She misses out on so much. Writing about her journey helped me to think about my own beliefs and to work through losses in my own life. If my granny did have an Egyptian spirit guide, I think he was probably reading over my shoulder and hopefully smiling!

I really hope that my readers enjoy Cleo, Alex and Rafe's story as much as I have enjoyed writing it. I also hope that it does offer some degree of comfort. As Cleo learns, love never dies but lives on in our memories and in our hearts. Please feel free to write to me and let me know your thoughts and feelings about this book or to share your supernatural experiences with me. I'd love to hear from you.

Finally, I need a favour! Reviews can make or break a book and it really helps the word to spread if a book has lots of reviews. If you enjoyed *Dead Romantic* and have the time to post a review on Amazon and Good Reads, that would be very much appreciated.

Thanks so much, and thank you too for sharing in Rafe and Cleo's story.

Brightest wishes,

x Ruth x

Ruth Saberton is the bestselling author of *Katy Carter Wants a Hero* and *Escape for the Summer*. She also writes upmarket commercial fiction under the pen names Jessica Fox, Georgie Carter and Holly Cavendish.

Born and raised in the UK, Ruth has just returned from living on Grand Cayman for two years. What an adventure!

And since she loves to chat with readers, please do add her as a Facebook friend and follow her on Twitter.

www.ruthsaberton.co.uk

Twitter: @ruthsaberton

Facebook: Ruth Saberton

Printed in Great Britain
by Amazon